SHERLOCK HOLMES
IN
AMERICA

EDITED BY
MARTIN H. GREENBERG,
JON L. LELLENBERG, and
DANIEL STASHOWER

MJF BOOKS
New York

Published by MJF Books
Fine Communications
589 Eighth Avenue, 6th Floor
New York, NY 10018

Sherlock Holmes in America
LC Control Number: 2017962115
ISBN 978-1-60671-393-8

Contents

INTRODUCTION: "AMERICAN, AS YOU PERCEIVE"
Jon L. Lellenberg and Daniel Stashower

"It is always a joy to meet an American," declares Sherlock Holmes in "The Adventure of the Noble Bachelor," "for I am one of those who believe that the folly of a monarch and the blundering of a minister in far-gone years will not prevent our children from being some day citizens of the same worldwide country under a flag which shall be a quartering of the Union Jack with the Stars and Stripes."

It should not come as a surprise, then, to find that the Sherlock Holmes stories are fairly bursting with Americans. The Great Detective's very first outing, *A Study in Scarlet*, features a lengthy flashback set in the Mormon community of Utah, while the novel *The Valley of Fear* turns on an account of nefarious doings in the coal-mining communities of Pennsylvania. Americans feature prominently in several of the most popular Holmes adventures, including *The Five Orange Pips* and *The Adventure of the Dancing Men*, and no less a figure than *the* woman, the legendary Irene Adler "of dubious and questionable memory" who bested Sherlock Holmes, hailed from New Jersey. If further evidence is required, one need only recall that Holmes himself posed as an Irish-American spy named Altamont to outwit the German spymaster Von Bork in *His Last Bow*.

Like his famous detective, Sir Arthur Conan Doyle was an enthusiastic admirer of the United States. In boyhood he was fascinated by the frontier tales of James Fenimore Cooper and Mayne Reid, and as a young writer he drew inspiration from Edgar Allan Poe, Oliver Wendell Holmes, Mark Twain, and Bret Harte. Over the course of his lifetime, Conan Doyle made four visits to the United States, and called for the creation of an Anglo-American society to promote understanding and friendship between the two nations. The dedication of his novel *The White Company* reads: "To the Hope of the Future, the Reunion of the English Speaking Races, This Little Chronicle of Our Common Ancestry Is Inscribed."

In that spirit, the present volume brings together a collection of new stories written by some of today's best mystery writers, in which Holmes and Watson strike out for the United States. "That's paying for brains, you see," as Holmes remarks in *The Valley of Fear*, "the American business principle." Some readers may balk at finding the Great Detective uprooted from his familiar Baker Street digs, but we believe we are playing the game according to Doyle.

"It air strange, it air," he once wrote, in a story called *The American's Tale*, "but I could tell you queerer things than that 'ere—almighty queer things. You can't learn everything out of books, sirs, no how. You see it ain't the men as can string English together and as has had good eddications as finds themselves in the queer places I've been in. They're mostly rough men, sirs, as can scarce speak aright, far less tell with pen and ink the things they've seen; but if they could they'd make some of your European's har riz with astonishment."

Indeed, as Sherlock Holmes once observed, "American slang is very expressive sometimes."

THE CASE OF COLONEL WARBURTON'S MADNESS
Lyndsay Faye

Lyndsay Faye is the author of the historical thriller *Dust and Shadow: An Account of the Ripper Killings by Dr. John H. Watson*, in which the Great Detective must trace the infamous serial killer in a pre-Freudian world, amidst the hostile censure of the gutter press, and at the risk of his own life. She spent many years in the San Francisco Bay Area, working as a professional actress. Lyndsay and her husband, Gabriel Lehner, now live in Manhattan with their cat, Grendel; she is a proud member of Actor's Equity Association and the Adventuresses of Sherlock Holmes. Visit her Web site at www.lyndsayfaye.com.

* * * *

My friend Mr. Sherlock Holmes, while possessed of one of the most vigorous minds of our generation, and while capable of displaying tremendous feats of physical activity when the situation required it, could nevertheless remain in his armchair perfectly motionless longer than any human being I have ever encountered. This skill passed wholly unrecognized by its owner. I do not believe he held any intentions to impress me so, nor do I think the exercise was, for him, a strenuous one. Still I maintain the belief that when a man has held the same pose for a period exceeding three hours, and when that man is undoubtedly awake, that same man has accomplished an unnatural feat.

I turned away from my task of organizing a set of old journals that lead-grey afternoon to observe Holmes perched with one leg curled beneath him, firelight burnishing the edges of his dressing gown as he sat with his head in his hand, a long-abandoned book upon the carpet. The familiar sight had grown increasingly unnerving as the hours progressed. It was with a view to ascertain that my friend was still alive that I went so far against my habits as to interrupt his reverie.

"My dear chap, would you care to take a turn with me? I've an errand with the bootmaker down the road, and the weather has cleared somewhat."

I do not know if it was the still-ominous dark canopy that deterred him or his own pensive mood, but Holmes merely replied, "I require better distraction just now than an errand which is not my own and the capricious designs of a March rainstorm."

"What precise variety of distraction would be more to your liking?" I inquired, a trifle nettled at his dismissal.

He waved a slender hand, at last lifting his dark head from the upholstery where it had reclined for so long. "Nothing you can provide me. It is the old story—for these two days I have received not a shred of worthwhile correspondence, nor has any poor soul abused our front doorbell with an eye to engage my services. The world is weary, I am weary, and I grow weary with being weary of it. Thus, Watson, as you see I am entirely useless myself at the moment, my state cannot be bettered through frivolous occupations."

"I suppose I would be pleased no one is so disturbed in mind as to seek your aid, if I did not know what your work meant to you," I said with greater sympathy.

"Well, well, there is no use lamenting over it."

"No, but I should certainly help if I could."

"What could you possibly do?" he sniffed. "I hope you are not about to tell me your pocket watch has been stolen, or your great-aunt disappeared without trace."

"I am safe on those counts, thank you. But perhaps I can yet offer you a problem to vex your brain for half an hour."

"A problem? Oh, I'm terribly sorry—I had forgotten. If you want to know where the other key to the desk has wandered off to, I was given cause recently to test the pliancy of such objects. I'll have a new one made—"

"I had not noticed the key," I interrupted him with a smile, "but I could, if you like, relate a series of events which once befell me when I was in practice in San Francisco, the curious details of which have perplexed me for years. My work on these old diaries reminded me of them yet again, and the circumstances were quite in your line."

"I suppose I should be grateful you are at least not staring daggers at my undocketed case files," he remarked.

"You see? There are myriad advantages. It would be preferable to venturing out, for it is already raining again. And should you refuse, I will be every bit as unoccupied as you, which I would also prefer to avoid." I did not mention that if he remained a statue an instant longer, the sheer eeriness of the room would force me out of doors.

"You are to tell me a tale of your frontier days, and I am to solve it?" he asked blandly, but the subtle angle of one eyebrow told me he was intrigued.

"Yes, if you can."

"What if you haven't the data?"

"Then we shall proceed directly to the brandy and cigars."

"It's a formidable challenge." To my great relief, he lifted himself in the air by his hands and crossed his legs underneath him, reaching when he had done so for the pipe lying cold on the side table. "I cannot say I've any confidence it can be done, but as an experiment, it has a certain flair."

"In that case, I shall tell you the story, and you may pose any questions that occur to you."

"From the beginning, mind, Watson," he admonished, settling himself into a comfortable air of resigned attention. "And with as many details as you can summon up."

"It is quite fresh in my mind again, for I'd set it down in the volumes I was just mulling over. As you know, my residence in America was relatively brief, but San Francisco lives in my memory quite as vividly as Sydney or Bombay—an impetuous, thriving little city nestled among the great hills, where the fogs are spun from ocean air and the sunlight refracts from Montgomery Street's countless glass windows. It is as if all the men and women of enterprise across the globe determined they should have a city of their own, for the Gold Rush built it and the Silver Lode built it again, and now that they have been linked by railroad with the eastern states, the populace believes nothing is impossible under the sun. You would love it there, Holmes. One sees quite as many nations and trades represented as in London, all jostling one another into a thousand bizarre coincidences, and you would not be surprised to find a Chinese apothecary wedged between a French milliner and an Italian wine merchant.

"My practice was based on Front Street in a small brick building, near a number of druggist establishments, and I readily received any patients who happened my way. Poor or well-off, genteel or ruffianly, it made no difference to a boy in the first flush of his career. I'd no long-established references, and for that reason no great clientele, but it was impossible to feel small in that city, for they so prized hard work and optimism that I felt sudden successes lay every moment round the next corner.

"One hazy afternoon, as I'd no appointments and I could see the sun lighting up the masts of the ships in the Bay, I decided I'd sat idle long enough, and set out for a bit of exercise. It is one of San Francisco's peculiar characteristics that no matter what direction one wanders, one must encounter a steep hill, for there are seven of them, and within half an hour of walking aimlessly away from the water, I found myself striding up Nob Hill, staring in awe at the array of houses.

"Houses, in fact, are rather a misnomer; they call it Nob Hill because it is populated by mining and railroad nabobs, and the residences are like something from the reign of Ludwig the Second or Marie Antoinette. Many are larger than our landed estates, but all built within ten years of the time I arrived. I ambled past a gothic near-castle and a neo-classicist mansion only to spy an italianate villa across the street, each making an effort to best all others in stained glass, columns, and turrets. The neighborhood—"

"Was a wealthy one," Holmes sighed, hopping out of his chair to pour two glasses of claret.

"And you would doubtless have found that section of town ap-palling." As he handed me a wine glass, I smiled at the thought of my Bohemian friend eyeing those pleasure domes with cool distaste. "There would have been others more to your liking, I think. Nevertheless, it was a marvel of architecture, and as I neared the crest of the hill, I stopped to take in the view of the Pacific.

"Standing there watching the sun glow orange over the waves, I heard a door fly open and turned to see an old man hobbling frantically down a manicured path leading to the street. The mansion he'd exited was built more discreetly than most, vaguely Grecian and painted white. He was very tall—quite as tall as you, my dear fellow—but with shoulders like an ox. He dressed in a decades-old military uniform, with a tattered blue coat over his grey trousers, and a broad red tie and cloth belt, his silvery hair standing out from his head as if he'd just stepped from the thick of battle.

"Although he cut an extraordinary figure, I would not have paid him much mind in that mad metropolis had not a young lady rushed after him in pursuit, crying out, 'Uncle! Stop, please! You mustn't go, I beg of you!'

"The man she'd addressed as her uncle gained the kerb not ten feet from where I stood, and then all at once collapsed onto the pavement, his chest no longer heaving and the leg which had limped crumpled underneath him.

"I rushed to his side. He breathed, but shallowly. From my closer vantage point, I could see one of his limbs was false, and that it had come loose from its leather straps, causing his fall. The girl reached us not ten seconds later, gasping for breath even as she made a valiant effort to prevent her eyes from tearing.

"'Is he all right?' she asked me.

"'I think so,' I replied, 'but I prefer to be certain. I am a doctor, and I would be happy to examine him more carefully indoors.'

"'I cannot tell you how grateful we would be. Jefferson!' she called to a tall black servant hurrying down the path. 'Please help us get the colonel inside.'

"Between the three of us, we quickly established my patient on the sofa in a cheerful, glass-walled morning room, and I was able to make a more thorough diagnosis. Apart from the carefully crafted wooden leg, which I reattached more securely, he seemed in perfect health, and if he were not such a large and apparently hale man I should have imagined that he had merely fainted.

"'Has he hurt himself, Doctor?' the young woman asked breathlessly.

"Despite her evident distress, I saw at once she was a beautiful woman, with a small-framed, feminine figure, and yet a large measure of that grace which goes with greater stature. Her hair was light auburn, swept away from her creamy complexion in loose waves and wound in an elegant knot, and her eyes shone golden brown through her remaining tears. She wore a pale blue dress trimmed with silver, and her ungloved hand clutched in apprehension at the folds. She—my dear fellow, are you all right?"

"Perfectly," Holmes replied with another cough which, had I been in an uncharitable humour, would have resembled a chuckle. "Do go on."

"'This man will be quite all right once he has rested,' I told her. 'My name is John Watson.'

"'Forgive me—I am Molly Warburton, and the man you've been tending is my uncle, Colonel Patrick Warburton. Oh, what a fright I have had! I cannot thank you enough.'

"'Miss Warburton, I wonder if I might speak with you in another room, so as not to disturb your uncle while he recovers.'

"She led me across the hall into another tastefully appointed parlour and fell exhaustedly into a chair. I hesitated to disturb her further, and yet I felt compelled to make my anxieties known.

"'Miss Warburton, I do not think your uncle would have collapsed in such a dramatic manner had he not been under serious mental strain. Has anything occurred recently which might have upset him?'

"'Dr. Watson, you have stumbled upon a family embarrassment,' she said softly. 'My uncle's mental state has been precarious for some time now, and I fear recently he—he has taken a great turn for the worse.'

"'I am sorry to hear it.'

"'The story takes some little time in telling,' she sighed, 'but I will ring for tea, and you will know all about it. First of all, Dr. Watson, I live here with my brother, Charles, and my uncle, the colonel. Apart from Uncle Patrick, Charles and I have no living relatives, and we are very grateful to him for his generosity, for Uncle made a great fortune in shipping during the early days of California statehood. My brother is making his start in the photography business, and I am unmarried, so living with the colonel is for the moment a very comfortable situation.'

"'You must know that my uncle was a firebrand in his youth, and saw a great deal of war as a settler in Texas, before that region was counted among the United States. The pitched fighting between the Texians— that is, the Anglo settlers—and the Tejanos so moved him that he joined the Texas Army under Sam Houston, and was decorated several times for his valour on the field, notably at the Battle of San Jacinto. Later, when the War between the States began, he was a commander for the Union, and lost his leg during the Siege of Petersburg. Forgive me if I bore you. From your voice, I do not think you are a natural-born American,' she added with a smile.

"'Your story greatly interests me. Is that his old Texas uniform he is wearing today?' I asked.

"'Yes, it is,' she replied as a flicker of pain distorted her pretty face. 'He has been costuming himself like that with greater and greater frequency. The affliction, for I do not know what to call it, began several weeks ago. Indeed, I believe the first symptom took place when he changed his will.'

"'How so? Was it a material alteration?'

"'Charlie and I had been the sole benefactors,' she replied, gripping a handkerchief tightly. 'His entire fortune will now be distributed amongst various war charities. Texas War for Independence charities, Civil War charities. He is obsessed with war,' she choked, and then hid her face in her hands.

"I was already moved by her story, Holmes, but the oddity of the colonel's condition intrigued me still further.

"'What are his other symptoms?' I queried when she had recovered herself.

"'After he changed his will, he began seeing the most terrible visions in the dark. Dr. Watson, he claims in the most passionate language that he is haunted. He swears he saw a fearsome Tejano threatening a white woman with a pistol and a whip, and on another occasion he witnessed the same apparition slaughtering one of Houston's men with a bayonet. That is what so upset him, for only this morning he insisted he saw a murderous band of them brandishing swords and torches, with the identical Tejano at their head. My brother believes that we have a duty as his family to remain and care for him, but I confess that Uncle frightens me at times. If we abandoned him, he would have no one, save his old manservant; Sam Jefferson served the colonel for many years, as far back as Texas, I believe, and when my uncle built this house, Jefferson became the head butler.'

"She was interrupted in her narrative as the door opened and the man I knew at once to be her brother stepped in. He had the same light brown eyes as she, and fine features, which twisted into a question at the sight of me.

"'Hello, Molly. Who is this gentleman?'

"'Charlie, it was horrible,' she cried, running to him. 'Uncle Patrick ran out of the house and collapsed. This is Dr. John Watson. He has been so helpful and sympathetic that I was telling him all about Uncle's condition.'

"Charles Warburton shook my hand readily. 'Very sorry to have troubled you, Doctor, but as you can see, we are in something of a mess. If Uncle Patrick grows any worse, I hate to think what—'

"Just then a great roar echoed from the morning room, followed by a shattering crash. The three of us rushed into the hallway and found

Colonel Warburton staring wildly about him, a vase broken into shards at his feet.

"'I left this house once,' he swore, 'and by the devil I will do it again. It's full of vengeful spirits, and I will see you all in hell for keeping me here!'

"The niece and nephew did their utmost to calm the colonel, but he grew even more enraged at the sight of them. In fact, he was so violently agitated that only Sam Jefferson could coax him, with my help, toward his bedroom, and once we had reached it, the colonel slammed the door shut in the faces of his kinfolk.

"By sheer good fortune, I convinced him to take a sedative, and when he fell back in a daze on his bed, I stood up and looked about me. His room was quite Spartan, with hardly anything on the white walls, in the simple style I supposed was a relic of his days in Texas. I have told you that the rest of the house also reflected his disdain for frippery. The bed rested under a pleasant open window, and as it was on the ground floor, one could look directly out at the gardens.

"I turned to rejoin my hosts when Sam Jefferson cleared his throat behind me.

"'You believe he'll be all right, sir?'

He spoke with the slow, deep tones of a man born on the other side of the Mississippi. I had not noticed it before, but a thick knot of scarring ran across his dark temple, which led me to believe he had done quite as much fighting in his youth as his employer.

"'I hope so, but his family would do well to consult a specialist. He is on the brink of a nervous collapse. Was the colonel so fanciful in his younger days?'

"'I don't rightly know about fanciful, sir. He's as superstitious a man as ever I knew, and more afeared of spirits than most. Always has been.

But sir, I've a mind to tell you something else about these spells the colonel been having.'

"'Yes?'

"'Only this, Doctor,' and his low voice sunk to a whisper. 'That first time as he had a vision, I set it down for a dream. Mister Patrick's always been more keen on the bogeymen than I have, sir, and I paid it no mind. But after the second bad spell—the one where he saw the Tejano stabbing the soldier—he went and showed me something that he didn't show the others.'

"'What was it?'

"He walked over to where the colonel now slept and pointed at a gash in the old uniform's breast, where the garment had been carefully mended.

"'The day Mister Patrick told me about that dream was the same day I mended this here hole in his shirt. Thought himself crazy, he did, and I can't say I blame him. Because this hole is in exactly the spot where he dreamed the Tejano stabbed the Texian the night before. What do you think of that, sir?'

"'I've no idea what to think of it,' I replied. 'It is most peculiar.'

"'Then there's this third vision,' he went on patiently. 'The one he had last night. Says he saw a band of 'em with torches, marching toward him like a pack of demons. I don't know about that. But I sure know that yesterday morning, when I went to light a fire in the library, half our kindling was missing. Clean gone, sir. Didn't make much of it at the time, but this puts it in another light."

Sherlock Holmes, who had changed postures a gratifying number of times during my account, rubbed his long hands together avidly before clapping them once.

"It's splendid, my dear fellow. Positively first class. The room was very bare indeed, you say?"

"Yes. Even in the midst of wealth, he lived like a soldier."

"I don't suppose you can tell me what you saw outside the window?"

I hesitated, reflecting as best I could.

"There was nothing outside the window, for I made certain to look. Jefferson assured me that he examined the grounds near the house after he discovered the missing firewood, and found no sign of unusual traffic. When I asked after an odd hole, he mentioned a tall lilac had been torn out from under the window weeks previous because it blocked the light, but that cannot have had any bearing. As I said, the bed faced the wall, not the window."

Holmes tilted his head back with a light laugh. "Yes, you did say that, and I assure you I am coming to a greater appreciation of your skills as an investigator. What happened next?"

"I quit the house soon afterward. The younger Warburtons were anxious to know what had transpired in the sick room, and I comforted them that their uncle was asleep, and unlikely to suffer another such outburst that day. But I assured them all, including Jefferson, that I would return the following afternoon to check on my patient.

"As I departed, I could not help but notice another man walking up the side path leading to the back door. He was very bronzed, with a long handlebar moustache, unkempt black hair, and he dressed in simple trousers and a rough linen shirt of the kind the Mexican laborers wore. This swarthy fellow paid me no mind, but walked straight ahead, and I seized the opportunity to memorize his looks in case he should come to have any bearing on the matter. I did not know what to make of the colonel's ghostly affliction or Jefferson's bizarre account of its physical manifestation, but I thought it an odd enough coincidence to note.

"The next day, I saw a patient or two in the afternoon and then locked my practice, hailing a hack to take me up Nob Hill. Jefferson greeted me at the door and led me into a study of sorts, shelves stacked with gold-lettered military volumes and historical works. Colonel Warburton stood there dressed quite normally, in a grey summer suit, and he seemed bewildered by his own behavior the day before.

"'It's a bona fide curse, I can't help but think, and I'm suffering to end it,' he said to me. 'There are times I know I'm not in my right senses, and other times when I can see those wretched visions before me as clear as your face is now.'

"'Is there anything else you can tell me which might help in my diagnosis?'

"'Not that won't make me out to be cracked in the head, Dr. Watson. After every one of these living nightmares, I've awakened with the same pain in my head, and I can't for the life of me decide whether I've imagined the whole thing or if I really am haunted by one of the men I killed during the war in Texas. Affairs were that muddled—I've no doubt I came out on one or more of the wrong Tejanos. So much bloodshed in those days, no man has the luxury of knowing he was always in the right.'

"'I am no expert in disorders of the mind,' I warned him, 'although I will do all I can for you. You ought to consult a specialist if your symptoms persist or worsen. May I have your permission, however, to ask a seemingly unrelated question?'

"'By all means.'

"'Have you in your employ, or do any of your servants or gardeners occasionally hire, Mexican workers?'

"He seemed quite puzzled by the question. 'I don't happen to have any Hispanos on my payroll. And when the staff need day labour, they almost always engage Chinese. They're quick and honest, and they come cheap. Why do you ask?'

"I convinced him that my question had been purely clinical, congratulated him on his recovery, and made my way to the foyer, mulling several new ideas over in my brain. Jefferson appeared to see me out, handing me my hat and stick.

"'Where are the other members of the household today?' I inquired.

"'Miss Molly is out paying calls, and Mister Charles is working in his darkroom.'

"'Jefferson, I saw a rather mysterious fellow yesterday as I was leaving. To your knowledge, are any men of Mexican or Chileno descent ever hired by the groundskeeper?'

"I would swear to you, Holmes, that a strange glow lit his eyes when I posed that question, but he merely shook his head. 'Anyone does any hiring, Dr. Watson, I know all about it. And no one of that type been asking after work here for six months and more.'

"'I was merely curious whether the sight of such a man had upset the colonel,' I explained, 'but as you know, he is much better today. I am no closer to tracing the source of his affliction, but I hope that if anything new occurs, or if you are ever in doubt, you will contact me.'

"'These spells, they come and they go, Dr. Watson,' Jefferson replied, 'but if I discover anything, I'll surely let you know of it.'

"When I quit the house, I set myself a brisk pace, for I thought to walk down the hill as evening fell. But just as I began my descent, and the wind picked up from the west, I saw not twenty yards ahead of me the same sun-burnished labourer I'd spied the day before, attired in the same fashion, and clearly having emerged from some part of the Warburton residence moments previous. The very sight of him roused my blood; I had not yet met you, of course, and thus knew nothing whatever of detective work, but some instinct told me to follow him to determine whether the colonel was the victim of a malignant design."

"You followed him?" Holmes interjected, with a startled expression. "Whatever for?"

"I felt I had no choice—the parallels between his presence and Colonel Warburton's nightmares had to be explained."

"Ever the man of action." My friend shook his head. "Where did he lead you?"

"When he reached Broadway, where the land flattened and the mansions gave way to grocers, butcheries, and cigar shops, he stopped to mount a streetcar. By a lucky chance, I hailed a passing hack and ordered the driver to follow the streetcar until I called for him to stop.

"My quarry went nearly as far as the waterfront before he descended, and in a trice I paid my driver and set off in pursuit toward the base of Telegraph Hill. During the Gold Rush days, the ocean-facing slope had been a tent colony of Chilenos and Peruanos. That colony intermixed with the lowest hell of them all on its eastern flank—Sydney-Town—where the escaped Australian convicts and ticket-of-leave men ran the vilest public houses imaginable. It is a matter of historical record that the Fierce Grizzly employed a live bear chained outside its door."

"I have heard of that district," Holmes declared keenly. "The whole of it is known as the Barbary Coast, is it not? I confess I should have liked to see it in its prime, although there are any number of streets in London I can visit should I wish to take my life in my hands. You did not yourself encounter any wild beasts?"

"Not in the strictest sense; but inside of ten minutes, I found myself passing gin palaces that could have rivaled St. Giles for depravity. The gaslights appeared sickly and meager, and riotous men stumbled from one red-curtained den of thieves to the next, either losing their money willingly by gambling it away, or drinking from the wrong glass only to find themselves propped insensate in an alley the next morning without a cent to their name.

"At one point I thought I had lost sight of him, for a drayman's cart came between us, and at the same moment he ducked into one of the deadfalls. I soon ascertained where he had gone, however, and after a moment's hesitation entered the place myself.

"The light shone from cheap tallow candles and ancient kerosene lamps with dark purple shades. Losing no time, I approached the man and asked if I could speak with him.

"He stared at me silently, his dark eyes narrowed into slits. At last, he signaled the barman for a second drink, and handed me a small glass of clear liquor.

"I thanked him, but he remained dumb. 'Do you speak English?' I inquired finally.

"He grinned, and with an easy motion of his wrist flicked back his drink and set the empty glass on the bar. 'I speak it as well as you, *señor*. My name is Juan Portillo. What do you want?'

"'I want to know why you visited the Warburton residence yesterday, and again this afternoon.'

"His smile broadened even further. 'Ah, now I understand. You follow me?'

"'There have been suspicious events at that house, ones which I have reason to believe may concern you.'

"'I know nothing of suspicious events. They hire me to do a job, and to be quiet. So I am quiet.'

"'I must warn you that if you attempt to harm the colonel in any way, you will answer for it to me.'

"He nodded at me coldly, still smiling. 'Finish your drink, *señor*. And then I will show you something.'

"I had seen the saloon keeper pour my liquor from the same bottle as his, and thus could not object to drinking it. The stuff was strong as gin, but warmer, and left a fiery burn in the throat. I had barely finished it when Portillo drew out of some hidden pocket a very long, mother-of-pearl handled knife.

"'I never harm the colonel. I never even see this colonel. But I tell you something anyway. Men who follow me, they answer to this,' he said, lifting the knife.

"He snarled something in Spanish. Three men, who had been sitting at a round table several yards away, stood up and strode towards us. Two carried pistols in their belts, and one tapped a short, stout cudgel in his hand. I was evaluating whether to make do with the bowie knife I kept on my person, or cut my losses and attempt an escape, when one of the men stopped short.

"'*Es el Doctor!* Dr. Watson, yes?' he said eagerly.

"After a moment's astonishment, I recognized a patient I had treated not two weeks before even though he could not pay me, a man who had gashed his leg so badly in a fight on the wharf that his friends had carried him to the nearest physician. He was profoundly happy to see me, a torrent of Spanish flowing from his lips, and before two minutes had passed of him gesturing proudly at his wound and pointing at me, Portillo's dispute had been forgotten. I did not press my luck, but joined them for another glass of that wretched substance and bade them farewell, Portillo's unblinking black eyes upon me until I was out of the bar and making for Front Street with all speed.

"The next day, I determined to report Portillo's presence to the colonel, for as little as I understood, I now believed him an even more sinister character. To my dismay, however, I found the house in a terrible uproar."

"I am not surprised," Holmes nodded. "What had happened?"

"Sam Jefferson stood accused of breaking into Charles Warburton's darkroom with the intent to steal his photographic apparatus. The servant who opened the door to me was hardly lucid for her tears, and

I heard cruel vituperations even from outside the house. Apparently, or so the downstairs maid said in her state of near-hysterics, Charles had already sacked Jefferson, but the colonel was livid his nephew had acted without his approval, theft or no theft, and at the very moment I knocked, they were locked in a violent quarrel. From where I stood, I could hear Colonel Warburton screaming that Jefferson be recalled, and Charles shouting back that he had already suffered enough indignities in that house to last him a lifetime. Come now, Holmes, admit to me that the tale is entirely unique," I could not help but add, for the flush of colour in my friend's face told me precisely how deeply he was interested.

"It is not the ideal word," he demurred. "I have not yet heard all, but there were cases in Lisbon and Salzburg within the last fifty years which may possibly have some bearing. Please, finish your story. You left, of course, for what gentleman could remain in such circumstances, and you called the next day upon the colonel."

"I did not, as a matter of fact, call upon the colonel."

"No? Your natural curiosity did not get the better of you?"

"When I arrived the following morning, Colonel Warburton as well as Sam Jefferson had vanished into thin air."

I had expected this revelation to strike like a bolt from the firmament, but was destined for disappointment.

"Ha," Holmes said with the trace of a smile. "Had they indeed?"

"Molly and Charles Warburton were beside themselves with worry. The safe had been opened and many deeds and securities, not to mention paper currency, were missing. There was no sign of force, so they theorized that their uncle had been compelled or convinced to provide the combination.

"A search party set out at once, of course, and descriptions of Warburton and Jefferson circulated, but to no avail. The mad colonel and his servant, either together or separately, against their wills or voluntarily, left the city without leaving a single clue behind them. Upon my evidence, the police brought Portillo in for questioning, but he proved a conclusive alibi and could not be charged. And so Colonel Warburton's obsession with war, as well as the inscrutable designs of his manservant, remain to this day unexplained.

"What do you think of it?" I finished triumphantly, for Holmes by this time leaned forward in his chair, entirely engrossed.

"I think that Sam Jefferson—apart from you and your noble intentions, my dear fellow—was quite the hero of this tale."

"How can you mean?" I asked, puzzled. "Surely the darkroom incident casts him in an extremely suspicious light. All we know is that he disappeared, probably with the colonel, and the rumour in San Francisco told that they were both stolen away by the Tejano ghost who possessed the house. That is rubbish, of course, but even now I cannot think where they went, or why."

"It is impossible to know where they vanished," Holmes replied, his grey eyes sparkling, "but I can certainly tell you why."

"Dear God, you have solved it?" I exclaimed in delight. "You cannot be in earnest—I've wracked my brain over it all these years to no avail. What the devil happened?"

"First of all, Watson, I fear I must relieve you of a misapprehension. I believe Molly and Charles Warburton were the authors of a nefarious and subtle plot which, if not for your intervention and Sam Jefferson's, might well have succeeded."

"How could you know that?"

"Because you have told me, my dear fellow, and a very workmanlike job you did in posting me up. Ask yourself when the colonel's mental illness first began. What was his initial symptom?"

"He changed his will."

"It is, you will own, a very telling starting point. So telling, in fact, that we must pay it the most stringent attention." Holmes jumped to his feet and commenced pacing the carpet like a mathematician expounding over a theorem. "Now, there are very few steps—criminal or otherwise—one can take when one is disinherited. Forgery is a viable option, and the most common. Murder is out, unless your victim has yet to sign his intentions into effect. The Warburtons hit upon a scheme as cunning as it is rare: they undertook to prove a sane man mad."

"But Holmes, that can scarcely be possible."

"I admit that fortune was undoubtedly in their favour. The colonel already suffered from an irrational preoccupation with the supernatural. Additionally, his bedroom lacked any sort of ornament, and young Charles Warburton specialized in photographic technique."

"My dear chap, you know I've the utmost respect for your remarkable faculty, but I cannot fathom a word of what you just said," I confessed.

"I shall do better, then," he laughed. "Have we any reason to think Jefferson lied when he told you of the ghost's earthly manifestations?"

"He could have meant anything by it. He could have slit that hole and stolen that firewood himself."

"Granted. But it was after you told him of Portillo's presence that he broke into the photography studio."

"You see a connection between Portillo and Charles Warburton's photographs?"

"Decidedly so, as well as a connection between the photographs, the blank wall, and the torn out lilac bush."

"Holmes, that doesn't even—"

I stopped myself as an idea dawned on me. Finally, after the passage of many years, I was beginning to understand.

"You are talking about a magic lantern," I said slowly. "By God, I have been so blind."

"You were remarkably astute, my boy, for you took note of every essential detail. As a matter of fact, I believe you can take it from here," he added with more than his usual grace.

"The colonel disinherited his niece and nephew, possibly because he abhorred their mercenary natures, in favour of war charities," I stated hesitantly. "In a stroke of brilliance, they decided to make it seem war was his mania and he could not be allowed to so slight his kin. Charles hired Juan Portillo to appear in a series of photographs as a Tejano soldier, and promised that he would be paid handsomely if he kept the sessions dead secret. The nephew developed the images onto glass slides and projected them through a magic lantern device outside the window in the dead of night. His victim was so terrified by the apparition on his wall, he never thought to look for its source behind him. The first picture, threatening the white woman, likely featured Molly Warburton. But for the second plate . . ."

"That of the knife plunging into the Texian's chest, they borrowed the colonel's old garb and probably placed it on a dummy. The firewood disappeared when a number of men assembled, further off on the grounds, to portray rebels with torches. The lilac, as is obvious—"

"Stood in the way of the magic lantern apparatus!" I cried. "What could be simpler?"

"And the headaches the colonel experienced afterwards?" my friend prodded me.

"Likely an aftereffect of an opiate or narcotic his family added to his meal in order to heighten the experience of the vision in his bedchamber."

"And Sam Jefferson?"

"A deeply underestimated opponent who saw the Warburtons for what they were and kept a constant watch. The only thing he stole was a look at the plates in Charles's studio as his final piece of evidence.

When they sent him packing, he told the colonel all he knew and they—"

"Were never heard from again," Holmes finished with a poetic flourish.

"In fact, it was the perfect revenge," I laughed. "Colonel Warburton had no interest in his own wealth, and he took more than enough to live from the safe. And after all, when he was finally declared dead, his estate was distributed just as he wished it."

"Yes, a number of lucky events occurred. I am grateful, as I confess I have been at other times, that you are an utterly decent fellow, my dear Doctor."

"I don't understand," I said in some confusion.

"I see the world in terms of cause and effect. If you had not been the sort of man willing to treat a rogue wounded in a knife fight who had no means of paying you, it is possible you would not have had the opportunity to tell me this story."

"It wasn't so simple as all that," I muttered, rather abashed, "but thank—"

"And an admirable story it was, too. You know, Watson," Holmes continued, extinguishing his pipe, "from all I have heard of America, it must be an exceedingly fertile ground for men of mettle. The place lives almost mythically in the estimations of most Englishmen. I myself have scarcely met an American, ethically inclined or otherwise, who did not possess a certain audacity of mind."

"It's the pioneer in them, I suppose. Still, I cannot help but think that you are more than a match for anyone, American or otherwise," I assured him.

"I would not presume to contradict you, but that vast expanse boasts more than its share of crime as well as of imagination, and for that reason commands some respect. I am not a complete stranger to the American criminal," he said with a smile.

"I should be delighted to hear you expound on that subject," I exclaimed, glancing longingly at my notebook and pen.

"Another time, perhaps." My friend paused, his long fingers drumming along with the drops as he stared out our front window, eyes glittering brighter than the rain-soaked street below. "Perhaps one day we may both find occasion to test ourselves further on their soil." He glanced back at me abruptly. "I should have liked to have met this Sam Jefferson, for instance. He had a decided talent."

"Talent or no, he was there to witness the events; you solved them based on a secondhand account by a man who'd never so much as heard of the Science of Deduction at the time."

"There are precious few crimes in this world, merely a hundred million variations," he shrugged. "It was a fetching little problem, however, no matter it was not matchless. The use of the magic lantern, although I will never prove it, I believe to have been absolutely inspired. Now," he finished, striding to his violin and picking it up, "if you would be so kind as to locate the brandy and cigars you mentioned earlier, I will show my appreciation by entertaining you in turn. You've come round to my liking for Kreutzer, I think? Capital. I must thank you for bringing your very interesting case to my attention; I shall lose no time informing my brother I solved it without moving a muscle. And now, friend Watson, we shall continue our efforts to enliven a dreary afternoon."

GHOSTS AND THE MACHINE
Lloyd Rose

Lloyd Rose, former chief drama critic of the *Washington Post*, has written for the *New Yorker* and the *Atlantic* and is the author of three Doctor Who novels for BBC Books.

* * * *

Excerpts from the journal of Mycroft Holmes, autumn 1874

25 September—Sherlock is bored.

This condition is not my doing, as I keep reminding him. I no more wanted this educational trip to the green wilds of American New England than he, but if between us we could not dissuade Father, then there's an end to it. *I* have accommodated myself most comfortably. This agreeable inn—a spacious, rambling, white-frame structure—has a number of airy porches furnished with wicker armchairs of generous proportion. While Father explores the golf links, I sit and admire the mountains, now shifting from green to crimson and gold, and concentrate on my Adam Smith.

Note: the Americans do whiskey atrociously but tobacco very well indeed.

29 September—I managed to talk my way out of a "delightful" hike to a local waterfall today while Sherlock did not. This was amusing.

2 October—"Even the people here are dull," he complains to me. I could retort that they are not much duller than the folk of the English countryside, but honesty compels me to admit he is not entirely wrong. The guests are almost exclusively members of the upper-middle classes from New York and Boston—pleasant enough, but intellectually limited, and with much the same sort of lives. Of the late war they appear to try to remember as little as possible, though I am certain that among the older generation many lost sons. Sherlock tells me that in a few of the local cemeteries he has explored for their native plant life, there are numerous graves of men who fell in battle ten and twelve years ago.

5 October—I overheard a ridiculous but nonetheless rather interesting conversation today. As a rule, I am fortunate enough to find a corner of the porch where I can be more or less by myself, but today a party invaded the area, taking over a table and ordering lemonade and a light lunch. There were two of them, both in banking, one a collector of ancient Byzantine (or perhaps, just perhaps, late Roman) coins and the other with a recent history of tuberculosis and an overdeveloped anxiety about rabbits. The former, whom I would have assumed to be the steadier of the pair, was regaling his companion with an extraordinary tale.

"I assure you," said he, "I am not inventing this. Nor have I succumbed to some delusional illness. And I was quite as sober as I am now."

"Nonetheless," replied his friend, "you can understand that I find your story difficult to believe."

"I should not have believed it myself if I had not seen. I scoffed when I first heard of the place."

"Which is called the Ghost Factory—"

"Ghost Shop."

"Oh, indeed!"

"That's only the derisive title of some of the natives who resent the invasion of so many tourists into their quiet town. The place is actually an inn run by a pair of brothers who, several evenings a week, hold mediumistic sittings in an upstairs room."

"My dear Daniel—"

"I know, I know, but hear me out!"

"I have heard you out. You say that musical instruments play themselves—"

"—are heard to play when no human hand could touch them—"

"—and that dozens of spirits of Red Indians appear—"

"Chinamen too! And child spirits."

"Popping up through a hidden trapdoor, no doubt."

This was my private opinion as well, but the storyteller shook his head emphatically.

"No indeed. That's part of the wonder of the thing. The place has been investigated by an expert in the detection of fraud who has had the floors and walls examined and is prepared to swear there are no secret entrances." At this point, regrettably, two young ladies joined the gentlemen, and the conversation veered off in a duller direction. I own myself intrigued. The idea of spirits is absurd, of course, but this sounds like quite a complicated hoax. If I can inquire without actually seeming interested in the nonsensical matter, I would like to find out more. Perhaps I can set Sherlock on the scent.

Later—Sherlock uncooperative. "Twaddle!" sniffed he, and proceeded to give me a patronizing lecture on human gullibility. He really can be most tiresome.

8 October—We were joined at dinner tonight by a gentleman Father had met that morning. Sherlock and I observed him with some interest from the door of the dining room, ourselves as yet undetected. He was a man of about forty with a short moustache and beard and an impressive, straight-backed presence.

"Military," said Sherlock, as if that were not obvious to anyone.

"From his air and bearing," I pointed out, "he is surely an officer of some rank. A colonel, I would think."

"And yet not a field officer," Sherlock murmured thoughtfully. "Look at his hands. No outdoor life or physical labor has roughened them."

He looked very smug as he said this, and I was forced to concede that he had a point. Fortunately, before I actually had to say so, Father noticed and beckoned us over. He introduced his companion as Mr. Henry Olcott, a reporter for *The Daily Graphic*. Sherlock and I exchanged glances.

"But with a military background, surely," said he.

"Possibly as a colonel," I added.

I regret to say that we rather displeased Father. He does not like us to "show off," as he puts it, and in this case went so far as to apologize for our rudeness. But when we hurried to voice our own apologies, Mr. Olcott genially waved them off. "They are completely correct," he said to Father, "and I would only like to know how on earth they worked it out." Father sighed, but told us to oblige him. "You will see," he remarked to our guest, "how simple it all is once they explain it." I believe Sherlock's vanity must have been tweaked at this, for he had the temerity to add, at the end of our account, "And you were a staff officer, sir, were you not?"

Father opened his mouth reprovingly, but before he could speak, Olcott exclaimed, "But that is wonderful. You are absolutely right.

I was a Special Commissioner to the War Department, in charge of investigating fraud in arsenals and shipyards."

This time Sherlock and I refrained from exchanging glances; indeed, we froze, pinned by the same certainty. But any questions we had were wiped from our minds by Father's next remark:

"And Colonel Olcott also served on the panel that investigated the murder of President Lincoln."

Needless to say, all else was forgotten as we listened to his account of the fate of that great and tragic man—of his assassination by the villain Booth, a sometime actor who knew well the interior of the theatre in which he committed his terrible crime. We listened as Colonel Olcott told us of Booth's broken ankle as he leapt to the stage; his escape by horseback; and his vanishing for twelve days while his fellow assassins—one of whom had attacked the secretary of state, one of whom was meant to kill the vice president but lost his nerve—were apprehended. He also told us of the murderer's eventual death in a burning barn, of the executions of the other conspirators. Colonel Olcott grew more and more somber as he recalled his story; even after nearly a decade, the sorrow and horror of it clearly have not left him. He spoke with great clarity and attention to detail, leaving an overall impression not only of inbred decency but of hard common sense. Indeed, as he went on, it seemed to me that I had injudiciously jumped to a conclusion—such a man could never be involved with the foolery of something called the Ghost Shop.

I said so to Sherlock later as we were preparing for bed, and he acknowledged as much. "Still," said he, "it seems almost too much of a coincidence that there should be two investigators of fraud here in this out-of-the-way part of the world at the same time," and I must agree that the odds of such a thing strike me as high.

9 October (midmorning)— The problem with Sherlock is that he has no respect for the other fellow's privacy. It never seems to occur to him that a man should be left alone, to smoke and read and mull and go about his business. He is always bustling about *discovering* things and drawing conclusions that invariably lead to his coming to me with some involved plan of action that involves stirring ourselves to a completely unnecessary degree. So, this morning, he popped up on the veranda just as I was settling in with my after-breakfast cigar, and announced, "It is he!"

I am a man who likes to enter the day gradually, and I did not immediately follow him. "Who?" I inquired irritably. "And whence this penchant for gnomic announcements, Sherlock? It's very irritating."

"I do apologize." He glanced at his watch. "I realize that I am all but waking you in the middle of the night."

"Go away."

He sat down. "I mean that Olcott is our expert on fraud! He has reserved a place on the afternoon train to Rutland and then a carriage to Chittenden—the town in which, my enquiries inform me, this so-called Ghost Shop is to be found."

I was dismayed at his industry. He must have been up since dawn, bothering people with questions and checking transportation timetables. "Well," said I, closing my eyes and hoping he would take the hint, "I gather from this enthusiasm that you're going to look into the matter after all. It sounds a fascinating hoax."

He did not immediately reply. I opened my eyes and saw that his expression was thoughtful. "It must be a very sophisticated one to have taken in Colonel Olcott. He really does not strike me as a man easily or willingly deceived."

"Nor I."

"So of course you will come to Chittenden with me to uncover the heart of this mystery."

I was actually rendered speechless for a moment. Finally, I sputtered, "Have you quite taken leave of your senses, Sherlock? Can you give me one good reason I should leave this comfortable porch for a train and then a jolting carriage ride into the wilds? These forests demoralized Burgoyne, you recall—"

"One hundred years ago," he scoffed, "and there has been at least one total deforestation since then. The trees are on average hardly twenty-five inches around."

"That is hardly the point—"

"The point, dear brother, is that if you are here this evening, you get to join Father at dinner with some gentlemen he has met who are up on all the latest theories of scientific agriculture."

Perhaps the journey will not be so bad.

9 October (late evening)—It was appalling. The train was primitive and the journey sooty—and as to the carriage ride, all I can say is that the American understanding of what is meant by "road" varies considerably from the English definition of the word. These rutted tracks must be nothing but mud when it rains. At present, there has been a drought for several weeks, so they are little but dust. And stones. At one point, there was concern we had broken a wheel. At another, we all had to dismount and ford a stream *by foot* so as to lighten the carriage for safe passage. Altogether, it was a miserable trip, not in the least helped by Olcott's good-natured stoicism and Sherlock's heretofore unexpected penchant for what I can only characterize as an exorbitant curiosity about the wilderness.

Still, I must admit the unpleasantness was considerably lightened by the story the colonel told us on the train. Sherlock had been a bit unsure how to approach him, but as soon as he found out we had heard about the events in Chittenden, he was immediately forthcoming.

He began with the history of William and Horatio Eddy, the men who, with their sister, Mary, run the Ghost Shop. It is in fact a large, two-storey farmhouse built about thirty years ago—the brothers lately added a wing so as to convert the place into an inn they call the Green Inn, doubtless to echo the name of the surrounding mountains. The brothers were raised there in what appear to have been horrible circumstances, comparable to something out of Dickens. The father was a religious zealot and tyrant who, when his sons began experiencing trances and visions, attempted to beat them—and at one point burn with scalding water—into normalcy. When this treatment proved ineffectual, he "leased" them to a traveling mountebank who exhibited them as mind readers and fortune-tellers—a dangerous business, as they were frequently mobbed, shot at, and run out of town. "The children got all the kicks and he got all the ha'pence in this transaction," the colonel observed with dry disgust.

When the father died, the brothers, now young men, returned to Chittenden to manage the family farm. Occasionally, they held medi-umistic sessions in a large parlour. As time passed, these sessions became more frequent, and at last they decided to enlarge the house and become innkeepers—in good part because, after the war, the area became a popular holiday destination and the audiences for their séances grew in number. Still, Olcott assured us, though they may make a better living than they did as farmers, the inn is not big enough for them to be earning much, and the expense of faking such elaborate manifestations would be beyond their means. In any case, they do not charge admission.

Despite the absurd subject of his story, there was something about the colonel's frankness and lack of pretension that made me unwilling to mock him. I could tell that Sherlock felt the same, for he had on his face that expression of polite interest with which he hides skepticism. Still, Olcott sensed our attitude and addressed it candidly.

He recited his own doubts and described in detail the way he and a carpenter—not a local man but one he hired at his own expense from New York—went over the room inch by inch, pulling up floorboards, tapping walls, searching for secret doors. They found nothing. Olcott personally climbed into the eaves above and discovered them to be so thick with cobwebs that no one could have hidden there to make noises or pull strings.

He was charmingly forthcoming about the possibility that he would be perceived as a mere gull. "It is the most natural reaction," he said simply. "Nor can I pretend to bring any special skills to my task—neither the profundity of the scientific investigator nor the acuteness of the police detective. I represent the layman of ordinary intelligence whose sole object is to discover the facts. Still," he could not help adding, "I am representing one of the great New York dailies. I take it for granted that my editor would not have engaged me if he had supposed me either of unsound mind, credulous, partial, dishonest, or incompetent.

"Now," here he leaned forward, "I am aware that your own Mr. Home in England has been caught out on occasion resorting to mere tricks. So, I must tell you, have the Eddy Brothers. But does it necessarily follow that they are fakes? The powers behind these manifestations are notoriously uncontrollable. On occasions when they fail, what should the poor medium do, with his audience so expectant and needy? He tries to smooth things over with some harmless bits of stage illusion and sleight of hand. How much of a generalization should be drawn from these petty subterfuges? I am not, I am happy to say, of that class of pseudo-investigators which rejects the chance of finding truth in these marvels because mediums sometimes cheat. The circulation of counterfeit coin is no proof that the genuine does not exist."

It seemed to me that those circulating counterfeit coin should not be depended on to provide the genuine, but I declined comment.

Olcott described in detail the room in which the séances are held—a large one on the first storey, at one end of which a platform and spirit cabinet have been constructed. In this chamber, nightly except for Sundays, audiences of up to thirty gather. Inside the cabinet, which is actually a small room some seven by three feet built entirely along one wall, Horatio Eddy is bound to a chair and the door shut. William Eddy stands on the platform to address the audience and take their questions. The spirits—old, young, white, Indian, male and female—emerge from the cupboard one at a time to speak or sing or answer questions. Apparently, they glow with an "unearthly light," the room itself being illuminated only by a single lantern at the opposite end from the cabinet and platform. As they speak, throughout the crowd, the ghostly touch of a cold hand will be felt on this shoulder or that wrist—but nothing seen. Empty chairs move across the room, but any impulsive fellow who grabs one finds no string attached. Musical instruments are heard to play. . . .

"How far away are these apparitions?" Sherlock asked neutrally.

"No more than four feet from those on the front benches. I myself have sat there often."

"You say these spirits have their own light," I said. "What are their skins like?"

"Well, the Indians have their usual hue. The whites are a bit grey to our eyes, even the children. I do not mean to imply that they shine like lanterns; the light flickers from their skin as they move."

"They are translucent, or solid?"

"As solid-looking as you or I."

"Are their voices unusual?"

"No. There is nothing 'spectral' about them, and they are appropriate to each spirit's apparent age."

"Clothing?" murmured Sherlock. His eyes had half shut.

"Also appropriate. Somewhat old-fashioned, of course."

"And have you touched them?"

Olcott emphatically shook his head. "They will not allow themselves to be touched. The Eddys have apologized for this to me, but of course they must do what the spirits request."

"And what do you think of the Eddys?"

Sherlock is sometimes quite inspired. It was exactly the right tack—away from the unreal, about which Olcott was intellectually defensive, and into the personal and emotional. The colonel was not expecting the question, and for a moment he hesitated. You could see on his face the struggle between his desire to be loyal to these strange friends and his commitment to a truthful account. "They are . . . difficult," he said at last. "With such a childhood, it is hardly surprising. My first weeks here were extremely unpleasant. I was snubbed, near-ignored, made to feel unwelcome. It was a slow process, gaining their trust. I do not blame them. They are too used to ridicule and disrespect."

"But of their character . . . " Sherlock persisted gently.

"They are honest, of that I am convinced. But you must understand," he continued earnestly, "that the character of the medium, his moral nature *as a person*, is irrelevant. These people have been endowed with a wonderful gift—an extra sense, if you will. They have no more control over their attraction of these powers than they have over seeing when their eyes are open. As the eye is a machine for receiving light, so they are machines for receiving otherworldly energies. A person of this kind may be a very bad man but a very good machine."

Sherlock smiled faintly—involuntarily, I thought—and asked no more questions. As for myself, I felt we had what we needed: Olcott's impression of what he had witnessed. There was no sense speculating further until we had seen these phenomena for ourselves.

After all this, I rather expected the Green Inn to be a gloomy, gabled manse out of some gothic novel. But upon arrival, we found a weathered but ordinary white clapboard house with a pleasant roofed porch along its front. There was no garden, but the expanse of grass was clipped and tidy, with here and there a hen pecking among the brilliant fallen leaves. The sun, though sinking towards the mountaintops, was bright, the air crisp, and the whole scene as far from ghostly as one could imagine. Visitors wandered the premises, talking animatedly. I could see no one who seemed to be our hosts, but on the porch a woman serving tea responded to Olcott's wave and he identified her as the sister, Mary Eddy.

Olcott led us round the wing accommodating the "séance room." This is a two-and-a-half-storey addition that gives the building a T-shape. The room in question is on the first floor; the end containing the "medium's cabinet" sits above the kitchen and a pair of butteries, and boasts a small but accessible window that Sherlock pointed out.

Olcott chuckled. "Yes, it is the first thing most people spot," he said. "But no ladder is owned on the premises. And I have covered the opening with mosquito netting and secured that with wax stamped with my own signet. The seals have never been broken, nor the netting torn except once during a windstorm."

It seemed to me that on such an extensive property there might be a ladder hidden *some*where, particularly as the forest started a mere fifty yards from where we stood. Sherlock must have shared my doubts, for as we walked past, he gave a quick, searching glance at the ground beneath the window. The drought had made the earth hard as iron, however, and he turned back to me with a shrug, shaking his head.

Dinner was a regrettable concoction of boiled beef and vegetables served with a harsh, tart apple cider. The experience so dispirited me

that I paid little attention to our fellow diners but sought the porch
and a cigarette as soon as possible, in spite of the gentleman on my
left having clearly spent several interesting years in Kyoto, a city I
would be tempted to visit had I any inclination to travel. (Sherlock, for
some curious reason of his own, has always expressed a desire to see
the fjords.)

Mary Eddy helped serve, but our hosts themselves had not appeared.
Preparing for the evening's performance, no doubt. As I was musing in
spite of myself on the form this might take, a figure came around the
corner of the house. As he drew closer, the porch lanterns showed me
a tall, strong-looking, sullen-faced fellow with deep-set dark eyes and a
thick moustache. He looked to be in his early forties and had remarkable
hands—calloused with farm labor, but long-fingered and strangely
sensitive in appearance. I knew who he must be. "Mr. Eddy?"

He stopped and eyed me indifferently. "Ayuh."

"I look forward to this evening's—" I almost said "entertainment"
but caught myself—"visitations."

He snorted. "English, are you?"

"Yes."

"We made a fool of you in '76."

"That wasn't me, I'm afraid," I said. "Perhaps you are confusing me
with one of my great-grandfathers."

He only stared.

"I am here with Colonel Olcott," I continued. "I was hoping to see
the room in which these mystic experiences occur, before the séance
starts properly."

"The devil you were," he said coarsely, and went inside, pushing
past Sherlock who was just coming to join me.

"Pleasant fellow," he observed. "A nice attempt, Mycroft, but he
seems unlikely to cooperate. However," he moved a few feet along

the porch to peer in the dining room window, "I see that both brothers have deigned to join their guests for coffee. We have a few moments. Quickly now." He took my elbow. "We must have a look at that room."

I shook him off. "You are not seriously suggesting that I sprint nimbly up some dark staircase to sneak around looking for clues?"

He looked me up and down. "You're right. Sprinting nimbly isn't in it for you. You return to the dining room and distract them."

And before I could object to this high-handed order, he was gone, silent as a cat, I'll say that for him. I hurried back to the dining room, aware that, as it is beneath the séance chamber, Sherlock was in danger of being heard at some point, no matter how softly he tried to move. I confess I was at something of a loss. Rapidly improvised actions are not my forte. I am a man who values careful planning. The best I could do when I rejoined the diners was request—impolitely, as they were just finishing—that I might also have coffee.

The Eddy I had met had been joined by his brother. He was a bit younger and had a higher forehead and a tiny patch of beard beneath his lip, but otherwise they were enough alike almost to have been twins. Both stared at me obstinately and were on the point of denying my request when, by a stroke of fortune, a young lady at the table requested a second cup for herself. Grudgingly, Mary Eddy returned to the kitchen while the brothers glowered at me. Olcott, whom my rudeness clearly embarrassed (greatly to my regret, but it couldn't be helped) introduced me, but they responded with little better than grunts. Attempts at small talk were met with the same response.

An uncomfortable silence took over the table, and I expected any moment to hear the thump of a footfall from above. So, like a buffoon, I rose from my seat, saying with forced jollity, "Perhaps your sister could use some help carrying the cups," and rushed into the kitchen.

This bizarre act stunned both my fellow diners and Mary Eddy, who regarded me with alarm as I bustled in. In truth, even before I rose, it had occurred to me that a look at the kitchen ceiling might be in order. Now I saw that it was simple plaster over lathe, obviously impenetrable. In the opposite wall, the doors of the two small butteries stood darkly open. "Some more milk perhaps?" I inquired idiotically and dashed through the right-hand door, followed by Miss Eddy's "Here now!" A glance upward showed me that the family had economized on the ceiling. It was not lathe and plaster but only naked beams, on which the platform and cabinet above sat, the underside of their shared floor exposed. I turned instantly back to the kitchen with a fatuous, "Dear me, it's dark in there, isn't it?" and returned to the dining room just as the brothers were rising to come after me. "My apologies," I said sincerely, for I had not enjoyed making such a fool of myself. "The lady did not need my help."

"Where's the other one?" said William Eddy (the brother who had met me on the porch) suspiciously, and to my relief, Sherlock's voice replied from outside, "Here," and we saw the glow of his cigarette through the window. He entered a moment later, not a hair out of place, and coolly took his former seat beside the colonel, to whom he leaned over with a whispered apology. I heard the words "too much cider at dinner," and, truly, if it had not been seven miles of bad road, I would have walked out then and there and gone straight to a hotel in Rutland. Instead, I sat where I was, inanely praising the very poor coffee Miss Eddy brought in, while the people around me exchanged embarrassed glances and the Eddys looked thunderous. A more unpleasant quarter hour I have never spent.

We were all ushered to the porch while the Eddys ascended to the upper room to prepare, and no doubt to see if there were any traces of meddling. Knowing Sherlock, I was certain there would not be. He had lit another cigarette and looked altogether too pleased with himself.

I took him down into the yard to tell him what he could do the next time he thought of involving me in one of his silly adventures, but he disarmed me by saying, "Well done, Mycroft. I know how unpleasant you must have found that, yet you did splendidly," and offered me a cigarette.

I took it.

We smoked for a few minutes. The stars were brilliant in the clear, cool night, and here in the mountains there seemed to be many more of them.

"Is it the window?" I asked him.

He shook his head. "The seals are in place, and the window frame is secure in the wall."

"They might have made an impress of the signet and reproduced it."

"I think it more likely that—"

But at this point we were summoned to the séance.

The upstairs chamber was a large one. Though distance was difficult to judge in the very poor light (as the colonel had said, there was but a single lantern, and that in a corner farthest from the cabinet and platform), I would hazard it was a good thirty feet from the rear wall to the edge of the platform, which itself appeared to be five or six feet deep. Sherlock whispered to me that there was roughly a yard between the door of the cabinet and the back wall of the house with its little window. "But I don't think they bothered with the window. The nailheads in the floor of the cabinet are much battered."

I nodded. All had become clear.

The Eddy brothers mounted the platform. With their deep-set eyes and surly faces, they looked grim enough, if not particularly spiritual. William gave a short speech about spirits and their nature and the responsibility of the medium and so forth; then he and Horatio entered the chamber, where he bound Horatio to a chair with thick rope. The audience was invited to come up one by one to observe this and to test the final result, which took several minutes, as there were nearly thirty people present. The dress of these revealed most of them as visitors, but there were several who appeared to be residents of the town. The latter did not bother to check the binding, and neither did Sherlock and I: no doubt the trick would be done well. Colonel Olcott too kept his place, up near the front and to one side, expectant but relaxed.

Finally, everyone was seated again. A curtain was drawn across the cabinet door and William Eddy repeated most of his speech. He moved to the center of the platform and shut his eyes. He swayed slightly. The room was hushed. From the cabinet, all was quiet. Then, from within, a violin began to play.

Sherlock winced. Whoever the spirit was, the violin was not his or her first instrument. The rest of the audience did not seem to notice the quality of the music, but gasped and murmured. They were equally impressed by the rattling of an invisible tambourine. However, the spirits did not seem to be in the mood for physical contact tonight. I saw no one flinch or start at a ghostly touch. Indeed, the presentation felt rather paltry. I suspect that mistrust of Sherlock and me had something to do with this.

Suddenly, William Eddy moved to the far right of the platform. The violin and tambourine fell silent. A tense moment passed before the curtain moved aside. The doorway was dark. Then a figure appeared and stepped solemnly out.

I found myself, quite unexpectedly, embarrassed. Embarrassed for the figure on the platform, for the audience around me, and for Colonel Olcott. I heard Sherlock sigh softly and realized he had had a similar reaction. Morosely, I examined the "apparition." It was a tall man clearly meant to be a red Indian, though a combination of wig and headdress so obscured his face that he might have been Chinese, or a woman. His hands were indeed, so far as it was possible to tell in the shadows, reddish, as if some rouge had been rubbed over a deep tan. And I suppose one could say that his face glowed if a couple of smudgy gleams from the half-hidden face could be called a glow. He began to chant nonsense syllables in a deep voice. William Eddy stood with his head respectfully bowed. My embarrassment faded to be replaced by boredom. If I could have left without notice, I would have.

But I was trapped for the evening.

And a long evening it was. "Spirits" trouped in and out of the cabinet, William Eddy pacing the platform and making some brief remarks between each appearance. There were more red Indians and a number of white people in clothing from a few generations past who, indeed, had slightly greyish skin where it wasn't streaked with phosphorous— some attempt to make them look misty, perhaps, though a more solid bunch I never saw. The audience had begun to recover from its dumb wonder, and a few bold souls ventured questions. Some of the "spirits" ignored them. Others nodded and then turned to William Eddy, apparently communicating with him through some thought process, for he was the one who answered. Still others answered, in a variety of voices, almost all of them bearing traces at the very least of the local accent.

The questions were what I suppose are the usual sort at these affairs. Will my crop yield be high or poor? Should I invest in this or that? The answers to these questions, I noted, were vague and "mystical," sometimes in rhyme. The otherworldly visitors were more specific when someone asked about a deceased relative: the loved one was always happy and always wished the survivor well. A few people, not all of them female, wept at this information. I felt myself growing angry and rather hoped Sherlock would have one of his impulsive urges and dart forward to unmask the impostor, but he remained still, indeed almost rigid, his attention fixed on the proceedings.

Apparently to vary the mood, some of the apparitions performed a trick by agreeing to improvise in rhyme on any subject. A number of these efforts were surprisingly agile and amusing, but most were on the level of these few lines, which I regret to say have stuck in my head:

Corn
Is when summer is born
On a hot July morn
Or earlier too
Depending on rain.
And it comes without pain
As a gift from the loving Lord to us.

At one point, a child "spirit," a little girl of seven or so with fluffy golden hair and dressed all in white, attempted to rhyme on the word "love" but, charmingly I must confess, collapsed in giggles and had to be led by William Eddy back inside the cabinet. Afterward, Colonel Olcott asked us whether we had not found her endearing: "I am always delighted by her."

"She comes often, then?" said Sherlock politely.

"Indeed, yes. She is a playful little thing."

We were on the porch again, with people hurrying to their horses or conveyances, as the Green Inn has only eleven rooms and most of the visitors were lodging with other residents of Chittenden who had a bed and a corner to spare. The night had grown chilly, and in the lantern light the colonel's face was flushed with cold as well as excitement. I did not know what to say to him, and I'm sure neither did Sherlock, but fortunately he was surrounded by people eager for his conversation. Soon, he was quietly but passionately addressing a small crowd, speaking of the "self-complacent disdain" of scientific men: "Last summer, at a meeting of this country's most prestigious scientific association, hours were devoted to a discussion of the habits and characteristics of the *tumble-bug.* A nice subject to be used as an excuse for neglecting to observe and analyze the unknown occult laws by which a spirit may clothe itself with a material form. These men bend in their laboratories to study wriggling insects and squirming reptiles, blind to the field of research that lies before them in the direction of the Inner World."

10 October— Sherlock and I did not have much to say to each other as we retired last evening in a small stuffy room at the Green Inn. I wrote in this journal while he went immediately to bed. This morning, the Colonel stayed on at Chittenden and we returned to Manchester on our own, though surrounded by enthusiastic and wondering spectators from the night before. It was not until we were walking from the train station back to our inn in Manchester, that Sherlock spoke. I was by now frankly bored with the whole matter, but he appeared disturbed, or at least distant. As we talked, he exhibited none of his usual eagerness and kept his eyes uncharacteristically down, watching the yellow leaves we scuffed from our path.

"The whole village is in on it," said he, "because the whole village benefits."

I nodded. "The Eddys' inn isn't large enough to accommodate or feed all the visitors, and the other residents take them in—"

"—And charge them well for a hard bed and a plain meal. Some of the villagers sit in the audience and assist with the 'ghostly' touches—"

"—Probably accomplished by nothing more complicated than an extending rod. Horatio Eddy escapes from his ropes with the ease of the practiced conjurer—"

"—And plays, after his fashion, the violin, as well as the tambourine. The spirits, in their costumes and phosphorus makeup, are the populace of Chittenden."

"They don't use the window, you say."

"Unnecessary. They come up through the floor in the cabinet."

"A possibility the colonel thought he had eliminated when he discovered no trap doors."

Sherlock snorted impatiently. "He looked for what he thought he ought to find and then didn't find it. It's a classic case of overcomplicating a situation. What need of trapdoors when you can merely lift the floorboards? The nailheads were worn, and the wood around them scarred, from repeatedly being hammered in again."

"Doubtless the nails had been shortened so that the boards pulled up as easily as opening a box."

"I am certain that was the case."

"The ceilings of the butteries were open to the beams above that supported platform and cabinet, you know."

He smiled at me. "Excellent, Mycroft. That answers the last of our questions. The 'spirits' climbed up on the beams and out through the floor, after being smuggled into the kitchen while everyone was upstairs. William Eddy, with his pacing and speeches, made enough noise to cover any sounds from below."

We walked on for a moment in silence.

"Well," said I at last, "no great mystery there."

"On the contrary," said he soberly, "there is a very great mystery indeed."

11 October—Much against my will, Sherlock inveigled me into accompanying him on a walk. I could tell he had something on his mind and was perfectly willing to hear him out, but I saw no reason we could not sit comfortably, possibly enjoying cigars, while he unburdened himself. He, however, was restless and tense and no sooner would he sit then he would be up and pacing, so I finally got

up myself and we went through the village and south along the verge of the road.

Having got me to go with him, he perversely fell silent. I put up with this for a few minutes before coming to the point. "It's this Olcott business, isn't it?"

He nodded. "I cannot understand it."

"But you've explained everything."

"Not *that*," he said irritably. "That sham and paste!"

"Then what?"

He looked at me seriously. "Surely you agree that Colonel Olcott is a highly educated and intelligent man."

"Of course."

"Nothing of the flighty about him."

"Nothing at all. Except this strange belief in spiritualism."

"Exactly! It hardly seems in character, does it?"

I acknowledged that it did not. "But most people are not rational, Sherlock."

"This is worse than that," he insisted. "Here we have a man who rose to the rank of colonel as an investigator of fraud, whose observational and analytical skills were so prized that he was chosen to serve on the committee that investigated a president's assassination. He clearly has a first-rate mind. And a mind is a machine. You cannot gum it up with shoddy ideas and expect it to keep functioning optimally. This is some morbid form of self-betrayal."

The passage along the main road was not particularly pleasant, the verge being narrow and the traffic heavy and dusty, so when we came to a pair of gateposts surmounted with marble figures of a sorrowing angel and a mourning woman, we turned in immediately. "Dellwood Cemetery," a sign read, and we found ourselves in a place more like a park than a graveyard, with winding lanes and handsome trees and example after example of memorial statuary: angels wept, families prayed, small children gazed down at stone lilies in their hands. Nothing further from the crowded church and city cemeteries of England could be conceived, and we wandered among the tombs in uneasy fascination. Somehow, I was not surprised when, in the distance, we saw Colonel Olcott.

He was standing in front of a pair of simple stones, and his attitude suggested contemplation rather than personal grief. I made to turn aside and leave him with his thoughts, but he saw us and waved in a comradely fashion. I glanced at Sherlock as we approached; his profile was hard and set. I sighed to myself. He had decided the colonel deserved the truth.

"Look at this, boys," said Olcott as we approached. His voice and manner were subdued as he gestured to the twin gravestones. Both were of young men, siblings by their name, who had died in 1863. Someone had recently left purple wildflowers on each grave. Olcott gestured across the expanse of the cemetery. "Dozens of them. And yet, that is nothing. In the graveyards of Pennsylvania, of Maryland and Virginia . . . " He trailed off for a moment. "I saw very little active duty, you know," he finally continued. "I am not ashamed; I had my job to do. I'm not like so many in the North who bought their way out of service so that some poor Irishman could die in their stead. I have been shot at in my time. I'm not such a fool that I wish I had been shot at more."

He fell quiet again, staring at the graves. We waited on his silence. "Over six hundred thousand men were killed in the war," he said softly. "I think it is important to use the word 'killed' rather than 'died'. They were shattered. Blown apart. There were battles in which twenty thousand were slain in a day. Even two days after, there would yet be . . . pieces of men lying in the bloody dirt. Or in mud. Dust. There were bodies no one will ever recognize. Those who loved them will never know . . . "

He squinted at the sky for a moment. "If I can demonstrate the genuineness of these phenomena," he said very quietly, "then all mankind may be assured that the sting of death and the grave's victory have passed away. Death itself will have died. No," he said fiercely, lowering his eyes again to the gravestones, "death itself will have been killed. And all the weeping will dissolve in joy. And all the blood will be as dew."

He stood there, still as the stones around him, and I realized he had forgotten us. I touched Sherlock's arm and we moved quietly away. I looked back as we reached the gates. Colonel Olcott had not moved.

All the way back to the inn, I waited for Sherlock to say something. But he never did. At last, as we mounted the steps, I could keep still no longer. "Well," I challenged him, "what of your plan to enlighten Colonel Olcott and save him from himself?"

He neither paused nor looked at me as he stepped ahead through the doors.

"A bad machine," he said, "may be a very good man."

Afternote:

The story of Henry Olcott and the Eddy Brothers is true. Three days after this tale ends, he met Madame Helena Blavatsky, and they went on to found the most far-reaching of the Victorian-era occult institutions, the Theosophical Society. Olcott wrote an account of his experiences in Chittenden, People from the Other World, *which I used as my main source; indeed, some of Olcott's words in my story, including "Such a person may be a very bad man but a very good machine," are direct quotes from that book. However, all speculation into his reason for belief in the Eddys are my own: the colonel remains a mystery.*

Excerpts from an Unpublished Memoir Found in the Basement of the Home for Retired Actors

Steve Hockensmith

Steve Hockensmith is the author of the popular Holmes on the Range mysteries about Sherlock Holmes–worshipping cowboy brothers "Big Red" and "Old Red" Amlingmeyer. The first book in the series was nominated for the Edgar, Shamus, Dilys, and Anthony awards in 2006, and since then, St. Martin's Minotaur has released several sequels. Hockensmith's first published crime story, "Erie's Last Day," won the Short Mystery Fiction Society's Derringer Award and appeared in *Best American Mystery Stories 2001*. Today, Hockensmith is a regular contributor to mystery magazines and anthologies, and his short fiction has been nominated for almost every major award in the field. Hockensmith and "Big Red" Amlingmeyer share a blog at www.stevehockensmith.com.

* * * *

Sherlockian lore is replete with tales of dusty manuscripts in musty vaults that, when found, shed surprising new light on the Great Detective. I myself have enjoyed reading many such "discoveries," even while (no offense to the discoverers) finding their provenance highly suspect. If there really were so many heretofore unknown Holmes chronicles floating around, there could hardly be a cellar, attic, or cupboard in the world that wasn't home to at least one, if not several.

I am no longer skeptical, however. Here's why.

In June of this year, I received in the mail a most remarkable (and rather dusty and, yes, musty) manuscript that—really and truly!—sheds surprising new light on the Great Detective. It was being sent to me, a cover letter said, because of my own small successes in the world of Sherlockiana. Perhaps I could act as literary agent for the party who'd unearthed it (who wished, for reasons I can't go into, to remain anonymous)?

The timing was fortuitous—practically miraculous, really—as I'd just been queried about a possible submission to this very collection. And here one was! And one of incalculable value to historians, as well, for it backs up one of William S. Baring-Gould's most interesting claims in his classic biography Sherlock Holmes of Baker Street: that Holmes once trod the boards, and in America, no less.

Unfortunately (or perhaps fortunately, as you will see), space does not permit us to present the manuscript in its entirety here. Not by a long shot. The verbiage is lush, thick, and, at times, tangled, and I had to hack my way through it like Jungle Jim through darkest Africa.

I think it was worth the slog, though. I hope you agree. If you don't, I would suggest this: Take a look in the attic. There's a good chance you'll find something there you like better.

—Stephen B. Hockensmith
Alameda, California
August 9, 2008

From *What a Piece of Work! My Life in the Limelight*
Chapter Fifty-Nine
"Some Notable Shame"

Oh, St. Louis, St. Louis—if only there were anything saintly about you. Anything heavenly, anything worthy of veneration. Anything not spackled with filth! But, no, alas. Praise for you I must limit to this: You are not Indianapolis.

And this, too, I will add upon further reflection. Your odors may have assaulted me, your citizens may have insulted me, your "theatre" may have been an insult to *the* theatre, yet at no time whilst walking your dung-paved paths (I cannot grace them with the appellation "streets") did I feel myself in danger of mortal harm . . . excepting, of course, that which I might inflict upon myself in order to escape you the quicker.

No, for that honor—the privilege of experiencing a fright worthy of Madame Tussauds Chamber of Horrors—I have Leadville, Colorado, to thank.

Leadville, of course, wasn't on the original itinerary for Sasanoff's tour of America. If it had been, I never would have signed on with the man's company. One glance at a map and I'd have seen that he was leading us deep into that infamous "Wild West" from which tales of savagery and death routinely gush like geysers of blood. At the time, the martyr Custer was but three years in his shallow prairie grave, and I certainly would have had no desire to become his neighbor. St. Louis was both as west and as wild as I ever intended to experience.

A few days before our engagement there was due to end, however, Sasanoff gathered the company to make an announcement. New Orleans would not be our next stop, as had been planned. There would be a "brief detour" to Colorado, where our *Twelfth Night* would help inaugurate "the grandest theatre west of the Mississippi."

Never mind that there was no such thing as a "brief detour" to Colorado from St. Louis, the journey from one to the other being nearly one thousand miles long. As for us opening "the grandest theatre west of the Mississippi," this was rich indeed given that we had yet to see anything approaching grand *east* of it, the stages of St. Louis, Chicago, Indianapolis (Oh! How my hand trembles to write that accursed word!), Cincinnati, Philadelphia, Hartford, etc., etc., being no more grand than an East End public house water closet.

The long delay in visiting New Orleans would be a bitter blow to the troupe, too. Most of us found American "culture" so woeful we were actually looking forward to the influence of (God help us) the French.

But Sasanoff quashed any hint of mutiny quickly, reminding us that we had all signed contracts that explicitly gave him, the acting manager, authority to add and drop tour dates—and company members—as he saw fit. If we didn't fancy a little jaunt westward, we could always remain behind . . . and make our way back to England alone.

This was an unveiled threat to most of us, of course. But I had the feeling it was intended for one of us—He Who Shall Not Be Further Canonized by My Pen—as more of an invitation.

[*First introduced in Chapter Fifty-Six ("The 'States' of America— Filthy and Repulsive"), He Who Shall Not Be Further Canonized by My Pen is never definitively identified. Even the most casual Sherlockian scholar should recognize him, however. To facilitate ease of reading, he is henceforth referred to wherever possible by the author's other nickname for him: "the Whelp." —S.B.H.*]

Our leading man's relations with the Whelp had continued their deterioration, and though the two rarely argued about the proper approach to acting any longer—a byproduct of not speaking to each other—Sasanoff had seen fit to demote the young dilettante. No longer was the Whelp our Malvolio. He was now Priest and

Musician #1 and Sailor #2 and other assorted nonentities a step up from scenery.

Yet the Whelp, with his usual arrogance, put up the pretense that he was *thankful* to be a mere spear carrier.

"I've played Malvolio for months," he said to me. "There was nothing more to learn from the part. Blending into the background in so many new guises, on the other hand—that's a challenge I look forward to."

As if it requires skill to *not* be noticed! It took all my own considerable powers as a thespian not to laugh in his face.

Unfortunately, much as it would have relieved us to be rid of him, the Whelp didn't rise to Sasanoff's bait, and our manager was still reluctant to sack him outright. When we set off for Colorado a week later, the company was intact.

I've written much already about the peculiar torments of American rail travel, so I won't dwell on them again except to say this: [*Approximately three thousand words have been omitted here in the interest of (perhaps unattainable, given the source) brevity. —S.B.H*]

All that was but preamble to the real tortures ahead, however. Leadville, it turned out, was a mining "boom town" not even two years old. No rail line had yet reached it, and the last hundred miles up from Denver required us to transfer to a pair of privately engaged coaches.

And when I write of traveling *up*, I do not mean we went north. Leadville actually lies to the southwest of Denver. It was further up into the snow-peaked mountains we had to go. And go and go and go. Mr. Verne and the other dreamers may assure us man will soon master fantastic flying machines, but if the like of Leadville is all we'll find in the clouds, I say it's not worth the bother.

After enduring nerve-racking rides along gaping gorges on rocky, hole-pocked roads plagued (the cackling drivers delighted in telling us) by both bandit gangs and bloodthirsty bands of Native warriors, we finally arrived at our destination: Gomorrah in the Alps. Or so it struck me at first. I would revise my estimation—*downward*—the longer I was there.

Surrounding the town on all sides were shoddily built shacks, tree stumps without number, and the yawning black mouths of the silver mines. Closer in was a fringe of tents—lodgings for newly arrived fortune hunters and the businesses (mostly "saloons" and drafty bagnios) that catered to them. And then at last we entered the city proper (if one could apply either word to Leadville) and found ourselves rolling down actual streets . . . broad ones comprised entirely of dirt and bracketed on both sides by only slightly sturdier variations on the canvas-topped groggeries and *maisons de joie* we'd just passed.

"To such a place as this we've brought the Bard," Sasanoff said with an incredulous shake of the head.

Only I was on hand to reply, Sasanoff having granted me the honor of sharing his private car while the rest of the company crammed themselves into the other coach like so much meat into an overstuffed sausage.

"Indeed," I said, and I reached out and gave little Master Sasanoff a hearty slap on one of his Lilliputian shoulders. "Dr. Livingstone himself couldn't have claimed to do more for the spread of civilization!"

Sasanoff's expressive features curled into a smirk.

"Nor could he have claimed to profit so handsomely by it," he said.

I chuckled through gritted teeth, for Sasanoff had favored me in another way, as well: by sharing an explanation for our presence in Leadville. The American silver magnate Horace Tabor had offered five thousand dollars for a week's run in the town's newly built opera house. Being under contract, of course, none of the players would see a penny's extra profit. The windfall would be Sasanoff's alone.

Uneasy lies the head that wears a crown, however, and Sasanoff's wee little head was soon uneasy indeed. Construction of the Tabor Opera House (the tycoon, with the usual humility of his ilk, had named the theatre after himself) was behind schedule, and our premiere there delayed at least a week. It had been hard enough for Sasanoff to put off our engagement in New Orleans. If we tarried too long, our run there—and our subsequent appearances in Atlanta, Richmond, and Washington—might be cancelled. The second half of the tour could collapse like a row of dominoes.

Predictably, the days that followed saw Sasanoff in the blackest of moods, and most of the company—terrorized by both their ill-tempered acting manager and the town he'd marooned them in—barricaded themselves in their hotel rooms. The Whelp, on the other hand, was rarely to be found in his: he quickly took to disappearing for hours at a time. In one of my few forays into Leadville's mud-splattered fray, I entered a low tavern (drawn, of course, by simple curiosity) and spotted him standing alone at the bar, watching all around him as if it were some great drama unfolding upon the stage. He seemed to be invisible to the ruffians infesting the place, yet upon *me* their attention seized instantly with hungry-eyed insolence. My ample frame and lordly bearing always served me well on the boards, but here it put me at a distinct disadvantage.

"Ho ho ho! Lookee who just walked in!" cried a miner so blackened with soot he looked like he bathed in cinders as the rest of us do water. He reached out a hand and took the obscene liberty of patting my stomach. "It's Santa Claus a whole month early!"

"If you please," I said, brushing away the man's grubby paw. But before I could utter another word in protest, the saloon erupted with more shouts.

"Where's yer sleigh, Santa?"

"Why ain't ya in yer red suit, Santa?"

"What'd ya bring us, Santa?"

Miners, "muleskinners," layabouts, even the lewd women such rough-hewn rustics consort with—all were jeering and laughing at me.

I turned to flee the raucous uproar. Before I could make my escape, however, I locked eyes, for just a second, on the Whelp. He was regarding me coolly, in that detached yet deeply probing way our fellow company members found so disquieting. And I could have sworn the young rascal was *smiling*.

I immediately relayed the incident to Sasanoff, taking an actor's license to give myself a more flattering exit line ("I would give you bounders lumps of coal, only I see it's smeared all over your filthy faces already!").

"He's the lowest utility player, consorting with rabble . . . yet he still thinks himself superior to us all," Sasanoff mused darkly. "I should have sent him packing weeks ago."

"Yes," I said. "You should have."

Sasanoff glowered at me—and a fine glower it was, too. The man may have been little taller than an overgrown squirrel, but he was undoubtedly one of the great Richard IIIs of his time.

Of course, Richard would have shown an impudent knave like the Whelp considerably less mercy than Sasanoff had, and why our otherwise irascible manager tolerated the stripling's cheek was a matter of much conjecture in the company. It had to do with an incident early in the tour, some whispered—a predicament the Whelp freed Sasanoff from with his sharp mind and even sharper tongue. Whatever the reason, even I, Sasanoff's closest confidante in the troupe, had not been made privy to the truth.

"Yes, well . . . you'd all better be on your guard," Sasanoff snarled at me now. "I'm in a foul enough temper to dismiss the whole company—myself included!"

I soothed his savage breast with the sweet music of gentle (feigned) laughter, then changed the subject to something more mutually amusing: the latest broadside in Catherine P_____ and Thomas B_____'s ongoing battle for the affections of Louis H_____.

[*A short passage has been excised here by request of the B_____ estate. —S.B.H.*]

My rendering of these inanities *d'amour* lightened Sasanoff's spirits considerably. And just in time, too. Horace Tabor and his wife were hosting a reception for the company in the hotel's paltry ballroom. It was time to kiss the backer's backside.

Tabor himself I found to be the epitome of the American ideal: a "self-made man." Alas, what he'd made of himself was vulgar in the extreme, and the making of him seemed to involve little more than a layer of dumb luck slapped over a foundation of slavering avarice. But, for all that, self-made he was. God certainly would want none of the credit.

The other town notables who turned out to greet us (and drink Tabor's flat champagne) I have even less to say about, except that they were "notable" only for their wretched clothing and abominable manners.

Still, let it never be said I couldn't play to the groundlings, and I was, as always, the darling of all. Sasanoff, as was *his* way at soirees, stuck close to the hosts (and the money), and I swooped in from time to time when it looked as though the conversation could use a little enlivening. Which was frequently. Tabor was the sort of man who grew forlorn and bewildered if the talk strayed far from commerce, while his wife . . . well, she made such a faint impression I can't, at this late date, recall her at all. In fact, I could barely remember she was present even when she was speaking to me.

I was giving the Tabors a comical foretaste of my performance as Sir Toby Belch, alternately huzzahing and haranguing as only the great old reprobate can, when I noticed Sasanoff scowling at something behind me. I glanced back to find the Whelp sauntering in a full hour late.

Usually, one might expect a sense of decorum—or, at the very least, self interest—to discourage public sniping between a leading man/manager and his supporting players. Yet (as exhaustively chronicled in previous chapters), Sasanoff and the Whelp had clashed at one gathering after another, and always on the same tiresome subject.

To wit, acting. That, so far as any of the troupe knew, the Whelp was a nobody from nowhere hadn't stopped him from airing his foolish views on proper dramatics. Sometime after leaving London, it seemed, he'd been infected by that always-fatal (to good acting) disease known as "Naturalism," and he'd increasingly insisted that Truth demanded the avoidance of "stylized bombast" (his phrase, not mine) and scrupulous attention to realistic detail. Sasanoff (and I, when sufficiently provoked) quite rightly countered that audiences don't care two figs about Truth. They crave Big—big characters, big emotions, big laughs, big tears. Any actor who chooses to be Small is also choosing empty houses over full ones. To which the Whelp invariably replied that he hadn't taken up the study of acting in order to enrich himself with *money*. Which was fine, it was always pointed out in return, because his approach to the craft would surely leave him penniless.

Round and round it ever went, and I certainly had no desire to see the circuit run again. Yet Sasanoff, sadly, couldn't resist a dig—the first, it turned out, in what would soon become a very deep hole indeed.

"Let me guess," he said to the Whelp. "You were studying your lines and lost track of the time."

The Whelp replied with a tight smile and a "touché" nod.

"I apologize for my late arrival," he said, addressing Mr. and Mrs. Tabor. "But I did indeed lose track of the time—while exploring this most intriguing community of yours."

I only barely stifled a roll of the eyes, but the Tabors (apparently afflicted with the same baseless provincial pride I'd encountered everywhere in America) grinned and cooed and practically adopted the Whelp on the spot.

"Think nothing of it!" Mr. Tabor said. "Why, there's so much to see around here, so much to do, I can understand a man getting a little lost in it."

"To be honest, I was surprised any of you *were* on time," his wife added with what I'm sure she imagined was coquettish levity. "Aren't actors always supposed to make a dramatic entrance?"

"Only the great ones," I said with a censorious sniff.

The Tabors just kept grinning idiotically, my point blunted by the impenetrable thickness of their plebeian skulls.

Mr. Tabor turned to Sasanoff.

"And what role will we see our young friend here playing come opening night?"

Sasanoff begrudgingly provided proper introductions, dismissively presenting the Whelp as "one of our junior utility players."

"What Mr. Sasanoff means," the Whelp said, "is that you will see me in a variety of roles. You won't, however, do much *hearing* of me. The parts are very small."

"Oh, that seems like a shame," Mrs. Tabor simpered. "You're such a striking-looking young man, and your voice is so—"

"It takes more than pleasing looks and stature to make an actor," Sasanoff declared, puffing himself up to his full height . . . which almost brought him even with the Whelp's chest. Of course, the woman hadn't mentioned the Whelp's height at all, but poor Sasanoff could never stop measuring himself against other actors—literally. I think that's one of the reasons he tolerated me. I was five times the man he was side to side, but toe to top of head he was nearly my equal.

"There's a deportment, a regality that sets the truly fine actor apart," Sasanoff went on. "Goliath himself would have made a poor player if he lacked *presence*."

"Indeed!" I chimed in. "Just look how little David upstaged him!"

My bon mot—and the quick change of subject to the weather I had planned—might have defused the situation if the doltish Mr. Tabor hadn't relit the wick.

"Well, son," he said to the Whelp, "you just keep studying Mr. Sasanoff here, and I'm sure one day you'll be a leading man just like him."

"Good heavens, I hope not," the Whelp replied. And then sensing—correctly—that he'd gone too far this time, he chuckled and tried to explain away his effrontery. "I find I prefer the small parts, Mr. Tabor. Roles sized to human proportions. I was drawn to acting as a way of better understanding how and why people *act*—which is to say, behave—the way they do. I was searching for the reality behind the artifice. Unfortunately, I've found it's almost impossible to see anything real when blinded by the limelight. So I'm happy to leave center stage to those who crave it. Truth, I believe, you'll more often find lurking in the wings."

Though he'd started out trying to soften the sting of his words, the Whelp had instead packed salt upon the welt, and even he knew it.

"Please forgive me," he told the Tabors with another light, self-mocking laugh. "You're not here to listen to the ramblings of a 'junior utility player.' My eminent associates here are the ones who should be sharing their wisdom. When it comes to acting and stagecraft, they're full of it."

And with that he excused himself and fled to the refreshments table—which was certainly no refuge for a sane man to seek.

[*A five-hundred-word aside on the supposedly life-threatening inedibility of "hinterlands victuals" has been cut here. —S.B.H.*]

At any rate, with the dazed expressions a pair of sheep might wear at a performance of *King Lear*, the Tabors watched the Whelp go to his culinary doom. They could sense that something was happening before their very eyes yet lacked the powers of perception to understand what it was.

There was nothing sheepish about the look on Sasanoff's face, however. It was so wolfish, in fact, I feared the man would bare his teeth and growl.

"So," I said, "is it always so beastly cold this time of year? The scenery here is beautiful—*beautiful*—but one risks frostbite with each pause to admire it!"

Predictably, the Tabors responded with a gushing rivulet of drivel about the incomparable splendors of a Colorado spring. And, as always at such moments, the actor's craft served me well, for I managed to project rapt interest, though I heard not a word after the first few bleatings about streams of fresh-melted snow sparkling in the sunshine of a golden-bright May morn, etc., etc.

Sasanoff's performance, on the other hand, wasn't nearly so convincing. He nodded and grunted out impatient *Hmms* and *I sees* more or less at random, all the while shooting dark scowls at the Whelp. At first opportunity, he found some pretext to extricate us from our hosts and drag me away to a quiet corner of the "ballroom" (which, in the interest of accuracy, I should report was hardly big enough for a *pas de deux*, let alone a proper ball).

"I've endured that amateur's slights for the last time." Sasanoff nodded over at the Whelp, who'd not only struck up a conversation with a rough-looking fellow chipmunk-cheeked with half-masticated *hors d'oeuvres*—some sort of local constable, we'd been told—but actually seemed to be *enjoying* it. "It's high time I taught him a lesson, wouldn't you say?"

"I not only would say, I've been saying it for weeks. So you're going to cashier the overweening rogue at last?"

Sasanoff's expression turned sneeringly sly, and he fed me one of my own lines from *Twelfth Night*.

"Wouldst thou not be glad to have the rascally sheep-biter come by some notable shame?"

I replied as per the Bard.

"I would exult, man."

"Then this is what we shall do. . . . "

And Sasanoff proceeded to lay out a plan of such diabolical ingenuity I hardly could believe he'd hatched it in a mere ten minutes. Yet I knew he'd done just that, for it had as its inspiration an anecdote Horace Tabor shared with us shortly before the Whelp arrived.

I myself had but one concern, every actor's first and foremost: the size of my role.

"What part do I play in all this?"

"Why, the most important of all," Sasanoff said. "You will be the audience. For what good is a great performance—or a great humiliation—if no one is on hand to witness it?"

I offered Sasanoff as deep a bow as my magnitude would allow.

"It shall be my honor to serve, thou most excellent devil of wit."

"It's settled, then. We must prove once and for all who the master actors are here." Sasanoff grinned as he again quoted *Twelfth Night*. "We will fool him black and blue, shall we not?"

The next midmorning, we attempted our first full dress rehearsal in the still-unfinished opera house, but it was a hopeless effort all around.

[*A lengthy account of the rehearsal—including critiques of various company members' performances and personal foibles, complaints about the "drafty cow barn about to be passed off as a theatre," and a condemnation of the "loutish workmen" who made concentration impossible by "hammering away at Art more successfully than their nails"—has been removed here. —S.B.H.*]

Eventually, Sasanoff saw the futility of it all and released us for the day. He'd seemed remote and distracted anyhow—and only I knew why.

The Whelp disappeared almost immediately, and I braved another outing into the town to seek him out. I found him in a little den of iniquity that was, difficult as this was to believe, even more iniquitous than the one I'd seen him in the day before. Instead of rotten boards for a floor, this one had only dirt liberally garnished with sawdust, and puddles I made it a point not to study at length. The clientele were of a sort to inspire the same policy, and between avoiding their surly, suspicious gazes and ignoring the repellent plashes at my feet, I practically had to navigate the place staring at the ceiling. That I made it to the Whelp's side without bumping into some thug's beer and sparking a "shootout" I count as a miracle.

"May I join you?" I said.

The Whelp was at a table in the corner, alone, his back to the rickety, warped-wooded wall. There were empty seats to either side of him, but given relations between us in the past, there was no guarantee he'd allow me to make use of one.

"If you wish," he said with more curiosity than cordiality. "But first, I would advise you to see Mr. Lonnegan there about a drink." He nodded at a grimacing old villain behind the bar, then down at an untasted beer on the table before him. "The price of admission, as it were."

I did as the Whelp suggested, purchasing a glass of frothy beer

(I didn't think it wise to inquire about port) before returning to his table and taking a seat. My chair—constructed, it appeared, from pasteboard and old kindling—squealed alarmingly beneath me, but after a moment's protest, it seemed to accept my ampleness.

I celebrated with a sip of beer . . . the celebration grinding to a halt the second the taste of it reached my brain. It took immense effort not only to swallow the stuff but to keep it swallowed.

"'Steam beer,' it's called," the Whelp said. "Vile, isn't it?"

I put the glass on the table and pushed it away to the edge furthest from my nose, for I'd noticed too late the swill's sour-milk aroma.

"You could have warned me," I said.

"And deny them their fun?"

I looked up to find the dive's other denizens chuckling gleefully at my distress. Seeing a gentleman's dignity assaulted obviously was, to them, the very apex of entertainment.

"Why do you keep coming to these filthy places?" I asked the Whelp in a whisper.

"The same reason I took up acting—a simple desire to better understand my fellow man. And I daresay I usually learn more in one saloon than any dozen theatres."

"Really? I wouldn't think such people as these would be so eager to advance your education. In fact, I'm surprised some ruffian hasn't thrashed you by now."

The Whelp picked up his beer and peered down into it, squinting at the stagnant yellow brine as if it were some laboratory experiment gone awry.

"Oh, several have tried," he said blandly. "I did go to a real college, you know. And the most valuable thing I learned there was boxing."

Several of the brutes around the saloon were still staring, and the Whelp raised his beer, saluted them with it, then took a long, glugging pull. When he'd managed to gulp it all down without retching, our grubby audience guffawed and turned back to their own, no-doubt sinister, business.

"So," the Whelp said, setting his now-empty glass beside mine, "you wished to speak with me?"

"More than that," I said. "I wanted to *warn* you. About Sasanoff, and the way you keep antagonizing him. I don't think you realize how close he is to dismissing you."

The Whelp shrugged, face impassive.

"I don't think you realize how close I am to giving notice."

"You don't fear being stranded in this godforsaken wilderness?"

"Do I *look* fearful?" The Whelp answered his own question with a carefree smile. "Leaving England, exploring a new land, a new people—and yes, new dangers. It's forced me to look at everything differently. I'm like an actor who steps down from the stage so as to finally see the play from the other side of the proscenium. Before, all I knew were my own little entrances and exits, my own marks. But now I see so much more. The whole stage, the whole theatre. The whole *world*."

I nodded as the Whelp babbled, all the while thinking him a fool. All the world's a stage, it goes without saying, but the opposite should be true for any real thespian: the stage is all the world. And upstage center—that's the only place to be in it.

"Yes, yes . . . I see your point," I lied. "But don't you understand that—?"

"You're Englishmen?" a croaky voice cut in.

Somehow, without my noticing, a troll had materialized beside our table. He was hunchbacked and wild-haired, with a scar running down one sallow cheek to disappear into a black briar patch of a beard. What one could see of his face was dark-tanned and deeply lined, and his left eye was narrowed in a perpetual squint while the right protuberated obscenely. His clothes were equally askew—baggy pants held up with frayed rope, a worn-elbowed coat that would have been skin-tight on a consumptive child, and a broad hat so floppy and stained and formless it could have been sewn together from a charwoman's old scouring rags.

"Yes," I said to It. "We are English."

"Cor blimey!" the wretched creature crowed in an accent that was unmistakably Cockney. "This must be me lucky day! New 'round 'ere, are you?"

"That is correct," I said. "We're actors—members of Michael Sasanoff's company. We'll be opening the Tabor Opera House . . . assuming the blasted thing ever *does* open."

"And you?" the Whelp asked. "You're from London, I presume?"

"I'm from all over, guv." The lumpy little man placed a gnarled claw on the table's only empty chair. "May I?"

"Well . . . " I began.

The gnome planted himself in the seat beside me.

"You can call me 'Goodfellow,'" he said, throwing shifty-eyed glances this way and that. "It ain't the name I was born wiff, but it'll do for now."

"It's a pleasure to meet you, Mr. Goodfellow," the Whelp said, and he looked over at the bar and held up a single finger.

Goodfellow hopped to his feet again, raging.

"Givin' the man the 'igh sign, are you? A trap, is it? Damn an' blast! I should've known this was too good to be—"

"I think you misunderstand, Mr. Goodfellow," the Whelp said soothingly. "I was ordering you a drink."

Goodfellow turned to stare at Lonnegan—who was indeed contaminating a glass with the fulvous suds of steam beer.

"Oh. Sorry, guv." Goodfellow sat down again. "I'm a bit jumpy, bein' 'ere. An' I got reason to be."

Goodfellow fell silent as Lonnegan stalked over and slapped the glass down before him, sloshing half its contents on the table. (And no better use can I think of for steam beer than cleaning furniture.) Then, as the tavern keeper stomped away, he leaned in toward us and went on in a low, hoarse murmur.

"I need 'elp, gents . . . an' it'll be worff your while to give it."

"Perhaps you didn't hear me," I said stiffly. "We're actors. If it's a poor box you're looking for, I suggest you try a church."

"I ain't no bleedin' charity case!" Goodfellow snapped back. "Fact is, there's a right wodge o' wonga in this for *you*—a bloody fortune—if you play your cards right."

"You'll have to excuse my skepticism," I sniffed, "but you don't very much look like a man with access to 'a right wodge of wonga.'"

"That's 'cause I can't get at it, mate." Goodfellow leaned even further over the table, the looming hump of his hunched back giving him the appearance of an immense, bearded mushroom. "*But you can.*"

"Mr. Goodfellow obviously has a story to tell," the Whelp said to me. "I suggest we let him tell it."

I harrumphed and settled back in my seat—which squeaked and creaked so piercingly I almost thought it about to explode into splinters. Fortunately, the chair held as Goodfellow held forth.

After a lifetime spent "knockin' about God's green earff," the man told us in a conspiratorial whisper, he'd ended up in Colorado trying to make a go of it as a prospector. His prospects, however, were more black than gold, and he soon went broke. But he did end up sitting on a pile of silver eventually—albeit another man's silver—as a guard for Horace Tabor's Matchless Mine. One day, he and three of his fellow guards were escorting a load of freshly milled silver down the mountain to town when they were attacked by bandits. It was a slaughter on both sides, and when the battle ended, only Goodfellow was still alive—and he just barely.

As he slumped against the wagon awaiting rescue, a bullet in his back, his face slashed, he pondered what future he had in even so humble a profession as the one that had brought him to this. The answer being none. Though he might survive his wounds a cripple, his nerves, he knew, were shattered beyond any mending at all. As gunman or laborer, he was through. Which left no future for him save starvation—a bitter irony, with so much silver so close at hand. He'd given his all for a treasure Horace Tabor wouldn't even miss, he was already so rich.

And that's when Goodfellow saw providence in his situation. No one but he knew how many men really had been in the gang. If he exaggerated their numbers—and said a surviving "desperado" made off with a packload of silver while he lay bleeding, feigning death—who could dispute it? Battered and bleeding though he was, Goodfellow's prospects were looking up.

He managed to dig a hole just big enough for a single small crate. In it he placed half a dozen bars of pure silver, and with his last ounce of strength he covered it with earth and rock. He finished in the nick of time, collapsing into a faint not twenty steps from his buried booty.

He awoke the next day to learn his party had been ambushed by the infamous Whelan brothers, Mike, Ike, Spike, and Dudley. The bodies of all four had been found, and they weren't known to ride with other bandits in the past. What, he was asked, had become of the missing silver?

Goodfellow had no choice but to stick to his plan, concocting a fifth member of the gang—a mysterious Indian who'd loaded his horse with silver before fleeing. The mine officials and law officers to whom he told this seemed skeptical, and eventually Horace Tabor himself came to his bedside to hear the story . . . and plainly didn't believe it.

Goodfellow's recovery was slow and painful and not entirely successful. (Here in the telling, he patted his hunched back.) And when it was through, he'd lost more than his youthful vigor. He'd lost his job, as well. The Matchless Mine dismissed him, and there were hints that he shouldn't linger long in Leadville. He wasn't trusted. He would be watched.

For six long months he'd been away, scraping by as best he could while growing his beard and weathering his features and dreaming of his silver. He'd returned just that morning, intending to hire a mule and set off up the trail disguised as an old prospector. But there was no disguise, he quickly learned, that could hide disfigurements such as his. He'd been spotted and accosted by a pair of mine guards. Their ultimatum: leave town by sundown or they'd fix his hump for him . . . with clubs.

So here he'd come, bereft, thinking to drown his sorrows in drink before abandoning his little hoard forever and slinking off to quietly die. And what should he overhear but two countrymen talking. Newcomers to Leadville. Men with the freedom to *act*.

"Us?" I scoffed. "What would you have us do?"

"Get your 'ands on the swag, of course," Goodfellow hissed. "It's just off the road to the mine, barely a mile from 'ere. But a mile's more than I'd make before bein' caught. The second I'm seen anywhere near that road . . . " He gave his shaggy head a slow, grim shake. "A gentleman tourist out for a constitutional, though? Nobody'd give that a second thought. Mind you, I wouldn't set off right away—the afternoon shipments'll be comin' through, and the guards'll be itchy-fingered no matter who it is they're passin' on the road. But as of, ooooh . . . four o'clock, say? Why, you'd 'ave nuffin' to worry about."

"And how would we find this ill-gotten plunder of yours, assuming we lowered ourselves to look for it?" I asked. "I'm guessing you didn't simply leave it under a leaf by the side of the road."

Goodfellow's eyes lit up with excitement—even the squinty one, which was a neat trick, I'll admit.

"There's a map," Goodfellow intoned portentously. "Drew it from memory soon as I was out of me sickbed and away from pryin' eyes. In case me memory went 'iggledy-piggledy. It'll lead you straight to the spot."

The Whelp hadn't said a word in minutes, and I turned to face him fully now. He was staring at Goodfellow like a man mesmerized.

No—I should rephrase that. There was nothing dulled or sleepy about his look. He was more like a man *enchanted*.

His eyes flashed with exhilaration, amusement, the thrill of danger. In all his slumming, he'd done little more than watch the riffraff flounder in the gutter. And now he'd been invited in for a wallow—and the idea excited him.

"Surely," I said to him, "you wouldn't involve yourself in something so . . . so . . . "

"Sordid? Perilous? Foolhardy?" The Whelp dismissed any such concerns with a casual shrug. "My curiosity is piqued."

As was his greed, it seemed.

"What would be my reward for helping you?" he asked.

Goodfellow stroked his beard and rolled his eyes.

"One bar," he said. "And before you try any 'agglin', just remember that'd be enough to get you back to England in style, and it's me what's paid the price for—"

"Done," the Whelp said. "Do you have the map with you now?"

"Strewth! I did walk into the right saloon, di'n't I?" Goodfellow gleefully groped beneath his grimy coat for a moment . . . then froze, his expression turning wary. "'Ang on a tick. 'Ow do I know you ain't gonna fiddle me out of me dosh?"

The Whelp regarded him coolly.

"You have my word, I have never fiddled with anyone's dosh."

"'Is word,' 'e says. Ha! I'll need a lot more than that before I 'and over me map. Why, you could scarper with the whole boodle and leave me with nuffin' but me bloody 'ump! No, no . . . a security, that's what's called for. To show your good faith."

"What sort of security are you talking about?" the Whelp asked.

Goodfellow looked him up and down, then pointed a knobby finger at the watch fob looping from the Whelp's vest pockets.

"That watch, let's say."

"My father gave me that."

"And I'll give it back . . . when you give me the silver."

Slowly, reluctantly, the Whelp pulled out a gold pocket watch and placed it on the table.

"Smart lad," Goodfellow said. After furtive glances left and right, he produced a scroll of paper and unrolled it on the tabletop just long enough to show it was, indeed, a crudely sketched map.

The Whelp swept the map off the table.

Goodfellow slipped the watch into a coat pocket.

"You stayin' at the Clarendon?" he asked.

The Whelp nodded.

"Alright, then," Goodfellow said, "I'll meet you behind the 'otel at nine o' clock tonight to do the divvy. Till then, I'd best keep out of sight."

He pushed away from the table, then paused before turning to go.

"Pleasure doin' business wiff you, guv," he said, and he gave the Whelp a wink with his bulging-wide right eye.

"I can't believe even you would sink so low," I said to the Whelp as the hunchback hobbled away.

As usual, my disapproval seemed to amuse the insolent jackanapes no end.

"Neither can I," he said with a smile. "Well . . . I suppose I should go, too. I shan't be leaving for another hour or so, but in the meantime I've preparations to make." He tugged at the sleeve of his black frock coat. "I'm hardly dressed for an expedition. Shall we return to the Clarendon?"

"You go ahead," I said. "Suddenly, I find I actually prefer the company here."

My show of pique merely gratified the Whelp all the more, and he headed for the door with such a jaunty spring to his step I wouldn't have been surprised had he started whistling.

I sat there alone, pretending to drink my steam beer so as to keep the saloon keeper at bay and avoid the curious (and hostile) stares of the other patrons. After a few minutes, however, I had company again: a hunched figure appeared in the doorway and came sidling toward me.

I greeted him with applause as he retook his seat.

"Bravo. A masterful performance."

My companion shrugged modestly.

"I had a receptive audience," said Sasanoff—for, as you've surely long since guessed, he and Goodfellow were one and the same. "He's so eager for adventure he would have believed me had I appeared to him as Admiral Lord Nelson. Now . . . what say we properly fortify ourselves for the cold?"

What I said was "yes," of course, and soon we were stoking up warmth with a surprisingly serviceable whiskey Mr. Lonnegan had on hand. Eventually, however, Sasanoff drained his glass and stood up.

"Come," he said. "All must be in readiness for the denouement."

I followed him out of the tavern with no little reluctance. Certainly, I wanted to see him deliver the *coup de grâce* with my own eyes. Yet by necessity he'd be doing it out of doors, while I very much wished to remain safely behind closed ones . . . preferably beside a roaring fire with a glass of port close at hand.

I knew better than to deny Sasanoff his audience, however, and soon we were hustling up the road toward the mine. Quite a sight I'm sure we made: Richard III and Falstaff side by side, both of them huffing and puffing in the thin, frigid air of the mountains. Though Sasanoff had given us plenty of time to beat the Whelp—the reason for his warning about the "afternoon shipments"—he still insisted on a forced march so swift it soon had my back slick with perspiration that would turn to icicles the second we stopped.

And worse was yet to come, for Sasanoff had selected a hiding place that required us to crawl on all fours into a dense copse of prickly bramble. Of course, frames such as mine are not proportioned for easy concealment, so we had to wriggle our way into the thickest of the thicket, briers tearing at my topcoat (and my pride). Sasanoff nearly lost his false beard in one particularly dense tangle, but after some struggling he managed to free himself, whiskers intact. I'd suggested he relieve himself of his disguise, but he accused me of lacking panache. (A charge that had never before been leveled against *me*!) A dramatic unveiling, he insisted, was key to the whole thing.

Once we were finally in place, I could see why Sasanoff had picked the spot he had, trying though it had been to reach. We may as well have been in box seats, for we had a perfect view down into the rocky basin in which the final act of the farce would soon play out.

Perhaps forty feet from us was a mound of loose stones piled up that morning by Sasanoff himself. Beneath it was a shallow hole just deep enough for the battered locker that had, not long before, housed my own little treasure: my clippings. I'd volunteered it when Sasanoff outlined his plan. Now it held but a single slip of paper, upon which had been scrawled these words:

YOU'RE SACKED!

—M.S.

The plan was this: We would wait for the Whelp; we would watch him unearth the box; we would witness his dismay upon discovering its contents; we would stand and announce our presence; we would reveal the true identity of "Mr. Goodfellow"; we would gloat; we would leave.

Curtain.

As it was, however, the first scene of our little production—the waiting—ran long. Every quarter hour or so, Sasanoff would pull out a watch and glumly mutter, "Any minute now . . . any minute, I'm sure." It heartened him considerably when I pointed out that the watch he kept consulting was the Whelp's own.

Just as my fingers and toes were going numb with the cold, we heard something moving toward us from the road.

"At last," Sasanoff whispered. "The fly enters the web."

And then someone finally stepped into the clearing below us . . . a mustachioed, bow-legged someone wearing a droopy, round-brimmed hat and rough clothes and mud-splattered boots.

In his hands was the map Sasanoff himself had drawn that morning—the one he'd given to the Whelp.

Hanging from the holster at his side was a revolver the approximate size of a small cannon.

"Who in God's name—?" I murmured.

Sasanoff shushed me.

The man moved slowly at first, glancing down and up, down and up, from the map to the glade before him. But when he spied the pile of stones (marked, but of course, with a thick-inked X on the map) he charged forward, cackling. When he reached the rocks, he began tossing them wildly aside.

Sasanoff's web, it seemed, had snared the wrong fly. And now it was about to snare two more.

As the man tore at the stacked stones, he glanced up, eyes darting this way and that. He was grinning madly, giggling, yet he seemed anxious, almost frantic, as well.

And then his giggles stopped, his grin wilted.

The man was staring directly at us.

Surely, he couldn't see us, I told myself. We were crouched low amidst a thick layer of shadow-eaved brush, and the afternoon sun had long since given way to the gray of approaching dusk.

Yet his gaze didn't waver. We might as well have been caught in the blinding light of a follow spot.

"Who's there?" he called out.

We said nothing.

"I know you're there, dammit!" the man bellowed. "I can see your breath!"

His right hand hovered over the butt of his gun.

"The better part of valour is discretion," I'd often said onstage as Falstaff. And I believed it and even lived by it, for "Run away!" I'd often said offstage as myself.

There would be no screwing of courage to the sticking place. I possessed no courage to screw.

I stood up with my hands held high.

Or tried to, at any rate. The thorns and vines clawed at me as I arose. When I was finally standing straight, I found Sasanoff on his feet beside me, face scratched, beard pocked with clinging thistles.

"Ummm . . . could you point us back to the road?" he said. "We appear to be lost."

"So lost you end up creepin' around the bushes?" the man spat back in an American accent as coarse and thick as his handlebar moustache and muttonchops. "Ha!"

"Oh, we were just looking for my . . . poodle," I said. "He slipped his leash when we were walking him, and—"

"Get down here," the man snapped. "*Now.*"

Sasanoff and I scrambled down the steep embankment side by side, kicking up dirt and stumbling over rocks and rotting logs.

"So," the man said when we were finally lined up before him, "who are you two workin' for? Tabor or yourselves?"

"I don't know what you mean," Sasanoff said. He was not so much a hunchback now as a hunch*buttock*: his hump had slipped down so low it looked as though he had a third cheek at the base of his spine.

The American took an angry step toward him.

"Are you mine police or bandits?" he demanded.

He was a tall man, obviously well built despite his bandy legs, and Sasanoff and I shrank back from him as one.

"N-n-neither," I said. "We're actors."

The American barked out a bitter laugh.

"Actors? Oh, I'll say you are! Bad ones, too, 'cuz I see right through you." He jutted a lantern jaw at me. "Judgin' by them lavender duds of yours—" he jerked his head at Sasanoff, "—and the rags on you? And you both talkin' all hoity-toity? I'll bet you're Pinkertons set after the missin' silver. Well, congratulations, boys. You done found it. You just ain't leavin' with it. I am."

"I assure you I have no idea what you're talking about," Sasanoff said with as much stiff-spined dignity as a man with a false beard and an extra rump can muster.

"Sir . . . if I may," I began, a whole new wave of sickly dread churning to life in the pit of my stomach. "How did you come to have that map?"

The American flashed me a smile sour enough for a Malvolio.

"You may not . . . but I'll tell you anyhow. I took it off a feller I followed outta Leadville. Word around town was he'd got his hands on an honest-to-God treasure map. So I caught up with him along the trail and, well . . . " He patted the butt of his gun. "I persuaded him to hand it over."

I could see Sasanoff go pale even beneath his grease paint. His performance back at the saloon had been *too* good, it appeared. It wasn't just the Whelp he'd convinced—it was all the eavesdroppers, too.

"Was your persuasion . . . fatal?" he asked.

The American shrugged.

"I didn't wait around to find out. Now, unless you want some of the same persuasion—" He backed off a few steps and nodded down at the mound of rocks nearby. "Get to diggin."

"But—" I began.

"*Dig!*" the American finished for me.

So dig we did, rolling aside the last of the stones covering the low hole in which my little trunk rested. I briefly considered turning and telling the brigand behind us that there was no stolen silver; it was all just a ruse we'd concocted to teach a much-needed lesson to a prattling malapert. I had the distinct feeling the man wouldn't see the humor in it, though. Best to feign ignorance and hope he'd take disappointment well.

Of course, I had the feeling he wouldn't do *that* either.

"By God," the American mumbled to himself as Sasanoff and I lifted the chest up out of the ground. "It was true. I'm rich!"

"Not necessarily," I said, trying to soften the blow before it fell. "Who knows what's inside?"

"Quite right," Sasanoff threw in. "Someone might have beaten you to it, then reburied the strongbox."

"Like who?" the American growled. "You, maybe?"

"Oh, no! I just meant—"

"Open it."

"But—"

"*Open it!*"

I let Sasanoff kneel down and do the honors. I wanted to keep my distance from that box both literally and figuratively.

Sasanoff reluctantly lifted the creaky-hinged lid—then stared down into the chest in stunned befuddlement.

"I-I-I don't understand," he stammered.

I leaned in close enough to peek over his shoulder, yet I couldn't see what had astonished him so.

There were the rocks he'd put in to give the box weight. There was the note he'd put in to give the Whelp his comeuppance.

But then I wasn't just glancing at the note to confirm its presence. I was *reading* it. And that's when my own eyes nearly popped from their sockets.

Instead of this:

YOU'RE SACKED!
—M.S.

I saw this:

I QUIT!
—S.H.

We both turned to measure the American's reaction to all this—and found the man gone. In his place was the Whelp.

In his clothes, too. The Whelp had simply stripped away moustache and muttonchops, and there he was, the transformation complete.

The Whelp swept off his hat and bowed deeply, as if our shock was an ovation for him to accept from the stage.

"But . . . how?" I said.

"Acting, of course," the Whelp replied blithely as he straightened up again. "Aided by the sort of quick change one must master as a utility player with four different costumes in the first act alone."

When this explanation did little to lift our dangling jaws, the Whelp went on.

"Instead of going to the hotel after leaving the saloon, I followed the map straight here to see what sort of burlesque you had planned for me. Once I'd made my own little alteration to the script, I returned to town, facilitated the necessary wardrobe change with the help of a local pawn shop—the same that supplied you with your costume, Mr. Sasanoff—then stopped by the opera house to avail myself of our makeup box. *Et voilà*."

He spread out his hands, inviting us to appreciate his makeshift disguise. Seeing him without his false whiskers, his legs no longer bowed, floppy-brimmed hat no longer drooping over his prominent brow, I was amazed that we'd ever been duped. The makeup hadn't been that heavy, really. He'd made little effort to conceal his features. No, much as it pains me to admit—and I'm sorely tempted to strike these lines out—it was the man's superior acting that had carried the day.

[*The above paragraph was, in fact, inked out with a heavy hand, and the content of the expurgated section was only discovered after painstaking X-ray analysis of the original manuscript. —S.B.H.*]

"I assume Mr. Tabor told you about the lost silver map swindle at the reception last night," the Whelp said. "It certainly couldn't have been one of the other guests, as you took such pains not to converse with them. I myself heard of the scheme in an altogether more direct fashion: in the course of my explorations of Leadville, I was approached by not one but *three* 'confidence men' plying variations on the tale. They were all most admirable thespians in their own way, and more convincing than many an Iago or Shylock I've seen. In fact, for all your successes in the theatre, Mr. Sasanoff, I daresay you wouldn't last a second as a buttoner in a public house. Your 'Mr. Goodfellow' had about him far too much of the actor's West End and not nearly enough of the Cockney's East."

This slap was, at last, too much for Sasanoff, and his surprise boiled away with the searing heat of rage.

"You arrogant pup!" he thundered. "I'll see to it you never appear on the stage again!"

The Whelp shrugged mildly.

"As you like it." He turned to go, then stopped and glanced back over his shoulder. "Oh, and by the way—you may keep the watch. I bought it in Indianapolis for a dollar."

And with that, his long legs carried him up the brushy incline slanting down from the road.

I never saw him again. Nor did I hear him spoken of until years afterward, and then in an entirely different (and eternally irritating) context.

For his part, Sasanoff refused to acknowledge the Whelp's existence or even his absence after that day. Queries from our fellow actors he answered with icy stares and silence. It was as if the man had never been with our company at all.

"You will not reveal what happened here. Ever. To anyone," Sasanoff growled as we trudged back to town in evening's gathering gloom.

I placed my right hand over my heart.

"I will never tell another living soul," I vowed solemnly.

It was, if I may allow myself a moment of immodesty, the finest performance of the day.

The Flowers of Utah
Robert Pohle

Robert Pohle is the coauthor (with Doug Hart) of *Sherlock Holmes on the Screen* (A.S. Barnes, 1977), and has made other contributions to Sherlockian filmography such as *The Films of Christopher Lee*. He is also a member of the Western Writers of America, and author or coauthor of a number of novels in that genre, including *The Fledgling Outlaw* (which features a Sherlockian vignette, and of which the late John Bennett Shaw, BSI, memorably wrote the author, "You do have everything in it except Bing Crosby as a drunken Irish priest!") Robert lives in Florida with his wife, Maryann, and part of the year in New Mexico with his daughter, actress-singer Rita Pohle. Having once argued, in the presence of Dame Jean Conan Doyle, that Holmes never visited America before the period of *His Last Bow*, Pohle is astonished to have unearthed the present manuscript by Dr. Watson.

* * * *

"Very sorry to knock you up before dawn, Watson," said Holmes, handing me a steaming mug of tea, "but it's the custom here in the West, you know—and we must get an early start if we're to overtake him."

"Thank you for not giving me any of that vile stuff that passes for coffee out here," I replied.

"It's the buffalo chips that give it body," murmured Deputy Marshal Ames, stirring under his blanket. "Don't go criticizin' American coffee, Doc."

"Don't fret," said Holmes, passing a mug his way, "I brewed you a cup of your own."

"'Sides, you know you're damn fortunate," continued the Marshal, taking a gulp and then slurping the excess liquid from the corner of his moustache, "gettin' either tea *or* coffee in Mormon country . . . let alone anything stronger," he added, pouring a thin stream from a glass flask into his mug.

Neither the Marshal nor I realized yet that the rattlesnake slithering toward his heel was shortly to send me on the ride of my life.

But I get ahead of my story.

Readers of *A Study in Scarlet* will recall that Sherlock Holmes had apprehended an American from Utah named Jefferson Hope for the London murders of two of his fellow citizens named Drebber and Stangerson. Hope, it appeared, was seeking revenge for the death at their hands of his lost love Lucy Ferrier. The case never came to trial because Hope died in prison of an aortic aneurism the same night Holmes presented him in handcuffs to Inspectors Gregson and Lestrade of Scotland Yard.

Scotland Yard, and indeed all those who look after the wheels of justice, appeared satisfied that those wheels had turned fully. But Holmes was not; far from it. For there was an accomplice of Hope's who got off scot-free: someone, apparently an athletic young man impersonating an elderly woman calling herself Mrs. Sawyer, who came brazenly into our very rooms at Baker Street in answer to a lure

Holmes had placed in the newspapers, an advertisement for a "found" wedding ring.

"Mrs. Sawyer" gave us a patently mendacious story about the ring belonging to her "girl Sally" who would be in dreadful trouble with a brutish husband named Tom Dennis if it wasn't recovered; but when Holmes followed her, clinging to the back of the cab, "she" gave him the slip by leaping out of it in full motion. And subsequently, when Holmes asked Hope who his accomplice had been, Hope had responded provokingly with a wink and replied, "I can tell my own secrets, but I don't get other people into trouble!" Though Holmes acknowledged that Hope's "friend" had done the job smartly, it still rankled him bitterly to leave this part of the case unclosed.

Finally, a ray of light appeared from a familiar quarter: a loud ring at the bell, an audible expression of resigned martyrdom from Mrs. Hudson, a patter of bare feet in the hall and on the stairs, a tap on our chamber door, and then the entrance of young Wiggins, with all the ceremony (or lack of it) befitting a minikin street Arab who was also chief of the Baker Street irregulars.

"Got 'er!" said Wiggins, with considerable satisfaction.

"Have you, by God!" cried Holmes, springing to his feet.

The boys, it transpired, had been circulating along the route Holmes had followed when he clung to the back of the four-wheeler. Holmes reasoned that the sight of an elderly lady rocketing from a moving cab might have excited comment—and indeed it had—and that a doorway that admitted a lady who exited as a gentleman might also have drawn curious eyes. This was the sort of territory where the irregulars were at their best, and it didn't take many questions before the exact address was run to ground.

"Ladies into gents is an easy one," said Wiggins.

"Is it really?" I asked.

"It's common as a ha'penny upright," said Wiggins.

"Good gracious!" said I.

"Capital!" cried Holmes.

"But how can you be sure it was the same person, Wiggins, after the, er, change?" I asked.

"Lord love you, Doctor!" the boy chortled. "The little girl wot seen the 'old lady' go in, tried to touch 'er for summat, you see, and noticed she was shy a fingernail on 'er right hand wot she swotted 'er with—and didn't the very same detail 'ppear on the gent who come out after, and swotted 'er too?"

"This is very good work, young Wiggins," pronounced Holmes, "on the young lady's part as well as your own! I've always said the Science of Observation—"

"Begging your pardon, sir," interrupted Wiggins, tugging on Holmes's sleeve, "but I've already read 'er that lecture, an' tipped 'er a tupenny piece as well for the nark job, which you'll see itemized in my expense list—so 'adn't we be going?"

The three of us were soon at the actual address, which proved to be a lodging house of a low sort. I was curious how Holmes would handle the situation, but he simply strode up to the desk next to the entrance and asked the clerk: "Is Mr. Tom Dennis in?"

"Sorry, sir," drawled the sallow youth under the grimy fanlight, "he just checked out this evening."

Holmes's disappointment was no greater than my astonishment at his correct guess of the name under which our quarry would be registered, and I said as much as we left.

"Oh, that was a trifle," he shrugged. "It's an elementary rule to never multiply names unnecessarily—the rogue wasn't likely to be bothered to make up a string of 'em without any need. But what now?"

Holmes looked down to find Wiggins tugging on the pocket of his frock coat.

"'Scuse me, Sir," he said, "but I natural left Simpson as a tail, an' he'll reliable report back to Baker Street."

Which indeed he did, but very late that night, with the news, alas, that Dennis had sailed for New York on the SS *Nephite*.

"Well, then, Holmes," I tried to reassure him, "all you need do is get Lestrade to cable the police in New York, and the man is shackled."

Holmes sunk deeper in his chair. "Ye-ess," he murmured, "except . . . I've been thinking . . . "

Something about my friend's tone worried me. "Surely, Holmes, there's nothing more for you to concern yourself with over this matter? You said yourself, only days ago, that this case was one of 'intrinsic simplicity'! And I quote you—I took notes."

Holmes grimaced. "My dear Watson, I shall watch myself more carefully if you are going to be quoting me back to myself like that. What bothers me is that I allowed myself to swallow so much of Jefferson Hope's unsupported confession, and then let slip away the accomplice whose testimony he tried to withhold from me. There's a piece missing, and I want it."

"Undoubtedly, the New York police will nab him and send him back," I predicted.

Events proved me wrong. In the upshot, Dennis was too slippery for the constabulary of that metropolis. But Holmes's reaction to this was curious: rather than increasing his frustration, as I had feared, it seemed to fire him with a nervous excitement.

Then we had what I suppose must be accounted a bit of luck— although when I was later careening around the precipitous crags of

Utah, and dodging bullets, I was not sure whether that luck was bad or good.

Holmes had cabled a colleague in America who had already helped immeasurably with this case: Police Superintendent Schmitt of Cleveland, Ohio, who confirmed that Tom Dennis was indeed the name by which our quarry had been known for some years, and also that he had been sighted in the proximity of Jefferson Hope while the latter was in that jurisdiction. And by the merest fluke, it happened that one of the Superintendent's sources had informed him that Dennis had recently slipped through Cleveland again—likely on his way back to Salt Lake City. Supt. Schmitt wondered if this tip would be of any use to Holmes in his enquiries.

He would not have wondered long had he been sitting in my chair in Baker Street when Holmes read Schmitt's cable, for Holmes burst up off his sofa like an exploding shell from a mortar.

"Watson," he asked, suddenly as calm again as if proposing a stroll across St. James's Park, "would you care to accompany me to the Country of the Saints?"

I rose to my feet, dumfounded. "Are you serious?"

"It would make for a change, don't you think?" he chuckled. "A change in perspective does wonders when you're having trouble with a case. We could grill that confounded Dennis once and for all; and then there's nothing like going over the ground of a case for yourself, I've always said. I have that nagging feeling that Jefferson Hope was not quite as forthcoming with us as he might have been."

"But my dear Holmes—I can certainly not afford it, even if you are able to."

"Oh, tut!" he said, waving his hand. "A wealthy old lady here in London who is a member of the Latter-Day Saints—we have them here, too, you know—wishes to retain my services. Mrs. Ponsonby-Mallalieu was dreadfully offended by that stupid piece of puffery Lestrade had inserted in the papers after Jefferson Hope died in prison—the one about 'romantic feuds and Mormonism' being behind the murders, even though there was no trial nor even anyone charged. So the good lady has offered me a generous retainer, plus expenses, to solve the case once and for all."

"But even with your gifts, my dear fellow," I expostulated, "with Hope dead that will take a miracle."

"Well, she believes in them," said Holmes. "Miracles, that is; and she doesn't mind paying for me to go to Utah, and I think she'll allow me a traveling companion. Even miracle workers need their coadjutors."

Holmes and I had crossed the ocean on the SS *Liahona* and then went west by train, eventually changing at Ogden, Utah, from the noble Union Pacific to the Utah Central, a Mormon-owned spur that took us right into Salt Lake City, arriving on July 1.

Brigham Young's "New Jerusalem" had been laid out by the Prophet himself a third of a century before, and although the city's population could hardly compare with London's millions, there were tens of thousands thronging its streets, readily apparent as our train came into the station.

"The Mormons chose their honeybee emblem aptly, Holmes," I said, gesturing through the travel-stained window of our car. "How do you expect to find Dennis amongst this multitude?"

"Well, well!" my companion chuckled. "We can but try! I fancy that Superintendant Schmitt's friend, Marshal Ames, may have a bone to throw us."

When our bags had been unloaded, we did not have to look for porters or cabmen, as our client had arranged for us to be met by her man of business in Salt Lake City, who turned out to be English, Mr. Edgar Smith.

"No need for surprise, gentlemen," he assured us. "You'll soon find that a fair percentage of our citizens are from the old country—why, the president himself is an Englishman!"

"What! Mr. Garfield?" I asked.

"No, no!" the man of business replied, in a hurt tone. "*Our* president, the Prophet—John Taylor: the president of our Church!"

Holmes gave me a rather sharp poke in the ribs, and we rode the rest of the way to our lodging demurely in Smith's carriage, our proud guide pointing out to us along the way the remarkable sights of Zion, like Brigham Young's "beehive" house, and the many-spired temple, still a-building after thirty years.

On the morrow, we asked our host for directions to the United States Marshal's office, since we were anxious to make contact with Supt. Schmitt's colleague while Dennis's trail was yet warm. When he learned that it was Deputy Marshal Ames whom we sought, Smith tried to warn us away from a person of, he claimed, questionable character. Finding us adamant, he sighed.

"At any rate, you're far more likely to find him in Robertson's than in the Marshal's office," he told us.

"Robertson's?" asked Holmes.

"A sort of private club," sniffed our host. "The fumes! We are teetotal here, you understand."

Holmes looked troubled. "When you say fumes, Mr. Smith, do you mean alcoholic?"

"That too, I fear!" tsked Smith. "But chiefly tobacco! Quite forbidden!"

"Oh dear!" said Holmes, turning pale. "I hadn't realized . . . but at any rate, Mr. Smith, we really must make the acquaintance of this officer, so may we beg you to direct us to this den of infamy. We shall steel ourselves in the name of duty."

"I can't corrupt a servant by sending one with you to that sort of place." Smith shook his head. "But if you must go, I'll draw you a map."

When Holmes and I were admitted to the club (production of our pipes at the doorway being equivalent to an occult handshake, we discovered), I had trouble at first adjusting my eyes to the dim light within. I don't know why I was surprised that the place was not dissimilar to an English club, or that an enquiry to the first person we happened to encounter—yet another Englishman, a Yorkshireman—brought us to Ames, who we discovered to be taller than Holmes, and wearing a frock coat that would have passed in London, but with his trousers stuffed into high riding boots. He had an aquiline face, which, again, curiously resembled that of my friend, save that his windblown tan was evident even in the subdued light. With his shoulder-length, rather greasy hair and drooping moustache, he put me in mind of some of the Afghans I'd known in my service days.

But when he spoke, his voice was pure Yankee prairie. "Glad to meet you gents," he said, wringing our hands with that excruciating American force to which I never became accustomed. "Schmitt wired me, and I reckon I can help you 'prise Tom Dennis outen his roost, but the jurisdiction may be kind of tricky."

"Really?" said Holmes, lighting the cigar Ames had offered him.

"You see," the Marshal continued, "we're in the City of Salt Lake, but also the County of Salt Lake, and of course the Territory of Utah. Now, of course I'm a Deputy United States Marshal, so I can collar the boy anywhere, theoretically."

"I'm not sure I like the sound of that 'theoretically,'" said Holmes. "This is an excellent cigar."

"Thanks, I get 'em made special and brought through the Isthmus. The problem is that we're also in the Country of the Saints, and President Taylor is King over Israel on the Earth, and just about every municipal, county, territorial, and federal officer is also one of Taylor's faithful. . . . Now, I'm not sayin' they have divided loyalties, but there is just a bit of bad feelin's between the Feds and the Church right now."

"Very bad?" I asked.

"Just a tad," he admitted. "What with Washington trying to make them give up their plural wives and their church property and all . . . So we'll have to tread easy."

"But you will help us apprehend Dennis?" Holmes asked.

"Oh, my pleasure," Ames assured him, downing what looked like a double whisky. "Apparently, your boy is engaged in movin' some kind of contraband between here and Wyoming."

I must have looked a little dubious.

"Oh, it ain't far," he said. "It's just over them mountains to the northeast—you must've noticed 'em. There's an easy trail for a good horseman—I used to ride it myself when I was in the Pony Express with Cody and Hickock."

This caught my attention. "Good Lord!" I cried. "You mean those chaps in the little soft-covered novels I've been buying in the train stations all along our route? I never dreamed they were real people."

"Oh, they're realer than most," he chuckled. "Leastwise, Bill Hickock used to be—damn fool fergot to sit with his back to the wall in Deadwood, a few years back. But I guess those dime novels keep him alive, and they're good publicity for Bill Cody—you might try 'em yourself, in your line of work, Mr. Holmes, bein' a sort of freelancer as you are."

Holmes made an expression of distaste. "I hope, Watson," he told me, "that you shall never contemplate such yellow puffery in my behalf, despite your tendency to take notes. But Marshal, do I understand you to suggest that this 'collar' will best be fastened somewhere outside the city, along this route you mention?"

"It'd sartainly keep the paperwork simpler," Ames chuckled. "I'd like to do 'er in one of the mountain passes better than in the middle of the desert, too . . . Don't want to give 'im a long view of our approach, y'understand. What kind of riders are you gents?"

"I'm afraid the Holmeses had left off being country gentlefolk by my time," deprecated my companion, "but I fancy I can sit a horse adequately to our purposes."

"And horsemanship was one thing I acquired in Afghanistan besides a Jezail bullet," I added modestly. "It was no jest riding in those mountains, either."

"Especially when slung bottom-foremost in the saddle by your orderly!" laughed Holmes. "At least your acquaintance with our four-legged friends is not limited to the wrong end of a bookmaker's tally-sheet!"

"Really, Holmes!" I replied. "I wouldn't have thought that a pint of beer would make you so merry! It must be the thin air at this elevation. I'm surprised the Mormons allow this much alcohol to be served here, too."

"Actually, they don't," admitted Ames, glancing about somewhat furtively as he drained another glass of his own. "It may well be that this is the sort of contraband that no-good Dennis is runnin'. Natcherly, I'm prepared to do my duty and put a stop to it, even if the rascal *is* performin' a public service."

So that, reader, is how I found myself encamped under the stars with Ames and Holmes.

"Don't move," hissed the motionless Holmes to the Marshal. "Watson! Have you got your service revolver?"

But I was too late. Even as I was shifting for my weapon, the snake—a spotted Massasauga rattler, we later confirmed—struck Ames's heel, and my shot an instant later tore off its evil head, but was out of time.

The three of us knew well enough how to deal with poisonous snake bites, and I had not outgrown the habit of carrying my medical bag everywhere, so we were easily able to save his life. But there was no question now of the Marshal riding the mountain trail in pursuit of Dennis.

"It'll be about all I can do to get back to town to the hospital, I reckon," he lamented. "Your boy will be over the border in Wyoming by the time I can get an officer detailed to you. Damn sorry! But no doubt Dennis'll make another contraband run sometime soon, he 'ppears to have gotten latched onto a going operation."

Holmes did not relish a delay, and I doubted our financial benefactress would approve it, either. "Could you not describe the route to us, Marshal," asked Holmes, "so Dr. Watson and I could secure Dennis on our own?"

Ames chewed his moustache and grimaced, either from the tourniquet we'd applied or the quandary we'd presented. "Well, the way is easy enough to see—bein' an old Pony Express trail," he mused. "And I s'pose I could deputize you; you ain't Americans, but that's never made much never-mind in this territory. But I still don't care for it much."

"Why not?" cried Holmes.

"You have to understand, we were cuttin' things mighty fine to begin with. We had to wait for the dawn because this trail is so durn precipitous some places that it would be risky even for an experienced rider in the dark. And shoot! Now that the sun's up, we've wasted so much time with this snake folderol that you'd have to do a Pony Express race just to catch up with Dennis before he crosses the border! And frankly, I'm fearful you gents might come to harm tryin' to go full-out 'round these mountains, unescorted-like."

"Oh, that's all right." Holmes waved his hand dismissively, and to my dismay said, "Dr. Watson is an old Afghan hand who can ride country like this in his sleep. But why does the territorial border matter if we have federal commissions?"

Ames squinted his eyes dubiously at me, as if his suspicions of my prowess as a horseman were much the same as my own. "Well, the federal writ runs both sides of the border, all right," he acknowledged. "But Jack Taylor has a rough set of Mormon guards up there, and you're far better off to snag your man before you have to two-step with the Temple brethren."

Holmes was thoughtful for a moment, and then turned to me. "That settles it," he said with an air of resolve. "Watson, since I am hardly in your league as a mountain rider, I must follow in your wake as best I can. You must start at once, at full speed, to overtake Dennis before he reaches the border."

"My dear Holmes," I assured him fervently, "I'm sure I cannot."

"Do so all the same," he replied.

Reader, I did.

Looking at the fire in those keen eyes, I had a prevision of the partnership that would outlast the shadows eternally shifting through those foothills. And though I confess that I heaved a sigh, my pulse racing a little, it did not take me long to saddle my horse, a fine mustang paint called Nestor, which Ames had broken himself, and climb into the stirrups. A few last minute instructions from both my superiors, and I set out at a brisk gallop.

Before long, though, the steepness of the climb and the sharpness of the turns forced me to slow Nestor to a walk. It seemed the pathway skirted one dizzying precipice after another the entire way! But we continued to make the best time we could, and when I looked down at the chasms below us, I blessed my beast's sure feet.

Sooner than expected, I heard the sound of voices drifting down from above and wondered at first if this might be some trick of the acoustics of the mountains. But not wanting to give our approach away, I stopped and tethered Nestor to some rugged bushes sprouting out of the side of the mountain wall.

Holding my pistol ready, I crept as softly as I could along the path until, rounding a corner, I suddenly found myself staring at a considerable flat expanse in which there was an encampment of several tents. A few young women were busying themselves at some activity, which I had no time to scrutinize because I hastily moved back out of sight. But I was too late. One of the women had seen me, shrieked, and pointed in my direction, and a moment later, a gunshot ricocheted off the rocks, spraying fragments inches from my face just as I leapt back.

This was a fine predicament! I could only reflect back on my Afghan experience for guidance, so I decided that since I knew nothing of the other party's strength, but knew all too well my own, I should gain little by delay, but might gain something by boldness.

Having a notion of the shooter's position, to make an impression, I darted out from behind my rocks and hazarded a quick couple of shots, one of which found its mark—for as I ducked for cover again, I was glad to hear a cry of surprise mingled with pain, followed by the sound of a body evidently fallen from some height. This was followed by an unmelodious chorus of feminine wails, and sounds of scurrying feet.

Hard-pressed to know what to do next, I was startled to hear a bold female voice close at hand, beckoning me: "You might as well come out, now, whoever you be—there's nobody left to shoot back, and I reckon you won't shoot women, will you?"

It sounds foolish, and I daresay it was, but this challenge to me as a gentleman provoked me to step out into what might have been harm's way. Instead, I almost stepped into the arms of a masterful-looking woman of perhaps forty years walking toward me, dressed in male western fashion, but rather attractive withal.

"Whoa!" she said, holding up a leather-gloved hand. "Put up that shootin'-iron if you don't mind. Ain't I already told you there's nobody but us women, now you've plugged poor Tom?"

"Tom Dennis?" I bellowed. "How badly is he hurt? I'm a doctor!"

She lifted one fine grey eyebrow. "You ain't much of one fer your Hippocratic Oath, are you? Or do you plug 'em first and then charge to mend 'em?"

"Don't bandy pleasantries when someone's bleeding!" I snapped. "My name is Watson. I *am* a doctor. I've chased that man all the way from London, and I want him alive!"

The woman sagged against the mountain wall. "Not Mr. Sherlock Holmes's friend?" she asked in a weak voice, and also, I noticed, a suddenly more cultured accent. "I thought—we thought—you were from the Church. . . . Tom's over here." She gestured toward a space behind the nearest tent, where I saw several young women huddled. "You only winged him, Doctor. He's more hurt from the fall."

As she led me where our long-sought quarry was now stretched upon a camp cot, she turned her fine profile to me over her shoulder and added, almost as an afterthought, "I'm Lucy Ferrier Hope." The words stunned me, and for a moment I simply stared in amazement. Her face, however, was filled with concern for the wounded man, and I realized that explanations would have to wait. Gathering myself, I knelt by the cot to attend to my patient.

Dennis was in considerable pain until I administered some morphia and he drifted off. My shot had been lucky for both of us, for I had stopped his shooting without doing him much harm beyond breaking his thumb, but he had broken his ankle in his fall from the eminence where he'd been doing guard duty for the camp. Just what the camp's purpose was, I had yet to find: were these young women the "contraband" Dennis was running?

After I had made my patient as comfortable as possible, my hostess led me to a set of canvas camp chairs at her campfire, offered me a mug of barbarous American coffee, and we talked a bit as we awaited the arrival of Sherlock Holmes, which I assured her was imminent.

"You notice I don't use that fiend Drebber's name, Doctor," she said quietly. "I don't count that as a marriage but as an abduction, of course."

"I quite understand," I told her. "But how did you escape? Hope told us he saw you stretched out dead on your bier."

She smiled in a way that made me shiver. "Why, so he did. Didn't he tell you also that he used to be the sweeper-out of the laboratory at York College, and learned a thing or two about drugs and medicines?"

"Poisons, you mean," I corrected her.

"Oh, poisons, too," she admitted. "But what he gave me was more like what Romeo's friar gave Juliet—a potion to give me 'A thing like death to chide away this shame, that cop'st with death himself to scape from it.' Something to make me sleep till he burst in and carried me off amongst all those 'mourning' Drebber wives. Oh, and wasn't I glad when I woke up!"

I was stunned, not for the first or last time in this case. "But he told us he only came in to take the ring off your finger!"

"I know," she replied calmly. "He told me when I visited him in prison. But that was one of his tallest ones! Why on earth should he have wanted the ring Drebber gave me? Jeff and I both hated Drebber."

My mind was swimming—each new revelation prompted at least two questions.

"How could you visit him in prison? He only lived one night! He wanted the ring for revenge, didn't he?"

"Oh, Doctor!" She shook her head, and her still-beautiful tresses, chestnut mingled with grey, fell about her solemn face as the hint of a reminiscent smile lit it. "Don't you think I'd been improving my time all those months we'd been in London? I was very active helping the Visitation Society, and it was no problem for me to get permission to visit Jeff. I'll tell you this, about those 'poisons' you mentioned: Jefferson Hope never poisoned anybody. But I wasn't about to let the man I loved languish in prison to die a lonely death from a burst heart, or at the end of an English noose for murders he never did. He taught me about drugs and poisons too! So there's my confession, and if you and Mr. Holmes want to take me back to London for it, I'll go quietly, after I've finished the work I'm about today."

My mother tried to raise her sons properly, but I have a dreadful feeling that my mouth was hanging agape at this point. I certainly wondered if it was I who was mad, or the lady speaking to me. "But Hope confessed," I said at last.

"I know that," she reiterated, as if she were explaining to a child. "He did that because he knew he didn't have long to live anyway." She wiped away a tear sliding down her sunburnt cheek. "And because he wanted to shield Tom."

The sun was now high in the Utah sky, and at last the light began to dawn in my foggy English brain as well. "Dennis killed them both," I said.

"Of course," Lucy nodded. "He hated Drebber and Stangerson far worse than Jeff or I did. You see, he hadn't been able to save the girl he loved. She really was dead."

"Sally Sawyer," I whispered.

Lucy looked at me, surprised. "How did you know?"

"Never multiply names unnecessarily," I recited, recalling Holmes's dictum as if from a dream. "Dennis told us the name himself, in the story he prattled when he came to try to get the ring from us. But come—how did Hope know of that visit?"

"Oh, goodness, Doctor!" Lucy laughed, for the first time, and I saw she was still a handsome woman. "What chatterboxes you and Inspector Gregson were in that cab on the way to Scotland Yard! Jeff told me all about it!"

I must have looked hurt, because she added, in a kindly tone, "Jeff said Mr. Holmes let slip a hint or two, also . . . and you have to admit that my Jeff was a resourceful man."

"More even than we credited," I agreed sincerely. Seeing sudden misery in her face, I reached across the distance between our two chairs and clasped her wrist. "You must miss him sorely."

"Every day!" she cried, raising her overflowing eyes to the empty sky, then turning them back to me. "But we had near two happy decades ranching in Wyoming before Jeff learned Tom was on Drebber's trail in Cleveland. Jeff determined to stop him from doing murder. He couldn't bear for Tom to have that sin on his conscience or his soul, no matter what the provocation." Now she was caught up in the full onrush of her story, and had to tell all.

"And I couldn't bear him to go without me, so we went together. We couldn't find Tom in Cleveland, but that foul Drebber spotted Jeff and had him jailed for a trumpery nonsense—and I couldn't bail him out at first for fear that Drebber would see me! By the time Drebber was gone and I'd got Jeff out, it was too late to stop Tom. That was how it went, across half the world, it seemed, using up our resources and Jeff getting more and more desperate, until finally we came to London.

"Jeff tried to do double duty hunting for Tom and guarding Dreb-ber and Stangerson, while I did what I could, too—though it wasn't much because I daren't let them see me.

"At last, at Lauriston Gardens, Jeff was too late by moments to stop Tom. It nigh broke his heart." She looked at me fiercely as if daring me to deny it.

"He wasn't too late to be observed by the constable," I pointed out. "And his presence there created all kinds of compromising physical evidence, although I always said that Holmes was too quick to theorize about a crime scene which he himself compared to the aftermath of a buffalo stampede."

"Jeff made up that stuff about going back for the ring," she said. "After you told him about 'Mrs. Sawyer' coming to your rooms for it, it was easy enough for him to figure out that Tom had lost Sally's ring there. Tom really wanted it back, you know; it was the one he'd given Sally himself, not like the one in my case."

"You mean Dennis and Sally had really been married before Dreb-ber had taken her away?" I exclaimed. "But that's infamous!"

"Oh yes," she sighed. "It's not unknown among the polygamists, you know. Sometimes plural wives are passed around—it's awful. Anyway, Jeff was too late again when Tom got to Stangerson, and I guess you know the rest."

"But why did the two of you go through all this to save Tom Dennis?" I asked, running my hand through my hair distractedly. "It's noble, of course, and I commend you both for it, but why should Hope risk the happiness of the woman he loved to save Dennis?"

"Because he didn't want his son to be a murderer."

I was suddenly as dizzy as if I had really plunged into one of those mountain chasms.

"Tom is Jeff's son from an attachment long before me," she

continued. "And now poor Tom is truly bereft over this; he understands, as Jeff always knew he'd do, about revenge not lightening his heart from sorrow. That's why he decided to join me in my good work."

"Good work?" I muttered blankly. "What work is that?"

"Why, helping plural brides to escape over the border into Wyoming and freedom!" she exulted. "Jeff and I had done it for years, and now Tom's taking it up with me, in Jeff's memory, and Sally's—or at least he was, until you laid him low with that lucky shot." She gave me a dark look under which I began to shift uneasily in my seat. I began to wish, not for the first time, that Holmes would arrive.

I'm not sure that her animadversion about my marksmanship did not rankle as much as the implication that I was somehow setting back the march of women's rights. "Oh, I'd love to do it all by myself!" she went on. "Maybe even be a Masked Rider like my old friend Bess Erne, but we can't get a passel of young Mormon women past the Temple guards without a man. The safest way's to pretend that we're a Mormon family traveling, a husband with his wives. Now I don't know what I'm to do! If I take these girls back, their families will never let them slip away again. They'll be watched too closely. And we can't camp here much longer; the relief squad for the guards will be coming."

She looked me full in the face with her piercing eyes. "Do you want them to end up like me—or Sally?" she asked.

I was silent. "No," she mused, after a few moments watching my face, "so I guess the only answer is for the fake husband to be you, or Mr. Holmes."

"Hah!" I laughed. "Holmes will never do it! You don't know his views about women. He couldn't carry the part off even if he did agree."

She smiled at me.

And that is how I added the women of a third continent to my store of dearly-bought knowledge. "How many of them are there in all?" I sighed.

"Seven."

"Oh dear," I muttered. "'As I was going to St. Ives . . . ' Introduce these young ladies to me," I said. "I must know their names if I'm to be plausible."

"Oh, that won't be any problem," laughed Lucy. "All seven are named for flowers, and four of them are named Violet."

When I returned exhausted to the foot of the mountain, the stars were out and I was wrestling with conflicting emotions. I felt pleased with my good deed, but also unsure of how to tell Holmes that I had left Dennis with Lucy Hope—or, for that matter, how to share any of my news with him. I confess I was also put out with him for leaving me to handle the entire matter myself, and I tried to keep that perturbation uppermost in my mind, so as not to contemplate the awful possibility that he might have attempted to follow me, but met with some mishap on the treacherous mountain pathway.

Consequently, it was with mingled relief and displeasure that I found both Holmes and Ames still at our campsite, in a cloud of tobacco smoke discussing possible Phoenician voyages to the New World, and the relevance of this to the Book of Mormon.

Holmes, when he spied me, seemed more annoyed than relieved. "What's this, Watson? Did you miss Dennis?"

"And you *as well*, Holmes," I replied testily.

"My horse took lame," he explained after a moment's hesitation.

"Deputy Ames," I said sternly, turning to the other miscreant, "you ought really to have started for the hospital long before this."

"Oh, a snake bite ain't nothin'," he chortled, taking a swig of his cure-all.

"Really, Watson," Holmes resumed, "I cannot congratulate you. Have we made all this trip for naught?"

"I don't know, Holmes," I replied, suddenly lighthearted, looking up at the starry expanse of the Western night sky. "You were right, as usual: a change in perspective does work wonders!"

THE ADVENTURE OF THE COUGHING DENTIST
Loren D. Estleman

Loren D. Estleman has published more than sixty novels in the mystery and historical western genres and mainstream fiction. He has received four Shamus awards from the Private Eye Writers of America, five Spurs from the Western Writers of America, and has been nominated for the Mystery Writers of America's Edgar Award and the American Book Award. His first Sherlock Holmes pastiche, *Sherlock Holmes vs. Dracula*, has been in print for most of the past thirty years. His latest novel is *Frames*, introducing Valentino, a film archivist–turned detective. Estleman lives in Michigan with his wife, author Deborah Morgan.

* * * *

Throughout the first year of our association, Mr. Sherlock Holmes and I were rather like strangers wed by prearrangement, mutually respectful but uncertain of the person with whom each was sharing accommodations. The situation was ungainly, to say the least, because upon the surface we were very different individuals indeed. When, therefore, it chanced that we should travel together abroad, we agreed without hesitation. As Mr. Clemens says (mortally assaulting the Queen's English), "I have found that there ain't no better way to find out whether you like people or hate them than to travel with them."

As it happened, both Scotland Yard and the *Times* of London, which was publishing a series chronicling the tragic events I have set down elsewhere under the somewhat sensational title of *A Study in Scarlet*, had asked Holmes to visit the place where the troubles involving Enoch Drebber, Joseph Stangerson, and Jefferson Hope had begun, and apply his formidable detecting skills towards eliminating a number of small discrepancies in the murderer's confession. This journey, with expenses to be paid by the *Times* in return for an exclusive report of the investigation, would take us to Salt Lake City, the capital of Mormon country in the Utah Territory, a strange and terrible place not unlike Afghanistan of darkest memory.

When I say that we did not hesitate to accept the offer, I do not mean to imply that we failed to discuss it at length in the privacy of our Baker Street digs.

"This is redolent of inspectors Gregson and Lestrade," said Holmes, flicking his long tapering fingers at the telegram from the *Times* as he lounged in his basket chair. "They were swift to claim credit when the boat seemed seaworthy, but now that it's sprung a leak or two they seek to abandon ship and let me go down with it."

"Undoubtedly. But if you're still certain of the soundness of the solution—"

"I'd stake my reputation upon it, were I to possess such a thing."

"Then," said I, "you have nothing to lose but a month or so from your studies here, and a holiday to gain."

"Holidays are for the overworked. I am singularly idle thanks to my magnanimity towards the Yard. The press perceived it to be a police case from start to finish until this moment." He made a motion of dismissal, exactly as if he were slashing his bow across the strings of his violin. Then his face assumed a quizzical expression. "You say 'you' as if I am to be alone in this excursion. What do I know of being a special correspondent? You're the literary half of this partnership, Doctor."

"That's flattering, but premature. I've only just begun arranging my notes, and there is no guarantee of publication, rather the opposite. I'm just one more returning veteran with a story to tell. Fleet Street must be crowded to the rafters with unrequested and unwelcome manuscripts like mine."

"Hardly like yours. There's romance in the business, murder, and not a line about troop movements or grand strategy. I'd read it myself if I didn't know the ending already. I never accept a pig without a poke. No, Doctor, I shan't undertake the assignment without a companion upon whose loyalty and discretion I can rely without question. What is your answer?"

"I was afraid you'd never ask."

His smile was shy, an emotion I had thought absent from his meager repertoire. We would be quite on the other side of our second adventure before such reticence vanished from our relationship forever.

Our crossing was not uneventful, despite calm seas; but the affair of the American industrialist and the Swedish stowaway presents facets of its own, and its appearance in these pages would only distract the reader from the circumstances I am about to relate. It is a story the world may be prepared to hear, but which I am unprepared to tell. As many times as Holmes has explained to me how a disparity between a ship's bells and the time on a pocket watch, *both equally accurate*, can coexist, I remain ignorant as to how he brought the matter to a satisfactory conclusion before we arrived in the Port of New York.

Ironically, the very questions that had brought us from our hemisphere and across the vast reaches of the North American continent proved easier to answer than the conundrum aboard ship. Suffice it to say that a minor but crucial player in the Hope tragedy lied to dissemble a sordid personal peccadillo, and that most of the burden fell to me as I struggled to turn a half-penny hurricane into four columns in the *Times*. They were printed, and our fare and lodgings were paid for without complaint, but from that day to this I have not received another invitation to submit so much as a line to that august institution.

We were left with a wealth of time and opportunity to broaden our experience of the world's curiosities. I circumnavigated the gargantuan lake in a hired launch, and Holmes made copious entries in his notebook about the practice of polygamy for a monograph upon the subject, but we were both eager to add to our education and were soon off to Denver.

On the way we were detained in a muddy little hamlet whose police force had been forewarned of a visit by the remnants of the Jesse James gang of notorious reputation, suspected because of our British accents and European clothes as bandits in disguise. While awaiting word from Washington, D.C., confirming the material in our travel documents, we were placed under house arrest in the town's only hotel. One of our guards was a friendly fellow with swooping moustaches and a revolver the size of a meat-axe, who taught us the rudiments of the game of faro. By the time we were released, Holmes had become an expert, and I had learned just enough to swear off playing ever again for the sake of my army pension.

Having lost several days, we elected to forego Denver as just another large city like St. Louis and turned south towards the territory of Arizona. There among weird rock formations and cactus plants shaped like tall men with arms upraised, I remarked to my companion that I was disappointed not to have seen a red Indian yet, to add to my observations of the aborigines upon three continents.

"In order to make an observation, one must first observe," said Holmes. "Those silhouettes are not the product of erosion."

I followed the direction of his pointing finger, but we had nearly drawn beyond range before I identified what had looked like broken battlements atop a sandstone ridge as a group of motionless horsemen watching the train steam past.

"Apaches, if my preliminary reading is accurate. Zulus are peace lovers by comparison." He laid aside his *Rocky Mountain News* and uncocked the Eley's pistol he was holding in his lap.

"You might have said something. I'm no babe in the woods, you know."

"Quite the opposite, Doctor. A seasoned warrior like yourself might have responded from instinct and training. That would in all likelihood precipitate an action we should all regret."

"I am not a hothead." I fear I sounded petulant.

"You've given me no reason to think otherwise. Now that you have so informed me, as one gentleman to another, I shall not repeat the mistake."

Ours was a difficult getting-acquainted period, as I've said. Even my dear late wife and I had an easier time of it; but then I'd had the advantage of having saved her life early in the courtship. I can't recommend a better approach when it comes to breaking the ice.

The gypsy life deposited us at length in the city of Youngblood, some forty miles north of Tucson. I'm told the place no longer exists, with nary a broken bottle nor a stone upon stone to indicate it ever did. I do not grieve over this pass.

Why we alighted in this vagabond jungle of canvas and clapboard, with an open sewer running merrily down its main street, is a question I cannot answer with certainty. We had not paused thirty seconds to take on water when Holmes shot to his feet and snatched his Gladstone bag from the brass rack overhead. Perhaps it was the scenery which inspired him. I vividly recall a one-eyed mongrel performing its ablutions on the platform and an ancient red Indian wrapped in a filthy blanket attempting to peddle an earthenware pot to everyone who stepped down from the train. A place so sinister in appearance seemed an ideal location for a consulting detective to practice his trade; then again, he may simply have been drawn to its perfect ugliness through some aesthetic of his own.

"Well, Doctor?" He stood in the aisle holding out my medical bag. His eyes glittered.

"Here?"

"Here forsooth. Can you picture a place further removed from Mayfair?"

For this I could offer no argument, and so I took the bag and hoisted my army footlocker from the rack.

Approaching the exit, Holmes nearly collided with a man boarding. When Holmes asked his pardon, the fellow started and seized him by the shoulders. "There's no call, stranger, if that accent's real and it belongs to Sherlock Holmes."

The reader will indulge me if I remind him that at this juncture in his long and illustrious career, my companion was no more public a figure than the thousands of immigrants then pouring into the frontier in pursuit of free land, precious metal for the taking, and the promise of a new life. To hear one's associate addressed by name so far from home was as much a surprise as to be struck by a bullet on some peaceful corner, and one nearly as unsettling. My hand went to the revolver in my pocket.

"I believe you have the advantage," said Holmes stiffly.

He did indeed. The stranger was as tall as my fellow lodger, and a distinct specimen of the Western type, with long fair hair, splendid moustaches, and a strong-jowled face deeply tanned despite the broad brim of his black hat. He wore a Prince Albert coat of the same funereal hue over a gaily printed waistcoat, striped trousers stuffed into the tops of tall black boots, and a revolver every bit as large as our erstwhile jailer's on his hip. I left my much smaller weapon in its pocket—albeit gripping it tightly—in the sudden certainty that any swift move by me would be met by one much swifter on his part, and far more deadly.

To my surprise, the man released his grip upon Holmes's shoulders and stepped back, dipping his head in a show of deference. "No offense meant. I feared I'd missed you, and charging square into you like a bull buffalo set my good manners clear to rout. Wyatt Earp, sir, late of Tombstone, and headed I-don't-know-where, or was anyway till I set foot in this hell."

The name signified nothing to me and was so unusual that I took it at first as a statement interrupted by gastric distress: "Why, at—urp!" was how I received his introduction. Having sampled in Colorado the popular regional fare of beans and hot peppers stewed and served in a bowl, I had been suffering from the same complaint for several hundreds of miles.

Holmes did not share this delusion, and he, who in later years would treat kings and supercriminals with the same cordial disdain, became deferential on the instant. "I am just off reading of your exploits in the *Rocky Mountain News*. This business in a certain corral—"

"It wasn't in the O.K., but in an alley down the street next to the photo studio of C.S. Fly; but I don't reckon 'The Shoot-out in Fly's Alley' would make it as far as Denver. It cost me a brother last March, and crippled another one three months before that. I'm not finished collecting on that bill, but it's not why I met this train. I saw a piece about you being in jail up north—"

It was Holmes's turn to interrupt. "Hardly a jail, although the condition of the hotel linens was a crime in itself. I'm curious as to the process by which you deduced I would proceed south from there, instead of east to Denver."

"You're a detective, the piece said, vacationing from England. I'm in sort of that line myself, tracking stagecoach robbers and such, and it occurred to me nobody who's truly interested in crime and them that commits it would bother with a place where there's a policeman on every corner. I wouldn't give a spruce nickel for a blue-tick hound that didn't head straight for the brambles."

"The brambles in this case being Arizona, where the savages don't all wear paint and feathers. It's crude reasoning, filled with flaws, but I warrant that within six months you'd make chief inspector at Scotland Yard." Holmes shook his hand firmly. "My associate, Dr. John H. Watson."

The sun broke in the man's features. "Doc, is it? Well, if that's not a good show card, I'll give up the game."

I accepted the grip of Mr. Wyatt Earp, late of Tombstone. When winters are damp, I still feel it in my fingers.

"I'm glad to see you traveling with a friend." Earp sipped from his glass of beer, which after thirty minutes was not half gone; he seemed a man who kept his appetites tightly in rein. "I don't know how things are in England, though I expect they've settled a bit since Shakespeare, but no matter how much attention a man pays to his cuffs and flatware, he needs a good man at his back."

Holmes said, "Dr. Watson is my Sancho Panza. You would have marveled to see his stone face just before I clapped the irons on Jefferson Hope."

We were relaxing in the cool dry shade of the Mescalero Saloon, a model of the rustic American public house, with a long carved mahogany bar standing in sharp contrast to the rough plank floor, cuspidors in an execrable state of maintenance, and the head of an enormous grizzly bear mounted on a wall flanked by portraits of the martyred Abraham Lincoln and James A. Garfield. Some marksman, possibly of a patriotic bent, had managed to put out one of the grizzly's eyes and its left canine without nicking either president. I felt distinctly out of my element, and ordered a third whisky-and-water. Our new acquaintance's tales of romance and gunplay in Dodge City and elsewhere required stimulants to digest. I was unclear as to whether he was a gambler or a road agent or a peace officer or a liar on the grand scale of P. T. Barnum. As a frustrated writer, I itched to commit his stories to paper, but as a man of science, I thought him a charlatan.

"I'm ignorant as to Hopes, but I pride myself on my Cervantes," said Earp. "My father wanted me to practice law."

"The errors of la Mancha and Richard III are most instructive in the legal profession." Holmes drank beer. I had the impression that among Mongols he'd have pleased himself with mare's milk. I never knew a man who assimilated himself so seamlessly with the natives. "However, we have not come to this place to discuss the classics."

Earp seemed to concentrate upon lighting a cigar, but it seemed to me all his attention was on Holmes. "They're set on hanging my friend. I don't mind telling you I'm against it."

Holmes's eyes glittered. Directness affected him like a chemical stimulant. "Dr. John Henry Holliday."

"I see you're a man who squeezes all the juice he can out of a newspaper. If you know his name, you know I'd never have walked out of that alley but for Doc. He killed two men who wanted me in hell, both in the space of a half minute."

"And he calls himself a physician? What about his oath?" My exposure to war had not prepared me for barbarianism in the humanitarian professions.

Earp's reptilian gaze was uncannily like Holmes's when he placed me under scrutiny. "Doc's a dentist, if it counts. He's separated more men from their teeth than their lives, but that was before consumption got the better of him. He came out from Georgia for his health. It don't look like the locals mean for him to find it."

He explained that he and "Doc" Holliday had left Tombstone to seek out and confront the conspirators who had slain Earp's brother Morgan and severely wounded Virgil, another brother. The precise cause of these attacks, and of the murderous street fight that had preceded them, was shrouded in territorial politics I could not understand. I gathered that this mission of vengeance had succeeded to some extent, but that Holliday had suffered a relapse of his corrosive pulmonary disease and gone into Youngblood for medical attention. When after a few days his friend arrived to look in on him, he found him in jail charged with murder.

"It happened last night; I just missed it. Doc don't make friends easy, but he draws enemies like flies to sorghum. They say he disagreed with a tin-panner over the proper number of aces in a deck. The tin-panner knocked him down, which you can do with a finger when Doc's ailing. They say Doc gunned him in front of a gang of witnesses down the hill an hour or so later."

"Is he guilty?" Holmes asked.

"He says he's not sure. He took a bottle back to his room after he got up from the floor and don't remember a thing till the town marshal pulled him out of bed and threw him in a cell."

Holmes asked if he'd been convicted.

"The town's just a mining camp with no authority. They can't hold a trial till the circuit judge gets here. That could take days or months, and these get-rich-now prospectors aren't inclined to be patient. Hank Littlejohn was well-liked by all but three, and the other two didn't dislike him enough to go up against a bunch of tin-panners with guns and a rope over the likes of Doc. I ask you now, does that look like a party that'd sit on its hands when hemp's so cheap?" He inclined his head towards a group of men in muddy overalls hunched at the end of the bar, drinking straight whisky and taking turns looking over their shoulders towards our table.

Holmes kept his eyes on Earp. "I noticed them when they came in. The former teamster is their leader. He is the only one who hasn't looked our way."

"What makes him a teamster?" Earp asked. "They all look the same in them Tombstone tuxedoes."

"Such muscular development as his is a common result of swinging a pickaxe or handling a team of mules or oxen. Since by calling them 'tin-panners' you suggest they haven't yet advanced beyond the stage of panning streams for nuggets, I must conclude they are not 'hard-rock' miners. That serpentine scar coiled round his neck ending at the corner of his jaw could only be the consequence of an accident with a whip—a hazard of the trade, based upon my observations since St. Louis. 'Bull-whackers,' I believe the men are sometimes called."

"You're a detective, for a fact. I'm glad to see the scribblers got it right for once. That's Elmer Dundy, Hank Littlejohn's old partner. When they got here, they quit the freighting business to find their fortune in the hills."

"Holmes, he's coming this way." I slid my hand into my pocket.

"Hold, Doctor. We can't shoot them all."

Elmer Dundy was burned the color of the native sandstone, with a great bald head sunk between shoulders built for a yoke. His eyes were tiny black pebbles above a broken nose and a thick lower lip that sagged to show a row of brown teeth and green gums. He'd been drinking whisky from a beer glass, which he held by its handle in a fist the size of a mutton roast.

"So you dug up some friends," he told Earp in a Londonderry brogue—filtered, it seemed, through cactus spines. "They don't look like the killers you run with regular. What's the matter, they fly the coop?"

Holmes intervened. "You'll pardon my speaking without invitation, but I'm unaccustomed to being discussed in the third person when I am present. If you wish to address a question to myself or my companion, be kind enough to do so directly."

Dundy regarded the speaker. Holmes was stretched languidly in his chair with one arm slung over the back and his stick resting alongside his legs, crossed at the ankles. "English!" The former teamster spat viciously, splattering the floor an inch from Holmes's boot, and swung the heavy beer glass at his head.

What happened then took place in less time than I can describe it. Holmes seemed merely to shift his grip on the handle of his stick, the ferrule end flashed so swiftly it was a blur, and dropping one shoulder and twisting the handle slightly, he inserted the stick between the oaf's ankles and sent him crashing to the floor.

Only when the building shook beneath this impact did I claw out my weapon, but before I had it free, Wyatt Earp scooped out his enormous revolver, thumbing back the hammer and leveling the barrel at Dundy's friends, stopping them in midcharge.

Belatedly, as it seemed, Dundy's beer glass, released as he fell, struck the floor with a thump. The gaggle of miners stared at it comically.

"Drag him out before he gives the place a bad name." Earp's tone was as hard and cold as steel.

"Wait." I got up to examine the insensate man. I asked the bartender for brandy.

That fellow had come around from behind the bar with a length of billiard cue in his fist, only to find the drama ended. "Busthead's all I got," he growled.

I looked to Earp for a translation, but it was Holmes who supplied it. "Whisky, in the regional argot; I'm assembling a glossary. The term may be ironic in the current context, but the spirits should prove more than strong enough, though the flesh be weak."

The remedy was produced—"Bill it to Dundy, when he's perpendicular," Earp instructed the bartender—and in a little while we were quit of the miners, who needed no further encouragement to conduct their friend outside.

Earp shook his head. "I must tell Doc. Your partner's slow on the draw, but I doubt even Doc would think to pull a bad tooth from a man I buffaloed. I'd hire you both in a minute, but apart from my interest in the faro game here in the Mescalero, I haven't a cartwheel dollar to pay you for your trouble. My luck's gone sour since the fight at Fly's."

Holmes finished his beer at a draught. "I shall play you for my fee when the thing's done, and accept your promise of payment should I win. When may I speak with Holliday?"

We placed our bags in the bartender's charge, with a warning from Earp to look after them as if they were his own, and repaired to the jail. The town's only building of substance was constructed of stone around an iron cage transported from some wild railhead that had been dismantled the last time the tracks moved westward; American civilization, I learned, was a portable thing in that rapidly developing wilderness. A gimlet-eyed deputy bit down upon Holmes's pound sterling, inspected the result, and gave us five minutes with the prisoner.

I have remarked frequently upon the ascetic gauntness of Sherlock Holmes, but he appeared well-fed in comparison with Dr. John Henry Holliday. Holliday was an exemplar of the attenuated Southern aristocrat, saffron in color, with the skull plain under a crown of pale thinning hair and a lank set of imperials blurred by days without a razor. He sat in a six-by-eight-foot enclosure on a cot, with a deck of sweaty pasteboards laid out on the blanket in a game of patience. A dirty collarless shirt, wrinkled trousers with the braces dangling, and filthy stockings, of good quality notwithstanding, comprised his entire costume.

"I detest this game," he said in lieu of salutation. "It's like making love to a mirror, with the prospect of humiliating yourself through failure."

"If it's the latter you wish to avoid, I should move the queen of clubs from the king of spades to the king of hearts."

The prisoner corrected the error with a throaty noise of self-disgust that turned into a paroxysm of coughing. He stifled it against a sleeve, which bore away with it a pink stain. His gaze, bright and bloodshot, took in Holmes. "God's wounds, an Englishman. Is business so good we're importing hangmen now?"

Wyatt made introductions. Holmes began his interrogation before Holliday could form another ironic comment. "Your friend said Hank Littlejohn was well-liked by all but three. Who, pray, are the other two?"

"Algernon Woods and Jasper Riley. Woods stopped playing poker with Hank for the same reason I did, and Riley got into a dust-up with him on the road here over a sporting woman they both liked in Bisbee; but I wouldn't waste my time trying to pin it on either one." He coughed and turned up another card.

"Are their alibis so sound?"

"Jasper's is. The Chinaman who runs the opium concession here swears he was in his establishment smoking up dreams the night Hank got it. Being a celestial, he's got no friends in town and no reason to lie."

"Lies don't always need reasons. What about Woods?"

"Algernon says he was working late in his shop alone. He's not your man, or even half of him. He's a dwarf, and fat besides. No one would mistake him for me even on a dark night, and there was a moon out big as a pumpkin."

"You said he has a shop. He is a merchant?"

"He's a combination tailor and undertaker. I was his customer once and it looks like I will be again."

"Where were you when Littlejohn met his fate?"

"Sleeping off a drunk in Mrs. Blake's boardinghouse. Whisky's a thief, but if I was to start killing poker cheats, I'd never be quit of it, and I'm a lazy man."

"Thank you. Dr. Watson and I will do what can be done."

Holliday chuckled, coughed, placed a red ten on a black knave. "I'd get to it directly. There's another big moon tonight, dandy for tying a knot and finding the right tree."

"I cannot understand such a man," said I, when we were outside the jail.

Wyatt Earp dropped his cigar and crushed it under his heel. "You get used to that honey-and-molasses drawl. The Wester he goes, the Souther he gets."

"I was referring to his character. My training tells me he's a consumptive in the tertiary stage, but that's hardly a reason to joke about hanging."

"Life's a joke to Doc. What part of it he's got left is too small to take serious."

"It's not so small to you, however," Holmes observed.

"Nor mine to him neither, comes to that. He's innocent."

"Of that I have no doubt. A man who's so willing to accept death would sooner lie and say he's guilty."

"It'd stick in his craw."

"Let us see if this Chinese opium seller suffers from that condition. There is no such thing as a watertight boat or an ironclad alibi."

Earp led us to a large tent pitched upon a slope so steep it would flood during rains and collapse before a mild rockslide. The moss growing upon it made it as dark as a cave inside, lit only by greasy lanterns suspended above rows of folding campaign cots, some occupied by men mostly insensible. Evil smoke fouled the air. Earp slid his bandanna over his nose and mouth while I buried mine in my handkerchief. Holmes took in a deep breath and let it out with a contented sigh.

"Wantee pipee?"

This invitation came from an Oriental in a black silk robe and mandarin's cap, round as Buddha and no taller than a child, albeit plainly in his sunset years. Gold shone in a wicked smile.

"No wantee pipee. Wantee straight talk, and not in pidgin. I know an Oxford accent when I hear it." Holmes held up a gold sovereign, snatching it back when a yellow claw grabbed at it.

The old man shrugged and folded his hands inside the sleeves of his robe. "The missionary who taught me was a retired don. If you are here on behalf of a wife or mother, you may browse among these wretches for him who is lost. I do not insist upon introductions and so am ignorant as to their names."

"If that is the case, how were you able to identify Jasper Riley among your customers the night Hank Littlejohn was killed?"

"I did not say I never pay attention to faces. In election years, many of my former colleagues in San Francisco went to jail because they failed to recognize the same undercover policemen who had arrested them before."

"Did Riley pay you to say he was here all night?"

"Had he been here and made the proper offer, I should have accepted; but honestly, do you think a common teamster could meet my fee for such a risk? I bring in more in a night than he sees in a month, and it is nothing to hang a Chinaman here."

"Very well. Here is your sovereign."

The old man left his hands folded. "That is not the coin you showed me. You are not the magician you fancy yourself."

Holmes grunted as if put out, slipped the coin into his waistcoat pocket, and produced another from inside his cuff. This the opium seller took with a mocking bow.

We went out, where Earp and I drew in great lungfuls of fresh air. Holmes chuckled, without mirth. "My good luck piece benefits me yet again. I took it from a German ironmonger who thought to ingratiate himself with Chancellor Bismarck by devaluing the British currency. Our educated friend inside is neither a liar nor a myopic. His price would exceed Littlejohn's ability to pay, and it's a very good counterfeit."

"Then we're licked," Earp said. "I met Woods. He's short as a rooster and fat as a hog. No one would confuse him with Doc with the moon out."

"I should like to see the scene of the atrocity."

We followed Earp to an open area a hundred yards from the nearest structure, barren but for rocks and scrub and grading downward from the mining camp, our guide reminding us to be alert for rattlesnakes. The dry earth was scored and spotted with wagon tracks and complex patterns made by overlapping hoof prints.

"A train of supplies and provisions came in from Tucson that night," Earp said. "Littlejohn and Dundy came out to visit, and the teamsters sat around passing the jug. They say Doc came in to the top of that rise, coughing and cussing and calling for Littlejohn to show himself. When Littlejohn got up from the ground, Doc plugged him in the belly. That's the story they told, anyway, to the last man."

"Where was Littlejohn standing when he was shot?"

"Right where I am."

"Doctor, will you stand where Mr. Earp indicated that Doc Holliday stood?"

I went to that spot.

"Mr. Earp, could you mistake Dr. Watson for Holliday under these circumstances?"

"No, sir. A bat wouldn't. Watson's a head shorter and twice as thick through the chest."

"What about at night? Disregard for the moment his mode of dress."

"The moon was just shy of full that night. What clothes he had on don't feature. You can make a skinny man look fat in the right clothes, pillows and such, but you can't make a fat man skinny, nor a short man tall, without a pair of stilts."

"I think it's time we met Mr. Woods."

A crude wooden placard hung suspended by twine above the open flap of a tent with wooden framework, reading *Tailor's Shop & Undertaking Parlor, A. Woods, Prop.* in whitewash. We ducked inside and were greeted by a man who rose from a canvas chair. The fellow was neatly dressed in a striped waistcoat, black garters, and grey flannel trousers, but the first thing one noticed was his unnaturally brief stature—four feet two at the outside—and cherubic roundness. He was highly colored and close-shaven, with clear blue eyes, and were I his physician I might have treated him for obesity, but never consumption. His welcoming expression became a frown when he saw Earp.

"Mr. Algernon Woods? I am Sherlock Holmes. This is Dr. Watson, my associate, and I believe you know this other gentleman."

"We've met." His voice, astonishingly deep for the size of its chamber, had a harsh edge. "He accused me of hiring someone who looked like Holliday to kill Littlejohn."

"I considered and rejected that hypothesis in the case of Jasper Riley. Youngblood is small and lightly populated as yet. Any local resident who resembled Holliday would be certain to fall under suspicion, and no stranger could fail to be noticed and questioned. In the absence of other suspects, I must conclude that one of three men is a murderer."

"Your man's in jail."

"I understand Holliday made use of your tailoring services."

"He's particular. Grey coats, never black, and he likes his shirts colored. I doubled the size of my scrap pile with the stuff he rejected." He indicated a heap of odds and ends of cloth between trestle tables covered with bolts of material.

"A man of distinction," Holmes said.

"A man who likes to stand out."

"In his condition he can hardly hope not to. As undertaker, did you conduct a post-mortem examination upon Littlejohn?"

"I dug for the slug, but it passed on through."

"Hardly thorough. Has he been interred?"

"Buried? Not yet; he's in back. What are you, Pinkerton?"

"I am merely a visitor who desires justice. Would you object if Dr. Watson examined the corpse?"

Woods began to speak, but at that moment Wyatt Earp spread his coat casually, exposing the handle of his revolver. The small man closed his mouth and led us with a waddling gait around the edge of a canvas flap bisecting the tent.

I won't belabor the reader with the clinical details of my examination. At Holmes's direction I probed the ghastly wound, then covered the naked body with a sheet and wiped my hands.

"Downward trajectory through the abdomen," I said. "Thirty degrees."

"Holliday was taller than Littlejohn," Woods said. "It's natural he would fire at a downward angle."

Holmes didn't appear to be listening. "Mr. Earp, would you say the ground sloped thirty degrees at the scene of the crime?"

"About that. I worked on a track gang once and learned a thing or two."

"Thank you. My compliments, Mr. Woods, upon your reconstructive skills. With rouge and wax you've managed to make Mr. Littlejohn appear in excellent health. Would you allow me to buy you a whisky at the Mescalero Saloon, to apologize for having wrongly suspected you?"

"I won't drink with Holliday's friend. I don't trust him."

Holmes took Earp aside. The pair spoke in low tones. At length the frontiersman left, but not before casting a dark glance back at Woods over his shoulder. "Mr. Earp understands and has recused himself from our celebration," Holmes said.

One whisky became three, then four. I am not a man of temperance, but neither am I bibulous, and I measured carefully my ingestion while marveling at the little man's capacity and Holmes's. Their speech grew loud, their consonants less crisp. I had not seen my companion in a state of inebriation and felt embarrassed for him and for my country. I became distinctly ill at ease as darkness fell and the saloon filled with teamsters and miners, all of whom seemed to share my tablemates' fondness for spirits. I remembered what Holliday had said about a bright moon being ideal for a hanging. The guard at the jail could not withstand them all.

Holmes was insensitive to the danger. He suggested we walk Woods back to his establishment, but in truth, when he rose he was as unsteady on his feet as was our guest. I kept my hand in my revolver pocket as we walked through that den of smoke and evil plans, feeling very much upon my own.

My fears for my companion's clouded faculties were realized when he steered Woods in a direction opposite the path to his tent. "Holmes, this isn't—"

He cut me off with a sloppy hiss, a finger to his lips and his other hand clutching the little man's collar, essentially holding him up; Woods was nearly walking upon his ankles. Holmes winked at me, and in that moment I knew that he was sober.

Confused and only partially encouraged, I accompanied the pair outside the mining camp and down the slope where the murder of Hank Littlejohn had occurred. "Holmes!" I jerked out my revolver. A group of men stood at the base of the descent. I recognized Elmer Dundy, Littlejohn's truculent teamster partner, and the miners who had been with him when he'd accosted us in the saloon.

"Spare them, Doctor," Holmes said. "They're witnesses."

"Let's get this done with." Dundy's tone now was free of bluster. I considered him more dangerous in this humour than ever. "I came prepared." He held up a length of rope ending in a noose.

"One moment. Mr. Earp?"

"Here." That fellow strode out of the shadow of a piñon tree into the light of a moon, in Holliday's words, "as big as a pumpkin." His revolver was in his hand.

Dundy and his friends fell into growling murmurs. Algernon Woods, who until this moment had been talking and singing to himself, grew silent, and to a great measure less incoherent. "What's this about? Where's my tent?"

"It's Holliday! He's busted out!" One of the miners pointed.

We turned to observe a tall, emaciated figure at the top of the slope, wearing a voluminous pale coat and a broad-brimmed hat that shadowed the top half of his face and the hollows in his cheeks. One bony arm stuck far out of its sleeve as the figure raised his arm to shoulder level and pointed a long-barreled revolver directly at Holmes and Woods.

Several of Dundy's friends clawed at their overalls, only to stop at a command from Earp, accompanied by the crackling of the hammer as he leveled his weapon at the crowd.

Holmes, with a foolhardiness I could attribute only to the bottle, left Woods weaving to ascend the slope. When he stood beside the figure at the top, he said, "Observe his stance. Is it habitual with Holliday?"

"Ask anyone," Earp said. "Only a fool fires from the hip."

"Mr. Dundy?"

The teamster conferred with his friends, nodded. He was hesitant. All could see that Holmes stood two heads higher than the man identified as Holliday.

Holmes produced a ball of string, one end of which he tied to the barrel of the gunman's pistol, then relieved him of it and assumed the former's stance. "Watson!"

I abandoned my weapon to its pocket, the better to catch the spool as he threw it in my direction.

"Mr. Earp, you are Littlejohn's height, are you not?"

"Give or take an inch. I only saw him horizontal."

"Kindly take Mr. Woods's place."

There was nothing kind in the way Earp shoved the little tailor aside and supplanted him. He stood, holding his aim upon the group of witnesses, as seeing Holmes's purpose, I unwound the spool.

"Taut, dear fellow! A bullet observes no principle other than the shortest distance between two points."

I pulled the string taut and placed the spool against Earp's person. It touched him high on the chest.

"Littlejohn was struck low in the abdomen. You will observe, gentlemen, that I stand at about Holliday's height."

No objections were raised. Holmes then returned the pistol to the much shorter man at his side, who raised it to shoulder level and aimed it down the slope. When at this angle I tightened the string, it touched Earp at his abdomen.

"Perspective, gentlemen. A short man standing at an angle thirty degrees higher than the man he is facing must appear taller; but the laws of physics are inviolate." So saying, he snatched the hat off the man dressed as Holliday.

"So sorry." The Chinese opium seller smiled and bowed to his audience. "One pipe apiece, courtesy of Mr. Holmes."

"The thing was simplicity itself," said Holmes, once we were settled in Mrs. Blake's boardinghouse, across from the room where Doc Holliday snored and coughed by turns, resting from his incarceration. "Woods knew Holliday's sartorial preferences and designed a similar wardrobe for himself whose cuffs fell short of his wrists and whose trousers swung free of his insteps; he was foolish enough to leave it among his scraps, where Earp found it while the rest of us sampled the fare at the Mescalero. The subliminal impression is of a man too tall for his garb, hence tall. A loose coat implies emaciation regardless of the portliness contained, and an undertaker's knowledge of cosmetics paints hollows in plump cheeks as easily as it fills in the ravages that scoop out flesh in the final stages of debilitating illness. I am guilty, through Earp, of burgling Woods's store. I also took the liberty of palming a spool of his string.

"Coughing and cursing, in Holliday's distinctive drawl, could only have contributed to the illusion," he continued. "As Woods said himself, Holliday is a man who likes to stand out. The rest was theater."

I said, "I'll wager it cost you another sovereign to enlist the Chinese's cooperation."

"I rather think he enjoyed performing, and would have done it for half. But what price a man's life, be it even so tenuous and sinister as Holliday's?"

"And what of Woods's? That tiny cell won't hold off Dundy's vengeance for long."

"Wyatt Earp has pledged to protect him until the circuit judge arrives. I do believe his sense of justice is equal to mine; as his loyalty to his friend is to yours."

This warmed me more than I can say. I felt that a barrier between us had fallen. "And what is your gain, beyond justice?"

He rubbed his hands. "The chance to drub Wyatt Earp at the game of faro. I take my profits as they come."

THE MINISTER'S MISSING DAUGHTER
Victoria Thompson

Victoria Thompson is the author of the Gaslight Mystery Series featuring Sarah Brandt and Frank Malloy, which was nominated for a 2001 Edgar Award by the Mystery Writers of America. In her previous life, she published twenty historical romances. A popular speaker, Victoria has taught at Pennsylvania State University and currently teaches in the Seton Hill University master's program in writing popular fiction. She is a cofounder and past president of Pennwriters and New Jersey Romance Writers, and past president of Novelists, Inc.

* * * *

I have mentioned previously how busy my friend Sherlock Holmes and I were during the years following his miraculous return from being presumed dead at the hands of the villain Moriarty. After selling my medical practice, I was able to devote my full efforts to assisting Holmes in whatever way he needed me, and since his previous clients had rewarded him so generously, he was able to involve himself in any investigation that took his fancy, without regard to financial considerations.

Holmes's reputation had grown so much by this time that hardly a day passed when someone wasn't trooping up the stairs at his lodgings in Baker Street, seeking his counsel or assistance. Holmes could hardly bear to turn anyone away without at least hearing about the case in question, and as a consequence, he had very little time for rest or relaxation and was seldom even able to sleep a night through without interruption. I began to fear for my friend's health and was, at length, able to convince him to travel with me on a holiday.

Holmes had dealt with many Americans through the years, and he had always found them interesting as individuals. He had also frequently expressed his desire that England and America might one day overcome the differences that had separated them and unite as one nation again. I thought he might be intrigued by the opportunity to present his arguments toward this end in person to our former colony, but only after several weeks of persuasion was I able to convince him to make the trip.

I naïvely believed that in America Holmes would find a respite from those seeking his help, but I had not counted on my accounts of his previous cases having made their way across the ocean ahead of us. We arrived in the city of New York to discover that Holmes was almost as well-known there as he was at home. Our only advantage was that the public at large did not know where he was staying, and that saved us from being overwhelmed by entreaties.

Still, those in certain circles were able to locate us, and we had not been in New York a fortnight before we were invited to dine at the home of Mr. and Mrs. Theodore Roosevelt. Mr. Roosevelt was rumored to be considering a position in the administration of the newly-elected American president, William McKinley, but for the moment he was still the commissioner of the New York City Police Department. As such, he felt obligated to entertain the famous detective Sherlock Holmes.

The party was surprisingly small. After meeting Mr. Roosevelt at his office at Police Headquarters and being assured he was *dee*-lighted with every aspect of our visit, as he seemed to be *dee*-lighted about nearly everything that happened to him, we had expected to encounter a legion of Mr. Roosevelt's friends, anxious to make the acquaintance of such an esteemed visitor. Instead, he seemed to have chosen his guests with care, and the party included only those who could converse intelligently with his honored guest and none of whom seemed to stand in awe of his reputation. I had begun to think we had happened upon the only remaining humans on earth who had no need of Sherlock Holmes's services. Then, halfway through the meal, when the fish course had just been removed, Holmes's dinner partner finally raised the subject of his unique vocation.

"Are you truly as perceptive as the stories about you would have us believe, Mr. Holmes?" Mrs. Brandt asked. She was an attractive woman of about thirty years of age who had been introduced as an old friend of Mr. Roosevelt's. "Or has Dr. Watson used more fiction than fact in his accounts to make you seem so?" she added, glancing over to give me a rather charming smile to take the sting out of her question. I returned it to let her know I had taken no offense.

"I have never claimed to have greater powers of observation than any other man," Holmes replied. "I have simply trained myself to use those natural powers to the fullest extent."

"May I ask you to demonstrate your abilities?"

Holmes raised one eyebrow at the strange request.

"Oh, dear, I've offended you," she exclaimed. "I'm very sorry. My mother will refuse to take me anywhere with her again." She glanced at the lady seated at Mr. Roosevelt's right to see if she had overheard, but she seemed engrossed in whatever our host was saying to her. "You see, Mr. Holmes, it isn't just idle curiosity. I have a reason for testing you."

"Very well, Mrs. Brandt," Holmes said with some amusement. "Shall I tell you what I have observed about you?"

This prospect seemed to please her. "Certainly."

Holmes took a moment, as if to study her, although I was certain he had long since taken her measure. "You are a widow, Mrs. Brandt. Although you are still a young woman, your husband has been dead for some years, and he was a man your parents considered socially inferior to you. They did not approve of the match, and you married against their wishes. You have chosen to remain in reduced circumstances rather than return to your family, and you have taken pride in your ability to make your own way in the world. Although you have not yet remarried, you have a gentleman friend who has engaged your affections, but he is also your social inferior. Your mother encourages you to mingle with her friends, but you seldom do, preferring your own circle of acquaintances."

She stared at him in amazement, so thoroughly awed she didn't even notice when the maid set the next course down in front of her. "How on earth could you know all that about me?" she asked, but then answered her own question. "Oh, of course, Theodore must have told you."

"I promise you that our host has told me nothing about your background," Holmes assured her.

"Then how could you possibly have known all that from simply meeting me tonight?" she challenged.

"You asked me to demonstrate my abilities, Mrs. Brandt, so I shall. First of all, I knew you were a widow because you were introduced to me as Mrs. Brandt, yet you are not wearing a wedding ring." She instinctively looked down at her left hand as if to verify his observation. "If you had been recently widowed, you would be in mourning, but enough time has passed since you lost your husband that you are wearing colors again and have removed your ring."

"I see," she said, nodding her approval. "But how could you know anything at all about my late husband's social standing?"

"The name Brandt is of German extraction, and even Americans are still a bit selective about whom they accept into the upper reaches of society. Your mother is obviously a member of that group."

"How could you know my parents didn't approve of my marriage, though?"

Holmes smiled apologetically. "Parents never approve when their daughter wants to marry a man they consider beneath her."

She conceded the point to him. "But how could you know I didn't return to my parents after my husband died?"

"I must apologize, but I can see that gown you are wearing, as lovely as it is, has been altered slightly to fit you, which means it was made for someone else. Your mother, perhaps? Did she lend it to you for the occasion because you had nothing suitable of your own and she was determined to take you out in society?"

She was speechless again, so Holmes continued.

"I surmised that you take pride in making your own way in the world because you have that air of confidence about you that women do when they are pleased with themselves."

"Is that a compliment, Mr. Holmes?" she challenged.

"Some men might not think so," he admitted.

"You're right there," she said. "And finally, what makes you believe I have a . . . a gentleman friend?"

"Because when Mr. Roosevelt introduced you and your mother, your mother made no mention of your many accomplishments or tried in any way to make Dr. Watson and myself think more highly of you."

"Why would she do a thing like that?" she asked in genuine confusion.

"Mrs. Brandt, Dr. Watson and I are bachelors of independent means. This makes us objects of interest to every woman with an unmarried daughter. The fact that we are also British for some reason makes us even more desirable here in America. You would hardly credit how many poor damsels have been thrust into our notice by their proud mamas since our arrival on your shores. Each and every one of them, to hear the mothers tell it, are paragons of virtue and achievement and perfectly suitable as wives to any Englishman, particularly Dr. Watson or myself."

By now she was covering her mouth to keep from laughing out loud. When she had recovered herself, she said, "Please accept my apology, Mr. Holmes, on behalf of all the desperate American mothers. I'm afraid they can't help themselves."

"Perhaps not," Holmes said. "But your mother feels no need to thrust you under anyone's nose, Mrs. Brandt. She knows your affections are engaged elsewhere."

The color bloomed in her face. "By yet another socially unacceptable man, I assume," she said, feigning bravado.

"Yes," Holmes said, "or else he would have accompanied you this evening."

"Perhaps he was simply otherwise engaged," she suggested.

"Then our hostess would have inquired about him."

Before she could reply, Mr. Roosevelt drew everyone's attention by making a toast to his English guests, proclaiming himself *dee*-lighted to have us in his home. Apparently, Mr. Roosevelt had been blessed with at least ten more teeth than most humans, and his smile displayed every one of them when he was *dee*-lighted. As I have already noted, this occurred frequently.

After the change of topic, Mrs. Brandt made no further mention of Holmes's vocation until much later, when the gentlemen had rejoined the ladies in the parlor after indulging in their brandy and cigars. Mrs. Roosevelt had claimed my attention, but Mrs. Brandt drew Holmes aside, as if by prearrangement with our hosts. After only a few minutes, however, Holmes summoned me to join him in the far corner of the room where he and Mrs. Brandt had found some measure of privacy.

"Watson, I would like for you to hear what Mrs. Brandt has been telling me about a very interesting case," he said, indicating I should take a seat beside her. "Mrs. Brandt, you may speak as freely in front of Dr. Watson as you would to me alone. Please continue."

"As I was telling Mr. Holmes," she began, "a young lady recently disappeared under mysterious circumstances. She is the daughter of one of the most highly respected ministers in the city, the Reverend Mr. Penny of Christ's Church. She was doing volunteer work in the church basement one morning, and she simply vanished, as if into thin air. No one has seen or heard from her since, and that was nearly two weeks ago."

"I believe I read something about this in the newspapers," Holmes said. "Although the accounts were a bit confusing, and some were even contradictory to others."

Mrs. Brandt shook her head. "The New York newspapers pay very little attention to accuracy, I'm afraid. They are much more interested in sensation, because it will sell newspapers. I've seen theories that Harriet Penny was abducted by everything from spirits from another world to Barbary Pirates."

Holmes smiled indulgently. "What is *your* theory, Mrs. Brandt?"

"Mine?" she asked in surprise. "I don't really have one. I only know what the police think."

"What do they think?" he asked with interest.

"That she was kidnapped and has been forced into a brothel."

I'm afraid I could not conceal my surprise that a lady of Mrs. Brandt's breeding would use such a word in polite company.

"I'm sorry if I shocked you, Dr. Watson, but Mr. Holmes was

correct when he guessed that I have continued to make my own way in the world, as he so politely phrased it. I am a trained nurse and midwife, and I have seen far more of the world than my parents would have approved, I'm sure."

By now I had recovered from my surprise, and of course Holmes had not even batted an eye at her candor. "I assume the police are searching for the young woman in the . . . the places where they might expect to find her," I said.

"Yes, but without success. There are so many of those places in the city, and none of them are likely to admit to keeping an innocent young woman against her will. As you can imagine, her parents are distraught, as are the people in her father's church. In fact, the sense of outrage by all decent people in the city is growing daily."

"A serious matter, indeed," Holmes agreed. "Is Miss Penny a friend of yours?"

"No, I don't know her personally, but her plight has affected me deeply, as it must affect all who know of it. I have determined to help in any way I can, even to enlisting the assistance of the best detective in the world," she added with her charming smile. "Do you think you could find her, Mr. Holmes? I know you aren't familiar with the city, but—"

"I would be glad to be of assistance," Holmes assured her, "if the police are agreeable to consulting with me."

"I know one of them will be. Mr. Roosevelt has already said he would give his permission if you were willing. I'll send word to Detective Sergeant Malloy first thing tomorrow to meet you at your hotel."

Holmes's expression never changed, but I knew he was thinking, as was I, that Mrs. Brandt had indeed given her affections to someone socially inferior if she had chosen a policeman.

Holmes and I had hardly finished our breakfast the next morning when the expected Detective Sergeant presented himself. From his expression, he either had a bad tooth or he deeply resented having to consult with Sherlock Holmes. He grudgingly accepted the offered chair and deigned to take a cup of coffee with us while he reviewed the details of Miss Penny's disappearance. We learned nothing that Mrs. Brandt had not already told us.

"When Mrs. Brandt told me about the case, I did not want to offend her by insinuating that it would be easy to solve," Holmes said, "but in my experience, when a young woman disappears, there is usually a young man or a theater troupe involved, often both. But surely you already know that."

"Of course I do," Malloy said impatiently. "But Harriet Penny is a minister's daughter, so she wasn't allowed to attend the theater. And usually, when a girl elopes, she climbs out of her window in the middle of the night and takes a carpetbag with her. Harriet Penny disappeared in broad daylight with nothing but the clothes on her back. Besides, from all accounts, she's twenty-five years old and as plain as an old boot. So far as I've been able to find out, no man ever looked at her twice in her entire life."

"Do the police believe she simply wandered off and found herself in the wrong section of town where she was taken in by a kindly madam?"

"No, they think she was tricked," Malloy explained with more than a touch of annoyance. "The madams employ young men they call cadets to find lonely girls and charm or seduce them into eloping with them. Instead of getting married, the girls end up locked in a brothel and forced into a life of shame."

"An innocent young woman like Miss Penny might easily be charmed by such a man," I pointed out.

"Indeed. What else can you tell me about Miss Penny?" Holmes asked.

"Not much. Everyone in the church knew her, but nobody could tell me a thing about her except to say she was devoted to her parents and to doing good works."

"Her friends?"

"She didn't have any close friends, anybody she confided in. She spent all her time with her mother, keeping her company."

"One wonders how any young woman could be lured away from such a delightful existence," Holmes observed wryly. "May I meet her parents?"

"They don't have any idea what happened to her, either," Malloy warned him.

"I'm sure they don't, but perhaps they can help us understand Miss Penny better."

"I'll ask her parents if they'll see you," Malloy said, although he didn't sound as if he held out much hope that they would.

But Mr. Malloy returned that afternoon with an invitation to visit the Reverend Mr. Penny and his wife at their home.

"May we stop by the church on our way?" Holmes asked as we were crossing through the hotel lobby. "I should like to see where she was when she disappeared."

"If you want to," Malloy said. "It's just a block from their house."

Malloy procured a cab for us, and after a harrowing trip through the crowded city streets, we found ourselves in a quiet neighborhood shaded with stately trees. The church was made of gray stone and boasted many stained glass windows. Inside, the dark wood gleamed brightly, and the altar was richly appointed. The congregation had been generous in their support. Still the building lacked the character of English churches, being only a few decades old, but in several hundred years or so, it might be considered a handsome example of some architectural period yet to be celebrated as classic. Malloy led us down a staircase to the basement and into a room where several partially filled barrels had been placed. Bundles of clothing were piled along one wall, and a table that had apparently been salvaged from a trash heap sat in the center of the room. Although it was likely used for sorting, it was bare now.

"She was sorting through the used clothing that people had donated for the missionaries," Malloy explained, indicating the stacked bundles of clothing. "They collect things and send them overseas in the barrels."

Holmes examined several of the bundles of clothing, then peered into the barrels, almost as if he expected to find Miss Penny hiding in one of them. But the barrels were only partially full, and not even a tiny child could have concealed herself in one of them for any length of time. "Is this the way they found the room after she disappeared, or did someone straighten it up afterwards?" he asked when had completed his inspection.

Malloy frowned. "This is how it looked when I got here. I don't think anybody would've had time to do anything to it."

Holmes nodded as if his answer held some mysterious secret meaning. "Does the basement have an entrance directly to the outside?"

Malloy led us down a dreary hallway to a door. It opened into the alley behind the church. Back gardens of the houses on the next street abutted the alley and were cluttered with ash cans and other refuse. People were passing by but not paying any particular attention to the three gentlemen who had just exited the church. They all seemed preoccupied with their own business and in a hurry to get somewhere else.

"What time of day did she disappear?" Holmes asked.

"In the morning, between nine o'clock and noon."

"No one missed her all that time?" Holmes asked in surprise.

"She was supposed to be working in the church," Malloy reminded him.

"Alone?"

"Her mother had come with her, but she got sick and went home. Miss Penny decided to stay."

"Then let's ask her mother about that, shall we?" Holmes said.

Malloy sighed in resignation and guided us down the alley toward the next street.

The church had provided a large, comfortable home for their minister. A young maid answered the door, an Irish girl who frowned at Malloy and actually glared her disapproval that two English gentlemen were invading her master's home. She showed us into a formal parlor that was fairly choked with the heavy furniture and the multitudinous bric-a-brac that people considered fashionable nowadays. A well-dressed couple of middle years awaited us.

Malloy made the introductions, and I noted that the Reverend Mr. Penny appeared to be familiar with my friend's reputation and expressed his heartfelt gratitude for our assistance. He was a well-groomed man of at least sixty, whose thick hair had gone a distinguished gray and whose middle had gone a bit soft.

Mrs. Penny had clearly been a beauty in her day and was still a handsome woman, although she was approximately the same age as her husband. She was practically enthralled by her visitors.

"Mr. Holmes, I understand Mr. Roosevelt himself has asked you to look into the matter of our poor daughter," Mrs. Penny said, plainly gratified by the attention of such an important person as Theodore Roosevelt.

"Although the police have been more than diligent in their efforts, Mr. Roosevelt thought perhaps a stranger would have a fresh perspective," Holmes quickly demurred, with a nod of recognition toward Mr. Malloy. Holmes never openly disparaged the police if he could help it, no matter how inept they might be. "Could you tell me about your daughter?"

"I'm not sure where to start," Mrs. Penny said uncertainly.

"What would be helpful to you to know?" Penny asked.

"Tell me about your family," Holmes invited. "Is she your only child?"

"Oh, no," Mrs. Penny said. "Not at all. She is the youngest of five."

"A surprise baby," Penny added, but without a hint of embarrassment or even the delight that people often displayed when describing such an event. "She came along years after we thought our family was complete."

"Which was fortunate," Mrs. Penny hastened to explain. "My health began to fail shortly after her birth, and she has been such a comfort to me. I remember when she was only a child, she told me her fondest wish was to live with her Papa and me forever and to care for us in our old age."

I could not help noting that in my professional opinion, Mrs. Penny looked remarkably well for a woman whose health had been failing for almost twenty-five years.

"Harriet is a beautiful girl," Penny said, contradicting what Malloy had told us and earning a look of shocked disapproval from his wife. "Her beauty is inner, however," he hastened to explain. "A beauty of the spirit."

"All my other children are quite handsome," Mrs. Penny wanted us to understand, implying that she should not be judged poorly because she had produced one child who failed to meet her standards. "But poor Harriet . . . So it was just as well she had no desire for marriage and a family."

"She has a good heart, though," Penny continued. "She kept up a voluminous correspondence with our missionary families and was always collecting things for them."

"How did it happen that she was alone at the church on the day she disappeared?" Holmes asked.

"I went with her that morning, of course," Mrs. Penny offered, almost defensively. "Just as we always do. We were sorting old clothes and packing them in barrels to send to the missionaries in foreign lands."

"Yes, Mr. Malloy explained that."

"But shortly after we arrived," Mrs. Penny continued, "Harriet said to me, 'Mama, I see that you aren't feeling well today. Why don't you return home and rest?' Harriet was always very solicitous of my health."

"So you left her there alone?" I could not help saying.

"Of course not!" Mrs. Penny exclaimed. "Mrs. Jenkins and Mrs. Smith were expected momentarily. She would have been alone for only a few minutes at most."

"And when did these two ladies actually appear?" Holmes asked.

"Never," Penny said before his wife could answer. "They did not come at all. There was some . . . some confusion about the day they were supposed to meet at the church."

"They thought they were supposed to come the next day," Malloy offered, as if to remind us this was his case and he was in command of all the facts.

"I will never forgive them for not being there," Mrs. Penny declared. "If they had been, our daughter would still be with us. Oh, Mr. Holmes, do you think you can bring poor Harriet back to us?"

"I will certainly try to locate her," Holmes said, being careful to promise nothing. "When you went to the church that morning, did you walk or take a carriage?"

"Oh, we always walk. It's just a step over to the church."

"Did Harriet bring anything with her?"

"A bundle of clothing. She had called on some of our neighbors to collect donations for the barrels. She was always thinking of others," she added.

"Did you see her sort the clothes she brought with her?" Holmes asked.

Mrs. Penny frowned. "I don't believe I did. We had hardly arrived at the church when Harriet suggested I return home, you see."

"You said that Harriet had no desire for marriage and a family, but had any young man expressed an interest in courting her?" Holmes asked.

Mrs. Penny shook her head sadly. "Dear me, no, Mr. Holmes. Poor Harriet is very shy, and she lacks those . . . those characteristics that make a young lady attractive to young gentlemen."

"And I am a clergyman, as you know," Mr. Penny added. "So Harriet had no financial expectations that might have overcome her lack of beauty and charm in the minds of potential suitors."

"Is it possible that in her entire life, no gentleman had ever so much as befriended her?" Holmes asked in astonishment.

Her parents exchanged a puzzled glance as they tried to recall and could not come up with a single candidate. I had begun to pity Miss Harriet Penny with all my heart.

When they failed to answer, Holmes said, "What sort of mood was Miss Penny in that morning?"

"Mood?" Penny asked, as if he were not familiar with the word.

"How strange you should ask," Mrs. Penny said, obviously familiar with it. "She was quite cheerful that morning. I can't recall the last time I saw her in such good spirits. Oh, wait, yes, I can. It was the time she beat Mr. Etheridge at chess."

"Who is Mr. Etheridge?" Holmes asked with interest.

"He was a student from Princeton Seminary who served his internship at my church last year," Penny said dismissively.

"He played chess with Harriet a few times while he was here. I believe he let her win," Mrs. Penny confided. "Harriet was never very good at chess."

"What became of Mr. Etheridge?"

"After he served his six months with us, he returned to the seminary." Penny said. "We haven't heard from him in almost a year."

"And you are sure that Miss Penny had not made the acquaintance of any other gentlemen recently? Someone at your church, perhaps, who had befriended her of late?"

"Absolutely not," Mrs. Penny said severely. "Harriet lived a quiet life. She did not go out in society like so many girls do today, and she had no interest in meeting gentlemen. As I told you, she had no wish to be married."

"Yes, she had dedicated her life to your well-being," Holmes re-called, and I must confess, I had to cough to keep from laughing out loud at his subtle sarcasm. Even Malloy had to rub his mouth to cover a smile.

The Pennys completely missed his barb.

"What could have become of her, Mr. Holmes?" Mrs. Penny asked with genuine concern. "Do you think—? I mean, the newspapers have said such horrible things." She shuddered.

"I would not like to raise your hopes just yet, but I would be happy to look into the case, if I may."

"Oh, yes," Mrs. Penny said eagerly. "Please do! Even if you learn the worst. Well, I can't bear to think of life without her by my side."

Holmes rose, and Malloy and I followed his lead. We took our leave of the Pennys, and the maid showed us to the door. "Are you a maid of all work here?" Holmes asked as she handed us our hats.

She stiffened, ready to take offense at whatever this Englishman might say to her. "Yes, sir, I am."

"And did you serve Miss Penny?"

"I did, and a sweeter lady there never was."

"Would you do me a favor and look through Miss Penny's clothes?"

"Whatever for?" she asked, not sure if she should do his bidding or not.

"Just to see if you find anything unusual."

"Do you mean if there's anything missing?" the girl scoffed. "Nobody's touched her things since she left that morning. I saw to that!"

"I believe you are mistaken," Holmes said. "If you will check her things, you will discover something unexpected. We will most likely call again tomorrow, and you can report to me then what you have discovered."

The girl frowned, obviously determined to show the Englishman he was wrong, and slammed the door a little too loudly behind us.

"I told you they wouldn't be able to help," Malloy reminded us.

"On the contrary, they were very helpful."

"Are you saying you know where the girl is?"

"I believe I do," Holmes said, shocking him. "I must return to my hotel and make some enquiries and send a telegram. As soon as I have received a reply, I will ask you to accompany us back to the manse to see the Pennys again."

A skeptical Malloy left us to find our own way back to our hotel. Holmes used the hotel telephone to make one call. Then he sent a telegram, as he had told Malloy he would. Since the day was still young, Holmes insisted that we visit the Natural History Museum. Although I asked him about the case, he declined to discuss it until he had received the answer to his telegram. The reply came shortly after luncheon the next day, and Holmes sent a message to Malloy. We arrived at the Pennys' home late that afternoon, with Holmes still refusing to enlighten Malloy or me until he had spoken with the Pennys.

The same maid admitted us, but today she treated Holmes with much more respect. She whispered a few words to him, her eyes wide with surprise over whatever news she was delivering. He nodded, as if he had expected to hear exactly what she told him, then allowed her to show us in to see the Pennys.

They were waiting for us in the crowded parlor again, their expressions expectant.

"Have you found her, Mr. Holmes?" Mrs. Penny demanded anxiously. "Is she all right? Will you bring her back to us?"

"Now, Mother, you mustn't get your hopes up," Penny cautioned her with a worried frown. "Even should Mr. Holmes succeed in returning her to us, she may no longer be the same girl she was, you know."

"I believe I can guarantee she will not be," Holmes said, startling a gasp from Mrs. Penny. "Although I am happy to tell you that your daughter is safe and in good health."

"But where is she?" Mrs. Penny cried. "And why hasn't she come home?"

"Because she left of her own free will and has no desire to return."

This time both of Harriet Penny's parents gasped. "That's impossible!" her father exclaimed angrily. "We know her disappearance could not have been voluntary."

"Not only was it voluntary, it was carefully planned. Shall I explain?"

"You had better, before I throw you out of my house!" Penny said, his handsome face mottled with fury.

"First of all, Miss Penny had arranged to be alone at the church that morning."

"How could she have done that?" Mrs. Penny asked.

"She had told the other two ladies they were to meet the following day, thereby ensuring they would not be at the church that morning. Then she suggested to you, Mrs. Penny, that you should return home and spare yourself the unpleasant task of sorting old clothes. No doubt she knew you could be easily persuaded to do so."

Mrs. Penny had no reply to this. She just stared at Holmes in silent outrage.

"When she was truly alone and unobserved, perhaps for one of the few times in her life, she left the church, walked to Union Station, and boarded a train for San Francisco."

The Pennys both protested vigorously, and even Malloy had to disagree.

"Nobody saw her leave the church," Malloy informed Holmes. "We asked everybody in the neighborhood."

"What exactly did you ask them?" Holmes asked.

"If they had seen a young woman leaving the church with a man."

"But she didn't leave with a man, and she wasn't forced or doing anything to call attention to herself. She would have walked calmly out and disappeared into the crowd. No one in that alley would have paid the slightest heed to her, just as they paid no heed to us yesterday."

"My daughter would never have left her home and family, much less boarded a train to anywhere at all!" Penny insisted. "She would never have caused her mother and me so much concern!"

"And why would she go to San Francisco?" Mrs. Penny asked. "We don't know anyone there at all!"

"Yes, you do. Mr. Etheridge lives in San Francisco. He accepted a call to a church there after he left Princeton."

"Etheridge? How would Harriet have known he was there? And why would she even have cared?" her father scoffed.

"I believe Miss Penny had developed a fondness for Mr. Etheridge, and he for her."

"Impossible!" Penny insisted.

"And they had corresponded in the months since he returned to the seminary."

"I would have known if she was corresponding with anyone!" Mrs. Penny wailed.

"Mr. Penny himself told us she corresponded with missionaries," Holmes reminded them. "She could have easily included her letters to Etheridge in those mailings and received replies in the same way."

"But . . . " Mrs. Penny cast about desperately for another argument to refute Holmes's claims. "She couldn't possibly have left voluntarily. She didn't take so much as a hairpin with her!" she tried.

"You yourself told me she was carrying a bundle of clothing when you left the house that morning," Holmes reminded her.

"Secondhand clothing," Mrs. Penny explained. "She collected it from our neighbors. I saw it myself!"

"But you told me you didn't see her sorting the clothes in that particular bundle. Would you ring for your maid, please?"

Startled at the seemingly incongruous request, Penny pulled the bell rope. The maid appeared almost instantly, her eyes still wide with amazement.

"Before we left yesterday," Holmes said, "I asked your maid to go through Miss Penny's clothing to see if anything was missing. Were her drawers empty?" he asked the girl.

"No, sir, they were all full, just like they should be."

"You see," Mrs. Penny said. "I told you!"

"Did you notice anything unusual?" Holmes asked the girl, ignoring Mrs. Penny.

"Yes, sir," the maid said, nodding her head vigorously. "None of the clothes in the drawers was hers!"

"Whose were they?" Holmes asked.

"I don't know," the girl said, "but they was all raggedy and old, like something you'd throw out."

"Or send to the missionaries in foreign lands," Holmes said.

"What are you talking about?" Mrs. Penny cried.

"Miss Penny had packed her belongings in the bundle that was supposed to be clothing for the missionaries and left the old clothing she had collected in her drawers. I am guessing she had secreted a carpetbag in the church at some time in preparation. When you left the church that morning, she put her own belongings that she had carried from home into it, and took it with her to the train. Then she used the ticket Mr. Etheridge had sent her and went to join him."

"This is all conjecture," Mrs. Penny exclaimed, her face now crimson with outrage. "I refuse to believe a word of it."

But Mr. Penny had calmed down a bit, and he was studying Holmes with a contemplative frown. "I believe, Mr. Holmes, that you have concocted this wild tale with the best of intentions, to reassure Mrs. Penny and myself that our daughter is safe on the other side of the country when you really believe her to be a fallen woman held captive someplace where we will never find her. If this is the case, I assure you, we are strong enough to hear the truth, whatever it may be."

Mrs. Penny's cry of anguish proved she wasn't as strong as her husband claimed, but Holmes ignored her. He reached into his coat pocket and pulled out the telegram he had received earlier today. "I took the liberty of telephoning Princeton Seminary yesterday. They were kind enough to give me Mr. Etheridge's direction in San Francisco, and I sent him a telegram informing him that Miss Penny's disappearance had caused a sensation in New York. He was completely ignorant of this unfortunate development. Most probably he and Miss Penny felt certain no one but her parents would even notice she was gone. Under the circumstances, they wish you to know that your daughter and Mr. Etheridge were married three days ago in San Francisco. I believe congratulations are in order."

Holmes held out the telegram, and Malloy snatched it from him before the Reverend Mr. Penny could gather his wits.

"It's true," the detective confirmed when he had scanned it.

"The ungrateful baggage," Penny snapped. "How dare she be so selfish? Frightening her mother and me so terribly and all for her own purposes!"

"Why, she asked me only a few weeks ago what I would say if someone wanted to marry her," Mrs. Penny recalled furiously. "I told her not to be ridiculous, that no one was going to marry her, and besides, her duty was to care for her father and me. Yet still she chose to desert us!"

"I've got some friends at the newspapers," Malloy said. "I'll give them the word. The real story will be in tomorrow's papers, and that should calm the city down again."

"You should also put an announcement of the marriage in the society pages," Holmes suggested. "To at least give the illusion that you approve the match. That will go a long way to stopping the gossip."

We left the Pennys still in shock at the treachery of the daughter they had believed to be without a mind or spirit of her own.

"Who would've believed Harriet Penny had so much gumption? How did you figure it out?" Malloy asked as we strolled down the tree-lined street in search of a cab. It was as close as he would come to complimenting Holmes.

"When you told me Miss Penny was as plain as an old boot," Holmes recalled with a small smile, "I wondered why one of those young men who work for the madams . . . What did you call them?"

"Cadets," Malloy supplied.

"I wondered why a cadet would select such an unattractive girl— who was already a bit old for the trade, by the way—when the city abounds with much more likely prospects. So the theory that she had been kidnapped to a brothel seemed unlikely. As I mentioned, when a young woman disappears, there is usually a man or a theater troupe involved. Since the minister's missing daughter never attended the theater, I simply had to identify the man, no matter how unlikely a candidate he might seem."

"She was clever," Malloy said.

"She had to be to escape from those two," Holmes said.

But not more clever than Sherlock Holmes.

The Case of Colonel Crockett's Violin
Gillian Linscott

Gillian Linscott is the author of the Nell Bray crime series, featuring a militant suffragette detective in Britain in the early years of the twentieth century. One of the series, *Absent Friends*, won the CWA Ellis Peters Dagger for best historical crime novel of 2000 and the Herodotus Award. She has worked as a news reporter for the *Guardian* and a political reporter for BBC local radio stations. She lives in a three-hundred-and-fifty-year-old cottage in Herefordshire, England, and in addition to writing, now works as a professional gardener. Interests include mountain walking and trampolining.

* * * *

"Admit it, Watson. Texas has not come up to your expectations."

My old friend lounged in a cane chair on our hotel balcony, the hint of a smile on his lips. Our days at sea had done wonders for his health and spirits. His face was lightly tanned, shaded by the brim of a Panama hat.

"It's not as I'd imagined," I agreed.

He laughed.

"You'd hoped for cowboys with lariats and six shooters, Indian chiefs in war bonnets."

Since that was pretty well the vision that had come to my mind when the unexpected invitation arrived on a drizzly day at Baker Street, I tried to hide my irritation.

"Certainly San Antonio seems peaceable enough," I said.

Two floors below, in the courtyard of the Menger Hotel, broad leaves of banana trees shifted gently in the breeze. Our suite, with its lounge, two bedrooms, and bathroom, was as clean and comfortable as anything you might find in London, perhaps more so. From where I was standing I could glimpse a corner of the town's plaza, with men crossing from shade to sun and back, looking much like men of business anywhere, though moving at a leisurely pace in the heat. A neat landau, drawn by a grey pony and carrying a woman in a white dress, trotted briefly into sight and out again.

"We've come too late for the wild days, Watson. Seventy years ago we might have arrived in a covered wagon, pursued by as many braves or Mexicans as your warlike heart could wish. I confess my preference for the Mallory Line."

We'd traveled in comfort down the coast from New York to Galveston on Mallory's three-thousand-ton steamer, SS *Alamo*, then on by Pullman car. The letter of invitation had implored us to make all convenient speed and spare no expense—both admonitions quite wasted on Holmes, who would spend time and money exactly according to his opinion of what was necessary and nobody else's. He stood up and joined me at the rail of our balcony, looking down at the courtyard. A gentleman in a white suit and hat had appeared from the reception area and was walking towards the foot of our staircase. Holmes gave a chuckle of satisfaction.

"Unless I am mistaken, Watson, here comes our client now."

Benjamin Austin Barratt was a gentleman of fifty years or so, still vigorous, straight-backed, and broad-shouldered, with thick dark hair and a small moustache on an otherwise clean-shaven face. His manners were courtly, asking after our health and our journey, as if his only purpose were to make us welcome in his native town. It was Holmes who cut short the preliminaries and brought us to business.

"You mentioned in your letter that you were writing on behalf of the Daughters of the Republic of Texas. Do we take it that you are their representative?"

"Indeed so, sir. You will surely be aware that before Texas became part of the United States of America it was an independent republic in its own right by virtue of—"

"We are aware of it, yes."

Holmes spoke with some impatience. Almost everybody we'd met, from our fellow passengers on the voyage down, to the lad who'd carried our cases to our rooms on arrival, had offered this fact as soon as setting eyes on us. Barratt showed no annoyance and went on with his explanation.

"The ladies thought it preferable that you should be approached by a businessman with some standing in our community. Since I have the honour to be one of the benefactors of their Alamo project and have an interest in the matter under discussion, it was agreed that I should write to you. You will have gathered something of our dilemma from my letter."

"The case of Davy Crockett's superfluous fiddle," Holmes said.

His tone was light. He'd responded to the letter in something of a holiday spirit because it piqued his curiosity. Barratt's posture stiffened for a moment and there was a hint of reproach in his tone.

"Colonel Crockett's violin, yes indeed, Mr. Holmes. The most famous musical instrument in our country's history. That it should have survived the battle is miraculous. That there are two of them is a matter so embarrassing that the ladies decided it could only be settled by the greatest detective in the world, who also happens to be an amateur of the violin."

Holmes nodded at the tribute, as no more than his due.

"Your letter spoke of urgency."

"Yes, sir. This year the Daughters of the Republic of Texas took on responsibility for safeguarding what remains of the old Alamo mission building, where the battle took place sixty-nine years ago. They plan to open it as a national shrine and a museum. Naturally, the very violin that Colonel Crockett carried with him when he brought his men of the Tennessee Mounted Rifles to join the defenders in the Alamo, the violin he played to hearten them all during the siege, will be its most precious exhibit."

"It is a fact that Davy . . . that is, Colonel Crockett, had his violin with him in the Alamo," I said. "There was one evening when he had a competition with a man who played the bagpipes and . . . "

I'd done some reading on the subject before we left London. All it brought me was an impatient look from Holmes.

"We can take that as established. But is there any explanation of how such a fragile thing as a violin escaped the destruction of everything else when the Mexicans stormed the Alamo?"

"One of the violins is in my possession," Barratt said. "I look forward to telling you its story when I hope you will do us the honour of taking dinner with us tomorrow night, but I believe its history is as well-authenticated as anybody could wish."

"And the other violin?" Holmes asked.

"I'm sure Mrs. Legrange will tell you that hers has a well-authenticated history too. I know she plans to meet you. One thing I should like to make clear."

For the first time in our conversation, his voice was hesitant. Holmes raised an eyebrow, inviting him to continue.

"There is no enmity between Mrs. Legrange and myself, none whatever," Barratt said. "She is a very charming and patriotic lady and we all admire her very much. We have both agreed that this business must be settled in a quiet and peaceable manner as soon as possible, and we shall both abide by your verdict. May I send my carriage for you two gentlemen at six o'clock tomorrow?"

Holmes told him that he might.

As Barratt crossed the courtyard, one of the hotel's messenger boys passed him in the opposite direction and came up the stairs to our suite carrying an envelope.

"I believe we are about to receive an invitation from the owner of the second fiddle," Holmes said.

A knock sounded at the door. I answered it and was handed an envelope by the messenger boy.

"Pray open it and read it aloud, Watson," Holmes said.

The signature was *Evangeline Legrange*, with as many curls and loops to it as a tangled trout line. I read:

My dear Mr. Holmes,

I hope you will excuse this informality of approaching you without introduction, but I wonder whether you and Dr. Watson would care to join us on a picnic luncheon outing to San Pedro Springs tomorrow. If I may, I shall send a gig for you at eleven.

Holmes told me to ask the boy to wait while he dashed off a polite line of acceptance on hotel notepaper.

"She gives no address," I objected.

"She has no need," he said. "If you look out of the other window, you'll see she's waiting outside in the landau with the grey pony."

And I thought he hadn't noticed.

I spent the rest of the day exploring San Antonio, while Holmes refused to be drawn from our shady balcony, smoking his pipe and reading a book that had nothing whatsoever to do with the subject under investigation. The town proved to be every bit as calm and prosperous as on first acquaintance. In whatever direction you might stroll, you were never far away from a river bank. Breezes rustled the groves of their strange twisted oak trees and freshened the southern heat. To my pleasure, I even saw several unmistakable cowboys in broad-brimmed hats and leather chaps, lounging on their raw-boned horses in saddles as large and deep as club armchairs. I climbed the hill to the barracks in the hour before sunset to watch the soldiers drilling, then walked back down to try to persuade my companion to take a stroll before dinner. There was no sign that he'd stirred all the time I'd been away and I might have failed in my purpose if his eye had not been caught by a flare of fire in a corner of the wide plaza.

"Good heavens, Holmes, has a building caught fire?" I cried.

"Nothing so calamitous. Shall we go and see?"

His keen senses had caught, as mine soon did, the smell of spices and the scent of charred meat. We strolled across the plaza in the dusk and found that part of it had been taken over by dozens of small stalls with charcoal braziers, tended by Mexicans. A band was playing jaunty music on accordions, violins, and a kind of rattling object, a woman singing in a plaintive voice that cut across the music and gave it a touch of sadness and yearning. We were surrounded by brown smiling faces with teeth very white against the dusk, women with silver ornaments twined in their black hair, and voices that spoke in murmuring

Spanish. It was as if our few steps across the plaza had taken us all the way to the far side of the Rio Grande and we were in Mexico itself. Holmes seemed delighted, as he always was by things unexpected. He even allowed a woman to sell him something that looked like a kind of rolled up pancake.

"Good heavens, Holmes, what are you eating?"

"I've no idea, but it's really very good. Try some."

Its spiciness made me gasp and cough. As we were walking back towards the hotel, a Mexican man came towards us out of the shadows. He was perhaps thirty years old or so, a handsome fellow and respectable in his manner.

"Excuse me, señor, you are Sherlock Holmes?"

He spoke in English. Holmes nodded. The man passed him a piece of paper.

"My address. I should be grateful if you would call on me."

He wished us good evening and stepped back into the shadows as smoothly as he'd stepped out of them.

"So you've got yourself a new client," I said, laughing. "He probably wants to consult you about a missing mule."

"Very likely," Holmes said.

But he seemed thoughtful, and I noticed he put the piece of paper carefully into his pocket.

Next morning, the gig arrived to carry us a mile or so north of the town to San Pedro Springs. It was as pleasant a park as I've ever seen, with three clear springs trickling out of a rocky hill and running between grassy slopes and groves of pecan nut trees. Our hostess had established camp in one of the groves, surrounded by preparations for an elaborate picnic luncheon, with folding chairs and tables loaded with covered dishes and wine coolers. Four black and Mexican servants were in attendance, serving drinks to guests who had arrived before us. Evangeline Legrange was sitting on a bank of cushions, leaf shadows flickering over her pale blue dress and white hat with a blue ribbon that tied in a bow under the chin. She jumped up with a cry of pleasure and came tripping over the grass towards us.

"Mr. Holmes . . . so kind . . . I can hardly believe it. And you must be Dr. Watson, such a pleasure."

Her small white-gloved hand was in mine, the scent of jasmine in the air around us. Her hair, worn loose under the hat, was the colour of dark heather honey and her skin white as alabaster. Close to, if one must be ungallant, she was older than she had looked under the shade of the tree, perhaps in her late thirties, but she moved and spoke with the freshness and impetuosity of a girl. She set her gentlemen guests to pile up cushions for us beside her, calling on one of the servants to bring us iced champagne. California champagne, as it turned out. Several people assured us that it was vastly superior to the French article. When we were settled, she clapped her hands at guests and servants alike.

"Now, leave us alone while I tell Mr. Holmes about my violin. You all know the story in any case."

They melted obediently away and this is the story she told us, in a voice as pleasant to hear as the stream flowing beside us.

"As everybody knows, the men in the Alamo were under siege with Santa Anna and his Mexicans camped outside. But for the local people, who knew the old building, there were secret ways in and out. Naturally, our brave defenders wouldn't use them. But people who were daring enough could get in to the fort, to bring food or nurse the wounded. Some of those daring people were women, and I'm proud to say that one of them was my grandmother on my mother's side, Marianne. She was only nineteen years old, and one of the defenders was her sweetheart. Five times that brave girl climbed out of her bedroom at night and carried food and water to him in the Alamo. The sixth time, they knew the end must be near. Colonel Crockett himself took Marianne aside and told her she must not come again. I can tell you the very words he said to her, as Marianne told them to my mother, and my mother told them to me. He said, 'I honor you for what you have done, but in the future, Texas will need its brave wives and mothers. Our duty is to die for Texas and yours is to live for Texas. Go and tell all the ladies that.'"

Mrs. Legrange's voice faltered. She wiped a tear from her cheek with her gloved finger.

"And the violin?" Holmes said brusquely.

He never did like to see tears. She smiled at him, disregarding his tone.

"Yes, his violin. That was when he gave it to Marianne. Again, I'll quote his exact words: 'I don't suppose there'll be much occasion for music in here from now on. This violin's been through a lot with me, but maybe it will enjoy a gentler touch.' So Marianne took it away with her and it's been the precious treasure of our family ever since. Here it is."

She reached into the cushions behind her and brought out a rectangular case, covered in white Morocco leather, tooled with gold. When she undid the gold clasp and opened the lid, we saw a violin and bow nestled in blue velvet. She signaled with her eyes that Holmes was to pick up the violin. He turned it over in his long-fingered hands, carefully as one might handle any musical instrument, but with no particular reverence. It was the copper-red colour of cherrywood and looked to me like the kind of country fiddle you'd expect a frontiersman to possess.

"Nobody has played it since Colonel Crockett," she said.

When Holmes simply nodded and handed the violin back to her, I caught a shadow of disappointment in her eyes. It was gone in a moment. She put the instrument carefully away and became instantly the gracious hostess, necessarily so because more guests were arriving. It seemed that most of the Daughters of the Republic of Texas and their friends and families had been invited to the picnic to meet Holmes and the grove was soon full of laughing and chattering people. They included Benjamin Barratt and his family and I noticed that Mrs. Legrange paid them particular attention, as if to emphasize to the world that there was no quarrel between them. From the way Barratt looked at her, I guessed there might have been some feeling of *tendresse* between them a long time ago. If so, it seemed to be replicated by Mr. Barratt's son Lee, a good-looking military cadet of twenty or so. He was always at Mrs. Legrange's side or running errands for her. When we left, Lee Barratt was even allowed to carry the precious violin to her landau.

That evening, we had the history of the other violin in the drawing room of the Barratt's fine home, after dinner. In this case, the instrument was a deep mahogany colour, on display above the marble fireplace in a glass case, with the Texas flag above it and swords with tasseled hilts flanking it on either side. Benjamin Barratt stood on his hearthrug, brandy glass in hand.

"I'm sure you gentlemen know the story. When he knew the case was hopeless, the commanding officer of the defenders, Colonel Travis, offered all his men a free choice: stay with him and die or leave without any reproach from him. Only one man chose to leave. His name was Louis Rose. Travis kept his word and did not reproach him, but the other men were naturally contemptuous. Colonel Crockett could not express his contempt directly, in the face of what Travis had said, so he did it another way. He gave his violin to Rose, with these words:

'Well, Rose, it seems you're no soldier after all, so maybe you'd better get practicing so you can make your living with this.' Rose took the violin, but he knew that San Antonio would be no place for him. My father had a reputation as a charitable man. Rose came to him at dead of night, begging for a loan of money to get away, offering the violin as security. My father gave him the money, on condition that he wrote a statement of how the violin came into his possession. He did so, exactly as I have told it to you. I have the statement in my desk, signed by Rose and witnessed by my father's servant. I shall show it to you. My father knew the money would never be repaid. We have guarded Colonel Crockett's violin ever since."

While Holmes was reading the document, our hostess, Mrs. Barratt, did her best to make polite conversation with me, but she seemed uneasy and kept glancing at the clock on the mantelpiece.

"Please excuse me, but I'm anxious about Lee. Mrs. Legrange was going on after our picnic to visit some friends who have a ranch north of San Pedro Springs. Lee offered to ride with her, which was only right and proper, but he should have been home long ago."

I wondered whether she was concerned for her son's safety or the effect of the lady's charms on the lad. An unworthy thought, as it immediately proved, because a clamour broke out in the hall. We all dashed out, to see Lee, with a bloodied bandage round his head, being supported by two of Mrs. Legrange's servants. Behind them was Mrs. Legrange herself, tears streaming down her cheeks, trembling like a trapped sparrow.

"It's my fault, my fault entirely. How can you ever forgive me?"

Barratt took charge of events with efficiency and had a couch made up in the parlour. I offered my services but also suggested sending for the family doctor, as a matter of professional courtesy. He arrived in a short time and confirmed my diagnosis of concussion as a result of two blows to the head with a heavy object, the patient's life not in danger, but absolute quiet and rest prescribed.

I returned to the drawing room, where Mrs. Legrange was huddled deep in an armchair, taking delicate sips of brandy, and Holmes sitting opposite her.

"Here's a how-d'you-do, Watson. It appears that some villain has snatched Mrs. Legrange's violin."

"The lad Lee kept trying to talk about the violin," I said.

"It's all my fault," Mrs. Legrange said again. "I should never have left him to carry it up. But here at home on my very doorstep, how was I to know?"

Between sobs and sips, she repeated the account for me. The visit to the ranching friends had lasted longer than expected, so it was dusk before she returned to San Antonio, with Lee riding alongside her landau. She'd gone straight upstairs, leaving the coachman to stable both horses and Lee to follow her with the precious violin in its case. Startled by a cry from below, she'd gone back downstairs to find Lee semi-conscious on the pavement and the violin gone.

"The coward had come up behind him. He never even saw his face. Did you ever hear of such villainy? And if poor Lee dies . . . "

I assured her that there was no fear of that, provided he was kept quiet.

With Barratt and his wife both occupied by their son, it fell to Holmes and myself to take Mrs. Legrange home in a hack and see her into the care of her housekeeper. Holmes behaved with unexpected courtliness, jumping ahead of me to hand her down from the hack, and even raising her gloved wrist to his lips as we left her in the hall. I smiled to myself, thinking that southern air and manners had made my old friend more susceptible than usual. We walked the short distance back to the hotel.

"If somebody went to such lengths to steal her violin, that must be because he believed it to be the authentic one," I ventured.

"A false conclusion, Watson. Might it not have been any sneak thief?"

"You surely don't believe that?"

"No, a thief bold enough to commit a violent robbery in a public place would choose some more disposable booty."

"So is Mrs. Legrange's the real Crockett violin? It surprises me, I must confess. I found Barratt's story far more convincing."

Instead of responding, he clapped his left hand to the pocket of his jacket.

"A one pipe problem. Now, which pocket did I put my pipe in?"

"Your right, surely."

At home, it always weighed down the right pocket of his dressing gown. He patted his other pocket, frowning.

"Not there."

"Surely it's not in your waistcoat pocket. Or did you somehow manage to slip it in my pocket by mistake?

I started slapping my own pockets. He laughed.

"My dear Watson, I may not have the polished manners of our Texans, but you surely don't think me barbarian enough to take my pipe to a dinner party with a lady present. It's where it should be, on the table back at the hotel."

"But . . . "

I stared at him.

"Think about it, Watson. By the by, you mentioned that young Lee had suffered two blows to the head. As far as you could tell, was one more violent than the other?"

"Yes, but that's not unusual. We may suppose that the thief's first blow was not hard enough to fell the young man, so he struck again."

"We may suppose anything we like, Watson. It's still only supposing."

I could get no more out of him that night.

The next day, Barratt had arranged to take us to lunch at his club, which occupied the same building as the opera house, opposite our hotel. The news of his son was encouraging: the young man had woken with a sore head but was rational and showing no signs of permanent damage. Holmes asked if he had any memory of his attacker.

"None whatsoever," Barratt said. "But at least we have the rascal in custody."

Holmes raised his eyebrows.

"Indeed. Has he confessed?"

"No, but he was actually seen half a mile away from Mrs. Legrange's home soon after the attack, carrying a violin."

"And he was arrested there and then?"

"No. The gentleman who saw him did not hear about the theft until this morning. Naturally, he remembered what he'd seen and as it happened, he knew the fellow by sight, a Mexican tradesman. Our sheriff's officer went straight to the thief's home this morning and arrested him."

"And the violin?"

"Found in his house."

"What's the name of this Mexican?"

Barratt looked surprised, clearly thinking that such details could mean nothing to Holmes.

"His name's Juan Alvarez. He lives on South Flores Street, down by the stockyards."

By this time, we'd arrived at the club. While our host was turned away, Holmes slid a piece of paper from his pocket and quickly showed it to me, his finger to his lips. I had to suppress a gasp of surprise. It was the slip of paper the Mexican had given him the night before last and the name and address were those of the man under arrest. Over the soup Holmes asked if he might have a word with the prisoner. Barratt was surprised.

"I hardly think it's a case worthy of your attention, but if it amuses you, by all means."

An hour later, the three of us were sitting in a small room in the county jail, with Señor Alvarez handcuffed to a chair in front of us. In spite of his predicament, there was nothing hangdog about the man. He met Holmes's eye and nodded recognition as if meeting an old acquaintance. Barratt started saying something about a cowardly attack, but Holmes held up a hand to silence him and spoke directly to the prisoner.

"I'm sorry I was not in when you called at our hotel last night," he said. "It might have saved you some unpleasantness."

Alvarez replied in the same civil tone.

"You had not called on me, as I hoped, so I came to call on you."

"Bringing the violin?"

"Yes, señor, bringing the violin."

Barratt almost exploded.

"You rogue, I suppose you were trying to get a reward from Mr. Holmes for bringing back Mrs. Legrange's violin. The nerve of the man."

"Except it wasn't Mrs. Legrange's violin, was it?" Holmes said.

"Well, whose else would it be?"

"I suggest we take a look at it. I assume it was brought in as evidence."

Barely restraining his annoyance, Barratt went to the door and called for a sheriff's officer. The violin was brought, wrapped loosely in a tablecloth, and handed to Holmes. He unwrapped it and held it up for us to see.

"You see, nothing like Mrs. Legrange's."

It was true. This was an entirely different fiddle, made of some pale wood and varnished the colour of light amber.

"Then what the thunder has happened to Mrs. Legrange's violin?" Barratt said. "And who attacked my son?"

Holmes stood up.

"If we may call on you this evening, I shall have an answer to both questions. Meanwhile, if you'll excuse us, Watson and I have work to do. I suggest that you tell them to release Señor Alvarez. Unless it's against the law to walk through the streets of San Antonio with a violin."

The hotel hired horses for us, and the cumbersome-looking saddles proved surprisingly comfortable. We rode past San Pedro Springs where we had attended our picnic, northward on a dirt track between broad and dry pastures grazed by cattle with horns wider than the handlebars of a bicycle. Holmes kept glancing from left to right and seemed to be sniffing the air like a hunting dog. Two miles or so along the track, he reined in his horse.

"Over there, in the trees."

We followed a narrower track to the left, towards a clump of live oaks. It was a lonely spot, not a barn or homestead to be seen. When we came nearer, we saw that the leaves of one of the oaks were scorched brown, with a small pile of ash on the ground beneath them. Holmes dismounted and kneeled down by the ashes.

"Cold, but still light and dry. This fire was lit yesterday afternoon or evening."

He picked up a stick and poked the ashes, then gave a sigh of satisfaction.

"Just as I thought. Do you recognize this?"

He was holding a piece of white Moroccan leather, singed at the edges.

"The case where Mrs. Legrange kept the violin," I said. "So where's the violin itself?"

He gave the ashes another stir.

"Here, Watson."

When we arrived at the Barratt house that evening, Holmes suggested to our host that we should first pay a visit to his son. Barratt took it as proper consideration for the invalid, but when we were shown into the parlor that was doing duty as a sick room, the look of alarm on the lad's face showed that he knew better.

"I'd be grateful if you'd leave us alone with Lee for a few minutes," Holmes said.

Then the older man looked alarmed too, but he withdrew. Lee sat up against a bank of pillows, staring at us. His face was pale, with dark circles round the eyes. Holmes took a chair by the couch.

"Was it your idea or Mrs. Legrange's?" Holmes said.

The lad said nothing.

"No matter," Holmes said. "I fancy the idea came from the lady. She stayed in the carriage and watched while you burned the violin. Then you returned home with her, as if you'd simply been on a visit, and carried out the next part of the plan. The harder part, I daresay. It must have taken some resolution on your part to kneel there and wait for the second blow."

Lee couldn't help wincing from the memory of it. Holmes smiled.

"You told Mrs. Legrange that she must hit harder to make it look convincing, and the second time she managed it. A blow with a heavy brass poker is no laughing matter, even from a lady."

"So she told you." Lee blurted it out, a flush on his pale cheeks. Holmes did not contradict him.

"Does my father know?" Lee said.

"Not yet, but he must learn of it," Holmes said. "It would come better from you than from me. Shall I send him in?"

Lee nodded, eyes downcast. We went out to the hall where Barratt was waiting anxiously, and Holmes said his son had something to tell him.

When the parlor door had closed on him, I turned to Holmes.

"How in the world did you know it was a poker?"

He smiled.

"You may have observed that I kissed the lady's hand. I could see from your face that you thought I'd fallen victim to her charms. In fact, I wanted to smell her glove. I'd already observed ash on one of Lee's boots. . . ."

"And then you smelled it on her glove. Admirable."

"No, I confess I expected to smell it. I should have known better. She'd leave such work to her male accomplice. The smell I caught was of something quite different: metal polish. Now, a lady of her standing would hardly polish her own household utensils; therefore she'd recently handled some metal object. In view of the young man's injuries, a poker seemed a near certainty, confirmed by his reaction."

"But why, Holmes?"

"Surely you can see. She knew I wasn't taken in for a minute by that romantic tale about the fiddle. Rather than have it lose the contest, she decided to destroy it—with the help of a besotted young man."

After a while, the parlor door opened. Barratt came out, stern-faced and led us through to the drawing room.

"Gentlemen, I must apologise to you for my son's deception."

"I believe it was Mrs. Legrange's deception," Holmes said.

"Lee would not stoop to putting the blame on a lady."

"Even a lady who deserved it?"

"I'm sure you cannot find it in your heart to blame her. She had believed in the authenticity of that violin."

"Just as you believe in yours?"

Holmes glanced at the instrument enshrined over the mantelpiece.

"That's one good thing to come out of it at any rate," I said, trying to lighten the atmosphere. "Mr. Barratt's violin is now the only one in the field."

Holmes and Barratt stared at each other. Barratt was the first to drop his gaze. Holmes settled himself in an armchair.

"Before we came here, Watson suggested that I should read the history of the Alamo." His tone was conversational. "As he knows, I dislike burdening my mind with useless detail. Nonetheless, there was one aspect that interested me. The person out of step is always more interesting than the ones in step, don't you find?"

I could not see where this was leading, but Barratt evidently did.

"Rose?"

"Yes, Louis Rose. The coward of the Alamo. The man who supposedly brought your father Colonel Crockett's violin."

"Supposedly? You doubt my father's word, sir?"

"I do not doubt that your father acquired that violin under circumstances exactly as you described. Equally, I don't doubt that he believed the vagabond at his back door to be Louis Rose. But he wasn't."

I expected an outburst from Barratt but he said nothing.

"I've done a little reading about Rose," Holmes went on. "One detail interested me. The man was illiterate. He couldn't read or write. You're an intelligent man. You must have done your own research. I think you knew that he couldn't have written that statement."

Silence from Barratt.

"But why should any man impersonate a notorious coward?" I said.

"Because whoever the man was, he needed money and had a violin he could sell," Holmes said. "He must have been sharp enough to realise that a hero's violin from the Alamo would be worth much more than any old fiddle."

Holmes took his pipe from his pocket and asked Barratt's permission to smoke. It was given with an abstracted nod.

"I played a trick on Watson when we were walking home from your house the other night," Holmes said. "I asked him which pocket I'd put my pipe in. He gave the matter his close attention, ignoring the obvious fact—that I hadn't brought my pipe at all."

"Really, Holmes, I . . . "

He ignored me, and went on speaking to Barratt.

"You take my point, I'm sure. The question you posed to me from the start was which one of two, hoping that little puzzle would distract me from other possibilities. As it happened, it was of small importance to you which I chose. The thing that mattered above all was that the violin which eventually went on display at the Alamo should be certified as genuine by none other than Sherlock Holmes. Who would question that? I believe you expected me to pick up that point about Rose and to be so pleased with myself that I would give the verdict in favour of Mrs. Legrange's instrument. Unfortunately, you neglected to inform Mrs. Legrange of your plan. Rather than have her violin slighted, she destroyed it—proving in the process that she'd never in her heart believed the family legend about it, or she couldn't have brought herself to do it."

"So neither of you believed in your violins?" I said to Barratt in astonishment. He raised his eyes and gave me a long look.

"There are things you believe with your head and things you believe with your heart. My heart said that violin should have survived."

Holmes puffed at his pipe.

"You remember Señor Alvarez wished to see me?" he said.

Barratt nodded, his thoughts clearly elsewhere. Holmes slid a rough-looking piece of paper from his pocket.

"Do you read Spanish, Mr. Barratt?"

Barratt shook his head.

"It seemed more likely to me that if Crockett's violin had survived at all, it would be in Mexican hands," Holmes said. "You know the saying—'to the victor, the spoils of war.'"

Barratt snapped out of his abstraction and stared at Holmes.

"You mean, the man Alvarez and his violin? Has he proof?"

Holmes said nothing, only smoothed out the piece of paper. I could see the struggle in Barratt's face.

"Crockett's violin, in a Mexican's possession?"

Still Holmes said nothing. Barratt paced the room, backwards and forwards.

"I put it in your hands," he said at last. "If you think the man's claim is authentic, then negotiate for us. I authorise you to go up to five hundred dollars if necessary."

"Thank you."

Holmes rose and thumbed out his pipe.

"You'll go tonight?" Barratt said.

"Certainly, if you wish. Come, Watson."

From my earlier wanderings, I knew my way to the stockyards area. The house of Señor Alvarez was a white painted cube of a dwelling, sandwiched between an ironmonger's shop and a baker's shop with a galaxy of brightly sugared pastries in its lamp-lit window. The house door was wide open, cheerful voices speaking Spanish coming from inside. When Holmes called, Juan Alvarez came out to meet us, like a prince welcoming an equal. We were led to seats by an open fireplace where something savoury was cooking in a pot, and introduced to his wife, children, and grandmother. After some minutes of this, Holmes brought us to business.

"You wished to talk to me about your violin."

"Yes, señor."

The violin, still wrapped in the tablecloth, was lying on a shelf. Alvarez took it down and placed it in Holmes's hands.

"Colonel Crockett's violin, rescued from destruction by my father's father, an officer in the Mexican army. He found it by Colonel Crockett's body and kept it in memory of a brave enemy. No man has played it since Colonel Crockett himself. I offer you that honour now, señor."

Holmes took the violin, nodded, and rose to his feet. A bow was produced. Holmes tightened the bow, tuned the instrument to his satisfaction, then began to play. The tune he chose was a simple melody that I had heard one of the cowboys singing, called "The Streets of Laredo." The sight of his absorbed face in the firelight, the rapt expressions of Señor Alvarez and his family, and the thought of all that this rustic fiddle stood for brought a tear to my eye. When he'd finished there was a little silence. He bowed and handed the instrument back to Alvarez.

"Mr. Barratt is offering you five hundred dollars for the violin," he said.

"To put in their museum?"

"Yes."

Alvarez stood for a while, deep in thought.

"It was our victory, not theirs," he said at last. "It was our country, not theirs."

Then he threw down the violin to the stone-flagged floor and stamped on it time and time again, like a man performing a Spanish dance, until he'd smashed it to smithereens.

"It is the greatest of pities," I said, still shaken, as we walked towards the hotel through the warm night. "To find Crockett's violin and then have it end like this."

Holmes laughed.

"My dear Watson, why should you think that fiddle was any more genuine than the other two? I'm sure Crockett was more likely to have died with his rifle beside him than his violin. No, Alvarez's family tale was as much a fiction as the others, though I think the man himself believed it."

"But the statement, Holmes, the paper in Spanish that you showed Barratt. Whatever it said seemed to be enough to convince you."

He laughed.

"Did I say so? I simply showed Barratt a paper, and he chose to draw his own conclusion. I admit I took a small gamble. If he had happened to read Spanish, I should have had to do some quick thinking."

"Holmes, what is this? What was on the paper?"

"You remember that first night, when we walked in the Mexican market, I found one of the local delicacies suited my taste. This morning, I descended to the kitchens of our hotel and was lucky enough to find a Mexican cook. She spoke few words of English but was obliging enough to understand what I wanted and write down the recipe. *Tamales*, I believe they're called."

"And you led Mr. Barratt to believe that this recipe was proof that—"

"I led him nowhere, Watson. He led himself. He had tried, for reasons that doubtless seemed honorable and patriotic to him, to take advantage of my reputation. This is a small revenge."

"But what shall you tell him?"

"That the Alamo Museum must, alas, do without Colonel Crockett's violin. Texas seems to be a resilient state. I hope it may learn to live with the disappointment."

The Adventure of the White City
Bill Crider

Bill Crider is the author of more than fifty published novels and numerous short stories. He won the Anthony Award for best first mystery novel in 1987 for *Too Late to Die* and was nominated for the Shamus Award for best first private-eye novel for *Dead on the Island*. He won the Golden Duck Award for best juvenile science fiction novel for *Mike Gonzo and the UFO Terror*. He and his wife, Judy, won the best short story Anthony in 2002 for their story "Chocolate Moose." His latest novel is *Murder in Four Parts*. Check out his Web site at www.billcrider.com.

* * * *

I have written little about Sherlock Holmes's adventures in the United States, not least because Sherlock Holmes himself requested that I refrain from any attempt to tell how he occupied himself there. Both he and I agreed that it was best for me to confine myself to setting down what he did in his native England, if I had to set down anything at all. His inclination always was to believe that I exaggerated somewhat when reporting the events of his career.

Now, however, because Holmes has left London again and lives in pleasant anonymity, enjoying his view of the Channel and his bees, I believe that he would not take it amiss if I were to set on paper at least one of his adventures in the New World. He said as much at one time. The story that comes to mind happened the year after the strange events at Wisteria Lodge, and Holmes and I had special reason to remember it, as we discussed one evening as we sat in our rooms at 221B Baker Street.

I remember the night well. The moon was full, and its light shone through the windows overlooking the street. The windows were closed, and a brisk wind swept down the street, occasionally rattling a somewhat loose pane. Holmes, whose powers of concentration far exceed my own, showed no sign that the faint noise bothered him, or that he heard it at all. He sat reading the day's news, and I said to him, "It must bother you a great deal, Holmes."

He lowered the newspaper, looked at me over the top edge of it, and said, "Whatever do you mean by that, Watson?"

"The fact that you share a name with one of the most shockingly brutal and cruel murderers of this century."

"You surprise me, Watson," said Holmes, lowering the newspaper into his lap.

"Furthermore," I said, "it must disturb you greatly that you were in the same city with him and knew nothing of his frightful depredations."

"You are positively brilliant this morning, Watson," said Holmes. "For those are my thoughts exactly. How, pray tell, did you come to fathom them?"

"I know your methods, Holmes," said I, perhaps a bit too smugly. All too often in the past, Holmes had amazed me by seeming to read my mind, when in reality he had merely been observing me. Being able to turn the tables on him was a pleasant diversion.

Holmes put the newspaper aside and went to the chimneypiece to fetch the Turkish slipper in which he kept his tobacco. Having done so, he reached into the pocket of his robe and brought out a briar pipe.

When Holmes had filled it with tobacco and lit it, he looked at me and said, "You, of course, saw the newspaper earlier and read about the trial of the notorious 'Torture Doctor,' known as H. H. Holmes, and surmised the rest." He paused and puffed on the pipe to make sure the tobacco was burning to his satisfaction. "I do not believe we have mentioned the similarity of the names before, but you are quite correct, Watson. It does bother me a bit that Mudgett should have chosen for himself my own patronym, but that is not his only alias. He has had many others."

"And he will soon meet his well-deserved end under the original name of Mudgett," said I. "Was the other point I mentioned also correct?"

"That I am bothered by having been in some proximity to Mudgett without knowledge of his crimes? Yes, Watson. I wish that I had known something of them at the time. With that knowledge I might have been able to put a stop to him before he had killed so many."

"How many? Is the number even known?"

"No," said Holmes. "Some surmise he may have done away with more than a hundred victims, but I suspect the number twenty-seven is much more likely."

He resumed his seat in the chair and took up the newspaper once more.

"I remember your desire to visit the Columbian Exposition in Chicago," I said. "And to see Buffalo Bill's Wild West once again."

Holmes had become quite a student of the history of Buffalo Bill Cody and the American West after his first meeting with the man. He put aside the newspaper again and glanced at the patriotic V. R. formed by bullet holes in the wall.

"Yes, indeed, Watson. Meeting Colonel Cody at the time of the Golden Jubilee was quite interesting. He and I have something in common, I believe."

I merely nodded at that. I did not have to ask Holmes what he meant. More than once he had expressed his opinion that the wild tales of Buffalo Bill, as related by Mr. Buntline and Mr. Ingraham, contained no more excesses than those I myself composed about him.

"While you did not hear about Mudgett while we were visiting the White City," I said, "you did find opportunity to exercise your skills in the service of good."

Holmes smiled a thin smile. "Ah, Watson. While you know my methods, I know yours. You are ever on the alert for something with which to fill your notebooks, some item you can later spin into a tale of adventure for your readers."

I laughed. "You have caught me out, Holmes, for that was indeed the very thought that crossed my mind. We are even, then, for I have read your thoughts, and you have read mine. I should very much like to tell of our American adventure some day."

"I do not believe the events of the story will be of interest to your readers, as they occurred so far away."

"Even in America there are many who know of you," I replied.

"Very well," said Holmes. "Perhaps in later years you will find occasion to tell the story."

And so at last I have.

After the bizarre affair at Wisteria Lodge, the idea of a trip to the White City to see "the highest and best achievements of modern civilization" had a great appeal to Holmes and me. We were certain that the sight of the Exposition's grounds would be one to inspire even the dullest of souls.

Surprisingly enough, Buffalo Bill's Wild West show was not a part of the fairgrounds. Colonel Cody had, I believe, wanted to be a part of the Exposition, but he was denied the privilege. He was too much of a showman, however, to let that stop him. He simply set up his tents just outside the grounds, taking up several blocks with his campgrounds and arena. His extravagant advertisements promised to introduce his "Congress of Rough Riders," with more than 450 horses, ridden by vaqueros, Cossacks, gauchos, Indians, cowboys, and more.

"Buffalo Bill's Wild West will be a show on a grand scale," Holmes remarked as we prepared to leave our hotel on the morning after our arrival in Chicago. "Even grander than the one presented before the queen."

"Perhaps we shall see the battle of the Little Big Horn enacted once again," said I, recalling a particularly exciting moment.

Just then there came a knock upon the door. Holmes's eyes widened, and I confess that I was startled. I had not heard the sound of anyone approaching, and I was certain that the same was true of Holmes, who rose and went to the door.

He stopped with his hand on the knob and said, "Colonel Cody, I presume."

Then Holmes opened the door to reveal the great showman standing there. He wore a wide-brimmed grey felt hat, black coat and britches, and western boots. His hair, moustache, and goatee were shot through with grey, and his piercing gaze lighted on Holmes's face.

"Mr. Holmes," Cody said, sweeping off his hat, "it is a pleasure to see you again. But how did you know who I was before you even opened the door?"

"Who else in this city but the great scout of the plains could move so silently through the corridors of the hotel that no one could hear him?"

Cody had turned his right ear slightly toward Holmes to hear the answer, and Holmes touched his nose surreptitiously so that only I could see. I ascertained his meaning, as I smelled the faintest odor of livestock, a clue that I felt we need not mention to Cody.

"I guess that's so," Cody said with a smile.

Holmes gestured him inside. "You remember Dr. Watson, I am sure."

Cody said that he did, and shook hands with me in his frank American way. After the re-introduction, Holmes offered him a chair. Cody sat down, both feet planted on the floor, his hands clasping his knees as he leaned slightly forward. He was about to speak, but Holmes raised a hand to stop him.

"Before you tell us why you have come to visit," Holmes said, "I would like to know how you learned we were in Chicago."

"Easy enough," Cody said. "I saw it in the newspaper." I suppressed the urge to tell Holmes that the article proved I was right about his being known in North America.

"Ah," Holmes said, with a glance in my direction as if to say he knew my thoughts. "I suppose some reporter or other noted our arrival at the railway station."

"Must have," Cody said, "and then he jotted it down in time for the late edition. As soon as I saw it, I decided to track you down."

Holmes walked across the room and rested his shoulder against the chimneypiece. "Not as difficult as tracking on the plains, I imagine," said he. "But you did not come here to talk about tracking."

"No," Cody said. "I came to ask for help."

Holmes took his pipe and the Persian slipper, brought all the way from England on our journey, from the chimneypiece. He filled his pipe with tobacco from the slipper, and when he had made sure the pipe was lighted to his satisfaction, he said, "I am not surprised to hear it. A man with your duties and responsibilities at this moment would not come merely for a visit. What is the nature of the problem?"

Cody leaned further forward as if to express his earnestness. "It's not real easy to explain. Have you heard that one of the exhibits here at the Exposition is Sitting Bull's cabin?"

Holmes looked in my direction. Taking my cue, I said, "We have read of it, but have not yet strolled the Midway. I believe there will be a daily 'war dance' performed at the site. It is, if you will permit me to say so, not unlike something from your own show."

"It sure is," said Cody. "Some folks might even see it as some kind of conflict, but that's not the problem."

"The problem has to do with the cabin, however," said Holmes.

"It does. I believe somebody wants to destroy it."

"But why?" said I. "And how?"

"How? Well, the plan is to burn it. Why? That's hard to say. Some people never have forgiven Sitting Bull for his part in the Custer massacre, and even his death at the hands of the Lakota police didn't end their desire for revenge. To destroy his cabin would be one way of striking at him even though he's dead." Cody sighed. "There's more to it than that, though. If the cabin's destroyed, at least some of the blame will fall on me and people in my show. Sitting Bull was with me for a little while, and even now I have some Indian performers that the government and a lot of the rest of the country would prefer to have living on the reservations. Destroying the cabin would be an act of revenge, and it would make me and my performers look bad."

"Have you informed the police?" I asked.

"Certainly," Cody said, "but I have a feeling they're not up to the job."

Holmes nodded his assent and added, "Their forces are spread too thin with the Exposition and all its visitors. It would be difficult for them to mount a twenty-four-hour guard on an exhibit on the basis of a rumor."

"It's no rumor," Cody said. "I'm sure of that."

"Then how did you come to hear of it?" asked Holmes.

"From Annie Oakley and Frank Butler. They overheard two men talking. One of them said, 'Burn Sitting Bull's cabin.' Butler says he heard him distinctly, and he heard the other agree. The voices came from behind a row of tents. Naturally, Butler ran down to the end of the row, but by the time he got there, the men had disappeared, lost in the crowd of people who work on the show. There are hundreds of them."

"And no one else overheard the conversation?" said Holmes.

"No one. The nearby tents were deserted, and it's a wonder that Butler happened to hear, considering the noise of the camp. Can you help me, Mr. Holmes, or do I need to go to somebody else?"

"Butler overheard nothing more?"

"Only nonsense. He could tell you himself if you'd come for a visit to my campgrounds."

"Very well," said Holmes. "Come, Watson, let us see what we can do to assist our American friend."

Colonel Cody expressed his thanks and settled his hat on his head. Holmes and I readied ourselves and went with him to the site of the great Columbian Exposition.

We went first to the Indian village on the Midway, as it was nearer the hotel. The site was across the way from the Lapland village, which had a board building covered with sod as well as a tent. Next to it stood the International Dress and Costume exhibit, which promised "Forty Ladies from Forty Nations, a World's Congress of Beauties." I was quite eager to have a look inside the building, but Holmes, of course was not interested.

"We did not come here to gawk, Watson," he said.

Further down the Midway was the immense Ferris wheel, towering 250 feet above the ground. I was thoroughly interested in that, as well, but Holmes had eyes only for the Indian village.

First, he inspected the sign that announced the war dancing. He said, "Make a note of the time, Watson." I did, and we entered the area and found the cabin easily. The outside walls were pocked with bullet holes and what I took to be splashes of blood, possibly a result of Sitting Bull's final moments.

An Indian stood near the entrance. He was clothed in full buckskin regalia and wore long braids and a feather in his hair. Cody spoke to him, the man moved aside, and we entered. As we did, another went quickly out the back door. He wore a loose shirt with crimson bands at the cuffs, elbows, and shoulders. A wide crimson "V" adorned the neck. Cody came in behind us and did not see him, but Holmes stood silently for a moment, looking toward the doorway.

The moment passed, and Holmes, as was his custom, examined the entire edifice with great care. I had no idea what he might have been looking for, as, knowing nothing of such a cabin, I saw nothing out of place. The place smelled of the smoke of many winter fires. The odor had infused the very wood of the walls, along with the smell of tobacco.

When Holmes had finished his inspection, he pronounced himself ready to speak to Butler, and Cody led us down the Midway, past innumerable wonders, though none was so grand as the Ferris wheel. We had a walk of several blocks beside the tracks of the Illinois Central Rail Line before reaching a crossing street, and then another long walk past the tents of Cody's show and livestock before reaching the campgrounds, which were located between the Illinois Central and the Exposition itself. Farther to the east was the vast inland sea called Lake Michigan, and a breeze from the lake cooled the air.

The campgrounds swarmed with men and women striding about in the colorful garb of all the nations represented by the Congress of Rough Riders, and of course American Indians and cowboys of all stripes. They seemed to have no purpose in mind, but Cody assured us that all had definite assignments. The air was thick with the smell of livestock.

"We had best talk to Mr. Butler as soon as possible," Holmes said.

"Before I left to find you, I asked him to stay in his tent," Cody said, and he led us through the crowds.

As we walked, I heard a veritable babble of languages spoken around us. I wondered if Butler had detected a distinct accent, and I was certain that would be among the first things Holmes questioned him about.

The tent to which we were led was somewhat larger and grander than most, if grand is a term that may be applied to tents. The flap was pulled back, and we went inside.

What I saw was quite different from the interior of Sitting Bull's cabin. The tent was furnished as well as the hotel room Holmes and I had engaged. Standing near a sofa was a tall man wearing a black coat. He had black hair and a black moustache, and he greeted Cody with a smile.

"Are these the gents you told me about?" he said, appraising us frankly.

"The very ones," Cody said, and performed the introductions. When those were done, Butler and Holmes sat on the sofa, while Cody and I took chairs nearby. I had hoped to see Little Sure Shot, but she was not in evidence.

"Annie's in the main tent," Butler said with a smile, as if he sensed my disappointment. "She's always practicing."

As usual, Holmes did not care for unnecessary information. He said, "Please tell us of the conversation you overheard, Mr. Butler. Word for word, if that is possible."

Butler explained that he'd been in his tent and heard the men talking outside. He couldn't hear the words distinctly, and, as Cody had said, the men were gone by the time he'd reached the spot where they had been.

"I heard one of 'em say they'd burn Sitting Bull's cabin," Butler told us, "but nothing else very clear. I can't give you a word-for-word reckoning."

"You heard nothing else?" Holmes said.

"I did hear a thing or two, but nothing that made any sense."

"Tell me, nevertheless," Holmes said.

"There was noise outside the front of the tent, and the wall's not as thin as it looks. At first, I heard something about a blustering wind and waving air. I wasn't really listening, and I don't hear too well, anyway, thanks to too many years of firing rifles off next to my ear. What they said didn't make a bit of sense, so I must've misunderstood. I perked up, though, when I heard the part about burning Sitting Bull's cabin."

Holmes looked thoughtful, though what he might have made of the weather report as delivered by Butler, I had no idea.

"Outside we saw people from all around the globe," Holmes said. "Many of them must speak only limited English. Did the men you heard speak it as if it were their native tongue?"

Butler considered it a moment before he spoke. "They spoke English, but they didn't speak it as good as you and me."

Holmes raised an eyebrow but made no comment. I, too, kept my peace.

"We have too many people to consider," Cody said, "and no way to winnow them down. It seems like too big a job."

"You don't know of anybody who has it in for you?" Butler said. "Somebody in the show, I mean."

"No," Cody said, with the assurance of a man who believes

he is beloved by all. "There's nobody like that, which is why I don't understand this even a little bit. Why would anyone who works for me want to harm the show? It's like a family."

I had been associated with Holmes long enough to know that there was always someone who wished harm on others even in the coziest of circles, but I did not see fit to mention that at the moment.

Holmes said, "Nevertheless, a problem exists, and I believe it to be more serious than I had first thought. Colonel Cody, do you have a list of your employees for payroll purposes?"

"Yes, but it's so long that you could never go over it all, not in time to stop anybody who plans to do something anytime soon."

"Still, I would like to see the list."

"All right, then," Cody said. "Come with me."

We thanked Butler for his help and followed Cody to another tent where a bookkeeper bent over his desk. Cody explained what Holmes wanted, and the bookkeeper provided the list. Holmes scanned it rapidly, as if he knew what he was looking for, as no doubt he did, though I had no idea.

"As I thought," Holmes said, handing the list back to the bookkeeper. He turned to Cody. "Kicking Bear and Short Bull are in your employ."

"They sure are," Cody said, surprised that Holmes knew the names. "They're two of the ones a lot of people would like to see confined to the reservation. I don't think they'd be the cause of any trouble, since they know what would happen if they were caught."

"There is another name," Holmes said. "Jack Wilson."

"I don't know him," Cody said after a pause. "I have so many cowboys that I can't learn all their names."

"Jack Wilson is the English name taken by Wovoka," said Holmes.

"Good Lord!" said Cody.

"Wovoka?" I cried in surprise. "The Indian messiah who started the Ghost Dance?"

Holmes had told me about it once: In a vision, Wovoka, who now called himself Jack Wilson, had come to believe the dance would lead to a new earth, covered with fresh soil that buried the white men. Meanwhile, the Indians would hang suspended in the air until green grass and trees grew upon the soil; and when the rivers ran afresh, and the buffalo again roamed the plains, they would be returned to the land along with the ghosts of their ancestors. It may have been an appealing dream, but while many Indians had adopted the new religion and danced the dance, it was to no avail. The Exposition was ample testimony to the triumph of the white man's way of life.

"Yes," said Holmes, "and Kicking Bear and Short Bull were with Sitting Bull when he was killed as a result of his involvement with the Ghost Dancers."

"Sitting Bull was my friend," Cody said. "He wasn't really involved in the Ghost Dance movement. His death when the soldiers came to arrest him was a sad mistake, no more than an accident."

"That may be, but it seems more than a coincidence to find Kicking Bear and Short Bull in your employ, and Wovoka on the grounds as well."

"It could be a coincidence," protested Cody. "Even if not, what does this have to do with the Ghost Dance?"

"You are connected by having taken the first scalp for Custer."

"The killing of Yellow Hand . . . " Cody murmured.

I began to understand. The killing of Yellow Hand was well known to all who had seen Cody's Wild West show, and it had been of particular interest to Holmes. I had always felt that the reenactment was what stimulated Holmes to read so much about the American West.

The event had been a highlight of Cody's career, and supposedly the turning of the tide against the Indians in the conquest of the American frontier.

"Custer," said Holmes. "Not bluster. Butler misheard. And you waved Yellow Hair's scalp in the air."

"So the conversation Butler recalled had not been about the weather after all," I said.

"Of course not," said Holmes. "I realized as much at once." He turned to Cody. "You still reenact Yellow Hand's death in your show, do you not?"

Cody acknowledged that he did.

"And the time of the 'war dance'?" Holmes asked me.

When I told him, he nodded. "That would be about the time the scalping scene would be performed in the Wild West Show. I am sure that is when they plan to burn the cabin."

"But why?" I asked Holmes.

"Not as revenge for Custer's death, but for Sitting Bull's," said Holmes. "They must see the chain of events beginning with Yellow Hand's death as leading inevitably to the failure of the Ghost Dance and the death of Sitting Bull."

"Do you suppose that they will perform the Ghost Dance at the cabin?"

"I do," said Holmes. "Do you remember the man who left the cabin as we entered, Watson?"

"Yes," I said.

"He wore a Ghost Shirt," Holmes said, "which is supposed to make one impervious to bullets. I suspect he will be involved in the dance today."

"Good Lord," Cody said. "We must stop them! They will discredit me and all the Indians who work for me if we do not."

"Watson and I will do our best," said Holmes.

I hoped that he had some plan to do so, as I could see no way the two of us could prevent the destruction. I feared a panic that would panic fair-goers and cause a stampede like that of the buffalo the Indians wanted to recall.

"You'll need help," Cody said.

"You must carry on with your show so that they suspect nothing," Holmes told him.

"This is Wovoka's work!" said Cody. "If the others are party to it, it's because of him."

"They may not be involved," said Holmes, "but we must waste no more time. Come, Watson, let us take up our station."

I did not know what or where our station was, yet I followed Holmes as always. As we hurried along and passed the big show tent, I found myself wishing I had brought my pistol, but I had left it behind in Baker Street. We were, I thought ruefully, a long way from home. I should have borrowed one of Cody's sidearms, but it was too late for that now. Holmes set a rapid pace, and I was hard pressed to keep up with him.

Between breaths, I asked Holmes what the Ghost Dancers expected to achieve, and how we might stop them.

"I believe they seek revenge on Cody for his imagined part in the events leading to Sitting Bull's death and the later slaughter at Wounded Knee."

Holmes's knowledge of the West's history far surpassed mine. I knew little of the latter event other than that after Sitting Bull was killed, a number of their tribesmen, including women and children, had been killed in a fight with the U.S. Cavalry at Wounded Knee, in the Dakotas three years ago.

"They may also hope to call attention to their plight," Holmes continued. "Most of them remain on reservation land no white man wants or could live on." He paused. "Or Wovoka might merely crave attention. Since the Ghost Dance's failure, he has lost influence and prestige."

Holmes was no believer in visions, and thought little of those who held to them, especially when others were likely to suffer because of them.

"We should arrive in ample time to prevent the burning of the cabin," Holmes continued, though he did not slacken his pace. "Did you not see the Fire and Guard building earlier?"

As always, Holmes's powers of observation outstripped my own. I confessed I had not. "You were no doubt looking at the Ferris wheel," he said. "The station is quite near the Indian village, and there are hundreds of guards. Perhaps a thousand or more, though of course not all in one place."

"You did not mention them to Cody."

"I was not entirely sure of their competence or presence, though having walked along the Midway, I am now more certain of their numbers. Did you not notice them?"

Once again I had to confess that I had not, though now that he mentioned it, I did recall a number of men in uniform.

"They were recruited especially to make the Exposition safe," Holmes said. "In spite of my earlier misgivings, I believe we can count on them for help."

I hoped he was correct. We reached the Midway, which bustled with a multitude of men, women, and children. The crowd at the Ferris wheel was especially impressive. We made our way through them, apologizing as we went, and soon came to the Fire and Guard building. Holmes went up to the door and asked a capped and uniformed young man there for someone in authority.

"I am in authority," the man said, his scanty moustache fairly bristling. "You can tell me what you need."

Holmes was not one to truckle, but this was an emergency. Instead, he said, "I believe someone plans to burn Sitting Bull's cabin in the Indian village. We must prevent it."

The young man did not hesitate. Fishing a whistle from a pocket, he blew a piercing note, and men ran to us from all sides as well as from within the building. The young man crammed his whistle back into his pocket and began shouting orders.

It was one of the few times that I ever saw Holmes appear dumbfounded. In fact, I cannot remember another. He had not expected such a reaction, but it seemed that the Guard had been waiting for an opportunity to show its value, apart from the usual petty annoyances of asking people for their admittance cards and harassing them for minor violations.

Unfortunately, the men were merely hired with the idea that their numbers and manner would prevent problems. Confronted with a true crisis, they dashed off in all directions, shouting at the crowds and each other, shoving people aside, and generally wreaking havoc along the Midway. Men and women clutched their children to them, while those whose offspring had wandered off looked wildly about and cried out for them.

"My word, Holmes!" I exclaimed as the mob surged around us. "What have we done?"

Holmes, though some would not expect it from him, was not without humour. He smiled a thin smile and said, "It seems my uneasiness about the Guard was justified, after all. However, if this massive disorder does not disrupt the plans for the fire, nothing will."

"But what of those who planned it? Will they not escape in the confusion?"

"It will be our job to stop them."

"How will we know them?"

"The Ghost Shirts," said Holmes. "We must look for the Ghost Shirts."

I recalled the man we had seen in the cabin earlier. I had, at least, observed that much. We forced our way through the throng and were pushed about in return. When we reached the Chinese theater with its tall towers trimmed in red and blue, Holmes tugged at my sleeve.

"There, Watson!" he said, and pointed.

I saw, over the heads of many people, a man dressed in a long black coat, his head covered by a black hat that almost concealed his face.

"That is Wovoka," said Holmes.

No Ghost Shirt could be seen. "He has taken to wearing the clothing of civilization so as to be unrecognized," Holmes insisted. "After him, Watson!"

We hastened in the man's direction, but Wovoka saw us coming. He must have known we pursued him, for he took to his heels. Thanks to the crowd, however, he could move no faster than we at first, but the multitude thinned quickly, as most were drawn to the cabin where the Guard had gone. Wovoka ran faster, as did we.

By the time Wovoka reached the Ferris wheel, we had narrowed the distance. Ahead of us, the gargantuan wheel rotated slowly on the mighty axle, its heavy cars rocking gently as it turned. To my surprise, we saw Wovoka leap up the stairs to the loading platform, thrusting aside those in line, and throwing several of them to the ground and impeding us.

Perhaps he hoped we would be afraid of the machine, or perhaps he thought that he could escape into the sky from its upper heights, and hang suspended while the Ghost Dance changed the world. First, though, he had to board it, but the operators made no attempt to stop the wheel, and the cars were secured by screened windows and locked doors.

Wovoka did not intend to be captured. He leapt from the platform and grabbed hold of the roof of a passing car. Within seconds he had pulled himself atop it. The passengers in the car stood from their chairs and watched in amazement.

"He has trapped himself," said Holmes as the car moved upward. "In the great circle, he can only come back around to us here on the platform."

For the barest fraction of a second, I thought of the Reichenbach Falls and of a figure dropping down, down. "Holmes," said I, "what if he chooses not to return atop the car?"

"Then he does not, but I believe he will, Watson. The Ghost Dance is a circle, and he circles now. He will return to close the circle."

When Wovoka reached the apex of the wheel's turn, we watched him rise to stand atop the car, look toward the sky, and spread his upraised arms. It was an amazing sight: the man of the plains rode atop the engine of civilization, stretching out his arms for something he sought, something beyond the power of man or machine to deliver. I do not know what answer he might have sought in the blue and the clouds, but I do not think he found it. He remained firmly fixed atop the car.

The wheel continued in its round, and as his car began its descent, Wovoka sat down cross-legged, his shoulders slumped. When the car reached the platform again, he jumped off, right into the waiting arms of Sherlock Holmes.

I believe he had hoped to be taken up into the sky, until the earth covered us over—me, Holmes, Buffalo Bill, the Exposition itself. Now, however, his eyes were empty of any hope whatsoever.

We sat in Cody's tent, one even more lavishly furnished than Frank

Butler's. The show was over, and Cody was there. Wovoka was with us, as were Kicking Bear and Short Bull, whom Holmes had retrieved from the Guard while I detained Wovoka at the base of the Ferris wheel. Neither of us had said much then, and Wovoka said little now. Cody did most of the talking.

"You have shamed me," he told the Indians. "But thanks to Sherlock Holmes, you have been prevented from doing any serious damage. It's lucky for you he was able to stop the Guard from injuring you, or anyone else."

Indeed. It was lucky for all of us that no one had been injured in the panic on the Midway.

"If I turned you over to the authorities and pressed charges against you," Cody continued, "Kicking Bear and Short Bull would be returned to the reservation. Wovoka would go to prison."

We had learned that Wovoka was, as Cody had suspected, the leader. He had talked the other two into one last attempt to bring back the old days and the old ways.

"I don't want to see any of you on the reservation or in prison," Cody said. I could not be sure, but I thought the Indians relaxed a fraction at those words.

"Kicking Bear and Short Bull can stay with me here, where I can keep an eye on them. Wovoka will leave us and swear never to return."

"Where will I go?" the Indian said.

Cody had no answer for that. He looked at Holmes, who had been sitting silent, as immobile as the Indians. His profile, indeed, resembled theirs as much or more than it did any of his own countrymen.

"Go wherever you please," Holmes said. "You must know now that the days you long for can never return."

Wovoka nodded, whether in agreement with the first statement or the last, or both, I never knew. He picked up his hat, which had rested on his knee, and settled it on his head. He nodded to Holmes again, and walked out of the tent without a glance at anyone else, and we never heard of him again.

That evening, Holmes and I rode the great Ferris wheel. We sat in the car with others, perhaps as many as fifty people, and all of us looked eastward. The fairground was bright with electric lights, and the people who streamed down the great street were tiny figures far below. We could see the outlines of imposing buildings stretching away to the dark inland sea beyond.

"I was wrong, Watson," said Holmes at last. I had to strain to hear him. He gestured to the vista before us. "Revenge was not Wovoka's motive. This is what he feared. This is what he wished to destroy with his final Ghost Dance."

"But Holmes," said I, "this sight is awe-inspiring. This is the future. Surely Wovoka must have realized that as he stood upon the car today."

The car dipped downward. If Holmes answered, I did not hear, and we never spoke of it again.

Recalled to Life
Paula Cohen

Paula Cohen (Lady Mary Brackenstall) has been a member of the Adventuresses of Sherlock Holmes since 1975. Born seventy-five years too late, she is a lover of the opera, Gilbert and Sullivan, Old New York, and all things Victorian. A previous short story, "The Adventure of the Dog in the Nighttime," appeared in *Ghosts in Baker Street* (Carroll & Graf, 2006). Her first novel, *Gramercy Park*, published by St. Martin's Press in 2002, is set in New York City in 1894; she is currently working on a sequel. Paula lives in Park Slope, Brooklyn, with her husband Roger, and her cat, Hodge.

* * * *

"New York City."

Such was the burden of the telegram I received recently, which, although terse, was instantly clear to me, as was the identity of its sender. Mr. Sherlock Holmes, from his retirement on the downs near Eastbourne, has been following my latest attempts to make known the singular successes of his career, and from time to time takes the trouble to suggest a likely candidate for, as he calls them, my "little romances."

Although it has ever been my desire to set down the most accurate accounts of his cases, I have never succeeded in convincing Holmes that the reading public needs more than the stark facts and ineluctable logic that guide his genius. That the public has nevertheless demonstrated an abiding interest in those "romances" has been a source of some annoyance for Holmes. For the particular case to which his recent telegram refers, however, Holmes himself must bear the blame if I fail to depict his methods in all their cold rationality. I was not present at its unfolding and must rely solely upon his own later account of it for the facts, and more than usually on my own imagination for the features.

It occurred, in fact, during that interval between the spring of 1891 and that of 1894, when all the world, including I, thought Holmes dead at the bottom of the Reichenbach Falls. Readers may recall that in April of 1894, and just after his "resurrection"—for so I have always thought of it—Holmes revealed to me where he had gone after his miraculous escape from death and Moriarty's minions. He spoke of Florence, of his two years in Tibet, of his time in Arabia and Persia, and his work in the Sudan at the behest of his brother, Mycroft, and the Foreign Office.

What I was unable to relate then, because the delicacy of many of the matters he undertook required that they not be made public until long after the participants were beyond either praise or blame, was that after leaving Khartoum, Holmes headed eastward yet again, across the Indian and the Pacific Oceans, to the United States.

America had always held a fascination for Holmes; and his freedom, as an ostensibly dead man, to travel when and where he willed under different identities, as well as the ability to use his remarkable talents in the service of his country, made a stay in America both logical and advantageous. The summer of 1893 found him in Baltimore, on America's eastern shore, once again carrying out a commission on behalf of his nation that would prove invaluable to her safety, and during which time Holmes developed a profound admiration for the American navy. He still ranks its Academy at Annapolis as every inch the equal of the Royal Naval College at Greenwich.

His assignment completed on the last few days of 1893, it was Holmes's intention to return to England. New York City, however, was the place from which he chose to embark, for the opportunity it would give him, during a fortnight of well-earned leisure, of briefly studying the ways of a city vastly different, and yet strangely similar, to his native London.

At the suggestion of a fellow passenger on the train up from Baltimore, he took a room at the Albemarle, a reputable hotel of middling size not far from Madison Square. As he made his way down to the dining room at eight o'clock that first evening in the city, his eye was caught by a quietly dressed man walking through the crowds of other guests and visitors, looking ever about him as if seeking someone he could not find. The public parlors were crowded with ladies and gentlemen in full dress, the corridors filled with parties heading out to the opera or other festive events, and Holmes, no stranger to the great houses of England, was struck by the opulence of some of the women's finery, which would not have been out of place at a royal audience.

Still, he kept the quietly dressed man in sight, and followed him at a distance through the glittering throngs, until he saw the man approach and then touch an exceptionally well-dressed youth lightly on the shoulder, then steer him into an alcove. The two exchanged a few quiet words, something changed hands, and the young man exited quickly from the corridor and disappeared hastily down the grand staircase.

The quietly dressed man examined what he had taken from the other, slipped it unobtrusively into his breast pocket, and eased his way back into the flow of the crowd, this time heading in Holmes's direction. As he neared, Holmes stepped aside to let him pass, but leaned toward him and spoke quietly into his ear.

"His companion is the elegant young woman in green," he said, "sitting just over there, beneath the clock. I believe that if you examine her reticule, you'll find the watch and chain you're seeking."

The man started and swiveled quickly to look at Holmes, sparing the seated woman one swift glance before he did so. His brown eyes were sharp. "Might I ask your name, sir?"

"My name is Greaves," said Holmes. "Simon Greaves."

"Then I would ask you to wait here for me, Mr. Greaves," the man replied, "and please not to leave this spot."

"By all means," Holmes said. "I will remain here."

With a last look at Holmes, the man turned and made his way across the corridor to the woman in green. As he bent to speak to her, he turned back the lapel of his coat slightly, and the woman flushed, half rose, and then fell back into her seat. Her hands shook as she opened her reticule, reached inside and withdrew something which glinted briefly in the light as she placed it in the man's upturned palm. A few more words were exchanged between them, and then she rose, and she, too, swiftly disappeared down the staircase, her face pale.

"You let them go," Holmes said, as the man returned to where he waited. "Was that wise?"

The man sighed. "They are very young, and this game was for the thrill of it, not for gain. Neither the watch nor the money has as yet been missed, and the gentleman from whom they were lifted will have received an object lesson in guarding his person when I return them to him."

"And the young couple?"

"Newlyweds, on honeymoon, and well able to afford to stay here. What they need, and what I gave them, is a good fright. They are not of the criminal class, and neither of them is suited to a night in a jail cell." He shrugged his shoulders. "If I'm any judge of character, they'll behave themselves from now on."

He gazed at Holmes. He was slim in build, an inch or two shorter than Holmes, but his eyes were cool as they sized him up.

"They say it takes one to know one, Mr. Greaves. You are from England . . . from London if my ear isn't wrong. Are you with Scotland Yard?"

"I am not, Mr. . . . ?"

"Battle. Robert Battle."

The detective extended his hand and Holmes took it. "A good name," he said, "for one in our line of work. I work independently. My practice is a private one, and Scotland Yard considers me an amateur."

Battle snorted. "An amateur? No one has ever 'made' me before, Mr. Greaves. I should say you are no amateur." He glanced quickly at Holmes's attire. "You arrived this afternoon, you have not left the hotel since, and you were near the dining room when you saw our young friend boost the watch and money from his victim's pocket and slip the watch to his wife. My surmise, therefore, is that you'd like your dinner, as would I . . . and as my shift is now over, might I invite you to join me, if you have no other plans? Just one moment, please, while I let my replacement know that I'm going off duty."

The headwaiter showed both men to a table with an unobstructed view of the entire dining room, and not too far from the entrance, permitting them to see everyone who came and went. Holmes took in the table's location and nodded.

"'When constabulary duty's to be done,'" he smiled at his host, "'a policeman's lot is not a happy one.' You said you were off duty. Are you not permitted to eat in peace?"

"*The Pirates of Penzance.*" Battle smiled in turn. "Strange you should quote from that. I was at the very first performance of *Pirates* on New Year's Eve in '79, here in New York, at the Fifth Avenue Theater. Sullivan himself was at the podium. It ran for three months in New York before it ever even opened in London," he said, with no small local pride, as he unfurled his napkin and laid it across his lap. "As for eating in peace, I prefer to be aware of what's happening around me. I must be able to observe my surroundings. Call it habit, if you will."

"Yes," said Holmes. "I agree entirely. We appear to have much in common, except that I trust I am correct in saying that you once served on the police force, Mr. Battle."

"What gives me away?" Battle laughed.

"Your manner of looking everywhere and nowhere at the same time. A good detective focuses on what will aid his investigation, but a policeman must be Argus-eyed and aware of what's behind him, as well as in front, to stop any mayhem before it begins. You have been on the streets."

Battle grunted. "For fifteen years, before I left the department. Worked my way up to captain."

"Yet you left?" Holmes raised a mollifying hand at the sudden tensing of the other man's jaw. "Forgive me, please. I meant no offense in asking, I was merely surprised."

After a moment of silence, Battle said, "I am largely ignorant of the inner workings of Scotland Yard, Mr. Greaves, but there are things in New York . . . politics and whatnot. Suffice it to say that much of what would put ordinary men behind bars is routinely practiced by the police here, and after a while I had had enough."

Holmes said nothing, and after a few moments Battle smiled again. "But I have hopes," he said, signaling the waiter. "Reform is in the air. And now, Mr. Greaves, what would you care to drink? I myself take no alcohol, as it does not agree with me. But please don't feel constrained on my account. The wine cellar here is quite excellent, and they have a bourbon—I don't know if you're familiar with bourbon—which I have heard roundly praised."

Holmes, though a man who generally loathed all forms of society, could be exceedingly charming at will, and was an excellent conversationalist; and in Battle he had found a rare kindred spirit. Throughout the course of a long and enjoyable dinner, the two men regaled each other with numerous "war stories," as Battle called them, of criminals with whom they had dealt, and as the coffee arrived Holmes was feeling unusually expansive.

"An aficionado of Gilbert and Sullivan such as you might, perhaps, enjoy other forms of music. Are you an opera lover as well?"

"I am, indeed," Battle replied.

"Do you enjoy Wagner?"

"Very much."

"Excellent! I was hoping to take in a performance of *Die Meistersinger* on Monday evening, and as I know no one in this city I was fully prepared to go alone. But if you are not working that night, Mr. Battle, and have no other encumbrances, perhaps you would care to join me? I can think of no more congenial a companion. And should you need any further inducement, Eames and de Reszke are singing that night."

Holmes spent the intervening days, and one or two nights, on the icy streets of New York City, disguised as an Irish laborer in shabby overalls, peacoat, and grimy cloth cap. The cold was severe enough that he needed no artifice to redden his nose and rime his brows, but the three-day growth of beard that appeared magically each morning had somehow vanished by evening as he sat down to dinner among the well-to-do of New York City.

"Admirable," Robert Battle chuckled, as he caught Holmes sauntering from the hotel one morning through one of the tradesmen's doors. "Did I not know who you were, Mr. Greaves, I'd have stopped you and asked you to turn out your pockets."

Holmes merely touched a finger to his cap and vanished into the raw January mist. His destination each day was different, and suggested to him by Battle, who knew New York as well as Holmes knew London. Within a few days Holmes had at least a nodding acquaintance with areas that were as foul as anything in Limehouse or Whitechapel.

"Remember, Watson," he told me later, "that London had been a great midden of humanity for more than a thousand years before the white man ever set foot on Manhattan Island, and then think of the depths of wickedness, cruelty, and despair that could create such squalor in such a brief period of time."

And as with London, so were the contrasts between the high and the low in the much younger city. On the following Monday night, Holmes and Battle passed through the bland, yellow-brick façade of the new Metropolitan Opera House and into a blaze of splendor wholly unimaginable to the denizens of airless tenements and filth-strewn streets. Battle had retained some of the friendships made during his years on the police force, and through connections had been able to obtain places for that evening in an unoccupied box in the first ring.

The two men settled themselves into their seats with time to spare, and Holmes took in the gorgeous scene around him. Present were many of the names that had made New York a byword for both riches and rapacity, and the wives and daughters who accompanied them glittered with gems. Battle quietly pointed out to Holmes the various well-dressed men, detectives all, stationed in key positions around the house to prevent anything that would interfere with the evening's enjoyment.

As the house lights dimmed, there was a flurry in the box opposite. Holmes, his eyes upon the unobtrusive detectives, felt Battle stiffen beside him, and saw his jaw clench. Following Battle's gaze, he saw two older men and a very young woman just taking their seats.

Dainty and exquisitely dressed, with pearls at her throat and in her dark hair, the young woman held fast to the arm of one of the men, her gloved fingers tightening on his sleeve, and shrank from the gaze of the audience below as they, and the occupants of the all other boxes, turned to look at her. A murmur arose throughout the house as her escort, silver-haired and straight-backed, settled her into a seat placed back from the rail of the box, where she would be less visible, then took his own seat.

But it was the second man at whom Battle stared, his fists closed into hard knots.

"You know him?" said Holmes.

"I know him," Battle replied, his eyes never wavering.

"An interesting trio," Holmes remarked. "May I ask who they are, and why the girl is of such inordinate interest?" The whispering of the crowd had not abated, and many eyes, although not those of Battle, were still turned to her as the conductor stepped to the podium.

"The taller man is Henry Ogden Slade. He is one of our leading citizens, rich as Croesus, and a great philanthropist." Battle's voice was quiet, and revealed nothing of the emotions that clearly gripped him. "The girl is his ward. She is, or so the received wisdom would have it, the daughter of a Jew banker with whom Slade has done business. He took her in several years ago, although no one knows why, and therein lies the mystery. There appears to be nothing whatever improper in their relations, although many would love to believe otherwise." Battle fell silent.

"And the other?" Holmes said. The object of Battle's relentless gaze was a portly, many-chinned man, shorter than Slade by a head. His spectacles and his small, perpetual smile gave him a pleasant, avuncular look.

"The other is Thaddeus Chadwick. He is Slade's attorney, and also his closest friend. Each is rarely seen without the other."

The first notes of the overture brought the conversation to a close. Holmes, with his keen ability to compartmentalize his mind, leaned back in his chair and became utterly absorbed in the music, his long fingers waving in accompaniment, but nevertheless remained aware of the fact that his companion was utterly insensible to what was occurring on the stage.

Wagner, as the world knows, is not succinct in his composition, and by the time the curtain came down on the first act, Holmes was grateful for a chance to stretch his legs. By common, wordless consent, he and Battle left the box and headed downstairs. Holmes waited until they were off to the side of the main vestibule, where the crowd was thinner, before he raised the subject of Thaddeus Chadwick again.

"I could not help but notice that his appearance was distracting to you. Please tell me if it is overstepping the bounds of our brief acquaintance if I ask you why?"

Battle set his jaw and answered. "Mr. Chadwick was the reason I left the police force. Or, rather, the reason I was thrown off it. I would rather not have told you this, Mr. Greaves, lest you think ill of me, for I have come to enjoy our acquaintance, but you will soon be returning to England, and your opinion of me will be of little matter."

"How could I judge you before I have heard the evidence?" Holmes said.

"How, indeed? But many have, and many who were once dear to me are strangers to me now." He took a deep breath and began.

"Mr. Chadwick's reputation as an attorney is above reproach, of course, and he has, in addition to Mr. Slade, many clients in the highest reaches of the city. But Mr. Chadwick is also known to the police. Threads leading back to him have been found in many unsavory schemes; and his name, through the names of those who front for him, is linked to some of the worst places, and some of the most ghastly conditions, to be found anywhere in the city."

Battle looked squarely at Holmes. "I will be brief. I said that Chadwick is known to the police, but not necessarily as an adversary. Many of the places you've seen these last few days sit on land owned by Mr. Chadwick, and although he takes no part in their actual business he still makes a great deal of money from them, and his hands are stained with their filth. I was investigating some of them, some houses where children, boys and girls as young as six . . . I will say no more, Mr. Greaves, for you know that places such as these exist. But I could have wiped at least some of them, and those who profit from them, off the face of the earth, and I was close, very close, to having my case airtight.

"But as I said, there are things in New York . . . Chadwick is open-handed to those who can help him, and many in the upper levels of the police . . . " He swallowed hard and wiped his face; his hands were shaking. "I was told to drop the case. I said I would not. I was told that if I did not drop it voluntarily, I would be made to do so. And still I refused.

"I took what precautions I could, but it was not enough, and those I had asked to guard me were paid to turn a blind eye. The night before I was supposed to present my evidence in court, a half-dozen men burst into my home. They overpowered me, held a chloroform-soaked cloth over my face, and dragged me out. I awoke hours later, in a room in one of the houses that I had investigated—alone, thank God—but reeking of alcohol, as though someone had emptied a bottle over me, and as I staggered to my feet I could hear whistles and screams. It was a police raid, and I was caught, just as surely as if I had been a patron there for years."

Battle sagged and leaned against a gilded pillar. His words were quiet now and matter-of-fact. "Instead of being in court that morning, giving evidence, I was in jail, and all the evidence had been destroyed. I had hidden it under some floorboards, but they didn't even bother to search for it . . . they took the quickest way, and just burned my house down, and the evidence with it. The fire was laid at my door, too . . . I was charged with knocking over a lamp, in my drunken state, as I left for the establishment where they found me. I've thanked God every day since then that no one died in the blaze, for I would have been accused of that as well.

"But the worst . . . I had no identification on me, you see, and to verify that I was who I said I was—even though the men who arrested me knew me—they brought my fiancée and her father down to the police station to identify me. Oh, yes, Mr. Greaves, I was engaged to be married. And there I stood, unshaven and stinking, in handcuffs and leg irons, still unsteady on my feet, and having been pulled out of that . . . that hell . . . with my beautiful Frances staring at me. And the look in her eyes . . . "

Holmes guided the man to an unoccupied bench against an adjacent wall and forced him to sit. The crowds were streaming back to their seats, and the vestibule was emptying quickly.

"Promise me that you will stay here," he said. "I will only be gone a moment."

Battle nodded, head bowed. Holmes returned in a few minutes with a glass of water, which he held to the man's pale lips.

"There is some whiskey in there," he said, as the man grimaced at the taste and started to push it away. "Not enough to harm you; just enough to bring the blood back to your face."

Battle drank again, then stood up shakily. "I don't know why I told you all that."

"Strangers are sometimes better confidants than friends one has known for years. But possibly you are being too hard upon your Frances. Would she not still believe in you, despite appearances?"

"I could not approach her again. Not until my name is cleared, which it never will be. How could I even dream of tying an innocent young woman to a man known as a sot and a debauchee?"

Holmes smiled. "Certainly, women are not my forte, Battle. But has she married anyone else since that night?"

"No. I have heard, through acquaintances, that she is still living with her father."

"Then she is probably stronger in her faith in you than you have given her credit for, and perhaps you should have more faith in her. And now," he said, as Battle set his glass on a nearby table, "the second act is well under way. Shall we return to our seats, or would you rather leave?"

"I would not cut your evening short. You wished to see the opera."

"That is of no consequence."

"No, I am well enough now. If you don't mind being seen with me, now that you know, then let us go back. . . . "

"Well, well, Battle," said the dry voice behind them. "I thought it was you, but I could not believe my eyes, so I came to see for myself. I really must ask the shareholders what they are thinking, allowing known degenerates in here."

Battle jerked about so quickly that he nearly fell, and Holmes put a light hand on his arm, to steady him. Chadwick gazed at them mildly. Now face to face with the man, Holmes could see behind his spectacles. His small, eternal smile never reached his eyes, which looked Battle up and down with utter contempt.

"Still drinking, I see," he said. He turned to Holmes. "I don't know who you are, sir," he said, "but I must warn you against associating with this man. His reputation is unsavory, to say the least."

Holmes tightened his grip on Battle's arm. "I thank you for your concern, Mr. Chadwick, but your warning is unnecessary."

"Ah, an Englishman. A visitor, perhaps, to our great city," Chadwick said. "Well, forewarned is forearmed, as they say. And since you appear to know my name, sir, although we have never met, may I know yours?"

"Simon Greaves."

"Then, Mr. Greaves, I will leave you and your friend now." He turned to go, snapped his gloved fingers as though he had forgotten something, then turned back.

"Oh, yes . . . some rumors have reached me, Battle, that you have secured employment at one of our better small hotels. I do not know what the management could have been thinking, or to whom they applied for references, but I will speak to them personally in the morning, and see to it that they have a true accounting of your history. No establishment can afford to risk its patrons with someone like you beneath its roof.

"What a shame," he said, "that you had to be here tonight. I had almost forgotten your existence. I am not likely to forget it again. Good night to you both."

They watched him bob across the vestibule on thin legs incongruous to the bulk of his upper body.

"A dangerous man," murmured Holmes.

"I will kill him." Battle was shaking.

"No, I think not. You would be an immediate suspect, for one thing, although I can well imagine that there are many besides you who would like Mr. Chadwick dead. No, you must leave that task to another, Battle.

"Besides . . . " Holmes said, continuing the conversation as the two men, having lost their taste for the opera, walked back to their hotel. An icy wind pushed them south down Broadway. "You do not want him dead before your name can be cleared and your reputation restored."

Battle stopped still on the pavement. "By all that's holy, Greaves, you heard him! What he's done to me so far isn't enough, he's out to crush me utterly! Do you think he would ever be a party to my reclamation?"

Holmes only smiled and pulled Battle along. "Let's discuss this over a hot supper when we get indoors. It's beginning to snow, which will benefit us greatly. It is just possible that we may bring Mr. Chadwick around."

The chimes of Trinity Church sounded half past nine on the following morning, as the card of Mr. Simon Greaves was handed in to Mr. Thaddeus Chadwick, Esq. Chadwick was a man of rigid habits, and the heavy snow that had fallen overnight had had no appreciable effect on his regular nine o'clock arrival, although the usual thunder of ironbound wheels and horses' hooves outside his office on lower Broadway had been replaced by the pretty jingle of sleigh bells and harness in an otherwise silent world.

Chadwick's office was large and comfortable, and a welcome fire crackled in the grate across from his desk. He kept his visitor standing before him for more than a full minute before deigning to look up from the brief he was reading.

"Well, Mr. Greaves," he said, tossing the papers aside and folding his thick fingers on the desk before him. "Who would have thought that we would meet again so soon?" He gestured languidly to a chair. "Do sit down, and tell me the reason for this unexpected pleasure."

Holmes complied. "I thank you for seeing me with no prior notice, Mr. Chadwick. I guessed that the snow would result in some gaps in your appointments, and I am glad to see that I guessed rightly."

Chadwick grunted. "And what have you come to see me about?"

"Stopping your persecution of Robert Battle."

Chadwick's small, perennial smile broadened with incredulity, creasing his many chins.

"Mr. Greaves, I am a very busy man, and have neither the time nor the inclination to deal with fools. You surprise me, I must confess, because my first impression of you was that you were a man of some intelligence. I will have you escorted out very shortly, but before I do I should like to hear your rationale for such a remarkable request."

"By all means." Holmes pulled a sheet of paper from his breast pocket and unfolded it. "You are a very busy man, as you say, so I will be very brief. Last night, between two and three in the morning, someone entered your office and opened your safe. That one," he said, gesturing across the room to a seemingly impregnable iron vault taking up half of the far wall.

Chadwick, startled, glanced involuntarily at it, then back at Holmes, chuckling.

"You amaze me! It occurs to me, Mr. Greaves, that you and Robert Battle are well-suited after all. Both of you are hopeless. That safe cannot be opened by anyone but myself."

"Yet it was."

"By whom?"

"By me."

Chadwick still smiled, but the first hint of doubt had crept into his face. "You lie, sir."

"Do I? By all means, please open it and see. And let me thank you for locating your chambers in a modern building, one that employs the latest in safety features, and has an iron fire-stair running down the back. Eight inches of snow have served to effectively obliterate any footprints I might have left. As for your locks, Mr. Chadwick . . . they were simplicity itself to open, and even your safe took me no more than five minutes to breach.

"I removed several papers from it, to wit . . . " he consulted the sheet of paper in his hand, "deeds showing you to be the owner, of many years' standing, of numerous pieces of property on Cherry, Baxter, Mulberry, and Water Streets. The unspeakable establishments at those addresses are well known to the police, although there are so many leases and subleases on the properties that it would be difficult, although not impossible, to trace you as their owner without the original deeds themselves.

"It was in one of those establishments, in fact, that Mr. Battle was found, ostensibly drunk, three years ago, as a result of which he was removed from the police force. That he was investigating it, and others like them, and had begun to follow the trail of ownership, was well known to many people, including his superiors and, through his superiors, to you. That, of course, was why you had to destroy him."

Chadwick's face had grown red, but he held out an imperious hand. "May I see that list?" he said. Holmes passed it to him, and sat silently while the attorney looked it over.

"There is no mistake, you see," Holmes said, when Chadwick had finished, and flung the paper back across the desk with a murderous glance. "No one could know the full list of properties who had not actually seen the deeds. And I do promise you that when you open the safe, you will find them gone."

"And just what do you propose to do with them?"

"Why, nothing whatsoever. No . . . no that is not quite true. What I propose to do with them—what I have, in fact, already done with them—is post them to England, to a trusted individual in the government, where they are beyond your reach forever. I have, however, no intention of extorting money from you, Mr. Chadwick, if that is what you fear. What I will do with your deeds is keep them safe. And I will require you to clear Mr. Battle's name of the stain you have placed upon it."

"And how am I to do that, Mr. Greaves?"

"That, Mr. Chadwick, is not my concern. You are, as I am certain you would be the first to acknowledge, connected to people in very high places in this city. What you caused you can no doubt remedy. I leave it to a man of your intelligence to determine a way."

Chadwick leaned back in his chair. "And what if I were to call the police, Mr. Greaves, and tell them what you have just told me?"

"What have I told you?" Holmes picked up the sheet of paper that Chadwick had flung at him, stepped across to the grate, and dropped in the paper, watching as it caught, flared up, blackened, and shriveled in the flames.

"Other than that list, now gone, there is nothing to prove that I know anything about the theft of your deeds."

Chadwick removed his spectacles and pressed his thick fingers to the bridge of his nose. His hands were shaking. It took him several moments to master himself, but he did, and replaced his glasses.

"And what do you get from all this, Mr. Greaves? Battle has nothing any longer. I saw to that when I had his house burned. What can he possibly pay you for what you have done for him?"

"Nothing whatever."

"Then I repeat . . . what do you get from all this? You have said that it is not money that you want. But what matters, then, if not money? I, unlike Battle, can pay you a very great deal for the return of those papers. I see that I was mistaken, thinking you a fool. You and I are both intelligent men. What is it you want? Name your price."

Holmes laughed and returned to his chair, stretching his long legs out in front of him, and knitting his fingers across his vest. "As I said,

I have no intention of extorting money from you. Those papers are merely a pledge of your good behaviour. Give Battle back his good name, and no one will ever know you to be the owner of a half-dozen of the worst hells in this city." His smile faded.

"But, since you asked, I do want more. You will close those places down, Mr. Chadwick, and see that they remain shut, forever. Not just sell them to someone else, who will continue to ply the same, age-old trade, but end them, for good and all." He leaned forward in his chair. "I am not naïve enough to believe that their elimination will stop this traffic. But at least, for a while, there will be fewer of them."

"Others will take their place," Chadwick said.

"Undoubtedly. But they will not be yours, and you will not be profiting from them. And please understand me . . . I will be leaving New York in a few day's time. Should something happen to me between now and then, or should I not return safely to England for any reason, the individual who will be receiving your deeds will know what to do with them. And," he said, rising from his chair, and walking to the door, "Robert Battle is under the same protection, except that for him there is no limit on the time.

"Pray that he remains safe and healthy, Mr. Chadwick. Should he be run down by a carriage, slip on the pavement and break his skull, or succumb to a sudden case of pneumonia, I will see to it that you are exposed."

"Who are you?" Chadwick, too, rose from behind his desk, and pointed a shaking finger at Holmes. "Who are you?"

"I will happily tell you, Mr. Chadwick, once I have reached London. Expect a telegram from me, informing you that I have arrived unharmed. You will, in fact, be the first to receive the news. In the meantime, I should waste no time in restoring Mr. Battle's good name."

The spring of 1894 was one of the busiest of Sherlock Holmes's long career. As the world knows, his return to London was heralded by the brilliant exercise that both solved the inexplicable murder of the Honourable Ronald Adair, and brought the infamous Colonel Sebastian Moran, the foremost of Moriarty's gang, to final justice. The news of Holmes's reappearance was met with universal elation by the highest in the land, as well as by the ordinary people whom he had so long aided, and the next few months were a blur of cases, with more petitions delivered to Baker Street than he could possibly accept.

My own domestic circumstances having altered during his absence, Holmes invited me to take up lodging with him once more in our old quarters, to which I gladly agreed. A crisp and clear January evening, the following year, found us ensconced before a pleasant fire, Holmes adding to his voluminous scrapbooks, and I reading. The sound of the doorbell, and voices in the hallway, caused Holmes to throw down his paste-brush with an air of distraction. So busy had he been, that his carefully organized reference works were beginning to suffer.

"Who on earth might that be?" he said. "I had hoped not to be disturbed tonight."

His irritation turned to intense pleasure, however, when he caught sight of the man whom Mrs. Hudson showed in a few moments later.

"Robert Battle!" cried Holmes, striding forward with his hand outstretched. "How very good to see you again! And it takes no great feat of detection," he said, turning to a darkly pretty woman that Battle drew forward, "to know that this must be Mrs. Battle. My hearty congratulations to you both. What brings you to London?"

"We are on our honeymoon, Mr. Holmes," Battle said as we took our visitors' things and made them welcome. "Our ship docked this afternoon, and we have just settled into our hotel. And then Frances and I could think of nothing, and no one, that we wanted to see more than you."

"Watson," said Holmes, as the introductions were made, "you remember that I told you of Robert Battle, and my little adventure in New York."

"Yes, of course," I said, shaking Battle's hand. "It is very good to meet you. And you, Mrs. Battle."

"I have waited for this moment," Mrs. Battle said, as Holmes took her hand, and her husband smiled at her fondly. "It is to Mr. Holmes that we owe all our happiness."

"It is, indeed." Battle's handsome face shone as he looked at his blushing wife. "She had waited for me, you see, just as you had said she would, and had never lost faith."

"You both chose wisely and well, then, in choosing each other. Watson, some glasses . . . we must toast Mr. and Mrs. Battle, and their happiness. Sherry for Mrs. Battle, please. Whisky or brandy for you, Battle?" he said, then stopped me as I reached for the tantalus. "Ah, but I remember. Mr. Battle does not drink. Forgive me."

Battle shook his head. "When we met in New York, I would have none of it," he replied, "because I had been tarred as a drunkard the night of my arrest, and I wanted no stink of the stuff on me, ever again. But since I am among the living once more, I do indulge on occasion. And I can think of no occasion more appropriate than now. Brandy, please."

With all four glasses filled, Battle rose to his feet and raised his glass, but was stopped by his wife's hand upon his arm.

"May I, Robert?"

Her husband looked at her, surprised, then yielded to her with a smile, and she, too, rose, as did Holmes and I. Her bright brown eyes were shy, but she lifted her glass high nevertheless.

"The first toast must be to you, Mr. Holmes, because you are the reason for all our joy. Like a magician or a guardian angel, you appeared and our gladness appeared with you. We can never thank you enough."

"Amen to that!" Battle cried. "To Sherlock Holmes!"

"To Sherlock Holmes!" I echoed.

Holmes lifted his glass next. "To Mr. and Mrs. Robert Battle. A most deserving couple!"

After we had drunk, Battle laughed, as we seated ourselves once more. "Actually, it's Captain and Mrs. Battle. I've been restored to my rank, and both my name and my record cleared. That's how I was able to call upon my Frances again. And speaking of names, had I but known, one year ago, that Mr. Simon Greaves was really Mr. Sherlock Holmes," he said, "I would have been much more circumspect with my professional advice during his visit to New York."

"Nonsense," said Holmes. "You know your city as I know mine, and your guidance gave a stranger invaluable assistance . . . and allowed us to rid the world of some places it can well do without."

"Some people, too," Battle replied. "You'll be interested, I know, to learn that Thaddeus Chadwick died this past October. Murdered," he added, "and not by me, though I certainly would have shaken the killer's hand, had I been able."

"Now that is news, indeed." Holmes gestured to the nearby table with its glue-pot and scissors and the substantial pile of newspapers on the floor. "I have had little time to read in the past several months, and have only begun to catch up. How did that come about?" He leaned forward, keenly attentive.

"He was stabbed, in his own home, by a young woman of his acquaintance."

"The motive?"

"None that we were able to ascertain." He smiled. "Yes, I worked on the case. I was back on the force by that time. But I must admit to not trying too hard to solve the matter. It seemed a straightforward enough domestic matter. The young woman was living with him at the time. And she died in the fire that resulted from their struggle, and had no relatives who might have shed any light on the situation . . . " He shrugged his shoulders.

"What was even more interesting than his death, however, was what was discovered about Mr. Chadwick several weeks later."

Holmes smiled, and turned to me. "Chadwick was a talented man, Watson. He dies in October, stabbed by a young woman who is residing with him, yet continues to be newsworthy in November." He turned back to Battle. "This is proving irresistible. Pray go on!"

"The short of it, Mr. Holmes, is that after his death a safe was found built into the wall of his bedroom. You will recall, of course, the gentleman and the young lady you saw with Chadwick, the night we attended the opera? The gentleman, Henry Ogden Slade, died barely a month after we saw him, and his young ward was left nothing whatever in his will. But a much more recent will was found in the safe in Chadwick's bedroom, and it left everything to the girl, whom Slade acknowledged as his daughter."

"The implication being that Chadwick somehow engineered his friend's death, and meant to take control of his fortune? A good friend, indeed. Well, it would not surprise me, when you remember that you and I deprived Mr. Chadwick of a very large portion of his income."

Battle shook his head. "I had nothing whatever to do with it, Mr. Holmes, which you well know. The credit is entirely yours, and your methods, although definitely unorthodox, were completely effective. A month after you left New York, I was summoned by the chief of police himself, and told that new testimony had been provided by several people, proving that I had been framed as I had claimed all along, and that I could have my old position back, if I wanted it. By that time, of course, I had received your letter, telling me what you had done."

Holmes laughed, clearly pleased with himself. "Yes, it was an opportunity that I simply could not resist. As I think I have mentioned to you, Watson, I have often thought that I would have been a highly successful criminal, had I been so inclined. And I could not possibly indulge myself similarly in London, of course—Scotland Yard would be less than amused if I took to 'second-story work' here—but in New York, who was to know? Besides," he said, raising his glass in the direction of the smiling Mrs. Battle, "the cause, in this case, was extraordinarily worthy.

"And what of you, Battle?" said Holmes. "What is in store for you on the police force? Is all forgiven?"

"More than forgiven. There are changes taking place, just as I had hoped, and shortly before Frances and I were wed, I was named an assistant to the new Commissioner of Police. You have heard of Theodore Roosevelt?"

"I have, indeed. A very good man."

"As good as they come, and as incorruptible. He is the new broom that will sweep all New York clean."

Rising to his feet, he raised his glass once more. "Another toast to you, then, Mr. Holmes. My cup runneth over, thanks to you."

We all rose, then. "My blushes, Watson." Holmes smiled, after we had drunk in his honour. "And now I think that we should all adjourn to Simpson's for dinner. I can think of nothing more satisfying on a cold winter's night than enjoying some good British beef with some excellent American friends."

The Seven Walnuts
Daniel Stashower

Daniel Stashower is the Edgar-winning author of *Teller of Tales: The Life of Arthur Conan Doyle* and a coeditor of *Arthur Conan Doyle: A Life in Letters*. He is also the author of *The Beautiful Cigar Girl: Mary Rogers, Edgar Allan Poe and the Invention of Murder*, as well as five mystery novels, the most recent of which is *The Houdini Specter*. His short stories have appeared in numerous anthologies, including *The Best American Mystery Stories* and *The World's Finest Mystery and Crime Stories*. His work has also appeared in newspapers and magazines including the *New York Times*, the *Washington Post*, *Smithsonian Magazine*, *National Geographic Traveler*, and *American History*.

* * * *

We have had some dramatic entrances and exits upon our small stage on East 69th Street, but I cannot recollect anything more startling and distasteful than the sudden appearance of Mr. Gideon Patrell, the celebrated sideshow entrepreneur. It was a brisk October morning in 1898 when Mr. Patrell presented himself at my mother's kitchen table and, after submitting his mouth to a thorough examination, promptly cleared his throat and began to regurgitate a handful of walnuts, summoning them from the depths of his stomach, one by one.

Mr. Patrell arrived at this singular moment by slow degrees. A tall, rail-thin gentleman of elegant bearing and impeccable wardrobe, he had arranged to join us for breakfast so that he might discuss the possibility of engaging the services of my brother, Harry Houdini.

Harry was all of twenty-four years old at the time; I had just turned twenty-two. Professionally, my brother had hit the skids. Try as he might—and no one ever tried harder—he couldn't quite manage to break out of the small time. Whatever small reputation he had rested entirely on his value as a novelty act. He spent weeks at a stretch working various odd turns in traveling circuses and midway tents, sleeping in swinging hammocks on carnival wagons and eating campfire meals at railway sidings. It was a life we both knew all too well. Harry and I had done an act together from the time we were kids, but of course that had changed five years earlier when he married Bess. From that day forward, she became his partner onstage and off, and I handled the booking and backstage work. To speak plainly, my duties as Harry's advance man were not terribly rigorous. In later years the theatrical world would unite in a roaring clamor for his services; in those days, the call seldom rose above a dull murmur. The note I had received from Mr. Patrell, mentioning a sudden vacancy in his program, was our first prospect of employment in several weeks.

I had arrived at my mother's flat early that morning. In those days I fancied myself as something of a man about town, and kept a room at Mrs. Arthur's boardinghouse several blocks away, so as to be free to enjoy the lively and vigorous social life befitting an eligible young bachelor in New York City. In point of fact, my social life was largely confined to solitary walks in the park and reading books at the public library. I lived in hope, however.

Harry continued to live at home even after his marriage to Bess, an arrangement that appealed not only to his all-encompassing sense of devotion to our mother but also to his frugal nature. Harry and Bess were already seated at the breakfast table when I arrived. Mother stood at the stove, as always, busying herself with a pot of oatmeal.

"Sit," she said as I came through the door. "I'll get you something to eat. You look thin."

"Good morning, Dash," said my sister-in-law. "Is that a new tie? It's very spruce."

"Not exactly new, Bess," I said. "They made me a deal at Scott's bazaar." I fingered the wide pukka silk tie at my throat, which, if I had unbuttoned the jacket of my double-breasted windowpane suit, would have displayed a grease stain left by the previous owner. "I was hoping to make a good impression on Mr. Patrell."

I turned to my brother. "Good morning, Harry," I said. He scowled and did not look up from buttering a piece of brown toast.

I looked back at Bess. "What's the matter with him?"

"He's sulking," she said. "He doesn't want to go back to the Ten-in-One."

"It's beneath me!" Harry cried, brandishing the butter knife. "Ten different acts for a dime! Ten performers lined up along the platform, displayed like prize hogs at a county fair! Jugglers and bearded ladies and rubber men and tattooed girls and—"

"All right, Harry," said Bess. "Calm down. It's just that there isn't much—"

"I am Harry Houdini, the justly celebrated self-liberator! The man whom the *Middletown Daily Argus* called 'a most winning and competent entertainer.'"

"High praise indeed, Harry," continued Bess in a soothing tone, "but even Houdini has to pay the rent. We haven't worked in nearly a month."

Harry grunted and resumed buttering his toast.

Bess pressed her advantage. "And Mr. Patrell was good enough to come and see us here at home, rather than bring us all the way downtown."

"Ha!" cried my brother. "Dash would have been perfectly happy to ride down to 13th Street. Mr. Patrell offered to come here only because Mama gave him a slice of blackberry torte the last time."

Harry was undoubtedly correct about this, as my mother's skills with a pastry brush and dough docker were legendary. "Look, Harry," I said, "the important thing is that he has an opening. Nobody wants to work in the dime museums forever, but we need to keep the wolf from the door. At least let's hear what Mr. Patrell has to say, all right? If you don't like his offer, we'll find something else."

"Very well," said Harry. "I will listen. Apart from that, I promise nothing."

At the appointed hour Mr. Patrell appeared at the door of the flat, greeting my mother with elaborate courtesy. His mood was buoyant, but his face looked pale and gaunt, and he wore his left arm in a heavy canvas sling. Stepping inside, he waved off our questions about his bandaged arm, assuring us that it was only a minor injury. Placing his dove-grey homburg on the sideboard, he took a seat at the breakfast table and grinned broadly as a slice of dobos torte was placed before him. Bess, meanwhile, chatted amiably with him about the potentially ruinous effects of the recent consolidation of New York's five boroughs. At length, when Patrell had submitted the misdeeds of Mayor Van Wyck to a lengthy analysis, my sister-in-law attempted to guide the conversation to business.

"Do I understand, sir," said Bess, "that there may be an opening at Patrell's Wonder Emporium?"

"Ah!" said the proprietor brightly, waving his good arm in the air. "Allow me to demonstrate!" Pulling a linen pocket square from his coat, he dabbed at his lips and gave a discreet cough. Then, with a brief flourish, he reached into his mouth and withdrew a large, whole walnut in its shell. "My mouth is empty," he said, turning to my brother to allow a brief examination, "and I shall take a sip of tea to demonstrate that my esophageal passages are clear. But see!" With a sweep of his hand he withdrew a second walnut, placing it beside the first on the edge of the kitchen table.

This peculiar display was repeated four more times until there was a neat row of six walnuts arrayed before him. "What do you think?" he asked, waving a hand over the harvest. "Rather good, is it not?"

I should perhaps explain that Mr. Patrell's exhibition was not without precedent. At that time the sideshows and carnivals were experiencing a modest vogue of what was called the "regurgitator act," an outgrowth of sword-swallowing and water-spouting. The regurgitator act would take many curious forms before the fad had run its course. Some regurgitators would swallow and then reproduce small stones and rocks, while other even hardier souls turned their skills to goldfish and frogs. One inventive practitioner found a means of swallowing assorted small objects—coins, thimbles, and the like— only to reproduce them in the order called for by his audience. It must be said that regurgitators were not my favorite class of entertainer, and I disliked sharing a stage with them. The act, depending as it did upon grotesquerie, tended to put the audience in a skittish, even hostile frame of mind. Worse yet, it produced a foul odor.

My sister-in-law shared my sense of distaste. "Mr. Patrell," said Bess, "I have always found acts of this type to be unseemly."

"Still," I said, eager not to offend a potential employer, "six walnuts! That's rather good."

"I can do seven," said Harry. "Plus a potato."

"Can you?" asked Patrell, looking a touch crestfallen. "Well, I'm still something of a novice. My difficulty is this accursed arm sling. I can't juggle with one arm, and if I can't juggle, how am I going to get the marks to pony up their dimes?"

It was a fair question. The sight of Gideon Patrell juggling a set of Indian clubs was a familiar one in New York City. He would stand on the sidewalk outside of his Wonder Emporium before each show doing wondrous cascades and showers as a crowd gathered to watch. This was his version of the time-honored "bally," the free act performed outside a carnival tent while the outside talker—we didn't call them "barkers" in those days—enticed the crowd to "step right up" and pay their admission. I was a competent juggler myself at that stage of my career, but Patrell was an artist. His overhand-eight pattern was a wonder to behold.

"Mr. Patrell," said Bess, folding her hands, "I am truly sorry for your difficulty, but surely there are better options than this? Do you honestly believe that coughing up a handful of walnuts will bring in paying customers?"

Patrell's face clouded. "What am I to do?" he asked. "I need something to go along with the spiel."

"I could do my handcuff act," said Harry. "That will bring them running!"

"God, Harry, don't start blathering on about that handcuff act again! What do I need with a—what do you keep calling yourself? An escapitator?"

"An escapologist."

"Whatever. Nobody's ever going to want to see a guy slip out of a pair of handcuffs, Harry. Stick with your magic act."

Harry folded his arms.

"You'll forgive me for asking, Mr. Patrell," I said, "but if you don't want Harry to do his escape act, why are you here?"

"I need a magician—I need a 'King of Kards.'"

"What happened to Addison Tate?" I asked. "Only last month you were telling me that he was the best card mechanic you've ever had."

"Tate!" Patrell's face darkened. "I took that man into my troupe when no one else would have him! Gave him two slots on the bill! And this is how he repays me!"

Harry leaned forward. "He skipped out on you?"

"Skipped out on me! No, Houdini—he shot me!"

Bess and I were too startled to speak, but Harry appeared delighted by this news.

"Ah!" he cried, bridging his fingertips. "A mystery!"

"A mystery? There's no mystery about it," cried Patrell. "He took out a gun and shot me! And when I get my hands on him, he'll regret the day he crossed my path. Even with one arm, I'll give him a thrashing."

"Your case fills me with interest," said my brother. "Pray give us the essential facts from the commencement, and I can afterwards question you as to those details which seem to me to be most important. Omit nothing. It has long been an axiom of mine that the little things are infinitely the most important."

Patrell stared. "I must say, Houdini, you're acting very strangely. What in the world are you going on about?"

The answer, of course, was Sherlock Holmes. My brother, though not a great reader, was a devoted admirer of the Great Detective, whose adventures he followed religiously in the pages of *Harper's Weekly* until the death of Mr. Holmes at the hands of Professor Moriarty, an event that left Harry despondent for several weeks. Even now, roughly five years later, Harry refused to accept that the detective's adventures had come to an end. Whenever the subject was broached, he would simply shake his head and insist that Dr. Watson's account of the events at the Reichenbach Falls must have been a deception of some kind. "The good doctor must have had his reasons," he would say.

If anything, Harry's enthusiasm had increased since the Great Detective's passing. The previous year we had been thrown quite inadvertently into the investigation of the murder of a Fifth Avenue tycoon, under a set of circumstances, as Dr. Watson might have said, that I have recorded elsewhere. Our unexpected success in this matter left Harry with the distinct, if unwarranted, impression that he had been anointed as the heir apparent to Sherlock Holmes.

"Perhaps you *should* tell us a bit more about this unusual turn of events, Mr. Patrell," said Bess. "I can't say I'm entirely at ease with the idea of a Ten-in-One where the performers are apt to shoot one another."

Patrell sighed and fingered one of the walnuts lined up on the table in front of him. "There isn't much to tell," he began. "Addison Tate joined the troupe in late July. He's a fine performer, and he is willing to step in wherever he is needed, but I had my doubts about him. We've all heard rumors that he served a stretch in prison as a young man. They say he shot a man in a gambling hall."

"He denies it," I said. "I've played cards with the man on many occasions. He says a crooked dealer got shot and the police arrested everyone at the table. He insists he had no part in any wrongdoing."

"I know what he says, Dash." Patrell picked up a table knife and began tapping at the shell of a walnut. "And I believed him. Truly I did. But almost from the first he began pumping me for more money. He told me his mother needed an operation! Of all the cock-and-bull—"

"I am sorry to learn that his mother is unwell," said Harry.

"Unwell? Houdini, his mother doesn't need an operation! That's the oldest line of patter in the book! I'm surprised he didn't try to sell me a share in a gold mine." Using his bandaged arm as a buttress,

Patrell wedged the blade of his table knife into the seam of the walnut and pried it open.

"This still does not explain how you came to be shot," Harry said.

Patrell picked out several pieces of walnut and began chewing. "The night before last, Tate brought every single member of the troupe to my office after the final show—the whole lot of them, even the bearded lady. He knew that I would be tallying the receipts for the week and preparing the pay packets. We'd had a fairly good draw, so there was a considerable pile of money sitting on my desk. Tate came to me with his hat in his hand and begged me to give him the entire week's receipts. He made a good show of it, I'll grant you. He said he had spoken with everyone and they had all agreed to put their salaries toward his mother's operation."

"The entire troupe was willing to do this?" I asked.

Patrell nodded. "I couldn't believe it. He said he would pay them all back as soon as he was able. He must have been remarkably convincing."

"It does seem extraordinary," said Bess, "but, if you'll forgive me, Mr. Patrell, what business is it of yours if your employees chose to give their wages to Mr. Tate?"

"You're quite right about that, Mrs. Houdini, but that wasn't all he was after. He wanted me to surrender the entire gate—every last dime I made for the week. It was quite impossible. I have overhead. It would have shut us down."

"You refused?" Harry asked.

"Of course I refused! And Tate assured me that he bore no ill will. We shook hands and parted as friends—or so I believed. But he returned later, when the others had gone. Said he was going to give me one last chance to do the decent thing. When I again refused, he informed me that I no longer had a choice in the matter. 'It pains me to do this,' he said, 'but I am a desperate man.' That's when he pulled out his gun."

"The Navy Colt," I said. "With the ivory grips."

Harry raised his eyebrows. "How could you possibly know that, Dash?"

"Harry, Addison Tate does a 'Wild West' act. He's the best trick shooter in all of New York. I've seen that pistol dozens of times. So have you. He treats that gun like precious jewel."

Harry stroked his chin. "A regrettable lapse. I saw, but I did not observe."

I turned back to Patrell. "I can't believe that Addison Tate would do such a thing. I know the man."

"I don't think he intended to shoot me, Dash," Patrell said, wincing slightly as his hand went to his bandaged shoulder. "I was so convinced of it, in fact, that when he reached for the money, I pushed him away and tried to scoop the money back into my strongbox. That's the last thing I remember, apart from the sound of the gun. When I came to my senses, the room was full of people and my shoulder hurt like the devil, but Tate and the money were gone."

"It must have been an accident," I said. "He keeps a hair-trigger on that pistol."

"Taking the money was no accident, Dash. And whether he meant to shoot me or not, it's all one and the same in the eyes of the law. I'll see him in Sing Sing before this is over. If only he can be found!"

"And so we come to the business at hand," said Harry, spreading his palms on the table before him. "You wish to hire me."

"Obviously," said Patrell.

"Yes, just so. Obviously. You should have consulted me sooner. By this time, no doubt, the police have trodden on any number of vital clues, but perhaps I might uncover the truth by questioning—"

"I must say, Houdini, you don't seem quite yourself today." Patrell brushed the last of the walnut shells into his handkerchief. "Do I understand that you fancy yourself a detective now?"

"You've come to the right man. I shall locate Addison Tate for you, and I shall solve the mystery of his disappearance, or my name isn't—"

"But there's no mystery about it, Houdini! He simply fled after the gun went off. The police will find him soon enough."

Harry's face fell. "No mystery? Then why have you come to see me?"

"You're still a magician, aren't you?"

"I am 'The King of Kards,'" said Harry, straightening his back. "The foremost pasteboard manipulator in the country, capable of making the cards—"

"—Capable of making the cards shimmer and dance upon your fingertips," said Patrell, finishing Harry's boast in the weary tone of one who had heard it countless times. "Well, Houdini, making the cards shimmer and dance is another service that Addison Tate had undertaken for Patrell's Wonder Emporium, and rather capably, I will admit. I need someone to fill his slot. I'd do it myself, but with my arm in a sling I couldn't possibly pull off a manipulation act."

"Harry would be very pleased to accommodate you," I said, assuming my de facto role as my brother's manager, "provided that you are willing to meet his terms."

"I'll pay him three dollars a week," said Patrell, "which is fifty cents more than I was paying Mr. Tate."

"My professional charges are upon a fixed scale," said Harry. "I do not vary them, save when I remit them altogether."

"What?" asked Patrell.

"Three dollars a week will be fine," I said quickly.

"Yes," said Harry, tapping his nose meaningfully. "Perhaps it *would* be best if I joined the company as a mere performer. We must not advertise the real reason for my presence. It would inhibit my investigation."

Patrell turned to me. "Dash?"

"Three dollars a week will be fine," I repeated.

"It is a perfect deception," Harry said, as he journeyed downtown to join Patrell's Wonder Emporium that afternoon. "I shall pose as a simple card manipulator. No one will suspect that I am silently observing each and every detail."

"Harry," said Bess with a sigh. "You *are* a simple card manipulator. Mr. Patrell told us to leave Addison Tate to the police. There's nothing to investigate."

"Bess is right, Harry," I said. "Don't mess this up. We need the money. Keep your mind on your act."

"I shall perform my duties with my usual skill and professionalism," said Harry. "Of that you may be assured." His voice took on a far-away quality. "The stage lost a fine actor when I became a specialist in crime."

"Harry . . . "

But he sank back in his seat and would say nothing more.

We were riding a horsecar down Seventh Avenue, with our collars pulled up against a stiff autumn wind. Bess wore a long cloak over the gauzy outfit that I always thought of as her "sugarplum fairy" costume, designed to show her legs to advantage. "I'm freezing," she said, pulling the folds of the cloak tighter. "I hope Mr. Patrell has managed to find a warm spot this time. Do you remember when he was running the show out of an old fish market? I thought I'd never get the smell of mackerel out of my hair."

Patrell's Wonder Emporium had occupied dozens of locations over the course of its twenty-year history. It began as a tent-show on the outer reaches of Central Park, in the days when Wild West demonstrations were still a familiar summer entertainment. Gradually, Patrell took his business downtown in hopes of attracting patrons throughout the year. It was his custom to swoop down whenever a warehouse or dry goods concern went out of business, buying up the remainder of the owner's lease at a discount and setting the run of his show accordingly.

We alighted at 14th Street and approached the Wonder Emporium from the west. From half a block away we caught sight of the banner line, a row of brightly-painted canvas panels depicting the "wondrous and edifying" novelty acts presented within—a bearded lady, a contortionist, a frog boy, a "Wild Man of Borneo," a snake charmer, a living skeleton, a "genuine leprechaun," a fat lady, a sharp-shooter, and a King of Kards. It should be admitted that the illustrations were eye-catching but also highly fanciful. The leprechaun, for example, was depicted as standing in the palm of a normal-sized man, brandishing his tiny hat and dancing a merry jig. "A tiny marvel!" read the bold, up-tilted caption. "Will you find his pot of gold?" The actual performer—Benjamin Zalor, with whom I often played a hand or two of whist—stood somewhat over four feet. If he had ever owned a pot of gold, he neglected to mention it to me.

"That looks nothing like me," said Harry, pointing to the panel depicting the King of Kards. This was certainly true. The figure on the canvas panel resembled a blond Satan, with playing cards shooting from his fingertips like lightening bolts. A trio of undersized red imps were seen cowering at his feet, averting their eyes.

"These are just stock images," I said. "Show people come and go. Patrell couldn't possibly have a new banner painted each time his snake charmer gets a better offer. None of these illustrations looks anything like the actual performer."

"I know that," said Harry, "but my public will be disappointed."

We had only twenty minutes until the start of the first show, and Patrell was waiting for us at the door. He led us inside and showed us to a makeshift stage—a narrow platform fronted with red and blue bunting that ran along one wall below a line of windows. The other performers had already taken their places on stage, waiting for Patrell to drum up the day's first audience. The proprietor made hasty introductions, then showed Harry and Bess to their place on the platform, between the living skeleton and the snake charmer.

This done, Patrell pulled out a large silver turnip watch at the end of a chain. "Five minutes, ladies and gentlemen!" he announced. "Dash," he said, turning to me. "Would you mind filling as frog boy?" He gestured to a strange assemblage of wood and cloth at the third position on the platform. At the center stood a raised column painted to resemble a tree stump. If you settled yourself behind the stump in a sort of crouch and poked your head through a hooded yoke of green cloth, it created the impression of a human head atop an elongated frog body. It was a nice effect, but tough on the knee joints.

"Don't tell me," I said, "Addison Tate was also filling the frog boy slot?"

"No," said Patrell. "Actually, we hired a young lady last month. Mathilda Horn. Lovely girl, but she hasn't turned up yet. I believe last night's events may have unsettled her."

"I'll need three dollars a week, just like my brother."

"Two."

"Two-fifty."

Patrell snorted as he reached into his pocket for a walnut. "Dash, it's not a talent slot." He picked up a rock from the "Wild Man of Borneo" exhibit and cracked the nut with it. "Your mother could do the frog boy act. I'm offering you two dollars a week until Miss Horn returns.

What do you say?" He held out the cracked walnut and I helped myself to half.

"Ribbit," I said.

The next three weeks passed pleasantly enough as we fell into the routine of the Ten-in-One. We did modest business throughout the afternoons, but drew rather larger and more boisterous crowds in the evenings, when young couples could be relied upon to be strolling past on their way to the theater or a dinner. I made myself useful by filling various slots behind the scenes as well as on the platform. After a couple of days, when Mathilda Horn returned to take up her duties as frog boy, I was promoted to the sharp-shooter slot recently vacated by Addison Tate. I should confess that I do not possess any native skill with a pistol, but the international success of Miss Annie Oakley— "The Peerless Little Sure Shot"—had created a public demand that every dime museum and carnival in America was now obliged to fill. Though I have never handled a live firearm in my life, only blank cartridges, I found as many others had done that sleight of hand offered an acceptable substitute. In my version of the sharp-shooter act, a volunteer from the audience made a selection from a deck of playing cards. After an appropriate interval of shuffling and cutting, I invited the spectator to throw the entire pack into the air. As the loose cards fluttered down, I gave a wild cry—the Rebel Yell, as interpreted by the son of an Orthodox rabbi—and fired my pistol. In short order the selected card was found to have a bullet hole in its center. The act drew enthusiastic applause whenever I performed it, but suffice it to say that Little Sure Shot had nothing to fear from me.

Harry, meanwhile, was doing yeoman service with his card manipulations, delighting the crowd with flashy overhand shuffles and hand-to-hand cascades, followed by platform effects such as the rising cards and the vanishing bird cage. If at times his stage manner appeared stiff, if not wooden, his audiences were generally forgiving. This may have had something to do with the pleasant addition of Bess striking poses at his side. She was easy on the eyes, I don't mind telling you.

Between shows Harry took every opportunity to make enquiries about the disappearance of Addison Tate. As a rule he did not mingle easily with other performers, but his path was greatly smoothed by the trays of pecan rolls that our mother sent along each morning for fear that our new friends—especially Mr. Grader, the living skeleton—were not getting enough to eat. Even so, Harry's attempts to strike up even the most casual conversation had the sound of a man practicing a new language. "Say, did you happen to see the newspaper this morning?" he would ask. "I see that Jimmy Sheckard got yet another hit for the Brooklyn Bridegrooms! He certainly is handy with a baseball bat, is he not? I wonder, was Addison Tate fond of baseball? Whatever happened to him, do you suppose?"

If these forays lacked subtlety, it emerged that our colleagues were not at all reluctant to discuss the abrupt departure of Mr. Tate. It was the custom of the performers to withdraw into a back room and pass around flasks of tea between shows. As the days progressed, the tea gave way to stronger restoratives, and the conversation flowed more freely. By the end of the second week, our new friends had advanced no fewer than a dozen explanations for Addison Tate's behavior, ranging from brain fever to a sudden impulse to run off and join the French Foreign Legion. "If you ask me," said Emma Henderson one afternoon, pulling off the "Bearded Lady" chin piece she wore, "he was up to no good from the moment he got here. I always saw him sneaking around behind the platform. Very odd, I call it."

"Sneaking around?" Harry asked. "How do you mean?"

"Nipping off to the back alley. Like he was looking for something, or meeting someone, but didn't want you to know. I never believed that business about his sick mother, not me."

"That's not what you said at the time, Emma," said Nigel Kendricks, setting his "Wild Man of Borneo" wig and mask on an empty stool. "You were willing to give him a week's pay, just like the rest of us."

"Oh, he was a charmer, I'll grant you that," said Miss Henderson. "He certainly charmed you, didn't he, Mathilda? Quite the rogue, that one."

Miss Horn looked away, her face flushing scarlet. "I'm sure I don't know what you mean, Emma," she said.

Miss Henderson snorted. "I've seen the way you looked at him, dear. A blind man couldn't have missed it."

I leaned forward and patted Miss Horn's arm. "There, now. One never knows what the future holds. There's always another trolley coming along, they say." I gave her what I hoped was a charming, even roguish smile.

Miss Horn glanced at me as though I were some simple-minded relation with whom she was obliged to make small talk. "Perhaps so," she said, "but I find I prefer to walk." She stood and brushed at the folds of the green cloak she wore for the frog boy routine. "If you'll excuse me, I must get ready for the three o'clock." She turned and drifted toward the platform, with Miss Hendricks trailing behind her. I stood watching them with my hands in my pockets.

"Strange how that woman manages to resist your charms, Dash," said Harry, sidling up behind me. "You of all people, with your experience of women that spreads over three separate boroughs."

"I'm just being sociable," I said.

"I wouldn't be *too* sociable," said Bess, laying a hand on my shoulder. "I believe Mr. Patrell has designs on Miss Horn."

"Why do you say that?" I asked.

"She missed a day and a half of work and he didn't fire her," said Bess. "For Gideon Patrell, that's something akin to a proposal of marriage."

"I'm sure Mr. Patrell is only concerned with the best interests of the show," I said. "I feel the same way." I pulled the Navy Colt from its holster and made a show of examining it.

"Perhaps," said Harry. "Still, it might be best for all concerned if you—that's very odd."

He was staring at me. "What is it?" I asked

He took the pistol from my hands. "You say this is Addison Tate's gun? The one he dropped after he shot Mr. Patrell?"

"The very one. Mr. Patrell gave it to me when I took over the sharp-shooter act."

Harry examined it cautiously and gave the barrel a tentative sniff. "This pistol has been fired, Dash."

"Of course it's been fired, Harry. I've been firing it eight times a day for the past two weeks. Ten times on Saturday."

"But you've been using blank cartridges, Dash."

"Blank cartridges still leave a heavy odor of gunpowder. That's what you smell."

"Indeed?" Harry waved a hand as though the remark was beneath his notice. He turned the gun over in his hands several times. "You've been rather careless with this firearm, Dash."

"How so? I'm shooting blanks. It's not as if I'm going to hurt anyone."

"The handle. You told me it was genuine ivory, did you not?"

I nodded.

He fingered a series of scores and ridges along the bottom of the ivory grips. "You told me that Tate was unusually careful with this gun.

He even had Mr. Patrell lock it up in the strongbox each night. Now it looks as if it has been chewed by a dog."

I took the pistol and examined the scarred grip. "Huh. I hadn't noticed that. It must have happened when Tate dropped it."

"Perhaps. It is but a trifle, of course, but there is nothing so important as trifles."

"Harry, why do you insist on making a mystery out of it? Next you'll be telling me that it's a three-pipe problem."

He sighed. "That's exactly what it is, Dash. What a shame that I don't use tobacco."

"Harry, face it. You're not going to get to the bottom of this one. Addison Tate shot Mr. Patrell and now he's on the run. With the money he took he could be anywhere. We may never know where he went."

"You're wrong, Dash; I will solve it. I'm simply looking at things the wrong way. I must shake things up—turn them upside down. And I know just how to do it." Harry smiled mysteriously. "Indeed, I have already taken the necessary measures."

"What do you mean?"

"I'll say no more. I must be discreet."

"What is he going on about now?" I asked Bess.

She slipped her arm through Harry's and led him toward the stage. "Hasn't he told you? He's written a letter to—"

"Shhh!" cried Harry, pulling us off to the side. "The others will hear!"

"Hear what?" I asked.

Harry looked around to make sure that no one else was listening before he continued. "Very well," he said, rubbing his hands together. "I shall confide in you. As the solution has thus far eluded me, I took the liberty of laying my case before an expert. I have written a letter to the world's foremost consulting detective."

"The world's foremost consulting detective?"

"Exactly."

"You wrote a letter to—"

"Sherlock Holmes. That is correct. I gathered the facts into a most interesting narrative, with certain literary flourishes that I hope will appeal to Dr. Watson."

"But . . . Sherlock Holmes. Harry, isn't Sherlock Holmes a—well, isn't he—"

"Dead? You are referring to the unfortunate happenings at the Reichenbach Falls? You know my views on that matter, Dash. Sherlock Holmes is not dead. He has simply withdrawn from public life for reasons that he is not at liberty to divulge. I feel confident, however, that when he hears the particulars of this case, he will make an exception."

"An exception?"

"Yes."

"An exception to being dead?"

"Yes, if you insist on phrasing it thus. He has undoubtedly heard of the exploits of the great Harry Houdini. I am the only escapologist in the world, just as he is the only professional consulting detective. He and I are two originals, charting a bold new course and bringing comfort to the downtrodden."

"Comfort to the downtrodden?"

He continued as if he had not heard. "It is a singular honor, but also a burden. He and I share this unique bond, like brothers. I wouldn't expect you to understand."

"Like brothers," I repeated, as we climbed the platform for the next performance. "No, I guess I wouldn't understand."

The following weeks passed quickly and we began to lose track of time, as one often does when caught up in the grind of a Ten-in-One. As the days melted away, the name of Addison Tate was heard less frequently among the performers, and even Mr. Patrell seemed eager to put the episode behind him. For my part I enjoyed the routine thoroughly, but for one detail. Though I persisted in pressing my attentions upon Miss Horn, she continued to resist me with polite but firm resolve. Each day at the end of the final show, she would hurtle through the door as if propelled from a cannon, vanishing from sight before I had a chance to offer to escort her on the walk home.

One morning in early December, as I arrived at my mother's flat to collect Harry and Bess, I found my brother slumped over the breakfast table looking thoroughly despondent.

"What is it?" I asked, glancing at my mother. "Is anyone—"

"His letter has come back from Baker Street," said Bess.

"Come back?"

"Unopened. See for yourself." A thick envelope lay on the breakfast table, addressed to "Mr. Sherlock Holmes, Esq." in Harry's blocky script. The surface was covered with postal markings and transfer stamps, and as I picked it up for a closer look, I could see a line of instructions printed along the bottom edge in a firm, slanting hand. It read: "Mr. Holmes no longer resides at this address. Return to writer." An arrow scrawled in the corner directed attention to the reverse side of the envelope, where Harry's name and address were carefully printed on the flap.

"Harry," I said, setting the envelope back on the table. "I'm sorry. You must be very disappointed."

"Extremely." His voice was heavy and listless. "I feel so terribly foolish."

"Still, you couldn't have really thought—I mean, you couldn't actually have believed—"

"That Sherlock Holmes would assist me in solving the case? Of course I believed it."

Bess reached across the table and placed her hand on his. "Let's put all this foolishness behind us and concentrate on the business at hand. Dash, we've been working for Mr. Patrell for nearly two months now. Don't you think it's time we—Dash? Dash?"

"Sorry? Were you speaking to me?"

"What is it? You have the strangest look on your face!"

"I—well—I'm not sure, but I think—I think—"

"What?"

I picked up Harry's letter and turned it over in my hands. "I think Sherlock Holmes just solved the case."

"It's bad enough that I have to spend eight straight hours standing on the platform. Now I have to remain afterwards?" Emma Henderson tore off her bearded chin piece. "And why does it have to be in Mr. Patrell's office? We'd all be more comfortable in the back room."

This was certainly true. Harry and I had asked all of the performers to gather in the relatively cramped confines of Patrell's office, which left most of us standing and others leaning awkwardly against the rear wall. It was a necessary measure. In answer to Miss Henderson's question, however, I merely shrugged.

"Be patient, Emma," said Mathilda Horn, gazing up at me with an unfamiliar expression of warmth and affection. "Dash has his reasons."

"Does he now?" asked Miss Henderson. "When did you two get so friendly?"

"You hadn't noticed?" asked Benjamin Zalor, settling his undersized frame on the edge of an unused packing crate. "They've spent half the day whispering at the back door."

Gideon Patrell took his usual seat behind his desk. "Are there any more of those pastries your mother sent, Dash?" he asked. "What did you call them again?"

"Kifli," I said. "And I'm afraid Mr. Grader has eaten the last one."

"Grader! I've never seen a living skeleton with such a sweet tooth," said Patrell.

"Sorry, boss," he said, patting his concave stomach.

"So, what's this all about?" asked Patrell, cracking a walnut with a juggling club. "Where is your brother, by the way?"

"Right here," said Harry, entering the room with the "Wild Man of Borneo" in tow. "Sorry for the delay. Mr. Kendricks and I needed to make preparations for this evening's performance."

"Performance?" asked Patrell. "We've done our eight turns today, Houdini. It's time to go home."

"Please indulge me for just a few moments longer," said Harry. "I've planned an encore, never before seen on any stage. Tonight, my brother and I intend to recreate the dreadful crime that took place in this office."

"Recreate the crime?" Patrell stared at him. "For what possible reason?"

"You have indicated that you would like to find Mr. Tate and recover your money."

"Yes, but he's long gone by now. And our money with him."

"Perhaps not." Harry straightened his tie. "Indeed, I believe the solution is closer than you think. Mr. Patrell, for purposes of our demonstration you will remain just as you are, behind the desk. Dash, you will be playing the role of Addison Tate in this evening's drama."

I stepped forward.

"Now," my brother continued, turning to the others, "Mr. Patrell has stated that Addison Tate returned to the office to demand the money after the rest of you departed. Dash—demand the money."

I shrugged. "Give me the money," I said.

"No, no," said Harry, stepping forward. "It is essential that you are believable in the part. Take out your gun! Threaten him!"

I pulled out the Navy Colt. "Give me the money," I repeated, somewhat apologetically.

"You're hopeless, Dash," said Harry, snatching the Colt from my hands. "Here's how it's done." He turned to Patrell and snarled at him across the desk, waving the gun menacingly. "See here, you low-down, four-flushing, no-account, miserable, rotten, lousy, cheap, dishonest—"

"I think we get the point, Houdini," said Patrell.

"Quite so," Harry agreed, in a much brighter tone. He set the gun down and turned away, twirling a juggling club carelessly at the tips of his fingers. "And then, when you refused to surrender the money, he shot you and stole away under cover of darkness."

Ben Zalor squirmed uncomfortably atop his packing crate. "We know all this, Houdini," he said.

"Indeed," said my brother, clearing his throat, "but later that same evening, something even more remarkable occurred. I believe that Addison Tate had no sooner fled into the night than he realized that he could not leave Mr. Patrell alive to tell what he knew. Tate would never be able to show his face again for fear of being arrested. The charge would be attempted murder."

Emma Henderson gave a horrified gasp. "You're saying that Tate came back here to finish Mr. Patrell off?"

"That's exactly what I'm saying, my dear lady. But Tate found himself in a terrible quandary. He knew that he had wounded his victim, but he could not enter the office and confront him directly. Patrell had likely summoned help by this time. What's more, Tate had dropped his gun earlier. He was unarmed. So what did he do? Ah, here was the genius of the thing. Creeping stealthily into the back room, Tate noticed a ventilator duct that communicated directly with Mr. Patrell's office."

"Ventilator duct?" asked Grader, scratching his skull-like head.

"Yes, for the circulation of fresh air. Essential in a property that had once been a fish market. Tate noticed a faint light glowing through the opening, which told him that Mr. Patrell was still in his office. The absence of noise confirmed that his victim was alone, possibly even unconscious from the gunshot. Tate seized this opportunity without hesitation. Reaching into the folds of his cloak, he withdrew a small but deadly swamp adder, the deadliest snake in India, which he had secured during his dealings with—"

"For heaven's sake, Mr. Houdini," cried Miss Henderson. "This is the most absurd yarn I've ever heard!"

"It's preposterous," said Patrell, reaching for another walnut. "And by the way, aren't you describing the plot of a Sherlock Holmes adventure? *The Speckled Band*, wasn't it?"

Harry waved the objections aside. "Perhaps that put the idea into Tate's head. In any event, the problem now remained of inducing the deadly snake to travel through the ventilator passage into Mr. Patrell's office. How could this be achieved? Searching through the back room, Tate chanced upon—" Harry broke off at the sound of a walnut cracking. An enormous smile broke across his face. "You see it, Dash?" he cried, springing forward. "You see it?"

"I see it, Harry."

"See what, Dash?" asked Ben Zalor. "I don't understand."

"Do you see what Mr. Patrell is holding in his hands?" I asked.

Zalor turned to the desk. "Your gun. What of it?"

"Do you see what he's doing with it?"

"He cracked a walnut. So what?"

"He cracked a walnut with the butt of an ivory-handled Navy pistol. We know he's done it more than once because there are markings on the handle that weren't there when Addison Tate cared for the gun."

"But what does it matter?" asked Miss Hendricks.

"Addison Tate didn't shoot Mr. Patrell," I told them. "Patrell shot himself. Again and again, we've seen that Mr. Patrell has a fondness for walnuts, and a tendency to crack the shells with whatever implement is at hand—a table knife, a rock, a juggling club. Tonight, Harry set the gun down on his desk and walked away with the juggling club. When Patrell had his next impulse to crack a walnut, he grabbed for the closest heavy object."

"The gun," said Zalor.

"Exactly. And the same thing happened on the night Mr. Patrell was injured—the night he claims that Addison Tate shot him. But Tate didn't shoot anyone. Gideon Patrell shot himself, accidentally, while cracking a walnut."

"Tonight, the gun didn't go off," Harry put in, "because Dash had adjusted the trigger mechanism. But Tate liked a lighter touch—almost a hair trigger—so the gun went off when Mr. Patrell cracked the handle against the nut. He's lucky he wasn't killed."

"This is absurd!" shouted Patrell, his face darkening. "It's crazier than the story about the swamp adder!"

"The wonder of the thing is that you did it twice," I said. "You'd think that a man who had shot himself once would be a little more careful."

"That's why I had to distract you with my spellbinding story," Harry said. "So that you wouldn't notice what you were doing. As long as your arm has been in that sling, you've simply grabbed for whatever object was close at hand."

Emma Henderson was staring at Patrell with an expression of fascination mixed with horror. "Why would he do such a thing? If it was an accident, why would he blame Addison Tate?"

"Two reasons," I said. "First, with Tate out of the way, he believed he had an opportunity to win the affections of Miss Horn." The young lady blushed deeply and turned away. "At the same time," I continued, "it allowed Patrell to salt away the money for himself. I have to give him credit. At the very instant that he shot himself, he figured out a way to turn it to his profit. He certainly showed a cool head."

"I don't understand," said Miss Henderson. "Why didn't Addison Tate simply speak up and defend himself? He left Mr. Patrell's office that evening when all the rest of us did. We would have vouched for him."

"Tate returned later that evening. That part of the story is true. He wanted to try again to convince Patrell to let him have the money. When Patrell refused a second time, Tate saw that it was hopeless. He turned to go, leaving his gun behind as he always did, to be locked up in the strongbox overnight. Later, when he heard that Patrell had been shot and the police were looking for him, he panicked and ran."

"Incredible," said Zalor. "So that whole cock-and-bull story about recreating the crime, about snakes in the ventilator—you were just waiting for Mr. Patrell to crack a walnut?"

"Exactly," I said.

"It's a pack of lies," said Patrell, his voice sinking to a menacing register. "You've made the whole thing up."

"Not at all," said Harry. "Once we realized what had happened, it was a simple matter to find Addison Tate—with Miss Horn's help, of course."

"You found him?" asked Miss Henderson. "Where?"

"Why, visiting his mother, of course," said Harry. "She's in the hospital awaiting an operation, just as Mr. Tate had said. He has been at her bedside every day, though he took the precaution of shaving off his 'Wild West' beard and moustache so that he wouldn't be easily recognized. This afternoon, he told the entire story to a friend of ours down at the police department."

"More lies!" insisted Patrell. "He'll be halfway across the Atlantic by now."

Just then, there was a stirring at the back of the room as the "Wild Man of Borneo" struggled to pull off his wig and mask, revealing not the familiar sight of Nigel Kendricks but a younger, smoother face.

Patrell gave a hoarse cry. "You! This is—"

"Hello, Gideon," said Addison Tate. "Would you mind returning my Colt?"

"But it was ridiculous!" I told Harry at breakfast the next morning. "Ridiculous on a grand scale!"

"All part of the plan," said Harry. "You told me to keep talking until he reached for the gun."

"I know," I said, "but really . . . a swamp adder in the ventilator?"

"I thought it was a rather tidy explanation," said Harry, reaching for a slice of brown toast. "And after all, there *was* a poisonous snake in the room, if you count Mr. Patrell himself. But come now, Dash, you still haven't explained how Sherlock Holmes provided the solution to the matter."

"No, I suppose not," I said. "Things got a bit chaotic last night."

"For a few moments I thought Tate really would shoot Patrell," said Bess. "And once the police arrived and demanded explanations, it seemed as if we'd never get out of there. Lieutenant Murray is a good man, but he's a fiend for details."

"Even he wasn't quite sure what to do with Mr. Patrell," I said. "Patrell never made a formal complaint against Addison Tate, so the nature of the crime is unclear."

"I overheard Mr. Patrell offering to pay the medical expenses for Tate's mother," said Bess. "I'm guessing that Tate will let the matter drop, especially if Mathilda Horn has anything to do with it. She clearly wants to run away with him and live happily ever after."

"A remarkable woman," I said. "She never wavered in her belief that he was innocent."

"Indeed," said Bess, patting my arm. "We knew there had to be some reason she was able to resist your attentions."

"But what about Sherlock Holmes!" demanded Harry. "My letter came back unopened!"

"Actually, Harry, it began with something you said. When the case began to get frustrating, you said something about 'turning things upside-down.' That put a seed in my head. Then, when I saw the letter to Sherlock Holmes, it all fell into place."

"But how?" Harry took the envelope from his pocket and studied it. "It's simply an unopened letter."

"With a message on the outside. And what is the message instructing us to do?"

"I don't understand. The message is simply telling us to—ah!" A smile broke across Harry's face. "The message is telling us to turn it over! Turn it over and look at the other side. Which is exactly what you did with the gun. You turned it over and looked at the other side."

"And once I did that, I saw that it hadn't been used as a weapon, but as a nutcracker."

"You turned things upside-down, just as I said." Harry leaned back and gave a sigh of satisfaction. "I must say, Dash, you have been positively brilliant in this business."

"My blushes, Harry."

"Almost as brilliant as—"

"As the man who wrote the message on that envelope?"

He fingered the envelope tenderly for a moment. "Really, Dash," he said, slipping it back into his pocket. "Now who's being ridiculous?"

THE ADVENTURE OF THE BOSTON DROMIO
Matthew Pearl

Matthew Pearl is the author of the historical novels *The Dante Club*, *The Poe Shadow*, and *The Last Dickens*. His nonfiction writing has appeared in the *New York Times*, the *Wall Street Journal*, the *Boston Globe*, and *Legal Affairs*. He has taught literature and creative writing at Harvard University and Emerson College.

* * * *

"More morphine!' 'More chloral!'" he cried, his eyes small and restless. "Oh, you wouldn't believe, Watson, how American patients order you about as if you were the stable boy."

This commentary I heard over breakfast with Dr. Joseph Lavey, the surgeon who had ministered to my injuries in Afghanistan, during my restorative tour through America. Lavey, formerly of London and now of Commercial Street, Boston, had remained in disconsolate and solitary spirits in the years since his wife had died of pneumonia. He was highly distracted and complained of matters large and small, whether the dwindled profits in his medical practice, or the incompetence in recent weeks of his housemaid.

"She has brought me plates of food never requested," he said about this. "She has spent daytime hours locked in her little room instead of at her duties!"

I could not know then what startling events the moody statements of my old friend Dr. Lavey portended.

Lavey's misery was so robust, I was relieved at the end of our breakfast to be left in peace with some free time and my guidebook to Boston. Two days later, Lavey returned to my lodgings at dinner. He was out of breath and had fear painted across his face.

"Why, Lavey, you are not well," I said. "Let us have something to eat." I wanted to get a closer look at him, thinking I had recognized in him some telltale signs of an opium eater.

He cried out in a muttering voice, his hands clapped to his brow, "Dead!"

"What?"

"She is dead, Watson! And the detectives' eyes are hot with suspicion. My dear Watson, I know you have experience in the line of queer criminal happenings. You are the only friend remaining to me in the wide world. You must help!"

During the night, Lavey said, he had been awakened to a loud thumping. Dressing hastily and taking a rifle from the wall, he nearly tumbled down the stairs before finding his housemaid, Mary Ann Pinton, lying dead on his kitchen floor. That was all he could remember. When next conscious, he was lying on top of her body with his rifle and the police were shaking him. It occurred to me that the whole fantastic tale had been some mental production of his opiates.

"Lavey, remain here with me in my lodgings," I implored him.

"No. She is gone; I must take care of her!" he said cryptically, and hurried away from the premises deaf to my pleas.

Opening the next morning's paper, I found news of the most alarming type: Dr. Joseph Lavey, the man to whom I owed my life, arrested for the murder of Mary Ann Pinton!

I cabled my friend and traveling companion, Sherlock Holmes, at once requesting that he depart on the earliest train for Boston. He had remained at our hotel in Portland, Maine, on business of a personal nature while I had continued our tour of New England.

During these same days, my name and Holmes's could be found in the Boston news columns. It was said that I had decided to hide Sherlock Holmes from the public of Boston. That when we had crossed through New Hampshire, I kept my coat draped over his face. That I had refused to make him available in any public appearances. Various editors called for Holmes to banish me back to England and replace me with an improved companion, preferably a Yankee. Meanwhile, I received piles of notes from portrait artists and photographers proposing Holmes the honor of sitting for them, and others from admirers offering up to twenty dollars for locks of his hair!

All this interrupted my attempts on poor Lavey's behalf. As I sat at my small desk writing letters to lawyers one afternoon, I was surprised in turning around for my water carafe to find that the armchair by the open window was now occupied.

"Holmes!" I cried.

"Boston is a city of overgrown college men," Sherlock Holmes said abstractedly.

I was overjoyed to have my friend back by my side.

Holmes had been suffering from the variety of mild ailments to the skin, nails, and lungs that many English visitors to United States cities experienced from the stale air and the lack of ventilation inside buildings and trains. Yet, as though his spirits compensated for his physical depression, Holmes had more than usual pluck and smartness in his slender, swift frame. I explained in detail what I knew about Lavey's case.

"You say your reunion with this man at this lodging house was less than pleasant?" Holmes asked, steepling his long fingers together.

"Lavey is by disposition a temperamental man. Still, he had been a well-meaning citizen at the side of his American wife, Amelia, a good and strong woman I counted as my friend. Since her death by pneumonia, I believe he has reverted to his former state, and turned to drugs for comfort."

"You had not seen him for many years, then."

"No. Yet I am fully inclined to give the old fellow assistance when requested—his dutiful services when an army surgeon having saved my life in the base hospital at Peshawar."

"That is an old grudge," Holmes observed.

"I should call it gratitude, not at all a *grudge*," I protested earnestly, "toward a man who kept me from death."

"You misunderstand, my dear Watson," said Holmes. "I mean the grudge to be on his part against you. There is nothing quite as trying as saving another man's life. He punishes you to this day. Yet, since you maintain a personal attachment, the case shall be ours. As you know, I cannot promise it will turn out as you want it to. But I should not mind terribly satisfying a long curiosity I've had by making a firsthand study of the methods of Boston detectives—the oldest department of detection in the United States, Watson. In my knowledge of Boston crooks, their crimes are by no means as clever as Chicago nor as desperate as New York, but they are singular to the degree their misdeeds are performed out of public view. One thing, Watson, have you seen Dr. Lavey since his arrest?"

"Yes. I visited the jail this morning and found he hadn't even a lawyer! He can hardly be of help to himself, I am afraid, Holmes. He mumbled pitiably how he could not be guilty of any crime if he could remember nothing of it."

"To be found lying on top of a murder victim is most unfortunate for the public perception. I should be interested in what he has to say about the girl. Miss Pinton, you say?"

I nodded. "He knows very little. Miss Pinton is twenty-three or twenty-four, from somewhere out west. Though quite attractive, she never married, has no family to speak of, never had a single visitor to the house."

"You are right that Dr. Lavey knows very little, but to our advantage. I am certain you have already considered that a housemaid may meet all kinds of ruffians on her errands for her master."

"Yes, Holmes, I did think just that. I asked Lavey to tell me the location of every household mission he had sent her on in the last weeks. I have recorded them on the map of Boston in McNally's guidebook, with a mark in red for his house." I showed this to Holmes, who seemed extremely pleased by it.

"Excellent, Watson! This shall be critical in time in understanding the crime."

"There was one other thing, Holmes. I thought it might be promising, but it turned out rather useless. When Lavey left here the other day in quite a state, I had urged him to remain but he said, 'She is gone; I must take care of her.' I thought it a queer phrase considering."

"Yes, I see why."

"This morning, I asked my friend in his cell, *whom* he had gone to take care of, whether it was perhaps a patient of his. It was my suspicion, as a matter of fact, that it was a mistress he was concerned about."

"A fine line of questioning, Watson. And did he tell you about the little animal?"

"Why, Holmes, you astound me still! Exactly!" I cried. "Lavey looked at me with a blank stare, then said, 'Oh, no. I meant only I had to take care of Mollie, the wretched kitten Mary had brought into the house the other day.' But Holmes, how did you know his strange words had referred to a pet?"

Holmes waved this away and smiled. "A trivial deduction little worthy of talk, Watson. If Lavey and his maid were united in the care of another being in their quiet household, by which Mary's sudden absence burdened her master, it was most likely to be a domestic animal and no doubt, with his recent mood, any pet too large or unseemly would have already met with expulsion. I shall say no more on the subject for now, so that we may begin to gather one or two important particulars you have failed to consider."

I visited the police headquarters. Detective Dugan, upon hearing the name Sherlock Holmes, immediately arranged for us to visit the scene. The modest three-story house was located in a dingy residential district near the waterfront of the city. Lavey had lived there for three years, having moved from a desirable street in Back Bay following his wife's death.

"We sealed the doors upon discovery of the crime, Mr. Holmes," Dugan said with a tone of professional pride. "The body was in the kitchen—over there. Dr. Lavey had fainted right on top of her, holding a rifle. I saw from the jump how it happened."

"She jumped, Detective Dugan?" I asked, looking around the kitchen.

"No, Watson," Holmes interjected. "'The jump,' if I am not mistaken, is like the start, the beginning. I have made a study of Americanisms since our passage, and consider doing a small monograph on the subject for publication upon our return to England. Please continue, Detective."

"I could see that she had been smothered and suffocated, Mr. Holmes, from the *moment* I saw her body," he said, with a sneering eyebrow at me. "The skin around her mouth was discolored and her nose was flattened and bruised as though it had been pushed down. He did not want anyone to hear him finishing her. There were no other marks or bruises on her head or body, and the rifle had not been discharged."

"Excellent! I would have asked you about the latter point, if you had not anticipated it," Holmes said.

Dugan was moved to a boyish smile by my friend's praise. "I also thought to check the doors, but none had been forced open."

"Was there anyone else seen near the house?" I asked the officer.

"The nearest neighbors did not look out until Dr. Lavey's shouts for help were heard before he fainted dead away. I am sorry to say the evidence is strong against your friend, Dr. Watson," said Dugan. "Firstly, they were the only two people in the house. Secondly, Lavey discovered the girl's body but says he cannot remember the circumstances."

"That is just it, Detective Dugan," said I. "It would surprise me greatly if Dr. Lavey had not turned to a habitual usage of opiates since Mrs. Lavey's death, which could explain his confusion and his untimely swoon. It is the vice of too many medical men here and in our own country."

"If you'd permit, Dr. Watson. Thirdly, it has become known that he has been complaining around the neighborhood in recent weeks about Miss Pinton's qualities as a housekeeper. Fourthly, as you testify, he had been a heavy user of opium as of late, and so could be prone to violence."

"The Boston detective force is extremely organized," Holmes said as an aside to me, with an amused air I could not share at the moment.

"As a point of fact, Detective," I remarked firmly, "it is my experience that those who take opium tend to be drowsy and depressed, rather than roused to violence."

"Even if that is the case, Dr. Watson, there is fifthly."

"Fifthly?"

"Ah, fifthly," Dugan resumed, "is that he feared, because of the sloppiness in her work, she was on the verge of resigning and looking for a new place, which could result in her whispering secrets of his habits around town. That would cause irreparable damage to his reputation as a doctor. There, that is the case in a nutshell."

"Do you not think," I said insistently, "that if a man is to take the trouble to suffocate a woman silently so that nobody will hear, he would not call for the police a moment later?"

"Narcotics can make a man act irrationally," the Boston detective replied after a pause.

Holmes looked back and forth at the kitchen. "I think we have learned all we can from this place. I wonder only where has the household pet gone?"

"Beg pardon?" Dugan nervously avoided looking at my friend.

"The kitten," Holmes clarified, speaking the word slowly and deliberately.

"Ah, yes," the detective replied. "Probably it has died of starvation and heat by now—gentlemen, spread out and look for that dead cat for Mr. Holmes to examine!" he ordered the two police officers that had accompanied us. When they had left the room, Dugan shifted to Holmes's side.

"Mr. Holmes, when we had first entered," he said in a contrite whisper, "the kitten was pawing at my shoe and mewing. I gave her a dish of milk, though I could hear the other men laugh at me. I had read in the paper of a new organization on Carver Street that condemned the practice of leaving cats in vacant houses to die. So before we left I placed the kitten in my pocket, beseeching the creature to remain quiet, and took her there straightaway."

"I perfectly understand," said Holmes. "You may rest assured your good deed will remain entirely quiet with us. I would not mind in the least seeing this organization."

Stopping on the way back to our lodgings, Holmes and I alighted at a three-story brick building bearing the name of the Animal Rescue League. Before going very far, we learned that the new organization had not escaped controversy, as circulars were posted on walls nearby with the following printed copy:

Humanity is sick of philanthropic fads and dilettante charities. The heart of Boston seems stirred over the distress of stray cats and the sensitive sympathies of the multitudes are awakened for some lonesome tabby that walks a back fence without a chaperon. But what of humanity? What of worse than homeless children of our city streets? Throngs appear to protect the sparrows, while little lives are perishing, one of which is of greater worth than many sparrows.

This was signed at the bottom by a Boston minister whose name meant nothing to Holmes or myself, but whose train of honorary degrees behind his name signified local prominence.

When the name of Sherlock Holmes was announced at the door, the president of the League was immediately sent for at his home as we waited in the parlor reading the literature about the place. A female employee worked diligently at a desk. A sign on the wall read, "If every person would give at least five cents we could care for several hundred more dogs and cats every year," and another, "Kindness uplifts the world." The latter phrase, displayed in bold lettering before us, seemed to perplex and entrap my friend Holmes's gaze as few things I had ever seen.

"It is an honor to have you distinguished gentlemen as my guests," said Colonel Brenton, the president, with a deep bow and hearty handshakes. "Our little League has been open to the public but a few months."

"I should like very much to see your headquarters, if you would be so kind," said Holmes.

Brenton led us into the League's parlors, where animals were gathered and being pet by visitors. Brenton explained how the League was the first and only central location in the city where homeless cats and dogs could be taken to be given new homes or put to death in a humane manner rather than to starve and suffer abuse and torture in the streets.

"We wish to spread a sympathy for dumb animals too often hardened inside our hearts. Why, sometimes even I will see a dumb animal I wish to help stuck in some ash barrel, and by the time I have reached it, I have thought about something else and forgotten all about it." He rubbed his thin moustache thoughtfully. "Sympathy is a good deal like electricity, gentlemen. The world is full of it, but before you can press the button with any effect you must have the line connected. And after connection is established the circuit is easily broken."

"There is much poetic sentiment in that, Colonel," Holmes said agreeably. "I wonder, though, if you might now turn over the guidance of our tour to the actual person in charge of the League. A woman, if I am not mistaken."

We both turned and stared at Holmes in awkward disbelief.

"Why, Mr. Holmes, I am the president of this organization! You may well look at the stationery for evidence of that!" he cried.

Holmes stood and waited. After a moment of shuffling and protesting, and Holmes still impassive, Brenton's face fell in inevitable surrender. "Wait here, gentlemen. I shall call for Mrs. Huntington Smith."

"Did you not see, Watson," Holmes said when we were alone, noting my confusion, "that the good colonel's steps inside were taken with a tentative, semi-familiar measure, looking ahead at all times, as one who has been inside a structure perhaps but three or four times. Nor did a single one of the animals having the liberty of the place note his presence with recognition or happiness. An animal knows its friend is present long before he is even in sight."

"I suppose you are right, but how did you know that a woman was the true head?" I asked, baffled.

"Simply enough, my dear Watson. If he is a man, then the real authority must not be. The only reason for his appointment would have been for the public legitimacy a man brings in the role. Then there is the fact that most organizations devoted to the humane treatment of animals and children are founded by women in this country, as in England, so that I had absolute certainty as to my trifling deduction. I had no desire to cause any embarrassment to the lawyer (or such I perceive him to be by his stance and inflection), but he can give us nothing we require."

I was about to ask what that was, as this all seemed to me a strange detour away from more pressing enquiries, but at this point there entered a small, quick-moving woman who presented herself as Anna Harris Smith, wife of Huntington Smith, editor of the *Boston Beacon*.

A mongrel terrier ran up and pawed at Mrs. Smith's leg for affection.

"Ah, there is a happy dog then!" I commented.

"You see," she said to us, "the animals are happy because this is not an institution, but a real home. We do not like to keep any animal in limited quarters. You need not explain who you are. I have read of your arrival in my husband's newspaper."

"I wonder if we might have the pleasure of seeing a specific animal under your care, Mrs. Smith," Holmes said. "Would that be much trouble?"

"We keep a very accurate account of the animals, entering upon our books every day where each animal comes from, in what condition it is when received, and how it is disposed of. When the animal is given away, an agreement must be signed in which a promise is made to treat the animal kindly, and if it is not desired, to return it to the League. We must be able to see for ourselves that the home is a good one. This may seem strict, but in this enlightened age there are still men and women who regard the lower animals as less than machines, using them if convenient, treating cats as animated mouse traps, then giving them less care than they would bestow upon a bicycle or a sewing machine."

"That is very true!" Holmes said exuberantly, as though he had worked a difficult case to its conclusion which, looking back upon the surprises of the case, it was very possible he had.

Holmes having described the circumstances of this particular kitten's arrival, Mrs. Smith took us at once to an enclosed room like a conservatory filled with fresh light from a roof of skylights. There, cats and kittens played, stretched, slept. Mrs. Smith began sorting through the menagerie with swift but gentle hands.

"When summer approaches, the number of animals given away or homeless increases greatly. It is a rather cruel habit of people to turn out their cats, or leave them inside to suffer and starve, while they leave Boston for the summer. Horses standing out in the heat become weak with thirst and hunger because of brutal owners who can pay less for another horse than to feed their own. They collapse in the street, or are taken by horse thieves and traded to be slaughtered. That is the end for the most faithful servant that mankind has. Does it not seem time to expect more of a Christian country?"

"There surely must be some recourse in the law, Mrs. Smith," I suggested.

"Not presently. This summer, we have kept a score of men constantly employed in the streets following the more wretched horses and listening for alarms of theft. Here. The ribbon on her neck said her name was 'Mollie.'"

The kitten had a flowing coat of orange and white, and she looked out and blinked at us with one blue eye and one granite gray.

"A beautiful puss," Holmes said after the briefest look. "Now that I see your labors, I am certain my colleague Dr. Watson would agree that we have taken entirely too much of your day."

On the way to the stairs, we passed by a room that held approximately a dozen boys and girls. They were playing very gently with some snoozing fat cat on a sofa and a sprightly kitten, while each youth stood up and told of a good deed performed toward an animal.

"That is our Kindness Club," said Mrs. Smith to us proudly. "The children come nearly every day through the summer vacation. Many of these children would spend their evenings on the streets if not for our club, boredom leading to abuse of each other and any helpless beings. If we can teach humanity to the generation growing up, there will be no cruelty to grapple with in generations to come."

One chubby boy was speaking about how he gave water to an emaciated horse on the street that was in weak, uncared for condition from pulling a heavy wagon. The other children applauded with sincere appreciation. After finding myself rather moved in observing, I turned back to see Holmes was speaking quietly to our guide. The only words I heard Holmes speak were "a good bargain." The strength in that woman's bright eye could only remind me of my very first glimpse at Holmes himself.

As we climbed into our waiting carriage again on Carver Street, an agent from the Animal Rescue League appeared at the window holding a small green bag with perforations along the side. He handed this into the carriage to Holmes. I presumed this package was connected to Holmes's hushed talk with Mrs. Smith. The agent said that yarn was the preferred plaything, but never to be ingested.

"I believe I saw a piece of yarn at the bottom of my wardrobe. Watson, did you notice it?" asked Holmes as we drove on our way.

"What is this about, Holmes?"

Holmes opened the top of the bag. Mollie peered over the side, then fell on her back as she tried to climb onto the carriage seat. For the next several days, Holmes hardly ever left the side of the mischievous kitten in the humble confines of our rooms.

I was often left with no occupation more pressing than to watch my companion dote on Mollie as she attacked a roll of yarn. Yet, it was my forehead she would pounce on in the still hours of the night and bat her claws into my nostrils. Mollie had grown attached to Holmes and after dinners would curl up in his lap as he read a Blue Book guide to cats he had secured inexpensively.

"My dear Holmes," I said at one point, "how long must *she* stay here while we attempt to concentrate on Dr. Lavey's case?"

"Watson, I am a little surprised at your impatience with the speechless creature. She has come very close to absolving your old friend of the grave charge of murder already."

Later that day, I sat with Sherlock Holmes at a fine restaurant he had pointed out in our guidebook among the elegant, tree-lined rows of aristocratic Boston. This outing took me quite by surprise, given my friend's thrifty tastes. Only once we were on our way there, did I realize he had carried Mollie with us in the green bag. I suggested that the restaurant would not permit her, and, even if we were to smuggle her inside, were she to begin meowing incessantly (as was her custom), we would be thrown out.

"I suppose you are correct, as this is not Paris, where they are permissive of animal companions," Holmes said. He tied a long ribbon he had in his pocket from her neck to a lamppost that could be seen from the restaurant's window. It was a rather strange sight, I suppose, to the American pedestrians. Shortly into our meal, two young women in expensive silk dresses stopped and reached down for Mollie, who backed away and looked coolly at them. After some unsuccessful inducements to prove their friendship, the women yielded. Later, as Holmes uncharacteristically ordered dessert, a more dramatic trial came for the poor creature. Two well-dressed boys began to throw rocks at her. Mollie cried out and tried to run toward the restaurant.

I rose from my chair and readied my walking stick as a weapon. To my surprise, Holmes did not stir.

"Holmes, would you allow such torment by those little devils?"

The imps now crossed to Mollie's side of the street, as their aim had been fortunately bad. Just as I was about to step into the fray, a hail of rocks flew at the perpetrators instead of the kitten. I craned my neck out the window and recognized three boys from Mrs. Smith's Kindness Club. Though they were smaller than Mollie's tormentors, they outnumbered the evildoers, successfully chasing them away and likely warning them never to harm helpless animals again without fearing their little club's vengeance.

"Do you not think it somewhat strange," I remarked when we exited, "those Kindness boys from Mrs. Smith's club would be in this part of the city!"

"I do not think it strange at all," replied Holmes, untying our little pet, and taking her up with one hand, "as I directed them to come. You must know I should want nothing to happen to our little colleague, Watson."

Leaving my companion afterwards, I visited my old friend Lavey, who was weeping with news that the prosecuting attorney brought the most severe counts against him in his indictment. He begged me to convince his jailers to allow me to administer medicine to him. By this, I knew, he meant his opium, as I watched him trembling, perspiring, and yawning uncontrollably.

Holmes, meanwhile, had spent the day in leisurely visits to scientific correspondents at the laboratories at the Massachusetts Institute of Technology and to the site near Harvard of the famous Parkman case. Knowing the remarkable character of Sherlock Holmes's mind, I had eliminated any doubt as to his commitment to Lavey's case. I was therefore not surprised upon returning to our lodging house when Holmes met me at the door and requested that I repair immediately to the police station and inform Detective Dugan that we wished to visit their prison in Charlestown in the morning. He also provided some particular requests for Dugan to fulfill for our arrival.

"Shall I tell him the purpose of all this, Holmes?" I asked.

"I see you wonder about my methods in this case, Watson. Were you to have considered the data and my actions at each step, you would cease to. Yet, your friendship with the suspected murderer has prevented that, I fancy, for you think about the welfare of the man, not about the logic of the crime, a fatal mistake that has reduced many a detective into a charitable worker. In this case the man was a simple clue, nothing more. As for Dugan, you may tell him that if he grants my peculiar wishes, I shall point out for him a brutal fugitive sought by the law across New England."

The next morning, we had no sooner arrived at the Charlestown prison than it was apparent to me that Dugan had carried out Holmes's requests with strict deference. Crowded into a small courtyard were no less than fifteen criminals guarded on all sides. Holmes, striding in, removed a lens from his pocket and examined their hands and arms as he walked. Without looking up at their faces, he stopped in front of a particular prisoner and waved for Dugan.

"Detective, what has this man been arrested for, and what does he claim as his name?" Holmes asked.

"Horse thievery, Mr. Holmes. His name is Julius McArthur, and he is serving two months."

"If I am not mistaken," replied Holmes, "you shall find McArthur a mere alias. His name is George Simpson, a murderer of a deputy sheriff in Brunswick, as well as a bigamist, a forger, and the true killer of Mary Painting—the housemaid you know as Mary Ann Pinton."

"Mary dead?" the man in question exploded at Holmes. "How could it be? I didn't mean to be rough, I only wanted her to come away with me! Mary, not my Mary!" he howled her name several more times as he fell to his knees and sobbed. Two prison guards ushered the pitiful beast away. I turned and stared at Holmes as did the detective. I could not, at that moment, remember him ever completing a case in so abrupt and unexpected a fashion as to locate the perpetrator already inside the walls of a prison!

"Why, Holmes, you have saved Lavey! But how is it you knew the girl's killer to be in this prison?" I asked. "And how, just by looking at the hands of this assortment of rascally men?"

"My dear Watson, you ask me to reveal my methods to an audience of eager ears in gray flannel who might put them to use. I have learned by telegram that we must soon depart at once for New York to attend to a grave affair with my old friend Hargreave. If Detective Dugan will accompany us on one final errand, I will happily explain the steps that have now brought a very bad fellow to justice. Detective, would you be kind enough?"

"I would not think of doing otherwise!" Dugan declared, still awestruck at the turn of events.

At Carver Street, we were ushered back into the parlor of Anna Harris Smith at the Animal Rescue League. I sat on an armchair with a cat as black as Poe's, the poor animal having been the victim of neglect but now recuperating nicely, while Detective Dugan shared the crimson sofa with the same lazy specimen of feline (who I now heard Mrs. Smith refer to as "Stuffy") who had been in that spot on our last visit.

"Mr. Holmes, I cannot wait a moment longer to hear!" Detective Dugan exclaimed with such fervor that even Stuffy seemed interested. Mrs. Smith stood to the side with a curious smile.

"Very well," said Holmes, placing down the green case. He opened the flap and our fluffy orange and white kitten, with the heterochromatic eyes, crawled out to check her surroundings.

"You know this kitten, Watson?" asked Holmes.

"Why, of course I do. It is our Mollie."

"The same dear kitten I saved from the residence of Dr. Lavey, and gave over to Mrs. Smith with my own hands," added Detective Dugan.

"Wrong," Holmes said.

Suddenly, a second orange and white kitten climbed into view from inside the bag. She was identical in every way, down to boasting one blue and one gray eye, though they had now switched places so that the blue was on the right and the gray on the left.

"Heavens above, Holmes! There are two of them. They are regular Dromios!" I cried, thinking of the dual figures in Shakespeare's *Comedy of Errors*, a production of which I had recently taken in with an artistic female friend at Terry's Theater, London.

"But what does this second cat have to do with the murder?" Dugan asked.

"Everything, my dear Detective!" Holmes answered. "When you

removed Mollie from the scene of the murder, Detective Dugan, you had unknowingly displaced the only revealing clue in the entire place. You shall see it for yourself. When I first heard that Mary had brought a young kitten into Dr. Lavey's home, I presumed at once that it was a gift someone had made to her. Mother cats are protective of their young, and do not part with their offspring willingly. A mother cat could meet with accident or malice, leaving her kittens behind, but the poor creatures in that circumstance will seldom survive a night, often contracting the diseases peculiar to their race or falling victim to other animals of the streets. So, the circumstances of Mary, not owning a cat, and then coming in possession of a healthy kitten, suggested that the animal had been presented to her from somewhere else."

"Yes, yes. That seems quite probable," Detective Dugan agreed.

Holmes continued. "Dr. Lavey, who had employed Mary for the last two years, said Mary never had visitors and had no signs of any friends or relatives. It might be noted that whenever a person seems to have no friends or relatives, the fact is almost surely just the opposite: that the person has friends or relatives of very formidable and oppressive natures whom the apparently lonesome soul wishes to avoid at all costs. It was a fact at hand that Mary had been distracted and depressed in recent weeks, which I surmised was a product of fearing the return of some old element in her life from which she was surely hiding. But to return to the kitten: I suspected that the gift was from one of the housemaid's supposedly nonexistent friends, perhaps one that Mary accidentally met while out in Boston. This feeling was confirmed when, taking possession of Mollie, I determined through a little research that she was a mix of an Angora and a Coon—two quite expensive and prized breeds of cat, often the winners, in fact, of the premium in recent years of Boston cat shows. It was sound logic that little Mollie had come, therefore, from a fashionable region of Boston, a suspicion made stronger upon

examining a map drawn up by Watson of the locations of Mary's errands in her final weeks. Choosing a place near where Mary had been
on an errand in the days before receiving the kitten, Dr. Watson will
now remember that we watched from a restaurant window as two young
women, aristocrats to the core, stopped at Mollie filled with surprise
and recognition. Their surprise was enhanced when Mollie behaved as
though she did not know them and had never before seen them. You
see, I counted on the fact that Mollie's mother had given birth to more
than one kitten and, hoping that at least some of the physical traits of
Mollie's brothers or sisters would be superficially similar, she would be
mistaken for having escaped from her home nearby.

"I had arranged for the services of several of Mrs. Smith's Kindness
Club boys to follow any persons who exhibited unusual interest in
the kitten while she remained tied on the street. This occurring, the
boys sent me back a note that night that the two fashionable young
Brahmins had knocked at a nearby mansion and saw to their surprise
this kitten, Miss Puff, Mollie's sister. I was fortunate, for the purposes
of my scheme, that this kitten was more remarkably like Mollie than I
could hope, and at a glance identical, except the colors of the eyes were
switched, which a person with no scholarship in optical matters would
rarely notice. Shown by a butler that Miss Puff was, in fact, sleeping
soundly by a breezy window, the girls were satisfied that they had been
mistaken in their recognition of the kitten at the lamppost. Now I knew
who had given Mollie to Mary Ann Pinton.

"Telephoning this woman, who had retired to a house by the shore
for the summer months, I inquired to whom she had given the second
kitten with prismatic eyes.

"'Why, to my poor dear friend Mary,' she said to me.

"'Forgive me, madam, I am a stranger here. Is it customary for a
woman of society to have a friend who is a housekeeper?'

"'No, Mr. Holmes, it is certainly not. Mary Painting was a school friend of mine when we were mere girls. We had all heard she had married and moved west. When I happened to see her on the street in the dress of a housemaid, my heart broke for her! She seemed aloof and nervous. My house girl, Betsy, said she had recognized the woman I had been speaking with from the intelligence office, and believed she kept a position with a Dr. Lavey over the last years. I thought having one of our beautiful kittens would bring her cheer.'

"'So you left Mollie the kitten for her?'

"'Not I, Mr. Holmes! That doctor resided in a neighborhood I do not dare enter myself without an acute loss of reputation. I had one of my domestics give her to Mary. Mollie, is that what she named her? Why, that sounds like a housemaid. Why not just name the poor thing Biddy!'

"From that point on, my path ahead to resolving Dr. Lavey's case was quite clear thanks to what Mollie's former owner had revealed. I consulted the city records and found that a Mary Painting had married one George Fitzbeck five years ago. The name immediately meant something to me. When I was in Maine last week, attending to personal affairs, I had read in the newspaper there about the fugitive George Smith who was wanted for murdering a deputy sheriff in Brunswick after a daring escape. Smith had been in prison there for bigamy and forgery, and had pretended to be insane so that he would be transferred to the asylum, where he easily managed an escape. The sheriff's men had found him with a stolen horse when Smith, without warning, fired from behind some rocks and blew off the deputy's head. The newspaper had listed several of Smith's aliases which included *Fitzbeck*.

"Whether or not Mary Painting knew what kind of man her lover was when she married him in her youth, we shall leave to the imagination. She moved with him out west, as her old Boston friends had correctly heard, where his criminal history records several outstanding warrants for horse theft in his youth and, later, for bigamy. When she recognized the extent of his character, or perhaps found out about his other wives, she returned to Boston and assumed a new name—Mary Ann Pinton—in order to hide. Penniless and likely disavowed long ago by her Boston family, she concealed herself in a humble station a universe away from her Beacon Hill girlhood, as a housemaid who told her employer she had never been married and had no family. There she remained safely hidden."

"Until Fitzbeck escaped," I said.

"Correct, Watson. Mary read of the escape and feared for her life. We have heard from Dr. Lavey that she had become distracted and emotionally shattered in the very weeks after his escape, and often locked herself in her room. Nor, we can safely imagine, did she feel she could tell Dr. Lavey without losing her station for lying about her history. Mary feared more than anything that her husband would find her, and she was right. Through means Detective Dugan may ascertain later in questioning the murderer, the fugitive discovered her whereabouts. Entering the house by the rear door, he found Mary in the kitchen. From Detective Dugan's accurate examinations of the injuries, I suspect Fitzbeck was attempting to convince her to leave with him, when she refused and tried to scream. He covered her face with his hand to stop her from screaming as he continued his attempt to persuade, but in her struggling against him his grip became harder, smothering her mouth and nose and suffocating her. When Dr. Lavey, in his habitual haze of opium, finally heard a noise and started down the stairs, the fugitive fled. The fugitive did not know he had just killed the girl, I might add."

"Astounding, Mr. Holmes! But how did you know the murderer would be found in our prison?" Detective Dugan asked.

"Quite easy, Detective Dugan. I assumed it was likely the ruffian waited near the house hoping to find a time to speak again with Mary. When he heard shouting for the police, he fell into a panic. It has been my longstanding observation that the instinct of even the hardened criminal when panicked returns to his earliest form of offense—in this case, horse theft. I knew from Mrs. Smith that, in addition to the usual work of the Boston police, the Animal Rescue League had begun to place a secret service of detectives around Boston to diminish the terrible effect of horse theft on the unwilling beasts. Therefore, I did not think it unlikely that by the morning, the stolen horse, if there were one, would have been traced to its captor. Now, Fitzbeck knows enough of police to know that if he resisted and was captured, he would be investigated closely and in all probability found to be a wanted fugitive. However, if he went quietly, protesting that he mistook the horse as his own, and giving a false name, he would be handed a perfunctory sentence of a few months. I telephoned the police in Maine to retrieve George Smith's Bertillon measurements, and then asked that Watson bring them to you with instructions to gather the prisoners that met those specifics."

"But Mr. Holmes, you were able to identify the murderer without looking at his face! I could hardly believe it!"

"Detective Dugan, I did this not to put on a spectacle, but because I knew nothing of what George Fitzbeck, or George Smith, looked like. A forger, by rule, is quite skilled at changing his appearance through small adjustments in habits of grooming and hygiene. However, knowing that he had fooled the police in Maine into transferring him to an insane asylum, I examined his hands and arms. Criminals wishing to appear insane will usually chew off their fingernails or make cuts across their wrists that appear to be suicidal marks but in fact remain superficial and harmless. These marks could not be concealed even three or four weeks later. Our man, I found, had both of these on him, and was taken in as a horse thief. Concluding that while in prison he had not yet heard that his encounter with Mary had left her dead, I counted on further confirmation of his identity on my mention of Mary's decease—as you saw with your own eyes."

"There is one point I don't understand," I interjected, turning to our hostess. "Mrs. Smith, when we arrived here you were quite adamant that a cat could not be taken out of this building unless it is to a permanent home. Yet, you allowed Mollie to come with us to be used as an accessory in this case."

"I am not deaf to reality, Dr. Watson," Mrs. Smith replied forth-rightly. "Our donations in these first months have been far more modest than we will need for our organization to survive more than a year. There are men and women standing high in religious and charitable enterprises who would celebrate our demise, who say that caring for animals is an affront when so much money is needed for men, women, and children. Even though when we receive a gift of one hundred dollars it is considered news, but if the new library or an institution of art receives ten thousand dollars, it is met with a shrug. But we will pass that by. Mr. Holmes assuring me that the League would be publicly credited with helping to save an innocent man from prison and capture a murderer, I agreed to his bargain. If the public can see the cause of an animal helping people, and the cause of people helping animals, we shall one day find our acceptance."

The two kittens, Miss Puff and Mollie, were now rolling around wildly and batting each other's heads with their paws. Mrs. Smith picked them up, one in each hand.

"I should think, Mrs. Smith, that Dr. Lavey will be quite pleased to take good care of Mollie, seeing that she helped save him from the gallows. And that his jail stay has released him from the demon grip of opium," Holmes said. "I shall make Mollie's good care our only fee to him for our services."

THE CASE OF THE RIVAL QUEENS
Carolyn Wheat

Carolyn Wheat's short stories have won her an Agatha, an Anthony, a Macavity, and a Shamus Award. Her book *How to Write Killer Fiction* (Perseverance Press, 2003) is a must-have addition to any writer's bookshelf. She teaches writing at the University of California, San Diego extension school and offers freelance editorial consulting services. She makes her home in San Diego and has added yoga and meditation to her teaching repertoire.

* * * *

The Hotel del Coronado's young bellboy was clearly overawed. Swallowing hard, he managed to squeak out the words, "Mr. Spalding would be grateful if you could spare him a moment, Mr. Holmes."

The mulish look on Holmes's face told me he had no intention of sparing Mr. Spalding, or anyone else, a moment. "We are here on holiday," he said curtly. "I do not wish to be disturbed." Holmes had taken against San Diego when he discovered that one of its more famous denizens, the legendary American lawman Wyatt Earp, had not gunned down evildoers in its city streets, but had instead opened an ice cream parlor. Holmes had formed his ideas of the American

West from the pages of dime novels and seemed affronted at every sign of gentility.

The boy said, "But it's Mr. *Spalding,* sir."

Holmes raised a single eyebrow. "I have no memory of that name," he said slowly, "which means Mr. Spalding is not a member of the criminal classes."

The boy gasped. I stifled a laugh and put an end to Holmes's ignorance. "In fact, Holmes, you have already made Mr. Spalding's acquaintance. Don't you remember the baseball game we saw in 1889? Mr. Spalding organized the tour and was the chief bowler. We were introduced to him at the reception following the game."

"Pitcher," the boy said with an air of reverence. "Mr. Spalding pitched for the Chicago White Stockings. He invented the Spalding twister." At our blank looks, he explained, "It's a curve ball. The batters never figured out how to hit it."

"A googly," I murmured. "I remember thinking the American game was faster than cricket. In fact, I thoroughly enjoyed our exposure to the American pastime."

"I vaguely recall some outlandish sporting event you insisted I attend with you," Holmes replied. He still lay at his ease on the chaise longue nearest the window, where the balmy Pacific breeze blew the sheer curtains to and fro. "I found it tedious in the extreme."

"Mr. Spalding is not only well known as a player," I said, realizing that I at least looked forward to meeting our visitor, "he is also the chief manufacturer of the balls used in the sport. He is, in short, a rich man and a leading citizen of San Diego."

"Very well, Watson," Holmes cried, leaping up from his place on the couch. "If it pleases you, we shall see this plutocrat." He exchanged his smoking jacket for proper afternoon wear and we made our way from our room to the magnificent Otis lift that would whisk us to the lobby floor. The Hotel del Coronado was as up to date as any resort in Europe, a fact that Holmes found intensely annoying, as he'd been looking forward to swinging saloon doors and sawdust on the floor. Ridiculous, of course, in the second year of the twentieth century.

A waiter led us through the wood-paneled lobby to the terrace where tea was being served. It was open to the ocean breeze and looked out over the Pacific. I wondered at first that we were not shown to the bar, and then realized the reason: Mr. Spalding had brought his wife. Albert Spalding was a solid man with a bushy moustache and hair parted in the center. He wore a black suit with a high collar and a thickly knotted tie. His wife wore a walking suit of lavender festooned with ecru lace. Together they looked the picture of well-to-do American respectability.

We made introductions and ordered tea. I mentioned the historic baseball game in which I had seen Spalding play. He nodded perfunctorily, as if to indicate that sport was the furthest thing from his mind.

"Mr. Holmes," he began after his wife had poured tea into each cup, "I am here on a matter of utmost importance. I would not dream of interrupting your holiday for anything less, I assure you. At first, I thought the matter was, well, a figment of my wife's imagination, but of late I have come to agree with her. Something is amiss at the Brotherhood."

"The Brotherhood?" Holmes looked as puzzled as I felt.

Spalding opened his mouth to reply, but his wife's words came first. "The Universal Brotherhood and Theosophical Society," she explained in a loud voice that would have been more appropriate on the lecture circuit. "Albert and I live on the grounds. I am very active in the Society."

I had heard that a branch of the Theosophical Society made its home in San Diego. Strands of gossip, such as one overhears in hotels, came back to me. "Godless heathens," I'd heard a woman say of the colony on Point Loma, "all dressed in white, dancing under the trees, speaking Greek."

I realized I'd stopped listening and came back to Mrs. Spalding's penetrating voice. "There have been incidents undermining Mrs. Tingley's excellent administration," she said. "Heinous acts designed to ruin the Brotherhood and bring disgrace to our Society. First, it was the silkworms, then the avocados, and finally, the disappearance of the queens."

I was about to ask what an avocado was when Spalding said, "I cannot agree with you about the silkworms, Elizabeth. I'm afraid they committed suicide. But those honeybees," he added in a firm voice. "I'd stake my life those bees were murdered."

I dared not look at Holmes. I had persuaded him to see the Spaldings, and now we were trapped at a tea table with two mad people.

To my surprise, the look on Holmes's face was one of rapt interest. "This Brotherhood," he asked. "Is it anything at all like the Mormons of Salt Lake?" Holmes had a fascination for secret societies and arcane religions, particularly those that found a congenial home in the former colonies.

Spalding hastened to reassure us that male Theosophists were content with a single wife. Mrs. Spalding added, "The chief goal of the Brotherhood is spiritual education, Mr. Holmes. We maintain a very successful school called the Raja Yoga Academy, and Mrs. Tingley has plans to open a college for the Revival of Lost Mysteries." She said the last with capital letters, and I sensed an excitement in Holmes. Perhaps this exotic Brotherhood would make up for the regrettable lack of gunfights.

Her husband continued the theme. "The Brotherhood has pioneered modern farming methods in California, Mr. Holmes," Spalding said. "We have a thriving apiary, and we are experimenting with the use of honeybees to pollinate avocado trees. It is most unfortunate that our experiment was undermined, as I am certain we would have revolutionized the burgeoning industry."

"Tell me more," Holmes said, choosing a tea sandwich and leaning back in his chair, clearly prepared to be entertained by our visitors. "I remember as a boy spending hours watching the bees on my grandfather's smallholding. Bees are fascinating creatures, are they not, Watson?"

I had few opinions on the subject of bees and had never heard Holmes speak of them before. He seldom mentioned his boyhood and I found myself wishing he would reveal a bit more to his biographer.

The Spaldings took turns explaining that they suspected a prominent member of the Theosophical Brotherhood of deliberately undermining the avocado experiment and the excellent apiary, which provided the group with a tidy profit as well as supplying honey and beeswax to the community.

"And I'm convinced she killed the silkworms, too," Elizabeth Spalding said with a stubborn set to her mouth.

"Silkworms are delicate creatures, my dear," her husband replied in a mild tone. "Give them one brown mulberry leaf, and they die. Let the temperature drop by one single degree, and they die. We are not the only community that has failed to bring the silk industry to these shores. I hardly think Mrs. Imbler can be blamed for the silkworms."

"Mrs. Imbler is the lady you suspect?" Holmes asked.

"She is the chief beekeeper," Spalding said. "It would be the easiest thing in the world for her to destroy the hives upon which our avocados depended."

"But why would she destroy the hives?" I asked.

Mrs. Spalding leaned forward in her chair and opened her blue eyes wide. "She wants to supplant Mrs. Tingley. I'm certain of it. She has made cutting remarks about the way things are run and hints that she could do better. She has even dared to challenge Mrs. Tingley on matters of Theosophical thought." She lowered her voice and almost whispered, "I fear for her life, Mr. Holmes. It pains me to say it, but I fear for Mrs. Tingley's very life."

This struck me as a wild exaggeration, but Holmes seemed entertained by the prospect of a visit to the Theosophists' frontier utopia, so we agreed to set off the next morning.

We could see the outline of Point Loma from the pavilion at the Hotel del Coronado. It was a peninsula that jutted out from the mainland and curved southward like the trunk of an elephant. Our peninsula, Coronado, was the bulbous end of a long narrow sand spit nestled under the elephant's trunk. Between Point Loma and Coronado, a sparkling bay separated the two land masses and opened out to the Pacific.

Our trip from Coronado to Point Loma required a train, a ferry, and a hired hack.

We bumped along a winding, dusty road in an open carriage drawn by a plodding horse, passing few cottages, several species of cacti, and huge swaths of scrubland. On the way, our driver regaled us with stories about Lomaland, as he called the Theosophical colony.

"Children torn from their parents, brought up by strangers," he'd said, in between copious spittings of tobacco juice. "The parents worship Hindu gods. But that's not the worst of it, sirs," he said, lowering his voice. "It's run by women, run by the Purple Mother, so called because she dresses in purple robes like a pagan priestess. It would be a disgrace—if it wasn't such a popular tourist attraction." He said the last with a tobacco-stained grin, and I realized with a start that we were no longer the only conveyance on the road. In the distance, charabancs and public omnibuses, filled with chattering visitors, stood in a line awaiting entrance.

"Some of them are staying at Camp Karnak," the driver said, and explained that the Society operated a tent city similar to the one next to the Hotel del Coronado. I marveled at the ingenuity of these Americans, who offered lodging at budget rates to travelers who enjoyed the same magnificent views and ocean breezes as the wealthy, the only difference being sleeping under canvas instead of a roof.

Beyond the line of carriages, I could see a sliver of the blue Pacific. The carriages entered the grounds through a magnificent gate decorated in Egyptian motifs. To our right, inside the gate, several large white buildings with colored domes gleamed in the bright California sun. One dome was covered in purple tile, another in aquamarine. Atop the domes were smaller globes of tinted glass. It was a fairyland, reminiscent of the Royal Pavilion at Brighton, where I'd been taken on holiday as a child. I wondered what it was about the seaside that brought out the fanciful in architects.

The cabbie stopped the hack at the gate and asked directions to the Spalding house. The guard pointed to a structure I'd taken for one of the temples. Like the largest building, it had a purple dome topped with a purple glass globe; it also boasted a circular staircase on the outside of the building next to a portico. Spalding was, I decided, the most uxorious man I'd ever met. Few husbands would have indulged a wife to the extent of living in such a monstrosity.

The cabbie pulled in the reins with a flourish next to a walkway lined with stone urns filled with geraniums. I alighted and knocked on the front door, noting the lavender stained glass blocks in the upper section of the windows. A servant answered, and before I could announce myself, she welcomed us and bade the driver bring in our Gladstone bags.

Inside, the sun's brightness was muted, and the large circular foyer glowed pale amethyst from the purple glass. Exotic bas-relief carvings decorated the columns in the foyer, which was circular and dominated by the rise of the dome.

Mrs. Spalding appeared on the landing and beckoned us upstairs to our rooms. We cleaned the dust of our journey from our persons and clothing and accepted our hostess's offer of a light lunch with Mrs. Tingley. We were to meet the Purple Mother in the flesh.

Katherine Tingley was a formidable woman in her early fifties, although she stood a mere five feet two in height. She had raven hair, large dark eyes, a determined chin, and the firm voice of a captain of industry. She was not dressed in purple, but wore a perfectly proper Nile-green dress with a double ruffle at the throat. I smiled; my fiancée would have told me the ruffles were a deliberate attempt to soften the air of command, to add a feminine touch to Mrs. Tingley's masculine directness. I wondered whether Holmes, unblessed by feminine confidences, would draw the same conclusion.

"I am delighted to make your acquaintance, Mr. Holmes," the Theosophist said. "And yours, too, of course, Dr. Watson. I have enjoyed reading your accounts of Mr. Holmes's amazing deductive feats."

I made the proper murmurs of self-deprecation, but I felt a glow of pride that my writings should be known in the hinterlands.

We did not speak of the problems at Lomaland. Instead, Mrs. Tingley turned to Holmes and said, "I understood from Dr. Watson's accounts of your adventures that you are a man who appreciates music. I should like you to know that at Point Loma music is regarded as much more than an amusement. It is a part of life itself, and it is one of those subtle forces of nature which, rightly applied, calls into activity the divine powers of the soul. Do you not agree, Mr. Holmes?"

Holmes did agree, warmly, and soon he was listening with great attention and respect to the methods of musical education employed at the Raja Yoga Academy. Only after the remains of our light luncheon were cleared away did the talk turn to the reason we had come. Mrs. Tingley said in her firm voice that she was grateful to the Spaldings for inviting Holmes to protect her, but that she had full confidence in Grace Imbler, the head beekeeper. "Indeed, she has promised me a treat tomorrow—fresh honey in the comb. We pasteurize most of our honey, but honeycomb is a special favorite of mine, and she always saves me some before she bottles the rest for the kitchen and the store."

We stepped away from the lunch table, thanked the Spaldings, and stepped out onto the circular porch. Down the steep, chaparral-overgrown canyon, a sliver of beach received silver-capped waves.

"I am eager to show you our community, Mr. Holmes," Mrs. Tingley said. "I think you will find it to your taste as a man of intellectual pursuits." Mrs. Tingley walked toward a large square building that from a distance looked like marble, but was wood covered in white stucco. Three smaller domes rose from the towered corners, and the edifice was topped by a huge aquamarine dome some three hundred feet in circumference.

"We call this the Homestead," she told us. "It is our headquarters. The small round building is our Temple." The Temple was no less impressive, and boasted two tiers of Greek columns, crowned by a spacious dome of amethyst.

Music sounded in the distance, but strange and discordant. I asked Mrs. Tingley about it and she smiled. "Our practice rooms," she explained. "Our students practice together, but they do not always play the same pieces. It is part of their discipline, to play their own music without allowing themselves to be distracted by their fellows."

I glanced at Holmes. A slight frown between his eyes gave evidence that he was disconcerted by the cacophony. What sort of music would the students play if they practiced in such chaos?

Children, young and old, passed us by, the younger ones walking in neat rows, attended by adults I assumed were teachers. They wore uniforms similar to those worn by any schoolchild, and I found myself almost disappointed that they were not in togas or saris or something equally outlandish.

Mrs. Tingley made up for the conventional costumes by referring to the young pupils as "Lotus Buds." Holmes's thin lips twitched in a near smile.

We learned that the small round buildings with mushroom-cap roofs were Lotus Houses, where the children lived. They did indeed live apart from their parents, who could visit them on weekends. This struck me far more humane than the British tradition of sending children as young as six to boarding schools several hundred miles from home.

We walked west, in the direction of the privately operated tent city. The land was hilly, and large canyons covered in scrub opened the vista to the sea. In the distance, I could see small white boxes and a larger whitewashed building without decorative accents. Next to me, Holmes pointed and said, "The apiary, I presume."

I was surprised and then realized I'd been visualizing the beehives of my youth, the moundlike skeps made of hay that dotted the English countryside.

"Nothing we do here is done purely for the sake of commerce," Mrs. Tingley said as we continued strolling along the bluff. "Our bee farm is not merely a source of honey, but also of inspiration. The bees have much to teach humanity about the virtues of cooperation and hard work."

She stopped walking and said, "This is where I live. I have some correspondence I must attend to. I will leave you to meet Mrs. Imbler on your own. Follow the path just past the theatre."

My eyebrows must have gone up, for Mrs. Tingley said, with more than a touch of pride, "We have just built the first Greek theatre in the New World, Dr. Watson."

Not only a theatre, but a Greek theatre! I saw wooden benches cut into the hillside, focused on a small flat patch of ground that served as a stage. I could not but marvel at the sight of an open-air theatre in the ancient Greek mode sitting on land once occupied by red Indians.

Holmes and I bade farewell to Mrs. Tingley, who went into her house, a much more modest affair than the Spalding mansion, and we made our way down the hill toward the neat rows of white boxes to meet the lady who might or might not be plotting Mrs. Tingley's demise.

As we drew closer, we smelled an overpowering sweetness in the air. Holmes remarked, "This must be the honey house" and strode forward to knock on the door.

Mrs. Imbler, a stout lady whose face and arms were brown from the intense sun, opened the door a fraction and peered out at us. She seemed distracted and not particularly pleased to have visitors, but she invited us inside after Holmes mentioned the magic name of Tingley. With forced good grace, Mrs. Imbler showed us how she used a heated knife to cut through the beeswax, and extract the honey, which drained into a can below the table. Heat would be applied to separate honey from melted wax and keep the honey from granulating. It was clear she'd given this tour before, but equally clear that she wanted to cut it short and send us on our way.

"I'm about to open the hives and check on my queen larvae," she said. "Queen work is the most exacting part of bee culture." Her tone said she would much rather perform these duties in solitude.

"I'm told beekeeping is farming for the literary soul," Holmes remarked. "Indeed, I recall reading about honeybees in Virgil's Fourth Georgic at school."

A thin-lipped smile graced Mrs. Imbler's weathered face. "In the first place, Mr. Holmes, no one really 'keeps' bees. Bees deign to live in our hives and allow us to steal some of their honey, but they are far from domesticated. In the second place, your Virgil was quite wrong when he wrote of 'kings' and 'warriors' in the hive. The queen rules the colony, and all the workers are female."

Mrs. Imbler seemed to come to a decision about our presence. She reached for one of the veiled beekeepers hats, which hung from wooden pegs on the wall nearest the door. She put it on and offered two others to Holmes and me. We put the hats on and secured the netting at chest-height with a strap. Mrs. Imbler took the extra precaution of putting on heavy gloves that reached to her elbow. She picked up an odd-looking metal canister with a bellows at one end and a conelike protrusion over the top. Smoke emerged from the cone. In her other hand, she held a long rectangular piece of metal.

"Come along," she said briskly and opened the door.

We stepped from the dimness of the honey house into the sun. Through the veil, the sharp-edged landscape took on a gauzy, painterly tone. It was as if a gentle fog had descended over Point Loma. I decided I liked the muted landscape better than the harsh one revealed by the California sun. Mrs. Imbler led the way toward the neat rows of white-painted boxes that lay nestled at the bottom of the canyon, about fifty feet from the water's edge. As we approached the hives, the sound of buzzing filled my ears. It was an otherworldly sound, and I found myself unable to conjure up a comparison. It was as loud as a foghorn on the Thames, as menacing as a tiger's roar, as angry as a raging mob. The hairs on the back of my head stood up, and I felt a fear so primitive that it shocked me.

I stopped. "Are you certain it is safe for us to proceed?" I had no wish to appear a coward, but neither did I fancy being stung by the thousands of little warriors that circumnavigated the hives.

"It is never safe," the beekeeper replied, and I sensed a smile I could not see through the thick veil. "The bees will die in defense of their hive and their queen. They see us as the enemy, and because we are bent on having their honey, they are right. We tend them, and then we rob them. That is the cruel reality of bee culture."

Holmes stepped closer to the buzzing hive and seemed to take a great interest in the worker bees flying to and fro. Several of them seemed to be engaged in what would be called a scuffle, had the participants been human. They zoomed and darted, thrust and parried, like guards repelling an assault. I said as much, and Mrs. Imbler remarked, "You are quite right, Doctor. These bees will repel any intruders who come from other hives to steal the honey."

"How can they tell these bees are intruders?" I wondered. "There must be thousands of bees in each hive."

"There are nearly fifty thousand at the height of the season," the beekeeper said. "And the bees know their own through scent, although they have no olfactory organs such as we would recognize."

The hives were tall rectangular boxes with three sections. The bees made their way in and out through a slit at the bottom. Mrs. Imbler explained that the top box was where the honey was stored, the middle box was where the bees kept the pollen they fed their larvae, and the bottom box was where the queen lived and laid her eggs.

"There is but one queen to a hive," she said, "and she is the only fertile female. There are a few drones, kept for mating with the queen, but they are driven from the hive at the end of mating season when they are no longer needed."

"It is a cruel society," Holmes murmured.

"Nature itself is cruel, Mr. Holmes," the beekeeper replied. "It is survival of the fittest."

Mrs. Imbler stepped toward one of the boxes, and I saw what the canister was for. She applied pressure to the bellows, and smoke emerged from the conical top of the device. Smoke encircled the hive, and the bees all flew inside.

"The bees believe their hive is on fire," the beekeeper said. "They are going inside to save their most precious asset: the honey. They will drink their fill and then come outside again, only they will be too heavy with honey to fight us."

I glanced at Holmes. I could not see his expression underneath the veil, but I knew he must have been thinking of the late Irene Adler, whom he had smoked out of her home, and who had also taken her most precious possession with her.

Mrs. Imbler walked behind the hive and motioned us to follow her. "Never stand in the way of the bees," she advised. "Always open the hive from behind." She set down the smoker and lifted the metal tool. She wedged it under the top of the hive and levered the top off. Bees streamed out the bottom of the box, but there were many more left inside, squirming and jostling one another. Mrs. Imbler lifted the top box and set it on the ground. Golden honey glistened in the sun, dripping from hundreds of six-sided combs.

Beside me, Holmes stood poised in what I began to realize was quivering excitement. "It is a city," he murmured. "A city as complex as London, with a hierarchy of work and government and productivity. Tell me," he said, eagerness in his tone, "how do the bees communicate? How do they know what to do, where to go?"

"You have put your finger on the great mystery, Mr. Holmes," Mrs. Imbler replied. "No one knows how bees do what they do. All we know is that they are able to communicate quite complex messages to one another, and that somehow the queen is the center of that communication network. She gives orders that are followed as far as five miles away—but exactly how she conveys her wishes is not scientifically established as yet."

As she spoke, Mrs. Imbler lifted the second box off the stack and set it on the ground. More bees tumbled over one another in writhing profusion inside the wax cells of the honeycomb. Several flew in my direction, and I lifted my arms to swat them away, and then blushed as I remembered the veil's protection.

She directed our attention to the third, lowest box. "Here is the birthing chamber," she explained. Holmes leaned in to look closer. I did not care to crowd him, so I stood back a few steps.

"Those little grains of rice," he asked, "are those the larvae?"

"Yes," the beekeeper said. "They will become workers or drones. They will make their way into the cells of the comb when it is time for their metamorphosis."

"Which is the queen?" I asked.

To my surprise, it was Holmes who answered. He pointed to a space deep within the box and said, "There. She is longer than the others and she has three black stripes on her back."

"However could you tell?" I asked. "They all look alike to me."

"It is a matter of seeing the anomaly," Holmes replied. "I could not have picked out the queen had she been alone, but I could see that one bee was not exactly like all the others. She is not only larger, but also more purposeful, and the other bees are crowded around, tending her. She did not fit the pattern."

Mrs. Imbler's response was tinged with something like respect. "You have the makings of a bee master, Mr. Holmes." She pointed to a section of the comb that contained closed-over cells, some of which bulged out like miniature wasps' nests.

"That is where the new queens are hatching," she said. "They are fed with a substance called royal jelly. The hive feeds several larvae, so there will be a new one when this one dies. The first to hatch will immediately kill all her rivals. There can only be one queen to a hive."

On that ominous note, we took our leave and asked directions to the avocado groves. They lay a hot and dusty distance from the main beehives, and I was perspiring freely by the time we arrived at the stand of glossy trees. As yet, I had learned nothing that justified our visit to this improbable place, but Holmes seemed to be enjoying himself.

Avocados, I learned, were alligator pears, and were particularly suited to the California climate. The trees were large and had thick spreading branches and dark green leaves that created a welcome shade in the burning sun. A small gardeners' shed stood at the edge of the grove. As we approached, the door opened and out stepped a wiry little man with ginger hair and a ginger moustache. He introduced himself as Jonas Imbler.

We must have looked startled, and I hastened to explain that we had just met Mrs. Imbler. The little man said, "My wife. We had a small bee farm in Alpine before we came here, but Mrs. Tingley believes that beekeeping is women's work, so my wife tends to the hives while I manage the avocados."

Holmes went straight to the point. "We were informed that you had a bit of bad luck with your pollination experiment."

Imbler motioned toward a beehive that stood between the avocado groves and the bluff overlooking the canyon. "I thought surely the bees would pollinate the trees better than any horticulturist could possibly do by hand."

"What happened?"

"The queen died," Imbler said shortly. "And when the queen dies, the bees get dispirited. They behave like rudderless ships, aimless."

"They no longer pollinate," Holmes said, "because without larvae, they have no need of pollen. Pollen is food for the larvae."

Imbler nodded. "You know your bees, Mr. Holmes. The queen is all in all to the hive. She is their reason for living, the beacon around which they all swarm and gather. Not unlike our own Mrs. Tingley." This last was said with a sly little wink, as if he'd made a mildly risqué joke. The image of Katherine Tingley sitting inside a giant beehive, surrounded by buzzing insects, was one I had no desire to contemplate. And yet, gazing around the peaceful grounds and remembering the white-clad students walking to and fro, I could not help but see Mr. Imbler's point. But for the queen, the hive would die. But for Mrs. Tingley, what would happen to the good people of Lomaland?

And yet, we had no evidence that anything of the sort was being contemplated. A dead queen bee and a dead Mrs. Tingley were two very different things.

The next day, Spalding surprised me by offering me a round of golf. The hilly desert landscape struck me as a highly unlikely place for the Scottish sport, but he assured me that his private course was as challenging as, and far more interesting than, any I had experienced before. Holmes encouraged me to play, suggesting that his day would be spent more profitably, perhaps, but with considerably less enjoyment.

The nine-hole golf course sat on the eastern edge of the colony. The putting greens, their emerald grass well tended and heavily watered lay amid roughs that were rougher than anything found in Europe. Stray balls hid behind cacti, rolled down the canyon, lodged in twisted branches of mesquite, and seemed bent on defying all attempts to get them safely onto the minuscule patches of grass. It was a most enjoyable game, and I thanked my lucky stars I had chosen to leave Holmes to the bees.

At the close of the game, I thanked Spalding and went in search of Holmes. I found him in the avocado grove gazing through his binoculars at the neat white beehives. The intense blue of the sky and the waves and the strong sun bouncing off the white buildings were almost painful to the eyes.

Suddenly Holmes turned and darted off in the direction of the Spalding house. I followed hastily and caught up with him just as he reached the porch. I followed him through the front door and into the kitchen. He took a wooden bowl, opened a sack of flour, and dusted the sides of the bowl. He opened the pantry, removed a jar of honey with the Lomaland label, and spooned a glob into the center of the bowl.

"Come, Watson," Holmes said, his eyes alight with the fervor of the chase. "Let us track our murderess."

Mystified, I followed as Holmes strode, bowl in hand, toward the North House, in the opposite direction to the hives. When we reached a bed of blue Nile lilies, he set the bowl on the ground near the flowers and motioned me to join him some several feet away. I watched as bees landed in the bowl and edged toward the glob of golden honey.

One of the bees, having drunk its fill, landed on one of the flowers. It rested there a moment and then moved off and flew in its drunken way to the next.

The look on Holmes's face was one I had never seen before. It held all the suppressed excitement I knew from past adventures, yet there was something alight in his eyes. I fancied I had a glimpse of the youthful Holmes studying bees on his grandfather's land. It stood to reason that a man of scientific bent had once been a boy of scientific bent.

We waited for about ten minutes as bees came and went. Finally, Holmes crouched closer to the flowering shrub and examined a bee that sat on a blossom. I looked closely, too, and realized that its underside bore a coating of white. The flour! This was a bee that had sampled honey from Holmes's bowl. Had it returned to the hive with its load of nectar and come back to this flower for more? And what did Holmes hope to learn from watching its progress?

When the flour-marked bee tired of this stand of blossoms, it zigzagged its way to the beds beside one of the Lotus Houses. Holmes picked up his bowl and moved it to an area four feet to the east of the flowerbed.

With each successive movement of the bowl, we moved further and further away from the Point Loma apiary in an easterly direction. Looking closely, I could see that now several of the bees wore white flour stockings on their little legs.

Following honeybees proved to be a tedious activity. We waited for the return of the flour-dusted bees to our little trap, and Holmes smiled when they brought others to feed on the glob of honey. At last we reached the end of the cultivated Lomaland grounds and entered the scrub wilderness at the edge of the settlement. We were heading away from the ocean and toward the mainland from which the elephant's trunk of Point Loma jutted. I trudged after Holmes with a thousand questions in my mind. Something pink in the distance resolved itself into a magnificent stand of rosebay bushes. Their pink blooms and dark leaves glowed in the strong afternoon sunlight. I marveled at the sight; everything else around us was scrub. Someone must have brought water to these flowers—but who and why? There was no habitation that I could see nearby.

Holmes raced toward the bushes as if Moriarty himself could be found at their center. I puffed as I ran alongside my friend, the pain in my leg growing sharper with every step. The heat of the day, combined with my English tweeds, produced a flood of perspiration that dripped from my forehead.

"Surely, there is no need for this immoderate haste," I said at last, bringing my gait to an exhausted walk.

Holmes slowed his step, but only slightly. "As to the need for haste," he replied, "I will not be certain about that until I find what I am looking for."

"And what," I puffed through gasps of breath, "is that?"

"Beehives," he said as he plunged into the wall of bushes, heedless of the hundreds of bees buzzing around the pink flowers.

"But, Holmes," I protested. "We know where the hives are." I gestured in the direction of the rows of white boxes, some two miles to the west.

As I pushed aside a heavy-laden branch, a bee buzzed at my face. I brushed it aside, and then realized my mistake. "Oh, I see," I said. "You mean there could be a natural hive out here."

Holmes's answer was grim. "There is nothing natural about this hive, Watson, or about the placement of it among these particular trees."

The blooms were lovely, the shade ranging from palest to deepest pink, the masses of flowers hanging with heavy profusion upon the dark-leaved branches. Rosebay, a lovely spring bloom, also known as—

"Oleander," I said aloud. My eyes opened wide; I understood Holmes's urgency. "One of the most poisonous plants known to man."

"Indeed," Holmes said. I could hear him ahead of me in the overgrown grove. I followed his voice and step, making my way through thick branches and increasingly agitated bees.

"Aha," he said at last. "Come quick, Watson."

I pushed aside the last branches and found myself in a small clearing. In the center, a large hollow tree stump buzzed with insect life.

"Honey made from oleander nectar will be as poisonous as the plant itself," Holmes said. "The keeper of this rogue hive made certain these bees would feed on oleander by locating the hive here."

Holmes took two steps toward the tree stump. I took two steps back. The honeybees, already agitated by strangers in their midst, buzzed loudly and menacingly. I felt a sharp stab of pain along the side of my neck and slapped at it automatically. "I've been stung," I cried.

"As have I, several times," Holmes replied. "It is the occupational hazard of the beekeeper."

Holmes inched closer and closer to the hive, and the bees, sensing danger, began to swarm around the hive and Holmes. Soon, he seemed enveloped in a cloud of angry, buzzing insects.

Bees were everywhere, crawling inside the hollow log. Holmes, brave as ever, crept closer to the hive and peered in. He shielded his face from the bees with his handkerchief, but I could see that this was wholly insufficient to guard him from stings.

He raised his head, and the look on his face chilled my blood. "The honeycomb is gone," he said. "There is no time to lose."

I understood at once. Mrs. Tingley had expressed a preference for honey straight from the comb. She might be eating her deadly treat at this very moment.

We were both stung over and over again as we fled the oleander grove and made our way as fast as we could back toward the colony.

Once back inside the Lomaland grounds, Holmes stopped the first person we saw, a young woman carrying a book. "Do you know where Mrs. Tingley is at this moment?"

"I believe she is taking tea at her house."

By the time we arrived at Mrs. Tingley's modest cottage, we were very much out of breath. Holmes flung open the door and we raced through the foyer and found Mrs. Tingley sitting with the Spaldings at a tea table on the rear porch.

In front of her sat a plate with a dripping honeycomb on it. She had lifted her spoon and was about to plunge it into the comb when Holmes whisked the plate away from her.

She raised an eyebrow and said, "What is the meaning of this, Mr. Holmes? I am quite looking forward to my little treat."

"This treat would be your last, Mrs. Tingley," Holmes said. "This comb is not from the hives Mrs. Imbler tends. Instead, it comes from a hive hidden deep inside an oleander grove. This honey is poisonous."

"I knew it!" Elizabeth Spalding said. Her plate contained bread and jam, no honey. "I knew I was right to bring Mr. Holmes here. He has saved you from that presumptuous beekeeper."

"But would this honey really have killed me, Mr. Holmes?" Mrs. Tingley asked. She seemed almost amused at the prospect of having nearly eaten it.

"It is not unknown for honey to be tainted with the nectar of whatever plants the bees feed upon," Holmes pointed out. "Cases have been documented in Greece and New Zealand. Those poisonings were, of course, accidental, but one who knows the principles of bee culture could easily arrange for his hive to feed upon poison flowers. Such was the case with Jonas Imbler."

I started, as did Mrs. Spalding. "*Jonas* Imbler?" she said with a gasp. "But surely it was Grace Imbler who wanted Mrs. Tingley gone."

"No, madam, your suspicions of Mrs. Imbler are quite unfounded. She did not create the rogue hive in the oleander bushes. Her husband, who is also a skilled beekeeper, did."

"Holmes," I protested, "you distinctly said you were hunting a murderess. Did you mislead me on purpose?"

He smiled. "I was referring to the bee. The workers are female; the workers made this honey; ergo, the workers are murderesses. Q.E.D."

"But why?" Albert Spalding protested. "Imbler has shown no interest in Theosophy and would never wish to become head of the

Brotherhood. What reason could he possibly have for murdering Mrs. Tingley?"

For once, I had an answer at the same time as Holmes. He opened his mouth to explain, but I found my voice first. "Not all husbands are as tolerant as you, Mr. Spalding," I said. "You are content to live here on Point Loma because your wife is a part of this community. You busy yourself with your golf and your civic activities and you are happy here. It was clear to me at our meeting that Jonas Imbler felt very differently. He chafed under the rule of a woman. He resented his wife's commitment to the Brotherhood and her responsibility for the beehives."

Holmes nodded and picked up the rest of the tale. "The bees failed to pollinate the avocado trees because their queen was gone," he explained. "Queenless bees cannot survive. They were queenless because Jonas Imbler removed the queen to start his rogue hive in the oleander grove. The sabotage of the pollination experiment was a mere byproduct of his larger scheme to murder Mrs. Tingley. Without her, he felt sure the Society would fail and his wife would be willing to leave Lomaland."

"It seems a strange way to commit murder, Mr. Holmes," Mrs. Tingley said. "Surely there are more straightforward methods available to one who is determined to kill another human being. Poisoned honey seems rather a roundabout way to do it."

"Roundabout, yes," Holmes replied, with a small smile. "But for Jonas Imbler, it had the virtue of poetic justice. He saw you, Mrs. Tingley, as the queen bee of Lomaland, and he felt that one queen deserved death at the hands of another."

Mrs. Spalding's face continued to wear its stubborn look. "How can you be sure," she asked, "that Mrs. Imbler was not her husband's willing accomplice?"

Holmes shook his head. "I am convinced that Mrs. Imbler knew nothing of her husband's activities. She might be capable of murder; I believe most people are. But she would never use her bees as weapons. She has far too much respect for them. It would be," he added, turning to me, "as if our own Mrs. Hudson were to put poison into her breakfast porridge."

I hastily agreed that this was not to be contemplated. I could see that Mrs. Spalding was not mollified, but Mrs. Tingley nodded her agreement.

"The soul is not invisible, Mr. Holmes," she pronounced. "It reveals itself in our every waking action. And Mrs. Imbler has shown me a soul devoted to order and peace. Her well-tended hives are her character reference."

We stayed one more night with the Spaldings before returning to the Hotel del Coronado. It was a night of sheer magic, for the magnificent orchestra played exquisitely as the sun lowered itself into the Pacific and the lights went on, one by one, inside the glass globes over the domes of Lomaland.

I stole a glance at Holmes. He was entranced by the music, and I saw another glimpse of the child he had once been as I watched a tall, slender boy of about twelve raise his violin to his chin and draw his bow across it.

THE ADVENTURE OF THE MISSING THREE QUARTERS
Jon L. Breen

Jon L. Breen, the winner of two Edgar Awards in the biographical/ critical category, has contributed to six previous Sherlock Holmes anthologies. He is the author of eight novels, including the Dagger Award–nominated *Touch of the Past*, and around a hundred short stories. His reviews appear regularly in *Ellery Queen's Mystery Magazine* and *Mystery Scene*, and frequently (and non-politically) in *The Weekly Standard*. His latest books are the comic courtroom novel *Probable Claus* (Five Star) and *A Shot Rang Out: Selected Mystery Criticism* (Surinam Turtle).

* * * *

Although I was a freelance American correspondent for several English newspapers, joining the crowds of ink-stained wretches attending the latest famous personality's arrival in Chicago was never part of my usual regimen. So it was purely by chance that autumn afternoon in 1907 that I was at Grand Central Station on West Harrison Street to see Sherlock Holmes's unheralded arrival. I had known him years before, and apart from my pleasure at seeing him again, I had hopes of an exclusive story to impress my Fleet Street masters.

"Clive Armitage, Mr. Holmes. We met—"

"I remember you well, Armitage, and I am pleased to greet a fellow Londoner. You are fully Americanized, I see."

"It's true I've been here several years now, and some say I'm developing an American accent, though I can't hear it myself. Why do you think me Americanized?"

"Your tiepin and cufflinks identify you as member of some sort of baseball supporters club, and the handle of your walking stick depicts an ornate American eagle. You appear to be chewing gum, a habit that has not yet infected British journalists in my experience."

"A representative of the Wrigley Company gave me some samples when I was working on a feature article about them," I said somewhat defensively. "Wrigley is something of a Chicago success story, and I was assured their products will one day span the globe, so be warned." Then, like a thespian belatedly remembering his lines, I exclaimed, "That was a truly amazing demonstration of your undiminished powers." It wasn't actually so amazing once he explained it, but I was not above flattery in search of a journalistic coup. "When I came to America, I feared I would miss reading about your adventures in *The Strand*, but *Collier's Weekly* has filled the breach. Didn't I hear that you had retired, though, beekeeping in Sussex or some such thing?"

"That is essentially correct."

"And how is Dr. Watson?"

"Well. I see little of him since his most recent marriage."

Finally, I reached the obvious question. "What brought you to America?"

The answer proved frustrating: "A matter too delicate to reveal. Perhaps one day the full story can be told. For now, consider me an ordinary tourist, hoping to see some of this invigorating young city before returning home. I seek no publicity of my presence here, and in fact explicitly discourage it."

"Do I gather though that you still do some detective work?"

"On rare occasions. A problem with truly singular elements is difficult to resist."

I immediately offered to be his guide to the city of Chicago, and he readily accepted. In the days to follow, we saw (and smelled) the stockyards, visited the site on De Koven where Kate O'Leary's cow kicked over a lantern and started the great fire of 1871, viewed such towering architectural masterpieces as the Rookery and the Schiller Building, rode the "L" trains, marveled at the great collections of the Art Institute, attended a concert of the Chicago Orchestra, and sampled the varied cuisines that immigrant populations offer a great city's diners. On his third morning in the city, I suggested a visit to the site of the World's Columbian Exposition, Chicago's 1893 world's fair, and casually asked if he would consent to meet a friend of mine while we were in the area.

"I am too much in your debt to refuse," he said, "but I trust I can rely on your friend's discretion."

"Absolutely. He's an interesting chap. Athletics coach. I met him when I was in France seven years ago covering the Olympic Games. A man of unshakable moral principles."

"They can only be deemed unshakable if they have been put to the test."

"Oh, his have. He was planning to bring several runners to the Games but cancelled the trip when he learned the finals of all their events would take place on Sunday. Then a cablegram from Paris said the French had decided to change the finals to a weekday, so he made the trip with his athletes after all. But when he got there, he found the original schedule still in place. He withdrew his team from the competition. Americans take the Sabbath seriously, you see. Don't ask my friend his opinion of the French. But he's a splendid fellow, really, has played and coached nearly every competitive sport under the sun. At present, he is most renowned for football."

"Is that Association football or rugby?"

"Neither. American football. Closer to rugby but different. It's a college game primarily, but some institutions have banned it on grounds of excessive violence, including fatalities. In response, the coaches keep adjusting the rules, whether to save the sport or outfox their fellows, I'm not certain, but it is enormously popular and draws huge crowds."

Conveniently for my ulterior motive, the former site of the World's Fair overlapped the campus of the University of Chicago, a highly experimental, daringly coeducational institution established only a few years earlier thanks to a series of gifts by John D. Rockefeller. For all the university's modernist innovations, its buildings were of a traditional gothic design, combining with the artistically landscaped quadrangles to create an aesthetically stimulating environment for learning.

"That gymnasium resembles a cathedral," Holmes remarked at one point of our walk across the campus.

"That's what Rockefeller thought. But in a way it's appropriate. One of the new ideas that enliven this place is a well-funded Department of Physical Culture and Athletics. It's given equal status with other academic disciplines and headed by an athletic director with professorial rank. And he, it happens, is the man we are going to see." As I pointed out to Holmes the buildings and other landmarks, I had been following the most direct route to the office of Amos Alonzo Stagg.

Stagg was a large, powerfully built man in his forties with chiseled features and a steady, penetrating gaze. Though he already had a visitor, he waved us into his office with a broad smile. As he walked around the desk extending his hand, he seemed to be moving somewhat gingerly, but his handshake was firm as ever. His younger companion, slight, pale, and alight with nervous energy, was Perry Garth, a reporter for one of the Chicago dailies. Respecting Holmes's desire for privacy, I introduced him as Mr. Benson. Shaking hands with Stagg and Garth, he nodded amiably but said nothing.

"Not given up, Perry?" I twitted my colleague.

Garth shrugged. "One can only keep trying." As always, his manner had a studied nonchalance, as if nothing in the world mattered, but I sensed an undertone of desperation.

Stagg explained, "Mr. Garth would like me to write some articles for his newspaper, and every time he darkens my door, he increases his offer. I have repeated over and over that it's not a matter of money, but apparently he subscribes to the notion that every man has his price. As the athletic director of the University of Chicago, I must make myself available to all of the city's daily newspapers equally. It would not be appropriate for me to favor one over the others."

"Sure, I can understand that," said Garth. "But with all the scandals and bad publicity visited on your sport in the last few years, I thought you would welcome the chance to defend it against the hordes of bluenoses. My editor agreed, and I sort of went out on a limb promising your cooperation."

"That's the danger of going out on a limb without testing its strength first."

"Maybe. But writing something for us about the character-building you do out on the practice field might be in service of a higher good, don't you think?"

Stagg smiled. "I hope I always act in service of a higher good, Mr. Garth." I knew they had rehearsed this argument many times before, and the journalistic grapevine suggested enticing Stagg to write for his paper was crucial to Garth. Some said his job depended on it.

But now Garth shook his head in comic resignation. "Anyway, before I leave, you can at least give me a good quote on the Carlisle game. You've already won the Big Ten. You've said this year's team is your best ever. Now you're up against Pop Warner and his Indians. You're not going to let a bunch of redskins take your scalp, are you?"

"I saw their game against Minnesota, and they are impressive indeed. Their speed is dazzling. Our men will need to play their very best to beat them."

"What do you think of Warner as a coach?"

After a moment's pause, Stagg said, "He's certainly a fine coach."

"I've been to Carlisle to interview him. Would you like to hear what he says about you?"

"Nothing profane, I hope. Glenn Warner can say what he wants to my face, and I don't take secondhand reports of anyone's comments too seriously. Not all journalists are as scrupulously accurate and professional as yourself, Mr. Garth."

Turning toward Holmes and me, Garth said, "You fellows caught the sarcasm there, didn't you? Was ever a man so misjudged as this humble scribe? Seriously, I don't know why I bother. Coach Stagg always says the same thing. Good day, gentlemen!" And with that, Garth was out the door.

Stagg, not fooled for a moment by my subterfuge, said to my companion, "It is an honor to meet you, Mr. Holmes."

"I congratulate you, Mr. Stagg," Holmes said. "We've never met, and I've managed to avoid publicity while in your country. Surely, you could not identify me from the idealized images conveyed by Mr. Steele in the magazines, or Mr. Gillette on the stage. I am innocent of that calabash pipe or that countrified deerstalker with which I am so often depicted. I haven't uttered a word since I entered your office, so you heard no accent to indicate my nationality. How, pray tell, do you know who I am?" As he spoke, Holmes cast a suspicious glance in my direction, which I returned with a show of injured innocence.

"No, Armitage didn't say you were coming. But he has mentioned that he knew you, and when he telephoned this morning that he was bringing to campus someone I would want to meet, your name immediately sprang to mind. Now, what can you deduce about me?"

"Apart from the fact that you are suffering from sciatica and are troubled by some sort of mystery, I can deduce little."

"How in the world do you know I have sciatica?"

"My friend Watson has schooled me in the diagnosis of limps."

"Maybe if the good doctor were present, he could suggest a cure," Stagg said ruefully. "I have covered the map of the United States seeking treatment, from Colorado to Arkansas to Indiana to Florida, with no lasting result. Laying that painful matter aside, what about this mystery you believe is troubling me?" Now it was Stagg's turn to look pointedly in my direction. "What has Armitage been telling you?"

"I've told him nothing," I said, "apart from the population, mean temperature, and annual meat-packing production of the city of Chicago."

"Then how did you know, Mr. Holmes?"

"Armitage must have mentioned many of his friends and acquaintances to you at some time or other. Why would the name of a detective spring to your mind if you were not in need of one?"

Stagg nodded. "It's true I could use your help. But I haven't adequate money to pay for your services, and anyway, time is too short."

"My time in your city is short as well. But I charge no fee for a brief consultation, and perhaps I could make some suggestions toward solving your problem."

"That's very kind of you. Please sit down, gentlemen, and I'll tell you about it. You know a bit of this, Armitage, but not the most recent development. When that reporter was here, he asked me my opinion of Glenn 'Pop' Warner, my opposite number at the Carlisle Indian School. You may have noted some hesitation in my answer. Glenn and I are unlike in many ways. I once planned to become a minister, changing course only because I couldn't preach for sour apples and believed I could serve God more effectively as a coach. Glenn by contrast trained as a lawyer. He is profane in his language. The strongest word my players ever hear from me is *jackass*, though I'll confess they hear that all too frequently.

"While I have tried to improve our game with my colleagues on the rules committee, Glenn has given us little help, but when we do change or introduce a rule, he is quick to exploit it. Last year, we allowed the forward pass for the first time, and no one has made more effective use of it than Glenn Warner. Sometimes, we have to make another new rule to close whatever loophole he has exposed.

"No one in coaching will soon forget Warner's hidden-ball trick against Harvard in '03: The Carlisle players pulled closely together to receive the kick-off, and the Harvard men could not tell who had the ball. One player—Dillon was his name—put his empty arms out in front of him as he ran down the field and was ignored by the Harvard defenders, who concentrated on searching among the other Carlisle players for the ball-carrier. Dillon crossed the Harvard goal line, produced the ball from the back of his sweater, and scored an unimpeded touchdown."

"Surely that's not cricket," I said.

"Obviously not," Holmes said humorously. "But is it American football?"

Stagg said, "Mr. Holmes, in that famous expression about cricket, your countrymen express a devotion to sportsmanship that goes beyond the importance of winning. To us in America, winning is the thing. We will honor the letter of the law, but not always the spirit. Glenn Warner will do anything to win within the rules, and I cannot in good conscience criticize him for that. I have always respected him as a coach and as a man, but now something has shaken that respect.

"I was pleased at your hearty endorsement of amateur sport in Dr. Watson's account of the 'Missing Three-Quarter.' Despite our minor differences in philosophy, in my country as in yours, the teamwork and ideals of sport mold boys into men, making my profession of coaching a sacred calling. Did not Wellington say, 'The battle of Waterloo was won on the playing fields of Eton'?

"But when I read that story of a missing rugby player, I never imagined that a similar situation might confront me. It has. A young man named Clayton Cumberland enrolled this year at the University and turned out for the team. I knew immediately he could be a player of great ability and versatility. He has shown in practice that he can do everything our game requires—run, block, punt, pass, tackle—and I have had the luxury of developing his potential slowly. Others did the job for me through the Big Ten season, but I believed I would need more in our upcoming game against Warner's Carlisle team. I was planning to unveil Cumberland as a sort of secret weapon.

"But the day before yesterday, a mere three days before the game, Cumberland suddenly vanished from his dormitory. His roommate had sensed something was worrying him but could provide no clue to where he might have gone. His professors say only that he had been diligent in his studies. With no evidence of violence, I could hardly enlist the efforts of the police. I was not so much worried about the game, Mr. Holmes, as the welfare of the young man. Then in this morning's mail, I received this."

He passed over a plain envelope addressed to him at the University.

There was no return address. Inside was a crumpled sheet of paper that Holmes and I looked at in turn. It had a Carlisle Indian School letterhead, and a typewritten message was crowded into the top half of the page, followed by a handwritten signature.

> *Dear Mr. Cumberland:*
>
> *As we discussed, there will be no problem in obtaining documentation of your Indian blood. We are delighted you will be joining our team here at Carlisle.*
>
> *Sincerely yours,*
>
> *Glenn "Pop" Warner*

"You see the implication," Stagg said. "Warner is now stealing players from other coaches by nefarious means. I don't believe Clayton Cumberland has any Indian blood at all. It seems Warner will do anything he can to gain an advantage. This goes beyond bending the rules. This is flat-out cheating."

"This is Warner's true signature?" Holmes said.

"I have seen his signature, and I believe it to be authentic. Mind you, I am no expert in handwriting analysis. But if this were merely a matter of Cumberland leaving Chicago to go to Carlisle, why would the young man not simply come and tell me what he was planning to do, or at least write his decision to me in a letter? Why just disappear one day?"

Holmes turned to me. "Armitage, if I may impose upon your time for a few hours more, it is possible we can make some sense of this." I readily agreed. For who would decline the chance to be substitute Watson?

We were fortunate to find the roommate, a young ministerial student named Chad Armbruster, in his dormitory room, and eager to talk to us. While Holmes continued to use the alias Mr. Benson, we made no effort to conceal that he was a detective.

"Are you English, Mr. Benson?" Armbruster asked. "Cumberland's parents were English."

"Indeed," said Holmes. "Are they living?"

"No, I believe they're both dead."

"You told Coach Stagg that Cumberland was worried about something."

"He certainly wasn't himself the past week or so."

"Did he say nothing to suggest the source of his worry?"

"Nothing."

"Did he say anything out of the ordinary that might help us?"

"There was one very odd thing, now that you mention it, but I can't imagine how it will help you. I returned to the room late one evening to find Cumberland sitting at his desk, just staring into space. I heard him say to himself, speaking in a low voice but very clearly, as if unaware I had entered the room, 'It all comes down to the missing three quarters.'"

Holmes and I exchanged a glance. "Could it have been the 'Missing Three-Quarter?'" I ventured tentatively. "There was a story in *Collier's Weekly* by that title. I can't recall the author."

"Can't you really?" Armbruster said with a laugh. "That was a Sherlock Holmes story, and a corker at that, but I doubt Cumberland read it. He is far too serious for any light literature. Anyway, he distinctly said 'missing three quarters.' Plural."

"Did you ask him what he meant?" Holmes asked.

"I did. He looked rather startled. He obviously hadn't known I'd heard him. He tried to laugh it off. 'I carelessly left three quarters on this table last week,' he said, 'and they've disappeared. I know you're too pious and holy to be a thief, Armbruster, but one of our visitors must be light-fingered.' Then he claimed he was hungry and suggested we go hunt down some sustenance. He was very eager to change the subject."

"So you didn't accept his explanation," I said, rather obviously.

"Not for a moment. But what could it all mean?"

"Did Cumberland ever typewrite his papers?" Holmes asked. An odd question, I thought, and Armbruster seemed equally nonplussed.

"No. I don't believe he knows how to typewrite. He has a beautiful hand, though. Perfectly legible."

With Armbruster's permission, Holmes looked through the books and other papers on Cumberland's desk. I saw him slip a sheet of paper and an envelope into his pocket, not ostentatiously but not with any obvious furtiveness either.

As we were leaving, Armbruster asked, "Mr. Benson, as a detective yourself, have you learned anything from reading about Sherlock Holmes?"

"Not a thing," declared Holmes. "A most inferior fellow. Dupin and Lecoq were both far more capable."

Ensconced in a cab that would take us back to Holmes's hotel, I ventured to ask, "What could the reference to the missing three quarters refer to? Cumberland's explanation was obviously a clumsy improvisation."

"I agree. But you have the advantage over me in these matters, Armitage. Does the expression have any significance in American football?"

"Well, the game is played in four quarters, but I don't know how you could be missing three of them. There is a position in American football called quarterback, but there is only one on the field at a time." Sudden inspiration struck me. "What about that reference in the note from 'Pop' Warner about Cumberland's supposed Indian blood? Perhaps Cumberland was one quarter Indian and Warner can only recruit full-blooded Indians, making the missing three quarters problematic."

My exultation at the brilliance of my theory was short-lived. Holmes shook his head. "It leaves too much unexplained," he said. "But there may be a clue in this letter. Also a clue to his present whereabouts, assuming, as I believe, his disappearance was at least semi-voluntary."

He handed over the letter and envelope, which I perused quickly. The envelope bore the address in the city of one James Gustavson, but the letter was unfinished, as if Cumberland had been interrupted in its writing. As Armbruster had proclaimed, his roommate had an attractive and easily readable hand.

Dear Oscar,

Thanks for your encouraging letter. Your old pal Saucy knew he could rely on a teammate. You are right that it was a breach of contract, and no one knows that blackguard O'Hara better than you. Don't know how you lasted out the season. But does receiving less than promised really mean what we would like it to mean? For now, I am staying on here, but if events make it necessary, I shall certainly avail myself

And there it broke off in midsentence.

"What does it mean?" I wondered. "He addresses the envelope to James and writes a letter to Oscar. And who the devil is Saucy?"

Holmes told me, "I have an idea about that, but time is short. We must go our separate ways for the next few hours." He instructed the cabby, then instructed me.

My assigned task was a puzzling one.

"You want me to do what?" I exclaimed. "But why?"

"There's no time to explain. Simply get it done and meet me back at my hotel at seven this evening."

Now I knew how Watson felt when kept in the dark. I grumbled a bit, but of course agreed to the mission.

The next morning, we were once again in Stagg's office, and this time young Clayton Cumberland, clearly unharmed but shamefaced, was present as well. I still did not know the entire story yet, and listened closely to Holmes as he explained it to Stagg.

"To begin with, that message from Warner was obviously faked. The signature was positioned right in the middle of the page, suggesting that Warner's secretary—I hardly think the great coach typewrites his own correspondence—is singularly lacking in the rudiments of his profession. Surely the body of the letter should be centered on the page, with the signature nearer the bottom. The implication was obvious: someone had obtained Coach Warner's signature on a sheet of Carlisle Indian School letterhead, probably on the pretense of being an autograph collector, then added the typewritten message after the fact. Every typewriter has its own peculiarities. The one used for the bogus Warner letter had a small letter 'e' that struck slightly above the line and a small letter 'o' that was filled in because of a dirty key."

"But, Mr. Holmes, who would do that, and why?" Stagg asked.

"Though I was puzzled as to his motive, I suspected Cumberland might have composed the message himself. However, his roommate told me that Cumberland does not typewrite, and I found no typewritten sheets among his papers that shared those characteristics."

"Then who was responsible for the false message?" Stagg demanded.

"Armitage came up with a good idea." (Had I? Not that I could remember.) "Could the person who faked the message be the reporter, Perry Garth? He told us that he was under pressure to recruit you as a writer, but you had spurned all his overtures. If he could make you angry enough about abuses by one of your coaching brethren, perhaps he believed he could get an exclusive story for his paper, and a lively one. We knew he had interviewed Warner at the Carlisle Indian School, so he could have obtained his autograph then. I asked Armitage to visit Garth's office and obtain a sample of his typewritten copy. The peculiarities of the type proved the same machine had produced the supposed letter from Warner.

"But to make his plan work, Cumberland had to vanish. How could Garth manage that? What hold did he have over Cumberland? An unfinished letter on the young man's desk gave me a clue. Stagg, you are well-known as a champion of amateur sports. Are your athletes allowed to play professionally?"

"Certainly not!" Stagg was outraged at the idea. "Playing professionally carries a stigma. It could result in disqualification and perhaps expulsion."

"And if a college player were to play professionally as well, could he cover his tracks?"

"He might play under an alias," Stagg said reluctantly, disgust in his tone.

"Exactly. Cumberland had addressed the envelope to James Gustavson, but the salutation of the letter was 'Dear Oscar.' In the third person, he referred to himself as Saucy."

Holmes turned to me. "Cumberland sauce, Armitage. I'm sure you've enjoyed it on game dishes many times, as have I. Any Englishman would know it, including Cumberland as the product of an English family, thus the odd choice of alias. As teammates, the two young men called each other by their assumed names, and other clues in the letter suggest that they were paid for their efforts. The words 'I shall certainly avail myself' I suspected might refer to an invitation from this Oscar to stay with him should Cumberland feel the need to leave the University abruptly."

Holmes gazed for a moment at Cumberland, who was looking more miserable by the moment.

"While Armitage was performing his errand at Garth's office, I went to the address on the letter, found the two young men, and got the whole story out of them," Holmes resumed. "Two summers ago, Cumberland briefly played professional baseball for a suburban team managed by a tight-fisted fellow named Brian O'Hara."

"O'Hara promised me twenty dollars but paid me only five," Cumberland muttered. "He claimed the box-office receipts had only been a quarter of what he expected."

"Thus," said Holmes, "the missing three quarters referred to by Cumberland. He asked some other players, including Gustavson, whom he knew as Oscar, if they had been similarly shorted, and learned they had not, but also that O'Hara was an unscrupulous employer who would cut every corner he could, and would often test new men by reneging on promises."

Cumberland turned to Stagg. "I was so mad, Coach, I quit the team then and there. I never thought of myself as a professional, and after that experience I never even wanted to be a professional. I found another job, and as soon as I could, I sent O'Hara's lousy five bucks back to him."

"And how did Garth come into it?" Stagg asked him.

"He'd heard about my mistake some way and approached me one day after practice."

"Blackmail?"

"That's not how he put it. Oh, no, he was my friend. He was going to help me out. He claimed O'Hara was threatening to go to you with the truth. Garth said he knew a way to deter O'Hara, but it would be dangerous for me to be on campus. Not dangerous to me, Coach! Garth convinced me that if his plan failed, and O'Hara made his information public, my presence on campus would destroy University of Chicago football, and your own reputation with it."

"And how was that to happen?" Stagg demanded skeptically.

"I don't know. I was confused. Gustavson is studying law and had it in his mind that O'Hara's breach of contract, plus my return of the one quarter he did pay me, somehow removed the taint of professionalism from my record."

"That's nonsense, boy!"

"I wasn't convinced either," Cumberland said ruefully. "I was working on that letter to Gustavson when a message came from Garth to leave the campus immediately. Coach Stagg, all I wanted was to play football for the University of Chicago!"

Stagg's features hardened, his stare intensified, and we glimpsed for that moment his practice-field visage. "You jackass! You should have come to me and explained what was happening! Perhaps I could have helped you."

"I didn't think you'd understand. Everybody knows how down you are on professionals. Of course, I know now that Garth never meant to help me. He just wanted me out of the way until after the Carlisle game."

"And he did all this to convince me to write for his newspaper?" Stagg said incredulously.

Holmes shook his head. "Garth was heavily involved in illicit gambling on college football games. He was depending on his wagers on the Carlisle Indians to erase a large debt to the bookmakers, needed Cumberland out of the way, and had uncovered the means to do so. Implicating Warner was secondary. His two aims fit neatly together, but his indebtedness to the bookmakers was the more dangerous problem."

Stagg shook his head sadly, his anger dissipated as swiftly as it had come. "We're all of us imperfect sinners. God willing, this incident made you grow as a man, Cumberland."

"You know, Stagg," I said tentatively, "once Holmes and I confronted Garth, he promised to destroy the evidence he had of Cumberland's secret, and leave town for points west. To make sure, Holmes and I accompanied him to the railroad station to bid him farewell, and he has every incentive never to return to Chicago. As for O'Hara, the man had no role in Garth's plans for the definitive reason that he died last winter. Thus, no one ever need know any of this. I shall be discreet, and I'm certain Holmes will."

"What are you suggesting, Armitage?" Stagg demanded.

"That Cumberland can still play for Chicago."

"But you did play professionally, didn't you, Cumberland?" Stagg said.

"Technically I suppose I did," Cumberland replied sadly, "even if what I got barely covered my carfare."

Stagg shook his head. "Then I'm sorry. Once you crossed the line and accepted money, even if you returned it, there was no going back. I sympathize with your desire to play, but I cannot knowingly violate a rule. If you had played any games for me in the regular season, I would have had to notify the Big Ten conference that we would forfeit our victories."

Cumberland nodded, accepting the coach's verdict. "Were you ever tempted to turn pro yourself, Coach?"

"Back in the eighties, six National League teams offered me pitching contracts. The highest bidder would have paid three thousand dollars for one season's work. I declined because of my loyalty to Yale and the low moral character of professional ballplayers. I am thankful football will never emerge as a professional sport, based as it is on school spirit and manliness and teamwork, everything that professionalism destroys." He extended his hand to Clayton Cumberland. "Good luck to you in your future endeavors."

When Cumberland had left the office, Stagg said to us, "I regret most of all that this scheme caused me to doubt my fellow coach Glenn Warner. While he will bend the rules at every opportunity, I should have known that he would never break them. It is good to know he is not a cheat."

"Can you defeat the Carlisle team without Cumberland?" Holmes asked.

"It will not be easy, even though their superb quarterback Mt. Pleasant was injured in the Minnesota game and may not be able to play. They are very fast, particularly a most talented end named Exendine. Some say one of their newer players, a young man named Thorpe, will be even better, though that is difficult to imagine. If Exendine breaks free of our defense, he will catch passes all afternoon. My plan is not to let him. My defenders will knock down Exendine and their other ends at the outset of every play, and not let them up until the play is over."

"And that is within the rules?" Holmes asked.

"Yes, perfectly."

"Wouldn't it be fairer," I ventured, "if only the man with the ball could be brought down? It would certainly reduce those grievous football injuries I'm constantly reading about."

With a slight smile, Stagg replied, "Perhaps I'll suggest that to the committee. But for now, I must take advantage of the rules as written if I expect to outsmart Warner. Mr. Holmes, you must be my guest on the sidelines, and you too, Armitage. It is the very least I can do to repay you for solving my mystery and easing my mind."

The University of Chicago's football stadium is called Marshall Field, a pun on the name of the real-estate developer who donated the land. On the day of the game, the skies were clear, the weather pleasantly cool, the grandstands filled. Someone estimated the crowd at between twenty-five and thirty thousand. At either end of the field, hundreds of spectators unable to get a seat watched standing on wooden platforms. Stagg had welcomed us cordially, but once play began, his focus was entirely on the game.

The plan to knock down the Carlisle ends proved quite effective for most of the game. Pop Warner was beside himself, smoking cigarettes incessantly as he prowled the sidelines. Probably (though I'm no lip-reader), smoking was not the only way he violated Stagg's purist standard of proper coachlike behavior. The injured Mt. Pleasant had been replaced by a chap named Hauser, and for much of the contest it seemed unlikely we would see his throwing arm tested.

Early in the fourth quarter, Carlisle had an eight to four lead, much too close to satisfy Warner. He called Hauser and the star end Exendine to the sidelines and gave them some quick instructions, as Stagg watched suspiciously from our side of the field. The center snapped the ball to Hauser, but Exendine, instead of running toward his inevitable knockdown, ran off the field and behind the Carlisle bench. Hauser evaded the Chicago tacklers as long as he could, then delivered a long throw downfield. Exendine, having run some twenty-five yards behind the Carlisle bench, ran back onto the field of play, and caught the pass with no Chicago defender near him. The Carlisle Indians went on to win by a score of eighteen to four.

"An admirable piece of misdirection," Holmes remarked in a low voice. "But is that stratagem within the rules?"

"I daresay it won't be after the next rules committee meeting," I said.

Amos Alonzo Stagg, who had come perilously close to violating his personal ban on profanity, had his own opinion. "That's unethical, unprofessional, dishonest, and dishonorable! Pop Warner is a cheat!"

Note: Two books were useful in verifying details of Armitage's account: Touchdown *(Longmans, Green, 1927), by Amos Alonzo Stagg and Wesley Winans Stout; and* Carlisle vs. Army *(Random House, 2007), by Lars Anderson.*

The Song at Twilight

Michéal Breathnach

"Michéal Breathnach" lives in his ancestral home in the Burren at Carrowney Cleary, County Clare, just a few miles from the market town of Lisdoonvarna and the rollicking seaside village of Doolin where, between the jigs and the reels, he occasionally gets some work done. For *Ghosts in Baker Street*, he contributed "The Coole Park Problem," co-written with his daughter, Clare, which was inspired by a long ramble in Yeats's haunted wood on Lady Gregory's old estate near Gort in County Galway. "The Song at Twilight" was suggested by the Canonical tale, "His Last Bow," with its tantalizing references to Holmes's time in Chicago and Buffalo. Michéal Breathnach is also the Irish *nom-de-plume* of the American writer, Michael Walsh.

* * * *

Chicago, July 1912

Mrs. Murphy's chowder was, of course, inedible, but then I was not here for Mrs. Murphy's chowder. I was here for Miss Maddie McParland.

Forgive me for being blunt. The finer points of literary style are Watson's, as my feeble effort concerning the business of the Lion's Mane so vividly illustrates. A few minutes' consultation with the *Britannica* and the solution to that mystery would have readily presented itself. Still, we all of us are human, all too human, as Nietzsche said, and I am not as young as I used to be.

How I do miss my amanuensis, my Boswell. I am not a man given to personal reflection, nor do I possess that experience with women on several continents which distinguished my long-suffering but ever-amiable companion when it came to matters of the heart. But Watson has finally abandoned me, and so cannot help me now, whether literarily or in the realm of *das ewig-Weibliche*, and so I alone am left to tell thee. I trust my allusions are clear and in order.

The chowder, as I said, was execrable, an eldritch admixture of corn, water—no doubt cheap liquor had been added to it as well—and some sort of meat stock dredged up from the bowels of the nearby slaughterhouses, whose stench permeates the insalubrious atmosphere of this most wretched of American cities. All it wanted was a pair of overalls to make the concoction complete.

So also the accommodations and the weather. Chicago is a fearful place at the best of times, but most of the time it is either blistering hot, as it was now, or frightfully cold. The people of this benighted metropolis walk head down, shoulders hunched, alternately nearly naked or bundled up like Esquimaux, cloth caps tugged down tight, like Irish peasants, too-small bowlers squashed onto too-large heads, dandy fedoras attached by strings to their bearers' lapels, so as not to go sailing away into inclement waters of Lake Michigan. The mere act of perambulation is one of the labors of Hercules.

For all of this, I blame my brother. Although it has been some years since one could truthfully say that Mycroft *was* the British Government, he nevertheless still wields enormous influence, especially since the accession of King George IV to the throne of England. Although *nil nisi bonum* and all that, my lack of regard for the former King, the late Edward, was well known, and I regularly rejected all honors and entreaties from His Majesty's Government during the mercifully brief reign of a man Watson chose to cloak as the King of Bohemia during our one unhappy encounter.

Too, the long-ago memory of Miss Irene Adler has long remained with me, and so it was with some reluctance that I welcomed my brother to my humble cottage on the South Downs, where I was content to live out the remainder of my life in peace and solitude, with only Mrs. Hudson and my apiary for company as I scribbled away at my magnum opus.

As always, on those infrequent occasions when I see my brother, I marvel at the physical dissimilarity between us. If ever, in matters of appearance, two men were less likely to be siblings, then surely he and I were those men: I, hawk-featured, even gaunt as I approach my sixtieth birthday, and Mycroft tending toward the portly as he advanced in both age and wisdom. And yet, in certain qualities of mind and rigorousness of intellect, I dare say that there is some distinct familial resemblance.

He ambled past Mrs. Hudson with the air of a man on a palanquin. "Damn it, Sherlock," he began without preamble, "if there is an excuse for your insufferable rudeness, I would very much like to hear it."

Unaccustomed as he was to physical exertion, my brother plopped himself unbidden into a wing chair as I discreetly signaled Mrs. Hudson for tea.

"You have come straight from Whitehall, I perceive," I said. After all these years, he was used to my little tricks of behavioural detection, but inevitably he rose to the bait.

"How on earth did you know that?"

"Elementary. Had you come from the Diogenes Club, you would have the tell-tale smudge of printer's ink on your left thumb and right forefinger, as you habitually wet your index finger as you turn the pages of the *Times*."

"Perhaps," muttered my brother, "but what about my attire or manner suggests Whitehall?"

"Again, child's play. Your right cuff is besmirched with sealing-wax, which strongly suggests you have very recently sealed an important envelope and then rushed here without a chance to change your cuffs. That, together with the presence of a Daimler outside my humble doorway, strong suggests that you are here on matters of state. Hence, Whitehall."

Mycroft looked at me for a moment, that look I knew so well from our childhood, and then moved straightaway to the business which had brought him here. "See here, Sherlock," he said. "Your country needs you and that is the end of it."

He then handed me the purpose of my mission: a sealed letter that I was not to open, but rather to deliver in person to a young woman in America of whom I had never heard. I glanced at the envelope, which contained only a single name: "Miss Maddie McParland." No address was given.

"You are wondering why I cannot simply post this," observed Mycroft, turning the tables ever so slightly, "but this is no task for the Royal Mail." His mien was deadly serious. "Make no mistake, brother, this is a matter of the highest urgency. I have given His Majesty my solemn word that, upon the honor of the family name, you will carry out this mission, personally deliver this missive to its intended recipient, and await her reply."

These were deep waters indeed, and I needed to tread carefully. "Who is this woman," I asked, glancing at the writing on the envelope, "this Miss McParland?"

"She is a native of Chicago, Illinois, living in what the inhabitants there refer to as the South Side. That is all, for the moment, you need know." He consulted his pocket watch, then replaced it in the folds of his waistcoat. "You are booked on the *Oceanic* tomorrow at this time. I trust your journey will be speedy, safe, and pleasant."

I ushered him out of my study. "Won't you stay for tea, Mr. Holmes?" asked the faithful Mrs. Hudson, bearing two steaming cups on a silver tray.

"My thanks to you, madam," he replied graciously, "but duty calls."

I saw him to the door. The Channel lay beyond the downs, shimmering in the grey light. But Mycroft's gaze was toward the east, toward the German Ocean. "Sherlock," he said quietly. "There is someone who would like a word with you." We stepped outside.

His motorcar was waiting, its engine running. There was a man sitting in the back seat, whom I immediately recognized as Mr. Asquith from his distinctive profile. As I moved to greet him, he rolled his window down and said, "You must fully understand, Holmes, that His Majesty cannot and will not acknowledge your presence in America. Should anything go awry, or should you meet with some misfortune, you are not to communicate with your brother or anyone else connected with this government. I cannot emphasize this point enough, and I trust I make myself clear."

"Perfectly, Prime Minister," I replied.

"Very well," said Mr. Asquith, rolling up his window. Our brief interview was over.

I turned back to Mycroft, puzzlement writ large upon my features. Instead of edifying me, however, my brother did something remarkable: he took my hand in his and held it for a moment before shaking it. It was not until his hand had been withdrawn that I realized he had pressed a small piece of paper into it.

"You have been through many rough adventures in which you have risked life and limb, Sherlock. I think at once of Dr. Roylott, and of the loathsome Milverton, and even of poor Jefferson Hope. I pray that this will not be another of them. And yet . . . " His voice trailed off.

"Many were the men, Moriarty's men, who have wished me dead, and I still live," I told him.

"Yes," he said after some thought. "Your strength has never failed you, nor your iron will, nor your keen mind. But it is a new world upon whose precipice we stand, and one that is not so readily accommodating to men such as we . . . such as we once were."

He clambered into the rear seat of the Daimler, and lowered the window as the driver made ready to engage the gears. "From now on, and until further notice, your name is James McKenna, laborer and former amateur boxer, of Liverpool. Good luck, brother," he said.

As they drove away, I looked at the piece of paper, which contained a single address: 3154 S. Normal Avenue.

"Mr. McKenna," squawked a voice in my ear. That would be Mrs. Murphy. Like other women of her race, she had a pinched, befreckled face, bony fingers that bespoke the miser and watery, pale blue eyes. "You haven't touched your chowder."

I had been a boarder at her establishment for several days, on the theory that if I was to pass for James McKenna, then what better place to pick up the plumage of this strange bird, the Irish-American, than in his native habitat?

I looked at the steaming bowl before me. "My appetite fails me today, Mrs. Murphy," I said, upon which voiced sentiment she whisked the vessel away and promptly set it down before another of the lodgers. "Then Mr. Callahan will have it, and that's the end of it. He'll no want of strength on the morrow, for the butcher's work ain't ne'er done but begins anew fresh each day."

Foregoing the chowder with gusto (as the Americans, with their unhealthy reliance upon Spanish words, say), I rose, took my leave, and set off in the direction my landlady had pointed me. I glanced once more at the piece of paper into which Mycroft had impressed my hand, though I had long since committed it to memory, perhaps as a kind of talisman.

I shall not trouble the reader with an account of the squalor and filth I encountered along the way. Suffice it say that half an hour's walk was never undertaken so briskly, with greater purpose, or more relief when at last my destination was reached: the intersection of W. 31st Street and S. Normal Avenue in a part of the city they called Bridgeport. I turned into Normal Avenue and walked south to number 3154.

The residence I sought was typical for the location or, in local parlance, the "neighbourhood." It was a small, two-storey building, what the locals call a "prairie bungalow," or perhaps more descriptively, a "shotgun shack." Miss Maddie McParland resided on the first—American, second—floor, and so a short trudge to the top of the stairs soon brought me face to face with her door knocker.

I knocked, then knocked again. At last, I could hear a voice on the other side of the transom: "Who is it, please?" The Irish lilt in her voice was unmistakable, even if her accent was wholly American.

"Mr. James McKenna, come all the way from London with an urgent message for you," I replied. "May I come in, please?"

The door opened. As Watson has told you, I am impervious to the charms of a well-turned ankle, but at this moment I wished I had his powers of description, so comely was the lass who now stood before me. "A message for me? There must be some mistake, good sir. But, please, come in and take some refreshment," she said.

The flat was rather more well-appointed that one might have suspected by its humble exterior. My own Mrs. Hudson could not have kept it neater or cleaner; there were books on the shelves and the satisfying smell of tea brewing in the kitchen.

I accepted her offer with gratitude and sat down in a comfortable chair near the fireplace while she sat opposite on a kind of divan. "I can't tell you who gave this letter to me, or why," I began, "but I can assure you this is no joke. Indeed, it is deadly serious."

"But how can something in London possibly concern me, Mr. McKenna? I'm an American."

Instead of a reply, I handed her the letter. At that point, my work was done and I should have taken my leave and set out on the long journey home. But, as I had no way of knowing whether it required a reply, I sat, waiting. At last, she took the hint and opened the envelope.

I cannot describe the look on her face as she read. Her eyes widened, her face flushed, though with embarrassment or anger I could not tell: I could swear a tear or two came to her eyes. But whatever awful news the epistle conveyed she otherwise bore with equanimity and strength.

She read the letter twice and then tucked it safely into the folds of her sleeve. For a long moment, she seemed to be struggling with herself, occasionally casting a glance my way, as if making up her mind about something. Then, wordlessly, she rose and motioned for me to follow her.

My nostrils flared with excitement as Miss McParland guided me down dark streets, little more than pig alleys. The beastly heat had brought out all manner of street life, with toughs lounging in every third doorway, while up on the roofs, women stood a constant watch. As we came around one corner, and into the filthiest street yet, one of the crones set off an unearthly howl. Others soon followed her example, banging pots and screeching. Soon, every eye was upon us.

And then the pelting began. Paving stones, flower pots, rotten fruit, and offal rained down upon us, most of which, I thought, was unmistakably directed at me. "Why are they doing this?" I shouted.

"They think you are a plainclothes detective," shouted Miss McParland over the din. "We must hurry."

Then I understood: I was in the very heart of gangland Chicago. A thrill ran through me. After all, I had been in correspondence with Inspector Byrnes of the New York City Police Department from 1886, when the great detective's magnum opus, *Professional Criminals of America* appeared, to his death four years ago. And to think that now I might be encountering in the flesh some of those whose photographs I had pored over for so long: the burglar Joseph Whalen, who went by the alias of Joe Wilson; "Jew Al," the confidence man; and the notorious pickpocket "Aleck the Mailman." Perhaps I would even encounter America's own Moriarty, lurking among one of the city's many Irish secret societies.

"In here," said Miss McParland, grabbing my arm. She darted down some narrow service steps and into the bowels of a nearby building as the mob outside howled like banshees and continued its aerial assault.

I had expected a dank, musty basement, crawling with lice and raggedy immigrants. Instead, I found myself in a kind of dance hall. Or perhaps a saloon. "What is this place?" I managed to whisper to my comely companion.

"A blind pig," she replied.

The place reeked of spilt beer and bloodied sawdust, where sawed-off shotguns and six-shooters were as plentiful as the rats who no doubt scuttled along the insides of the walls. A mediocre player pounded a hideously out of tune piano in a corner, while whores and second-storey men danced with shameless abandon. On balance, however, it was no worse than the East End dives and opium dens I had often visited in the course of my detective work. "Ain't this a swell ballumrancum?" asked a swaying tough with half an ear missing, and I replied that I was sure it was.

Miss McParland was speaking with a hard, scarred fellow behind the bar, who looked me over with what I fancied was approval. Indeed, a big smile was crossing his bluff Hibernian countenance, and he wiped his hands on his soiled apron and moved toward me.

"Abe Slaney, I presume," I said, but my little joke was lost on him.

The force of the blow sent me reeling across the room. It was like being back in the ring with McMurdo, Bartholomew Sholto's manservant. Had I been struck with a Penang lawyer, I could not have felt the assault more forcefully. The last thing I recall seeing was the treacherous visage of Miss Maddie McParland, smiling sweetly at me, her expression a mixture of pity and revenge, as I descended into that unexpected night.

Of the next few weeks, I have little memory. Most of the time I was kept drugged—opium, I am quite sure—and was chained to a metal cot in a back room while the gang debated about what to do with me. Occasionally, the big man who had knocked me out—they called him "the Boss"—and some other fellows would enter my room and "grill" me. Some of them argued for my speedy demise, but the Boss demurred, saying I might well be put to better use. I knew that in order to survive, I was going to have to play along, no matter what the humiliation. Besides, I was burning to know what role Miss McParland had played in all this, and what the contents of my brother's letter to her were, which had brought me to such a pretty pass. But of her, however, I saw nothing.

What they could not know, of course, was that my long experience with cocaine and opium had rendered me resistant, if not immune, to the drugs, and thus I was able to keep my "character" in front of me at all times. I told them, over and over, that I was Jim McKenna of Liverpool—

my Liverpudlian accent more than rose to the occasion—and that I could still lick any man in the room if they would only set me free.

At last, my moment came. The door to my cell opened and there stood the Boss. He entered and sat down next to me. I could smell his foetid breath. "So, it seems that you are who you say you are. We've checked you out six ways from Sunday with our lads in Liverpool and mister you are jake in my book. You're a tough old bird, I'll give ya that; then you're more than welcome to join us and fight for our people and Mother Ireland, Mr. James McKenna." I breathed a small sigh of relief. Mycroft had "set me up" well enough to pass the scrutiny of this lot.

"But," the Boss continued, ominously, "if you turn out to be some dirty copper, well, buddy, you have come to the wrong place. Because we in the brotherhood know how to police our own. Sure, we've had many years of experience, if you catch my drift."

Now the scales fell from my eyes—these were not just gangsters, but Fenians, one with the Irish Republican Brotherhood, and dedicated not only to Davitt and Parnell and Home Rule, but outright independence. And I, a loyal subject of His Majesty, was being forced to join them. Was this what Mycroft had in mind all along? It seemed inconceivable, but however improbable, it was the nearest thing to the truth—or at least a working hypothesis—that I had. "OK," I said, starting to pick up the lingo.

The Boss brought his smelly face close to mine. "Will you fight for us, old man?" he breathed. "Will you fight for Eire, and freedom?"

I swallowed hard. "I will," said I.

"Stout lad." And with that, he unlocked my chains and told me to stand up.

What happened next was a blur. I had the sense of being rushed, my shirt ripped from my back. Then a searing pain in my back, beneath my left shoulder blade. The unmistakable scent of burning flesh filled the air with its noisome acridity.

As they released me, I dropped to my knees and then collapsed across my bed. Only had Tonga's dart found me on the Thames could the pain have been more intense. How long I lay there in my misery, I have no idea, but it must have been several minutes. Then I gradually became conscious of soft hands, gently rubbing some healing lineament in my wound, and then a softer voice, whispering in my ear.

"How does it feel?" said Maddie McParland. She grasped my chin and turned my face toward hers. Even in my anguish, I could see the fire in her eyes, the beauty in her flushed cheeks, the passion in her touch. "Tell me, for I must know: *How does it feel*?"

Buffalo, February 1913

My room at the Altamont was simple, Spartan, sufficient. A single bed. A washbasin and a chamber pot that I had to empty myself. More flophouse than Michelin, but still, it was better than Chicago, and I no longer yearned so fervidly for the tender mercies of good Martha Hudson. It was a good place for the gang to "lie low," as they say, and, besides, Miss McParland was there.

My wound had healed, although absent a mirror I still could not see what they had done to me. The best I could manage was a dim, gas-lit reflection in a window against the darkness of Lake Erie that stretched out like a vast, frozen inland sea beyond my window. But even then, I could only make out the seared flesh, and not what lay beneath.

Lost in my ruminations, in my half-naked state, I was startled by a knock at the door. Hastily, I donned my shirt but I was too late: the door opened and there she stood. How forward these Americans are, and how little they care for propriety! I turned quickly away, still struggling with my shirt.

"It's healing nicely," she said, inviting herself in.

I could stand the suspense no longer. "For God's sake, please tell me how they have marked me!" But my pleas fell upon deaf ears. Perhaps it was my distressed state, but at this moment, she looked—dare I say it?—ever more beautiful than before. And yet she was the one responsible for my condition. The heart is a strange regulator.

She fixed me with that otherworldly Celtic-blue stare, at once so foreign to our earthy, sturdy Anglo-Saxon stock and yet so beguiling.

"I am sorry you were treated so roughly in Chicago, but we had to be sure. About you and your suitability for . . . " She grew pensive for a moment, and then suddenly her eyes widened and her cheeks flushed with anger. "God, how I hate them!" she cried.

Her outburst startled me.

"Hate them for what they did to my father, hate them for what they made him do, hate them for what happened to him." She threw herself at me like a tigress, pounding her fists against my chest. "I hate them, do you understand! Hate them! And I'll have my revenge on the whole rotten lot of them before I'm through!"

I could not, of course, account for this sudden, passionate outburst, but as her anger subsided, she collapsed upon my breast, sobbing. She—perhaps at Mycroft's urging—had pulled me into this underworld, and yet apparently was now denouncing the very people to whom she had betrayed me. How I wished I had Watson to advise me at this moment.

There was nothing for me to do but to put my arms around her; mystified though I was, I was nevertheless still a gentleman. In which embrace the Boss found us moments later.

"Now, Morey, will you look at them lovebirds," he said to a man standing beside him. "It looks like our little daughter and the old man have gotten mighty fond of each other in a short time. I t'ink you've been aced out of the racket. Ha ha!"

The man called Morey turned red. "Damn it, Maddie," he shouted.

"You know how things stand between us." He tried to push past the Boss, but was blocked by one hairy arm thrown across the doorway.

Miss McParland released herself from my embrace, turned toward them, and addressed Morey: "Listen to me, Charlie," she said. "I'm not yours now, or ever. I thought I made that perfectly clear. I belong to no man, except the memory of my father, and until I have either his vengeance or his benediction, no man shall ever possess me." She looked wildly around the room, and then at me. "Oh, God, I am so confused!" she cried, rushing out.

For a moment, there was silence. And the man called Morey (to whom I had taken an instant dislike) muttered, "Dames."

Now he turned his baleful attention to me. He was a big man, almost as big as the Boss, and from the rippling sinews of his arms, I knew he would be a formidable opponent in combat. "And who might you be?" he barked.

"Jim McKenna," I replied, and then he hit me. The blow wobbled me, but I stood my ground.

"You sound like an Englishman to me. What's your name?"

Once again, I said, "Jim McKenna, of Liverpool." This time two blows followed in quick succession, but I had steeled my midsection and so, while painful, they were resistible.

"I'm only going to ask you one more time, old man," he said, his voice gleaming with menace, "so you'd better get it right. *What's your name?*"

My promise to Mycroft and my obligation to my country steadied my resolve. As did one other: Miss McParland's honor. "My name is Jim McKenna of Liverpool and Chicago. If you disbelieve me, then strike me again, but make sure you kill me, for otherwise it will go very hard with you, Morey."

Morey scoffed as I put up my dukes. As Watson has told you, I was a passably fair boxer in my prime, having battled the great McMurdo, and I had long since taken the measure of Irish bullies from the London underworld, where Moriarty had made ample use of them. He swung once more, but this time I ducked his punch and came up with my right fist just under his chin. Rocked back, he was an easy mark for a left to the solar plexus, and down went Morey in a heap. The great Mendoza himself could not have executed a finer one-two.

The Boss let out a roar of laughter. Morey let out a groan, and then glared at me from the floor. "It's just you and me now, Jim McKenna," he said evilly, skulking off.

The Boss brushed his threat aside. "This is war. Ireland needs all her sons, even gorillas like Morey, no matter their land of birth or their personal indispositions toward one another. If a man like your own good self has had his conscience pricked by the indignities heaped upon our most distressful nation, and you wish to join us in our struggle, then . . . this is where it begins."

"Then let it begin," I replied.

In the days, weeks, and months that followed, the Boss and his men did nothing less than to rob me of my Britishness and turn me into an Irishman—or, rather, an Irish-American. I was schooled in the lore of that island, and in its resentful, aggrieved history. I was taught the finer points of counterfeiting, of bomb-making and pistol-shooting, loosening my British inhibitions against the straightforward use of violence. At one point, my mind flashed back to that moment in what Watson had called *The Adventure of the Three Garridebs*, and I realized that never again would I strike a ruthless criminal such as "Killer" Evans with my pistol when I could more easily shoot him in lawful response to his attempted murder of Watson and myself.

As the Boss said, this was war.

I learnt of the Irish underground railroad, which moved fleeing Fenians through Boston, New York, Philadelphia, Buffalo, New Orleans, Chicago, St. Paul, and San Francisco. I realized for the first time the immense amount of money being collected in the States to be remitted to Ireland, apparently to finance a very big operation to be forthcoming. I heard names bruited, names not unfamiliar to me, but never in this context: Casement and Childers and a man they called "Dev." The thought that men such as these could possibly be traitors to the Crown stunned me.

There was more, even darker. Cut off from civilization as I was, I had little recourse to newspapers. But the ominous wind blowing from east had not gone unnoticed, even in here Buffalo. The possibility of war with the Kaiser's Germany was now openly being contemplated across the Atlantic and, to judge from the tenor of my companions' remarks, it was something devoutly to be wished—and they made no secret where their loyalties lay.

As a "cover," I was sent to work with a motor-car mechanic. Americans were mad for motor cars, and with my natural aptitude for gadgetry, I was soon on a first-name basis with starters, sparking plugs, oil pumps, and the like. To enhance my Americanness, I even began to sport a small, although hideous, goatee beard, which lent me an uncanny resemblance to "Uncle Sam."

That was by day. In the evenings I often visited with Miss Mc-Parland. Why she had betrayed me in Chicago, I still had no idea. She would not respond to any questions on the subject, but instead fixed me with that penetrating gaze I had come to know so well. Once, I dared ask her what was in the letter I had delivered, but her expression was that of a kindly teacher toward an especially dim pupil, and so I dropped the subject for the nonce. Instead, she handed me a "dime novel" about Custer's Last Stand and asked me to read it aloud.

I had not got ten words into it when she stopped me. "No, no," she said. "Listen to me, then imitate." Treating me as an especially dim pupil, forcing me to repeat words, then phrases, then sentences, correcting my pronunciation at every step, as if she were my Svengali and I her Trilby. The object was to change my manner of speaking, to expunge all traces of Britishness in my speech, and to adopt the harsh and unlovely tunes of the American. I made rapid progress.

One evening, exhausted by my labors at the motor-car shop, as I lay smoking, she entered, but this time without a book. Directly, I made to rise, but she held up her hand in that forward way American girls have, and bid me to lie still. She took the bedside chair, and without preamble, she began to sing. It was a curious, melancholy waltz, but with a kind of serenity about it that I found utterly captivating. And her voice . . . it was of such perfection that the angels themselves must have been sitting at her feet, listening. "Just a song at twilight / when the lights are low / and the flick'ring shadows / softly come and go . . ."

"What is it?" I asked when she had concluded.

"'Love's Old Sweet Song,'" she whispered. "Come on, James—sing it with me now."

It was the first time she had called me by my Christian name, and even though it was not really mine, I felt a thrill run through me.

And so we sang. The song ended. She searched my face for what seemed like hours, questions unposed flitting across hers. "You know, Jim," she said at last, "you're really something."

And so time passed . . .

In the portrait that Watson has so generously drawn of me, you may perhaps have noticed that disguise comes as second nature with me; indeed, I think I do not flatter myself by acknowledging that the stage in fact lost a great talent when I chose instead to become the world's first private consulting detective. Still, no role I had played, neither stable boy, nor wizened bookseller, nor even Sigerson—when the world, including Watson, thought me dead after Professor Moriarty's unfortunate accident at the Reichenbach Falls—could rival my new persona as Jim McKenna. With every passing day, he was becoming more and more real to me, and there were days when I hardly thought of Mr. Sherlock Holmes of Baker Street.

The irony was unmistakable: in search of the solution to the greatest mystery of my life, I had become my own client.

Therefore, I could not help but reexamine many of the tenets of my previous faith. Of course, it was impossible that I could descend to the level of the common Irish among whom I found myself. And yet, perhaps my forcible indoctrination was offering me another perspective on a people I had long dismissed as either congenital drunkards or habitual criminals—if often, like Moriarty and Moran, criminals of genius—whom I had now come to see, mostly thanks to Miss McParland, as human beings.

It was in the midst of this brown study that I took my place at our evening table, Mrs. Murphy's boardinghouse writ large, but with as dangerous a band of cutthroats as I had ever associated with. As a series of names was called out, it was clear to me at once that the die had finally been cast: Lefty Louie, One-Eye, Happy Jim, and Paddy the Priest; the Americans were on a first-name basis with the world. And then . . .

"Jim," said the Boss. "And Maddie. That's the team. You leave two days hence for New York."

Morey rose in anger. "But Boss—," he sputtered. "What about me?"

"Shut yer gob, Charlie," retorted the Boss. A parcel bound up with twine landed with a plop in front of me. New clothes, to complete my transformation from British gentleman to Irish-American ruffian. Among the accessories, I noticed, was a revolver. "Wear it in good health, Jimbo," he said. "And use it if you have to."

Once again, all eyes were upon me, Morey's most especially. Only this time, it was not a rain of brickbats and chamber pots, but rather the hushed breath of expectancy that accompanied their attention. Though her gaze was modestly diverted, I could sense Maddie's blushes from across the room. "Terrific, Boss," I said, then turned my glance to her. "Let's blow this dump, Maddie. I'm goin' bughouse here."

The plan was that she and I were to pose as father and daughter. But Maddie demurred, arguing that despite our difference in age, it was far more common among our class that an older man take a younger wife than be seen traveling with a marriageable daughter. And so it was agreed. Over one objection, as you might well imagine. Indeed, Morey had been quietly but steadily seething in a corner of the room, and I did not like his look.

We were but small cogs in a much greater wheel of intrigue, so the exact use to which our "charitable" funds were to be put was never spelled out. But I had long since caught the drift: the Fenians, the IRB, and the Irish Republican Army were planning some kind of an uprising in the near future, perhaps in conjunction with some agents of the Kaiser based in rebellious Ireland; there were mutterings about the Dutchmen, which I knew was an American term for the Germans, and a rendezvous in Skibbereen.

And then it struck me—this was, perhaps, the reason Mycroft had sent me on this mission: to infiltrate the gang and find out what the Irish-American brethren were planning for the Ould Sod. What a fool I had been to mistrust him!

There was just one last missing piece of the puzzle. And only she could help me, help me see what I could not see for myself. At long last, I was piercing the veil.

Silently, she came to me that night. We spoke not a word. I slipped off my shirt. With her tender hands, she traced the markings on my back: a triangle within a circle. And suddenly, it was all clear to me. It was the same brand that Birdy Edwards once bore, and the corpse he had so devoutly wished to pass off as his own at Birlstone in order to make his escape from the Scowrers of Vermissa Valley a quarter of a century ago. The hand of a man long dead had reached out and touched my shoulder. The hand of Fate.

She kissed the back of my neck and then, moving lower, the wound, kissing the brand, kissing the mark of Cain that had been forever laid upon me.

I could hear the rustle of her shift as it dropped to floor, then felt her warm flesh upon mine. "Now we're both comfortable," she said.

There was revelry the next night in what passed for the Altamont's ballroom to celebrate our departure on the morrow. The beer and spirits flowed.

Morey had been glaring and glowering at me all evening, and I smelt trouble brewing from this bonehead—trouble for which I was fully prepared, or so I thought.

"Come, Jim, let's dance," said Maddie. "If we're to," she blushed, "pretend . . . to be married, then we ought to act like it." I took her sweet hand in mine and led her to the dance floor.

In a flash, the glowering Morey was upon us. "Take your filthy paws off her, you damned bastard!" he shouted. "Or, by God, I'll send you straight to hell." He shoved me, hard.

"No, Charlie," cried Maddie.

"You belong to me!" he snarled.

"No," she replied, with a quiet dignity that I shall never forget. "I belong to him, and there's the end of it."

Enraged, Morey lunged for her, bringing him directly into my path. I could not bear to let Morey's Irish temper spoil that which now lay before me, nor its promise of happiness.

I struck him in the face with all my might. The same strength that unbent my poker after Dr. Roylott's ministrations was summoned forth one last time. The whole room could hear the crack of the bone. For an instant, I thought I had killed him.

He stumbled backwards, reaching for his pistol as he fell. A shot rang out. I felt nothing. He had missed! I moved in for the kill. My Irish, as they say, was well and truly up. As I made ready to finish him—

—I heard my Maddie cry out. Instantly, all thoughts of further violence were forgotten; I turned to see her, lying on the floor. As I rushed to her side, I could see at a glance that the wound was fatal.

"Water!" I shouted.

The best I could do was make her as comfortable as possible before her final journey into that land of *Mor* that the Irish know so well. I cradled her dear head in my arms. Her eyes were wide and so blue.

"Be true to me, Jim," she gasped. "On the blood of my father, be true to me!"

"Birdy Edwards," I said, quietly. Her eyes told me the truth. She had known all along.

The chastened crowd moved forward, to hear the dying colleen's last words. "God, how I hated him for his treachery, even as I admired him for his bravery. How I love the people he betrayed! And how I love him for betraying them!"

Somehow, she found the strength to raise her arms and point at the people in the room, sweeping them all up in her dragnet. "And you!" she cried. "How I hate you for what you did to him, and for what you made him do." Her head dropped back into my arms.

Her strength was gone, and I knew the end was near. Somehow, she found the power to extract something from the folds of her dress and press it into my hand. It was the letter from Mycroft, now stained with her blood.

I put my ear to her sweet lips. "Promise me, Jim, you'll never waiver. Never despair. Never falter."

"I promise, Maddie."

"Tell me you love me," she said, the fierce light in her eyes subsiding.

"As no other." It was just moments now. "And forever."

"Then sing to me. One last time. The song at twilight." She gasped and shuddered.

I sang: "Still to us at twilight / comes Love's old song / comes Love's old sweet song . . . "

I never stopped singing to her, even after she lay quite still and silent in my arms.

The rest of my story is quickly told. I chased Morey across the sea, to Ireland and Skibbereen. He had gone to ground, seeking shelter with the IRA, but of course it was child's play for Jim McKenna, a fellow Irish-American, to find him. As I had done so often in London, where young Irish boys had been legion among my Baker Street Irregulars, I quickly organized a flying column of street Arabs, which fanned out across all the public houses of the town. In less than a day I had my answer: "The Wild Geese."

I slipped in incognito: cap tugged down low, hunched over, a tremor in the hand that held my walking-stick. Morey, on the other hand, was his usual loud, vulgar, and expansive self. I spotted him at a table in the corner, gesticulating wildly at a Prussian gentleman whose monocle and dueling scar proclaimed both his ancestry and his attitude.

As I edged closer, I heard him say, " . . . von Herling. Now a deal's a deal and if you've even half a mind to double-cross me well, buster, you had better watch your step."

The German sneered across his beer. "Do you think you can impress me with this belligerence?" he asked with a deprecatory laugh. "Look around this room; there are twenty men I could hire to work for us. Why do I need you?"

I noticed there were four empty pint glasses in front of Morey. Two went flying as he gestured wildly. "Damn you, I thought we were on the same side!" he shouted.

"Simply because the enemy of my enemy can be my friend does not mean that you and I have to like each other," replied the German. "Quite the contrary."

Morey's face flushed and he started to rise. I could not let him do anything rash, not with my revenge so near to hand. I needed a diversion and the pint of Guinness in my left hand would do nicely.

The stout splashed him from head to toe. Enraged, he leapt up, the Prussian temporarily forgotten. Feigning unawareness in my senility, I passed through the side door, the one the urchins used to nip in and out of as they dragged foaming growlers back to their drunken fathers at home.

"You there! Old man!" he screamed, but pretending deafness, I ignored him. The room jeered as he struggled to his feet.

I was in the alley and waiting for him when he burst through the door. Cap off, upright and cold as death was I. "McKenna!" he said, staggering back against the door. This was just the effect I had hoped to produce, for our confrontation needed to be quick and final; the intrusion of strangers would have been most unhelpful at this point.

"Go for it," I said.

He went for it.

I fired two shots to his one. Both mine found their mark. His did not.

Morey's body sagged, then sat heavily as his life's blood ebbed away. I could hear pounding on the other side of the door as the pub's denizens were roused by the commotion. I waited just long enough to watch the light in his eyes flicker out and then into the rubbish went the elderly McKenna's hat, stick, coat, and as much else as I could strip off in the few moments allotted to me, revealing the oil-stained, motor-car tradesman's garb beneath.

I walked round to the front of the pub and entered just as a few men had managed to push the body aside and force open the door. As the hue and cry for the police went up, I took a seat near the German and tugged ever so slightly on my goatee. He looked at me and gave me a small nod of acknowledgement, but not of betrayal.

"What'll it be, sir?" asked the barmaid.

"Nothin'," I replied, my Irish-American accent plain. "I've changed me mind." I nodded in the direction of the German: "Good evening to you, fine sir," and took my leave.

For a short while, the local constabulary were very much mystified, especially when they discovered the old clothes and the American revolver, but they were used to drunken Irishmen murdering each other, and quickly lost interest in the case, and so I made my way across the Irish Sea and on to London without further incident. The next day, I was back on the South Downs, among my bees, making some observations upon the segregation of the queen.

Sussex, July 1914

It did not surprise me when Martha announced Mr. Mycroft Holmes. By rights, I ought not to have received him. That such a conniving mind could comfortably reside within such a portly and indolent exterior . . . I realized that, not for the first time, I had underestimated my own brother.

It had been, I had to admit, sheer genius on his part to insinuate me into the Irish-American underworld of Birdy Edwards's own hometown, and send me to the one person who could have successfully infiltrated me into the mob. But how did he know she would? I took the letter, stained with her blood, from my billfold and, smoothing it out, laid it flat upon my study table. "Show Mr. Holmes in," I said.

"Sherlock!" he exclaimed, as if he had half-expected never to see me again. He extended his hand, but I let it dangle, as we said in Chicago.

"I brought this back to you," I said, gesturing toward the letter. "Full circle."

For a moment, my brother was something he almost never was: nonplussed. The sight of the blood—her blood—on the letter, I believe, unnerved him. But he quickly regained his composure.

"We had had our eye on the girl for some time," he began. Was there a hint of apology in his manner? "Ever since the tragedy of Birlstone, in fact. After the death of her father, we sent her small anonymous remittances and made sure our agents looked in on her from time to time. In fact, it was we who suggested the alias, McParland, to protect her from the Moriarty gang's American henchmen. A most conflicted, troubled young woman. A tragedy."

I said nothing. My silence was remonstrance enough.

"Damn it, Sherlock, what could I do? If I had told you what His Majesty's Government was about, you would have refused outright, Asquith or no Asquith; after all, you'd already turned Grey down. And I knew that your love of a mystery would keep you in the Great Game, as it were. And you have done brilliantly. I am very proud of you."

At last, I found my tongue, and it was all I could to tame it. "All of this—for what? For me to 'keep tabs' on a few Fenians? And at what cost?" I felt myself growing hot under the collar. "If His Majesty's government cannot watch a few sad-sack revolutionaries in Dublin, then what hope is there for it?"

Mycroft looked me up and down, as if I were still his younger brother, playing with tin soldiers and hobbyhorses in our bedroom so many years ago. "You still don't understand, do you?" he said at last.

At this point I must confess that I lost my temper. "What is there to understand?" I cried, clutching at the letter. "Your own words condemn you!"

His eyes shuttled back and forth inside his head, and not for the first time was I reminded of the very strong affinity, intellectually speaking, between Mycroft Holmes and the late Professor Moriarty. Both of whom now had the blood of the McParland family on their hands. I looked down at the letter, her red bloodstains fading, the paper already taking on the appearance of parchment, receding into history along with what was left of my heart.

"We—*I*—trusted her to do the right thing. And so, it appears, she did. Read it aloud, please."

My hands were shaking as I looked at the epistle. "'My dear Miss Edwards: The gentleman who bears this letter is the man who both saved your father from the gibbet and yet condemned him to death. He is in need of a redemption that only you can provide. Do with him as you will.'"

There was nothing further to read, but the letter's contents did not end there. At the bottom, instead of a signature, there was simply a mark: a triangle within a circle. Her blood had swamped this bit, rendering it a dark brown stain, like the brand I had seen on Birdy Edwards, and the corpse at Birlstone. Like the brand I now bore on my back. The Trinity and Eternity. The solution to the final problem.

I let the missive flutter to the ground. At last, I understood.

"This has nothing to do with the Fenians, Sherlock. Or the Irish. It was always about the Germans, who mean to have war, and war they shall get. They would never have trusted an English turncoat, especially not one of recent vintage. Furthermore, although you were retired, we needed you out of the country, that the memory of Mr. Sherlock Holmes of Baker Street and the South Downs might fade. But an Irish-American named James McKenna . . . "

"Is dead," I said. "And dead he shall stay." My promise to Maddie overrode everything, even my loyalty to the Crown, even my blood ties to my brother. Sherlock Holmes's undying loyalty was and always would be to England, but Jim McKenna would never betray her. There was another sort of loyalty, that which Maddie had taught me, and if that were the higher, then so be it.

"Very well, then. May he rest in peace. But there is now a nobleman of the Hun persuasion in fact, who very much desires to meet with you. In fact . . . coincidentally . . . he is living not far from here. I think you take my meaning."

I smiled, reflecting the memory of her last smile, a memory that would never leave me. Where Mycroft was concerned, there was never a coincidence; in the chess game of life, he was always two moves ahead. "What is this *Junker*'s name?"

Mycroft exhaled in relief. "Von Bork. Funnily enough, a colleague of your friend, von Herling, whom you encountered in Skibbereen. You shall enter his service on the morrow."

So Maddie had not died in vain. For King and Country, and for the United States of America, she would always live. "Agreed," I said, my nostrils flaring. Truth to tell, I was looking forward to a second encounter with the sneering Prussian and his agent in my country.

Business settled, he rose to leave. "One last question," Mycroft said, on his way out the door. "If James McKenna is dead, by what name shall you call yourself?"

"Altamont," I replied.

MORIARTY, MORAN, AND MORE: ANTI-HIBERNIAN SENTIMENT IN THE CANON
Michael Walsh

Michael Walsh, the former music critic of *Time* magazine, is the author of the novels *Exchange Alley*, *As Time Goes By* (the prequel/sequel to the movie *Casablanca*), and *And All the Saints*, a winner of the 2004 American Book Awards for fiction. His latest novel, *Hostile Intent*, was published in September 2009 by Kensington Books. Under the name "Micheál Breathnach," he contributed "The Coole Park Problem" to *Ghosts in Baker Street*. For good measure, he co-wrote with Gail Parent the 2002 hit Disney Channel movie *Cadet Kelly*.

* * * *

Few figures embody both a place and an era like Sir Arthur Conan Doyle. Fewer still conceal such a welter of internal contradictions beneath such a confident—but deeply misleading—exterior.

The very image of the late Victorian British Empire, Conan Doyle was born in Scotland's capital, Edinburgh, and came to consider himself the very soul of Englishness, and yet—on both his father's and his mother's side—was descended from a long line of Irishmen, and Catholics to boot. A Catholic in a Presbyterian city—no matter its large number of his co-religionists; an Irishman in England; and an

Englishman to the world: it is little wonder that these stresses would so bedevil their author that only his most famous creation could give them voice, and resolution.

"I am half Irish, you know," Conan Doyle once said, explaining an outburst of temper, "and my British half has the devil of a job to hold the hotheaded rascal in." So far, so stereotypical: the image of the quick-tempered Hibernian was one already long established in the British hierarchy of racial classification. And, indeed, Conan Doyle himself seemed to accept the conventional archetypes of Irishness, using them as a kind of handy shorthand to explain some "un-English" behavior or other. Stumping for a Liberal Unionist candidate, he recalls in *Memories and Adventures* that he found himself being pushed on stage to address an audience of three thousand: "I hardly knew myself what I said, but the Irish part of me came to my aid and supplied me with a torrent of more or less incoherent words and similes which roused the audience greatly, though it read afterwards more like a comic stump speech than a serious political effort." Temper and the gift of the gab: two hallmarks of the stage Irishman, which Conan Doyle obviously, desperately, did not want to be.

For at the same time, he was dead set against Gladstone's policy of Home Rule for the perennially fractious colony of Ireland. As Britain moved inexorably toward the twin crises of the Great War and the Easter Rising, Conan Doyle, at the peak of his literary fame, was essentially a collaborator with the enemy.

It is my contention in this brief monograph that Conan Doyle's distaste for his own Irishness, lightly and comically alluded to in the excerpts above, was in reality deep-rooted and far-reaching. It is largely masked in his letters, now available in *Arthur Conan Doyle: A Life in Letters*,[1] but we need not trouble ourselves with mere mundane reality.

---

1 Edited by Jon Lellenberg, Daniel Stashower, and Charles Foley (New York: Penguin

The proof is precisely where it ought to be: in the Canon, which is a veritable feast of anti-Hibernian sentiment that would make the most bigoted Englishman blush. Do we want a villain? And not just any villain, but the Napoleon of Crime, the spider at the center of a vast web of criminality that affects all England? Very well, Conan Doyle—through the amanuensis of a sturdy Scotsman, Dr. John Hamish Watson—gives us a corker in Professor Moriarty, the Napoleon of Crime.

Does Moriarty want a second? A man of ruthless cunning and one of the finest shots in the Empire? Very well, then—Colonel Sebastian Moran is just your man. Throughout the Canon, Irishmen are nearly always portrayed in an unflattering light, as men of either overt criminality or, at the very least, violence. In addition to Moriarty and Moran, consider McMurdo, the former prizefighter and servant to Bartholomew Sholto in *The Sign of the Four* who, tellingly, had once boxed with Holmes. "If instead of standin' there so quiet you had just stepped up and given me that cross-hit of yours under the jaw, I'd ha' known you without a question."

McMurdo—a name with deep significance for Conan Doyle, as we shall see—oft recurs (or perhaps "occurs," given the sequencing of the stories) in the Sherlock Holmes novel that is itself a veritable symphony of anti-Hibernian sentiment; I refer, of course, to *The Valley of Fear*.

In this novel, which no Irishman or Irish-American can read without shuddering, we find proof positive of not only Conan Doyle's self-loathing, but his active support of the forces that would crush the brave Irish men and women of Vermissa Valley. Adumbrating Liam O'Flaherty's classic about the Irish revolution, *The Informer*, Conan Doyle presents us with a "hero" who goes by a number of names, including Jack McMurdo, Birdy Edwards, and John Douglas. This traitor, working for the despised and brutal Pinkerton Agency,

Press, 2007).

infiltrates the Scowrers in a Pennsylvania coal town, where they are fighting for justice, and eventually breaks them. Like Gypo Nolan, Edwards flees his treachery and heads for California, where he strikes gold. Later, in England as "Jack Douglas," he is acquitted of murder, but is eventually lost overboard as he flees again, this time by sea. So, in a sense, the story does have a happy ending after all.

What are we to make of this?

These are very deep waters, indeed. And without resorting to armchair psychoanalysis, it seems clear that Conan Doyle, in a successful attempt to penetrate English society, masked himself *à la* Birdy Edwards—and later, most ominously, as Holmes himself—and yet felt such a sense of self-loathing that he was forced to confess his sins to his alter ego, Dr. Watson.

And so it is in the pages of the Canon that we see the Conan Doyle psychodrama played out, where the Irishman battles the Englishman with the Scotsman as referee. And the Irishman—or in one particular case, the Irishwoman—always loses.

There is no question that his Celtic heritage was a source of endless fascination for Conan Doyle. Edinburgh has, since the Irish exodus of Black '47, hosted a large Irish minority, as do several other British cities, including most prominently Glasgow and Liverpool. Looked down upon, often despised, the Irish were to the English what the Africans and the Indians were to eighteenth- and ninetheenth-century Americans: a dark and savage people, by turns childlike and murderous, given to song and dance but appallingly prone to sudden outbursts of the most appalling violence. Incapable of controlling their thirst for drink—"the Creature," in Irish parlance—they were clearly second-class citizens (if indeed citizens at all).

The Doyle family had been in Britain for generations, but the Foley

family—Sir Arthur's beloved mother was the Irish-born Mary Foley—
brought him close to his origins. "My real love for letters, my instinct
for storytelling, springs from my mother, who is of Anglo-Celtic stock,
with the glamour and the romance of the Celt very strong marked."
(Even when discussing his own mother—"The Mam"—Conan Doyle
felt compelled to resort to Irish stereotype.)

But that was the happy face of the Celts. The dark side, the Creature-
obsessed, was symbolized by none other than his father, Charles
Altamont Doyle, whose powerful thirst damaged a promising career
as an artist—the wreck of whom we have visible evidence in the six
drawings he made for his son's *A Study in Scarlet*, featuring a bearded
Sherlock Holmes.

So . . . *Mor*iarty, *Mor*an, Mc*Mur*do, even *Mor*gan the poisoner.
All Irish names, each one beginning with some variant of "mor," the
linguistic signifier of distress and death. The most powerful resonance
of all, of course, is the Irish phrase *An Gorta Mor*—the Great Hunger—
referring to the famine of the mid-nineteenth century, which changed,
changed utterly, the fate of That Most Distressful Nation.

Can you see the pattern emerging here?

Mordred. Fata Morgana. Even Tolkien's fictional Mordor—each of
these Celtic formulations indicates danger and darkness. For Tolkien,
"Mordor" was the Black Land, an etymological throwback to the roots
of our common tongue and the source of our word "murder." Clearly,
in the works of Conan Doyle, the prefix "mor" immediately indicates
that the person named is not to be trusted, is not only dangerous but
*mur*derous—someone with whom an interaction may well be fatal.

So let us now consider three Canonical stories of the utmost
significance to our discussion: *The Final Problem*, *The Adventure of
the Empty House*, and *His Last Bow*. And then let us conclude with
a fourth that may well feature the most surprising character in all

the Canon. Someone who puts Moriarty and Moran in the shade—Sherlock's most dangerous opponent, but one without whom he could never have survived the plunge over the Reichenbach Falls. Someone who is, in many respects, the most crucially overlooked figure in the Canon—which is exactly the way Conan Doyle wanted it.

In many ways, *The Final Problem* is the most straightforward of the lot, and certainly makes an ideal curtain-raiser to this discussion of anti-Hibernianism. I need not recount the story here; suffice it to say that it not only introduces us, in person, to Professor James Moriarty, it also engenders a whole discussion of precisely how many Moriartys there actually are, and whether they are all named James. Certainly, the Professor is an unlovely physical specimen, devisor of a binomial theorem of genius or not. Physically, he resembles a reptile, and upon meeting Holmes he promptly insults him by expressing disappointment in the size of his frontal development. (Of course, we have only Holmes's word for this, since Watson can only report the hearsay encounter from Sherlock's testimony.)

But the Professor is the *primus inter pares* of declared Sherlockian villains, and there can be no question of the mortal danger he poses to Holmes. Holmes, on the verge of rounding up Moriarty's gang, convinces Watson to travel with him to the Continent, where Holmes has his final confrontation with his now-discomfited nemesis.

And so Moriarty dies. But like his shape-shifting predecessor, Fata *Mor*gana, he is almost immediately reincarnated in the form of his henchman, Sebastian Moran, who (we learn in *The Empty House*) bombards Holmes with boulders as the Great Detective scrambles away from the Reichenbach abyss. Holmes imagines he hears the late Professor's voice screaming at him from the bottom of the falls, and then suddenly Moran appears, bent on malevolence, as if summoned from the depths of Hell. His subsequent attack on Holmes from the empty house in London is entirely to be expected, but Holmes outwits him and the "second most dangerous man in London" is captured and charged with the murder of the Hon. Ronald Adair.

Then something entirely miraculous happens. Holmes and Watson are restored to their old rooms in Baker Street, which despite fire and gunshots are found to be in essentially pristine condition, maintained by Mycroft Holmes and Mrs. Hudson, with "all the old landmarks in their places," including the chemical corner, the acid-stained table, the scrapbooks, the violin, the pipe rack, and the Persian slipper.

And Holmes's encyclopedia of biographies, where in addition to Morgan the poisoner, Merridew of abominable memory, and Matthews, who knocked out one of Holmes's teeth, we find Colonel Sebastian Moran, London-born son of Sir Augustus Moran, the former British Minister to—Persia.

By now, it's clear that the combination of murder and magic, so quintessentially Celtic, is powerfully at play here. Like Conan Doyle himself, Professor Moriarty and Colonel Moran have a patina of Britishness to overlay their Irishness, but Hibernianism in the blood can take the strangest forms, and in this case it took the form of two respectable "Englishmen" who were, of course, really disguised Irishmen. Exactly like Conan Doyle himself.

And so we come to *His Last Bow*, that moody, mysterious and moving *ave atque vale*, written in the third person—as if by Conan Doyle himself—in which all of the Literary Agent's obsessions can at last be viewed in full flower. Secret identities. Irishness as a marker of betrayal. A false identity, as false as that of "Birdy Edwards" during the Pinkerton man's undercover work in Vermissa Valley. Holmes learned American gangland slang in Chicago, joined an Irish secret society in

Buffalo, and got into trouble with the constabulary in Skibbereen as he polished his anti-English credentials. Then (in collusion with Martha, the ever-faithful Mrs. Hudson), he sprang the trap on the German spy, von Bork. And when the imperious kraut vows vengeance, how does Holmes respond? "The old sweet song. How often have I heard it in days gone by"—an allusion to the famous American popular chanson written by the Irish-American James L. Molloy in 1884, "Love's Old Sweet Song."

Says Holmes: "It was a favorite ditty of the late lamented Professor Moriarty. Colonel Sebastian Moran has also been known to warble it. And yet I live and keep bees upon the South Downs."

And yet I live. Keep that in mind. We'll come back to it in our final peroration. And what identity, of all possible identities, does the master of disguise, the man who could impersonate stable hand and wizened bookseller alike, employ? An Irishman. An Irish-American.

An Irish-American named Altamont. As in Charles <u>Altamont</u> Doyle.

Sir Arthur's father.

The pinnacle of Sherlock Holmes's career—his greatest service to England—comes as an Irish-American named "Altamont."

In this valedictory, in which Holmes utters the memorable lines: "Stand with me here upon the terrace . . . ." Conan Doyle sums up all his ambivalence about his own nature and his own family, and seems to reconcile it at the very end. Holmes and Watson, together for the last time, with the proximate enemy, von Bork, vanquished, but an east wind coming, an east wind such as never blew on England yet. God's own wind . . . And then, embarrassed by this most un-British display of sentiment, Holmes turns his attention to von Bork's check for five hundred pounds and rushes off to the bank to cash it before the Kaiser can stop payment on it.

Thus does Holmes's quintessential Englishness assert itself.

And yet I live. Why does Holmes say this, at this particular moment, and in this particular context? Why would he *not* live? After all, many years before, he had vanquished Professor Moriarty with his knowledge of baritsu, and dodged Colonel Moran's rocks and avoided his exploding bullet. By the time of *His Last Bow*, on the very eve of World War I, Holmes had survived every attempt on his life, every battle, every boxing match, Dr. Roylott's swamp adder in *The Speckled Band*, even Tonga's poisoned dart in *The Sign of the Four*.

On the eve of World War I . . . when just across the Irish Sea a storm was gathering that would culminate with the Harp flying, however briefly, above the G.P.O. in Dublin . . .

When both the British Empire and Conan Doyle himself stood, however unknowingly, not on the terrace but upon the precipice, into which both would soon hurtle. As Britain would lose her Empire, Conan Doyle would lose his faith, and embrace spiritualism; the father of the ultra-rationalist, "no ghosts need apply" Sherlock Holmes, would not only *reject* the faith of his fathers, he would *embrace* a far older and more primal faith: the faith in the spirit world.

The faith of the ancient Celts, who could cross over between the dark land of Mordor and the living.

Who knew that Life and Death were and are two sides of the same coin, inevitably twinned, not to be feared but embraced as a necessary duality. Like sun and moon. And: Male and female.

Which brings us to the last and most important story link in our chain: *The Sign of the Four*.

In which Holmes and Watson meet another "mor" character. Who turns out to be Holmes's deadliest enemy.

Mary *Mor*stan.

Or, as she was briefly known, Mrs. John H. Watson.

Whose pivotal, vital, and indispensable role in the Canon is not sufficiently understood or remarked upon. For if Sherlock as "Altamont" was a partial salvation of Conan Doyle's father, can it not be said of Mary that she is nothing less than "the Mam"?

Moriarty, Moran, Morstan. From Holmes's point of view, the three greatest challenges of his career, each one inextricably linked by ethnicity and etymology. Moriarty and Moran we have already considered. Let us now turn our attention to the formidable Miss Morstan.

The literary parallel between her and Colonel Moran should be obvious. He was an officer in the Indian Army; her father was an officer in the Indian Army. Their names are, in fact, nearly identical, and indeed "Morstan"—with its wonderful *frisson* of implicit death—is anagrammatical for "St. Moran." Thus, Mary Morstan is the "good side" of Colonel Moran.

Holmes, however, takes an instant dislike to her. When at the conclusion of *The Sign of the Four* Watson announces their engagement, Holmes coldly tells his Boswell that he cannot congratulate him. For Holmes has instantly sensed an enemy, however innocuous she might appear, and realizes, with the chill wind of death blowing past him in the shape of Tonga's dart, that the world will not be able to contain both him and Miss Morstan.

One of them will have to die.

Now, it may be objected that Mary Morstan is not Irish. Apparently born in India, her mother dead, she is sent to school in Edinburgh (much like Watson himself, who was packed off to boarding school in the Scottish capital as a youth), and later comes down to London. But consider the evidence:

1) Her Christian name is Mary, the most common Irish name for a girl. Conan Doyle's own mother was named Mary.

2) By her own admission, she has no relatives in England.

3) She goes to school in Edinburgh, with its large Irish population.

4) She earns her living as a governess, a standard occupation in England for an unmarried Irish girl.

5) She is described by Watson—a man who boasts of great experience with women—as blonde with pale skin and large blue eyes: typical physiognomy of the west of Ireland, with its heavy Viking influence.

6) While the name Morstan is unusual, there is a district in County Down, near Belfast, called Morstan Park.

It's very likely, therefore, that Captain Arthur Morstan—interesting choice of a first name—was born in Northern Ireland (there's the Home Rule problem again), raised in Edinburgh, joined the Indian Army, not the regular Army (which might indicate that he was a Catholic, not a Protestant). In charge of a convict settlement in the Andaman Islands—a fit duty station for an Irishman, perhaps, but not an Englishman—he later dies of heart attack brought on by an attack of furious temper.

When Watson marries Mary Morstan, Holmes's world is shattered. Other than scorn, he has no way to fight back. With Dr. Roylott, he could unbend the poker; with Moriarty, he could jiu-jitsu him over the side of the Reichenbach Falls; with Col. Moran, he could outsmart him and deliver him into the hands of the police.

But against Mary, he could do nothing.

And so Holmes "dies" at the conclusion of *The Final Problem*, the best and wisest man Watson had ever known.

There follows the three years—note the symbolic number three—of the Great Hiatus, during which we read of the remarkable explorations of a Norwegian named Sigerson, time in Tibet, a meeting with the

Dalai Lama, a visit to—tellingly—Persia, Mecca, and Khartoum (just after the death of General Gordon, whose portrait hung upon the wall in Baker Street), and the coal-tar derivative research in Montpelier. Complete bunkum, of course, as Edgar W. Smith, the best and wisest member of the Baker Street Irregulars, pointed out. Holmes did nothing of the sort. Without the linguistic skills of Sir Richard Burton, the look-in at Mecca would very likely have ended at the business end of an Arabian scimitar.

For the truth is, during the period of the Great Hiatus, Sherlock Holmes was, in fact, dead. As dead as Mordred and Mordor and Moriarty.

And what recalls him to life? What brings him back to face the villain Moran (and thus the ghost of Moriarty) in *The Empty House*? Only one thing.

The death of Mary Morstan. The shape-shifter, Fata Morgana's sister. Without Watson's sad bereavement, there can be no return of Sherlock Holmes.

In order for Holmes to live again, Mary must trade places with him.

Thus does Holmes's greatest enemy make the most heroic sacrifice. Mary Morstan gives up her husband and returns Watson to the embrace of Sherlock Holmes, Mrs. Hudson, and Baker Street.

Just as "the Mam" had to sacrifice herself for her family in the face of Charles Altamont Doyle's alcoholism and penury, so does Mary Morstan sacrifice herself that "Altamont" might live. After all, it was "the Mam" who entreated her son to resurrect Sherlock, after his death in *The Final Problem*; and upon relenting, what did Conan Doyle say to her?

He still lives.

Just as Conan Doyle had to kill first the Irishman in him and later the Catholic, so that the Scottish-born English gentlemen and knight of letters could fully flower, so must the Irish girl die that the Englishman and his Scottish amanuensis—the two presentable sides of Sir Arthur Conan Doyle—may fully live again, reborn through a woman's love. It is one of the noblest and most moving self-sacrifices in all of fiction—and for Conan Doyle, one of the most daring self-portraits in all literature.

How the Creator of Sherlock Holmes Brought Him to America
Christopher Redmond

Christopher Redmond grew up in Kingston, Ontario, graduating from Queen's University. He received his MA from the University of Waterloo, where he is currently director of internal communications, editing the university's daily news bulletin. Redmond is the author of *In Bed with Sherlock Holmes*; *Welcome to America, Mr. Sherlock Holmes*; and *A Sherlock Holmes Handbook*. He was formerly editor of *Canadian Holmes*, the journal of The Bootmakers of Toronto, Canada's Sherlock Holmes society, and now operates the Web site Sherlockian.Net. Redmond is a member of several Sherlockian societies, including the Baker Street Irregulars of New York.

* * * *

Arthur Conan Doyle—the creator of Sherlock Holmes and so many other characters and achievements—lived, from his birth in 1859 to his death in 1930, precisely 25,978 days. A little arithmetic shows that the exact middle of his life came on December 14, 1894, a winter day that saw him, at the age of thirty-five, aboard a ship in the North Atlantic, returning home from his first visit to North America.

Conan Doyle was British through and through, but nevertheless he loved America and visited the continent four times, and enthusiasts can trace many of his steps on this side of the water, and imagine how he felt as he saw views that we still can see today.

At thirty-five, Conan Doyle presumably considered himself a young man still, even if now carrying the responsibilities of middle age including two children and a wife, the former Louise Hawkins, who was slowly dying of tuberculosis. Young though he might still be, it was because of his considerable achievements already that he had been invited to come to North America to tour and lecture. He had managed to acquire an education—something not to be taken for granted by a youngster growing up in poverty in smoky Edinburgh, capital of Scotland—and then a medical training. After a few false starts in his medical practice, he had managed to earn a respectable income from it, in the Southsea suburb of Portsmouth, England's largest Channel port. He succeeded there sufficiently, supplementing his medical income with occasional modest payments for magazine stories and newspaper articles, to become a principal source of financial support for his extended family, and be able to start a family of his own. He had married Louise in 1885, and initially they had lived in Southsea and then in South Norwood, a modest suburb of London, but Louise fell ill and they spent time at a number of resorts in the hope of finding a climate that would bolster her health.

Eventually, he abandoned medicine for writing as a career. He had produced scores of short stories in a number of magazines by then, some intended for boys and some for adults. By the time he sailed for America in 1894 he had published seventeen books of fiction, in fact, including three historical novels of which he was particularly proud. Most important, of course, he had invented his Great Detective, and had presented him to an increasingly enthusiastic public in two novels and twenty-four short stories. That little industry he had just brought to an end, however, against the advice of the author's friends and family. The detective was not only wearing out his welcome with his creator, but taking time and attention away from what Conan Doyle considered his more important work, particularly his historical fiction. In December 1893 he published the short story called *The Final Problem*, in which he invented an arch-enemy for Holmes, one Professor Moriarty, and disposed of them both at an encounter in the Swiss Alps.

With Holmes making no more demands on him, ACD moved on to other projects. He and his ailing wife spent the fall of 1893 to the summer of 1894 in Switzerland, at Davos, which was not yet a ski resort, but was considered to have a splendid climate for lung patients. He spent time with her and their new acquaintances there, enjoyed winter sports and had skis shipped to him from Norway, and worked diligently at his desk. This period accounts for his semi-autobiographical novel *The Stark Munro Letters*, and it was also at this time that he created one of the three great characters of his literary career, Brigadier Gerard, a picaresque cavalry officer in Napoleon's service.

In every sense, he was in the middle of his work and the middle of his life. That was the position when an invitation came from Major James Burton Pond in New York, who was in the business of bringing celebrity speakers to platforms across the United States. An earlier generation had welcomed educational lecturers, but by the 1890s the biggest audiences turned out for speakers who could be entertaining as well as improving, and Pond was the top of his profession, acting as manager to the likes of Henry Ward Beecher and Mark Twain. (He surely did not imagine that a device that had been demonstrated earlier in 1894 by Thomas Edison, a gadget that could throw an image of a moving photograph onto a wall, would soon almost entirely replace lecturing as a form of entertainment.)

Major Pond thought there would be a receptive public for Arthur Conan Doyle, and made him an offer of fixed fees for some lectures and a percentage of the box office for others. ACD agreed to go on tour from the beginning of October until the first of December. (In the end he stayed a few days extra.) He landed in New York on October 2, accompanied by twenty-one-year-old Innes Doyle, taking leave from the British Army to be his older and famous brother's traveling companion throughout the tour.

Conan Doyle stepped off his ship into a land that perhaps was stranger to him than he realized. His idea of America had been shaped largely by his childhood reading, including the frontier novels of James Fenimore Cooper and Mayne Reid and the historical works of Francis Parkman; and as soon as he had the opportunity, he headed north to what he liked to call "Parkman Land," the territory in and around the Adirondacks where the French and Indian War had been fought. In this region nearly every name was magic to him: Fort Edward, Bloody Pond, Ticonderoga. Now he was able to compare the genuine terrain with the descriptions he had already drawn in his novel *The Refugees*, much of it set in this borderland between America and Canada. "It was very much as I had pictured it," he reported later, "but the trees were not as large as I thought."

For a few days he was able to indulge himself as a tourist. He had hoped to do one other thing early in his American trip: pay a respectful visit to Boston and shake hands with Oliver Wendell Holmes, the great old man of American literature, whose name he had borrowed for his own detective. But Oliver Wendell Holmes died on October 7, 1894, at the age of eighty-five, while ACD was deep in the northern woods, staying at a six-bedroom hunting lodge near Saranac Lake made available by a friend of a friend. By the time he emerged from Parkman Land and was able to visit Boston, the best he could do was to place a wreath on Holmes's grave.

It is exhausting just to list the places Conan Doyle visited during his lecture tour that fall. He spoke repeatedly in New York and Chicago, and made single appearances in Indianapolis, Cincinnati, Detroit, Washington, Baltimore, Elmira, Glens Falls, Schenectady, Jersey City, and some twenty other places. He gave the same lecture thirty-four times in two months, and other lectures or readings a total of five times, and the biggest variation seems to have been the opinions of local reporters about what his accent was like. One of them called it "a mixture of English, Irish, Scottish, and cold," and it is no wonder if he came down with a virus after so many nights consisting of straining his voice to speak in a gigantic hall, being delivered to the railway station at midnight, catching a few hours' sleep aboard a train, arriving in a new city the next morning, seeing a few of the local attractions, having dinner with local literary figures or social climbers, then lecturing once again, and repeating the process, day after day with few breaks.

A typical day of the trip was Thursday, November 1, when ACD travelled from Boston to Worcester, Massachusetts. He was a guest of the Woman's Club of Worcester, which had invited him to give one of the lectures in the series it was sponsoring that season. All 827 seats in the downtown Association Hall were filled when Conan Doyle appeared at eight o'clock on a stage decorated with large palms, ferns, and white chrysanthemums. The speaker was introduced by the president of the club, the wife of a local manufacturer and state legislator, and she explained Conan Doyle to the audience as "the author of those famous detective stories which have entertained, delighted, and mystified two continents." After the lecture, which lasted about an hour, the ladies carried their guest off to a reception at the home of another local industrialist and his wife. Arthur and Innes, as well as the leaders of the Woman's Club, shook the hands of about 175 people in the receiving line before there was finally a chance for some rest. Experiences of this kind, in which local dignitaries missed no opportunity to meet the celebrity author, were repeated day after day through the exhausting ten weeks of the trip.

As for Conan Doyle's lecture itself, it was the same almost every night, under the title "Readings and Reminiscences." He had come to North America hoping to give several literary talks in rotation, including one about the novelist George Meredith, whom he considered to be the greatest author of his time—but sponsors and audiences were not interested in George Meredith. What they wanted to hear about was Sherlock Holmes, and Holmes is what his obliging creator talked about, time and again. Newspaper reports of his successive lectures quote various sentences and paragraphs, to the point that it is possible to reconstruct the entire hour's ramble about how he became an author, together with some comments on Holmes and some on the writing of his historical novels. Many sentences and whole paragraphs of his talk later found their way into his autobiography, *Memories and Adventures*.

Here is one anecdote from childhood mentioned only briefly in the autobiography, but told more fully in the lecture from 1894: "I can remember that into the little flat in which we lived there came one day a great man—gigantic he seemed when viewed from the height of two-foot-nothing. His shoulders, I remember, spanned the little door and his head was somewhere up near the gas chandelier. His voice, too, was as big as his body and I have since learned that his heart was in the same proportion. I can still remember the face of the man, clean-shaven, pugilistic, with an old man's hair, a young man's eyes, and a child's laugh. Above all I remember his nose, which fascinated me by its strange distortion. Long after I had been tucked into my little crib I could hear him roaring and rumbling in the next room, and his bare personality left as vivid an effect upon my three-year-old mind as his name and fame could do upon the thousands who knew him as William Makepeace Thackeray."

Along with the reminiscences came the readings, which included two passages from Sherlock Holmes—the classic section from *The Sign of the Four* in which Holmes examines Watson's pocket watch and deduces more about Watson and his family than Watson was prepared to hear, and a brief section from "The Greek Interpreter" in which Holmes and his brother Mycroft match observations about people in the street below, from at the window of the Diogenes Club in Pall Mall. Then, just about at the end of his performance, Conan Doyle set Holmes aside to read an entire short story from his other work, which seems generally to have been one that had only just been published in *The Strand Magazine* in England and a number of American newspapers, *The Lord of Chateau Noir*. It would eventually form part of the collection *The Green Flag and Other Stories*, issued in 1900. The tale is fairly gruesome, in keeping with a theme of physical mutilation that surfaces repeatedly in Conan Doyle's writing, especially his stories of crime, including *The Cardboard Box* and *The Crooked Man*, but also his general and historical fiction. After the lecture in Worcester, for example, the local newspaper, the *Evening Gazette*, complained that it had been a mistake for the visitor to read such a thing, calling it "painful," "brutal," and "unpleasant."

What emerges from these sources is not just the story of one lecture tour, but a portrait of social and literary America in 1894.[2] He did not see the whole country, going no further south than Washington, D.C. and no further west than Milwaukee, but within that scope there was plenty for him to see, plenty of people to meet, and plenty more he might have enjoyed meeting if the pressure had not been so intense and continuous. After shaking those 175 hands at the reception in Worcester, he may have felt mixed enthusiasm for getting up the next

---

2 See the author's *Welcome to America, Mr. Sherlock Holmes* (Toronto: Simon & Pierre, 1984).

day, traveling to Amherst, and giving the same talk all over again, this time for an audience of college men. But there were clearly good times as well. One of the best may have been his day in Indianapolis, where he stayed at a hotel that was also home to the local poet laureate, James Whitcomb Riley. They met with mutual enthusiasm, and apparently spent several hours talking in one or both of their rooms upstairs— and anyone who knows of Riley's habits will suspect that while they talked, a bottle and a couple of glasses were not far away.

In Yonkers, New York, Conan Doyle had dinner with John Kendrick Bangs, the writer best known now for using Sherlock Holmes as a character in his comic novel *The Pursuit of the House-Boat*. A biography of Bangs tells how everyone went upstairs to change for dinner, and what happened after Conan Doyle came down and took a seat in Bangs's library: "As Bangs crossed the hall to the wide doorway of the library, he saw the back of Doyle's head above the plush comfort of a chair which had been drawn up before a blazing fire on the library hearth. At the same moment he was shocked to see his son move swiftly upon Doyle from the rear, and, with a Gollywog Doll poised on high, bring it down upon the crown of the distinguished creator of Sherlock Holmes. Doyle like a flash seized the boy and went to the floor in a wrestling match, easily bringing the attacking party to complete subjection. Looking up and smiling, Doyle eternally subjected Bangs also. 'Oh, never mind, Mr. Bangs,' he said. 'This is only another example of the irrepressible conflict between Old England and Young America!'"

Newspaper reporters sometimes asked him about exactly that sensitive issue. Conan Doyle told an audience of American literary men at New York's Lotos Club that Britons "exult in your success and in your prosperity," but at a dinner in Detroit he took exception to some derogatory remarks about the British Empire made by an intoxicated speaker late in the evening. "You Americans," he rose and said in reply, "have lived up to now within your own palings, and know nothing of the real world outside. But now your land is filled up, and you will be compelled to mix more with the other nations. When you do so you will find that there is only one which can at all understand your ways and your aspirations, or will have the least sympathy. That is the mother country which you are now so fond of insulting."

Conan Doyle visited Brattleboro, Vermont, to have Thanksgiving dinner with an expatriate Briton, Rudyard Kipling, and his American wife and in-laws, and they astonished local residents by playing a game of that newfangled sport, golf, across a nearby cow-pasture. In Philadelphia, he had dinner at the home of publisher Craige Lippincott in Rittenhouse Square. In New York City, he met with a less affluent publisher, S. S. McClure, and gave him a check for a thousand pounds sterling by way of investment in his struggling magazine—an amount he afterwards said accounted for the entire net proceeds of his lecture tour, worth about $100,000 in today's money.

And there were a number of literary luncheons at which he met the writers and would-be writers of the day. These tended to be events for gentlemen only, but there was one particularly festive lunch in Chicago, at the home of a distinguished banker, at which ladies were present as well as businessmen, a prominent clergyman, and two noted authors of the time, Eugene Field and Hamlin Garland. Field took the opportunity to tease Conan Doyle a little by asking him to sign a copy of one of his books—a cheap, badly printed, pirated edition of *The Sign of the Four*, at a time when copyright and literary piracy in America were continuing aggravations for British authors. This one took the joke well: next to his signature in the book he drew a skull and crossbones, and wrote a doggerel verse about pirates. He also signed a copy of the printed menu for the event, and all the guests did likewise. That menu is still in existence, owned by a private collector.

Some souvenirs of the trip are preserved in institutions now. The public library in Niagara Falls, New York, has the autograph-book maintained by the owner of the inn where Conan Doyle stayed overnight. The illustrated menu for the Lotos Club dinner, whose talk by Conan Doyle that night follows, is framed on the wall of the club's grill-room. Among the most touching documents of all is the diary kept by Lydia Kendall, who saw him lecture at the City Hall in Northampton, Massachusetts, and wrote at length about the experience. "He is a fine-looking man of thirty-five," she wrote, "very tall and well-proportioned." That firsthand evidence of the tour is now in the archives at Smith College, where Kendall was a student at the time.

Anyone who wishes to stand where Conan Doyle once stood, and imagine how Lydia Kendall saw him 115 years ago, can have that experience in Northampton, for the City Hall on Main Street still stands. So does Plymouth Church on East Hampshire Avenue in Milwaukee; so does the Brooklyn Academy of Music on Lafayette Avenue; so do many other halls in which audiences heard his "Readings and Reminiscences." Similarly, today's pilgrim can walk in the footsteps of the visiting author to Cooper's Cave in Glens Falls (though it is no longer open to tourists as it was then), and even spend a night in Naulakha, Kipling's house in Vermont where Conan Doyle spent the Thanksgiving holiday in 1894.

The tour ended in early December, as Conan Doyle was eager to get home for Christmas. He and his brother sailed from New York on the Cunard liner *Etruria*, landing in Liverpool on December 15. By this time he was the author of two more books than when he had departed for America. *Round the Red Lamp* was a collection of medical short stories, most of them previously unpublished, which had come out in October, in time for the reviewer in Worcester, the one who didn't like *The Lord of Chateau Noir*, to complain about its sordid and painful content as well. And *The Parasite*, a creepy and sexual story about hypnotism, had appeared at the beginning of December.

That December, the first of the Brigadier Gerard stories, *How the Brigadier Won His Medal*, appeared in *The Strand Magazine*. Conan Doyle had apparently written it shortly before leaving for the United States, and at one of his lectures, making a change from his usual material, he read it aloud from the proof-sheets that he had been correcting. Now, back at his desk, he started turning out more adventures of the Napoleonic swashbuckler, as well as a story of English prize-fighting in the same period, the early nineteenth century, that would become the novel *Rodney Stone*. For the toast of literary America, returned to his British roots, there was never any lack of things to be written.

The Romance of America
A. Conan Doyle

Sir Arthur Conan Doyle (1859–1930) was the creator of the most successful detective of all time, Sherlock Holmes, whose exploits took on a life of their own to thousands of mystery readers around the world, and still resonate with a large audience today. His creator studied medicine at the University of Edinburgh, served as a senior physician at a South African field hospital during the Boer War, and was knighted in 1902. His writing career had been well established by then, with the tales of Holmes and his chronicler and companion John Watson passing from literature into legend.

* * * *

(Toward the end of his first trip to America, on November 18, 1894, Conan Doyle was given a dinner in his honor at New York's distinguished Lotos Club, attended by many leaders of New York public and literary life. "Dr. Doyle is not more than thirty-five years of age, closely fulfilling his own conditions of the man most to be envied—'a writer of romances who has not passed his thirty-third year,'" said the club's twenty-fifth-anniversary history (A Brief History of the Lotos Club by John Elderkin, Lotos Club: 1895). In his remarks, Conan Doyle demonstrated that if some Americans were unfriendly toward the British Empire, as he found

on his speaking tour across the country, he was nonetheless a Briton enchanted by America.)

* * * *

There was a time in my life which I divided among my patients and literature. It is hard to say which suffered most. But during that time I longed to travel as only a man to whom travel is impossible does long for it, and, most of all, I longed to travel in the United States. Since this was impossible, I contented myself with reading a good deal about them and building up an ideal United States in my own imagination. This is notoriously a dangerous thing to do. I have come to the United States; I have traveled from five to six thousand miles through them, and I find that my ideal picture is not to be whittled down, but to be enlarged on every side.

I have heard even Americans say that life is too prosaic over here, that romance is wanting. I do not know what they mean. Romance is the very air they breathe. You are hedged in with romance on every side. I can take a morning train in this city of New York; I can pass up the historic and beautiful Hudson; I can dine at Schenectady, where the Huron and the Canadian did such bloody work; and before evening I have found myself in the Adirondack forests, where the bear and the panther are still to be shot, and where within four generations the Indian and frontiersman still fought for the mastery. With a rifle and a canoe you can glide into one of the black eddies which have been left by the stream of civilization.

I feel keenly the romance of Europe. I love the memories of the shattered castle and the crumbling abbey; of the steel-clad knights and the archer; but to me the romance of the redskin and the trapper is more vivid, as being more recent. It is so piquant also to stay in a comfortable inn, where you can have your hair dressed by a barber, at the same place where a century ago you might have been left with no hair to dress.

Then there is the romance of this very city. On the first day of arrival I inquired for the highest building, and I ascended it in an elevator— at least they assured me it was an elevator. I thought at first that I had wandered into the dynamite gun. If a man can look down from that point upon the noble bridge, upon the two rivers crowded with shipping, and upon the magnificent city with its thousand evidences of energy and prosperity, and can afterward find nothing better than a sneer to carry back with him across the ocean, he ought to consult a doctor. His heart must be too hard or his head too soft.

And no less wonderful to me are those Western cities which, without any period of development, seem to spring straight into a full growth of every modern convenience, but where, even among the rush of cable cars and the ringing of telephone bells, one seems still to catch the echoes of the woodsman's axe and of the scout's rifle.

These things are the romance of America, the romance of change, of contrast, of danger met and difficulty overcome, and let me say that we, your kinsmen, upon the other side, exult in your success and in your prosperity, and it is those who know British feeling—true British feeling—best, who will best understand how true are my words. I hope you don't think I say this or that I express my admiration for your country merely because I am addressing an American audience. Those who know me better on the other side will exonerate me from so unworthy a motive.